The
Awaited
One

TERRY SHOULDERS

BALBOA.
PRESS
A DIVISION OF HAY HOUSE

Balboa Press books may be ordered through booksellers or by contacting:

Balboa Press
A Division of Hay House
1663 Liberty Drive
Bloomington, IN 47403
www.balboapress.com
1 (877) 407-4847

Because of the dynamic nature of the Internet, any web addresses or links contained
in this book may have changed since publication and may no longer be valid. The views
expressed in this work are solely those of the author and do not necessarily reflect the
views of the publisher, and the publisher hereby disclaims any responsibility for them.

The author of this book does not dispense medical advice or prescribe the use of any
technique as a form of treatment for physical, emotional, or medical problems without the
advice of a physician, either directly or indirectly. The intent of the author is only to offer
information of a general nature to help you in your quest for emotional and spiritual well-
being. In the event you use any of the information in this book for yourself, which is your
constitutional right, the author and the publisher assume no responsibility for your actions.

Any people depicted in stock imagery provided by Getty Images are models,
and such images are being used for illustrative purposes only.
Certain stock imagery © Getty Images.

This is a work of fiction. All of the characters, names, incidents, organizations, and dialogue
in this novel are either the products of the author's imagination or are used fictitiously.

Print information available on the last page.

ISBN: 978-1-9822-0070-1 (sc)
ISBN: 978-1-9822-0072-5 (hc)
ISBN: 978-1-9822-0071-8 (e)

Library of Congress Control Number: 2018903654

Balboa Press rev. date: 05/16/2018

Contents

Acknowledgments

I deeply thank my wife Juna, for her support,
encouragement, editing, and patience
during the time needed for me to complete this story.

Also, I applaud my friends, who heard countless times that
my manuscript is almost finished!

Thank you to authors Naomi C Rose and Anne Snowden Crosman
for your professional advice and gracious suggestions.

Thank you Goodness of All Things!

May messages found within "The Awaited One"
help create a better world in which to live 'together.'

Terry Shoulders

Prologue

Crystola, A Galaxy Of Majestic Marvels

Prismacia

There is a galaxy in a far away star system. This galaxy is Crystola. While each galaxy throughout the Heavens is truly unique, Crystola's spectacular majesty has but few rivals.

Within Crystola exists an extraordinary planet. It is Prismacia! When viewing Prismacia from afar, one is awed by the sight of such a celestial jewel glistening in the deep vastness of the Heavens.

You see, Prismacia is a planet of crystals. It's hot molten core, forming billions of years ago, thrust crystals of all sizes, colors, and shapes onto most of the surface areas. And, whether lit by it's Mother SunneLavva, or Mother MoonLunna, it literally sparkles!

Prismacia encompasses beautiful and sometimes foreboding landscapes too. Towering crystal mountain ranges surround vast deserts and seas — all offering unknown beauty, and dangers should you venture into them!

The incomparable black sand Carbonian Desert, with seemingly endless sand dunnes, stretches to the vast horizon, far, far away. There it connects with the deep sea-foam blue waters of the "Sea of The Forgotten Place." This sea is home to the underwater city of Neptuna.

Simple terraced lands surround the central governing center called Spectrum. The city of Spectrum is where the High Council of the Voice Of One resides, as well as XennaOne, the spiritual and mystical HighPriestess of the Voice of One. The name given to this beautiful area of Prismacia is Amythesia.

Amythesia is rich with abundant varieties of sea life, plant life and floral life, sustaining the existence of all things and all Beings, known and unknown.

Unchartered and mostly unexplored distant lands, where one may seek sanctuary to discover their truth, or to simply disappear, also exists on Prismacia.

Finally, there are impactful secrets hidden here — of great significance. Secrets hidden from those of Amythesia and those from beyond.

Secrets soon to be revealed!

Chapter 1

The Gathering

It is time for the truth to be known

Looking down from a dark dunne, her eyes glittered from the starlight of emerging stars.

Ah, they are all here. I must join them soon ... then it will be time!

She knew what must be done.

A 'Twinkling' floated by her. She playfully propelled it on it's way.

All were gathered by a beautiful oasis near the edge of Oneness. As the Mother SunneLavva sank beyond the Carbonian sands, a slight cool crispness began to hover. Evening temperatures slowly dropped, and early night winds began gently caressing the cooling sands, buoying tiny desert dust balls, called Twinklings, upward into their floating nomadic wanderings.

Above those gathered, it darkened rapidly.

Extraordinary heavens appeared, giving all cause to pause and yield to their mysteries. The distant and ancient beginnings of both time, place, and life— and unknown origin—once again unfolded before them. Beings were resting on rocks and reclining on the sands. Some were standing. All wore their wraps to lessen the coolness that the evening promised and always delivered.

It was captivating.

And, while anxious anticipation and unknown expectations lingered in the air, a calm and peacefulness blanketed the small gathering. Stars hidden by the light emerged into the darkness. The meaning behind the gathering drew near. They all waited in eagerness ... they had no idea of what was to come.

The story leading up to this gathering

began a long, long time ago and far, far away,

but I will start its tale from about one year ago

in the small city called Spectrum.

The High Council of the Voice of One

is assembled to hear an argument

presented to them

from one named ... Poona.

whether by reason or by chance

what will happen to us in time

will come to pass...

what will happen to us in time?

... time starts now

Bocc

poet, and Initiate of Brightness on the Wisdom Path Journey
Prismacia
UGT 20,872

3

Chapter 2

I Am Here To Advocate For The Inclusion Of Laurra Of Emeralsia

A time of trial

It was early as Poona, Annuj, and Laurra walked up the steps and onto the Pathway Hall of the Voice of One. Spectrum, the Seat of Amythesia, was awakening and the Mother SunneLavva was just breaking the horizon to offer the day an assurance of warmth to come. Early gentle winds, caressing their faces, were soft and comforting. Exotic chimes, ringing their tones in harmony, gave Poona a feeling of lightness. A sense of promise surged through her.

A good omen, she thought.

As protocol dictated, they were all wearing the gown of Council. It had been decided long ago that when addressing the High Council of the Voice of One, all participants, including the High Council, were to wear simple attire with no decoration of any kind. The consensus being this would lessen any distraction while presenting or listening to requests and argumentation. Poona thought this to be an interesting concept to adhere to—nevertheless, one with merit.

In a short while they were summoned and ushered to their Council table.

"The chamber feels austere and official looking," whispered Annuj, contemplating the intimidating room housing the Voice of One.

"Yes," said Poona, smiling. "It definitely could use a woman's touch."

They all shared Poona's smile and silently chuckled.

XennaOne, the HighPriestess of the Voice of One, had sequestered herself in the balcony to observe the proceedings. Unknown to anyone else, she possessed a secret Poona had entrusted to her years before, and the proceedings today were vital to this extraordinary secret. She remembered...

Poona, a woman I did not even know, requested a personal audience and informed me of extraordinary events that were to unfold including the forthcoming implementation of those events. She asked for my approval, input, and discretion. And I, after hearing her story, gave my approval and blessing.

"I have kept your secret, Poona," she whispered softly to herself.

Abruptly, XennaOne reconsidered her decision to sit in the balcony.

As the spiritual and mystical HighPriestess of the Voice of One, it may be wiser to sit as an impartial observer where I can be seen by all parties involved.

She smiled. *"Impartial" may not be exactly the correct word! My presence might be influential in the outcome. I will move!*

On the floor below events were proceeding and when acknowledged by the Council chair, Poona rose. She walked confidently forward. Standing before her audience of seven, she began to address them.

"Honored ones of the Voice of One, I am..."

Suddenly the Council chair raised his hand in a halt to the proceedings and arose, as did the six other members. Together they bowed their heads. Poona, Annuj, and Laurra, not understanding these actions, turned to see the HighPriestess XennaOne walking down the aisle toward them. They too stood, and bowed in respect as she approached. Passing by Poona, XennaOne ever so slightly nodded in acknowledgment.

"I sincerely apologize for this untimely interruption," she said, slowly looking at them all, "but I have chosen to be seated here."

She pointed and smiled.

"I will add that discussion regarding the subject of Poona's argument is long overdue for serious consideration and action. I believe a fair and compassionate resolution will emerge, given the depth of consciousness and wisdom I see standing before me today—on both sides."

Gazing assuredly at the Council, XennaOne remarked...

"Honored Council, time appropriately continues to honor some traditions, but traditions in and of themselves can become passé, needing to be amended—or deleted entirely."

Pausing, she let her words resonate to all present.

"And if so," she continued, "to be replaced with laws that accurately reflect present conditions. I believe that all things that come to be, will come to be in their time. But that said ... time starts now! Time waits for no one! So it is only when we deem it appropriate that the time for change is at hand, that beneficial change is enacted."

Annuj, captivated by the presence and command that HighPriestess XennaOne exuded noticed that the Council listened intently to her every word.

Regal radiance is the only descriptive term available, she thought.

She also silently noted, *The HighPriestess is of the same tonality as I am. Intriguing!*

HighPriestess XennaOne gracefully nodded to the Council and gestured for the proceedings to continue. She seated herself in a pew directly between the three young women and the honored Council.

Known to be wise and just, everyone felt an elevated importance to the proceedings due to the influence of HighPriestess XennaOne's presence and statements. Her attendance was not just curiosity, but concern regarding the outcome.

Poona gave a respectful bow, and continued.

"I am Poona of Emeralsia. As you may be aware, we are those of spirituality. It is an exceptional honor to be in the presence of the High Council and XennaOne, the HighPriestess."

Placing her hands over her heart in a gesture of respect, Poona said,

At this time, allow me to present to you, Annuj, the Initiate of Brightness from Lapisia, attending in the capacity of authentic witness as required by the codes and statutes of the Voice of One."

Standing, Annuj bowed.

Lifting her arms slightly, as if encompassing them all, Poona stated,

"As you undoubtedly noticed in the dossiers, which you requested, there are actually three matters in question. First, I will address the addition of a trained and qualified caregiver to accompany the Initiates of Brightness on the Wisdom Path Journey. Without question, on an unpredictable journey such as this, unfortunate incidents may require a caregiver. The caregiver must be fully able to see to any needs of the Initiates should such an incident occur. It is best to deal in what-ifs beforehand, rather than should-haves after the fact."

"Am I clear thus far?" Poona asked.

The Council members nodded affirmatively.

"Second, and relating to Laurra of Emeralsia, it is only just, that a nominated and selected Initiate, if physically and mentally capable, be allowed to participate in what certainly will be a life-changing experience— not only for themselves but for present and future generations of Beings to come. I am here to advocate for the rightful inclusion of Laurra of Emeralsia."

The Council listened intently.

XennaOne, placed her fingertips on the temples of her mind, earnestly awaiting Poona's next statement.

"Expediency is pressing! Because of Laurra's past illness, we have recently been notified that she may be replaced. However, I must emphasize that Laurra's condition has improved dramatically." Turning to Laurra, Poona said...

"Allow me to present Initiate Laurra."

Rising, Laurra bowed and calmly spoke.

"High Council of the Voice of One, please know how deeply honored I am to have been selected to represent my Quin, Emeralsia, as an Initiate of Brightness. I realize that my participation in the Wisdom Path Journey will involve unknowns regarding health and safety, as it will for all the Initiates."

Pausing, Laurra moved around the table to stand directly in front of the High Council. Pleasantly, she stated with conviction...

"With regard to my health, it is clear you must make a determination as to whether I am capable of this privileged journey. Please be assured that I am. I cannot elaborate enough on the compassionate care given to me by Poona, my friend. Poona's inclusion as caregiver should erase any doubt as to my well-being and add welcome relief for any concern regarding misfortune along the way for any Initiate. Besides Poona's extraordinary gifts of healing and knowledge, her presence alone will offer comfort for both the Initiates and their loved ones at home. I thank you for your attention and what I know will be a just consideration."

Laurra bowed, and sat down.

Rising, Poona stated...

"In summation, oh honored ones, Laurra was chosen, and she is physically and mentally capable. We are requesting her inclusion on the journey. I offer myself as the qualified caregiver for all the Initiates."

Chapter 3

Part 2 Of Poona's Appeal

Poona paused briefly allowing for anticipation to set in before addressing the Council.

"As to the third and final appeal, I now present another consideration long past due. It relates to the Initiate's selection program. Given equal qualifications, equal promise and equal gifts, I propose there be two candidates from each Quin awarded the honor instead of only one. Also, I glaringly observe we have no selected Initiate involvement from the underwater kingdom of Neptuna, or from Spectrum, the governing center of our lands."

"Oh honored ones, it is only right that Initiates from both be included in the Initiates of Brightness program. Selection of the gifted must represent all areas of the population. It is imperative for the promise and future of Amythesia, Prismacia—and perhaps ultimately the Heavens themselves."

"In summation, Oh Voice of One, we trust in your fairness and wisdom. We believe you will grant our requests, as they are warranted. And, as to existing laws regarding the selection process, it is our hope that you will introduce both ethical and fair resolutions thus deepening the pool of promise for the future.

Your discrimination and judgement in these matters will be crucial, Oh Honored Ones. This cause is just. A favorable decision to honor these requests placed before you will be for the ultimate good of all!"

HighPriestess XennaOne smiled inwardly at Poona's ability to both praise and challenge — with grace. She was pleased.

The absence of Initiates representing Spectrum and Neptuna is a matter of outdated tradition needing to be remedied immediately. The time is now, she thought. *It will be interesting to hear their decision.*

The Chair of the Voice of One considered his thoughts before responding. "You have prepared admirable arguments, Poona of Emeralsia. You were clear, and not in the least superfluous. The Council will now adjourn to deliberate. I will add that we of the Voice of One are privileged to have such promise for the future as those sitting before us today." Standing, he turned to XennaOne, and bowed.

Chapter 4

The Judgement

The time seemed to pass slowly, but did eventually pass, and when summoned, everyone took their seats in the Chamber. The High Council slowly returned to the hall, chatting quietly amongst themselves. All were seated and the Chair of the Voice of One addressed Poona.

"Let me begin by stating the obvious Poona — your presentation for requests was impressive. Regarding your appeal for the inclusion of Initiates representing Spectrum and Neptuna, which has regrettably been long overlooked …

it has been approved! When we convene for our next session it will be entered into law."

"Also, the Council collectively feels that your request to extend the number of Initiates to two per Quin is laudable. However, Poona, in determining that which is right and just for all, it was brought up that the probability of a plausible scenario, involving perhaps three, four, or more gifted Initiates, equally deserving of selection and of the same Quin or areas of population, could arise. This, of course, would be exciting, even euphoric for Amythesia. Nevertheless, at some point, and I enter this under the heading of unfortunate, we determined there must be a limit to the number of Initiates selected for the Wisdom Path Journey."

"Therefore, Poona, the Council, with the blessing and assistance of the HighPriestess XennaOne, will appoint a committee to look into this. An initial thought put forth is to create a special Academy located here in Spectrum, to accommodate all those deemed "gifted," but not participating in the Journey itself.

A commendable consideration."

He paused to let his remarks be considered and glanced at the HighPriestess XennaOne before continuing.

"Now, Poona, let us consider the first part of your appeal involving Laurra and the inclusion of a caregiver. We realize the ceremony for the

Initiates of Brightness is due in three days hence, and Laurra's participation hangs in the balance. Thus, the importance of making an expeditious decision is imperative."

Rising to Stand before the three young women, he declared...

"We, the High Council have decided to allow Laurra's selection as Initiate to stand — and to allow your inclusion, Poona, as caregiver to the Initiates."

Delighted, Laurra, Annuj and Poona arose, turning to each other and hugging in joy over these determinations. Beaming, they bowed in a gesture of thanks before sitting again.

Appearing quite happy himself, the Chair of the Council continued.

"It should be understood, Poona, that there may be a time, when, because of unforeseen events, a caregiver can not be present with all the Initiates. We determined that although the Wisdom Path Journey is generally presented as a group endeavor, it is as much an individual journey. A time may present itself, by chance or by choice, when one or more of the Initiates chooses an alternative path than that of the others. It is a possible scenario."

"However, keep in mind, that to a degree, all the Initiates have been schooled in self-healing. It will be the caregiver's decision to determine which Initiates to accompany, as you can only be responsible to those within your immediate area of influence. Having a qualified caregiver present on all subsequent Wisdom Path Journeys for the safety and care of any Initiates will be mandatory from this moment forth."

"We, the High Council of the Voice of One, thank you, deeply."

All stood, and turning, bowed in respect to XennaOne, the HighPriestess of the Voice of One.

Chapter 5

Far, Far Away, And Deep In The Rogue Galaxy

MorQ stood alone — and frightened

Languishing deep in the Heavens, and far, far away from the inspired and promising events taking place on the planet Prismacia there existed a mostly barren and bleak planet known as Rogue.

Standing alone and frightened, MorQ, a diminutive man in stature was gazing out his viewport at this desolate planet, and beyond into the vastness of the Rogue Empire. Cloistered within three small rooms aboard a large sinister craft called the RogueEmpire Complex, he contemplated the undeniable promise of his demise if for any reason he would be subjected to the absolute and instantaneous punishment of the void outside his protective viewport.

One word, one nod, one flip of a finger from Emperor CodL is all it would take, he thought, shaking his head in wonder at the frailty of his existing situation.

How much longer can I endure this, or even justify my existence in its present form. It can only be construed as slavery. I am trapped and in-prisoned.

He placed his head in his hands and shuddered. *This is so unjust. After all, I am a Being, and the Chief Engineer and Scientist aboard this vessel. Like all living Beings I just ask to be allowed my dignity. I have done nothing to be treated otherwise. But to CodL I am beneath contempt! I just can't go on like this.*

For the past few days MorQ had sequestered himself away, awaiting the arrival of Spacial Rogue galaxy probes from their exploratory mission. Once their results were analyzed he knew it would mean subjecting himself to the humiliation of yet another tense few moments before "the self-exalted" Emperor CodL.

It always seems to last a lifetime, he grimaced.

A wave of anxiety suddenly rushed through him and once again he felt fear seeping into his consciousness — as if it ever left. MorQ purposefully kept his small accommodations dimly lit in the hope of lessening the chance for anyone in a surveillance mode to detect his cunning scheme. He carefully glanced around his darkened room. With quivering legs MorQ turned from his viewport and slowly walked over to his work station. He just knew the "eyes and ears" he swore were watching — were watching! Ever so casually he pulled a few folders out from his files, selected one, and hunched over, shielding it.

I will simply appear as if I am working on a project. Which I am!

But, the truth be known, MorQ had another agenda in mind. Once again he went over every detail of an escape plan he had carefully concocted. He etched it into his memory and entered the plan, in code, on various pages of an inane report describing a scientific breakdown of molecular structures in the Heavens.

The probability of my secret, hidden within the lines of facts, would be nearly impossible to discover, he reasoned.

Soon," he uttered. "Something must happen soon!"

The anxiety rushed in once again. He shivered and cautiously glanced over his shoulder.

Chapter 6

They Prepared

The Initiates and the caregiver

Annuj...

Awakening from her late afternoon nap, Annul stretched, and gazed from her bed into the vast, galactic Heavens of Crystola. Night time rapidly approached and the twinkling light of stars rebirthing had begun.

She lay back and day dreamed.

Ah, the Mother SunneLavva has already descended below the distant horizon here in Spectrum. Far, far, to the north, at home, the Lapisian MoonXena is just beginning it's monthly odyssey around the northern tip of Prismacia.

Quin Lapisia is where it all began.

She smiled.

I became a Future Seer, an apprentice of the Healing Arts, and am mastering the skills of Past Recaller.

Jumping out of bed, she softly said...

"I feel so very fortunate."

Her light hazel-green eyes shone bright with anticipation and her dark-amber skin glowed in the promise of the evening to come, for tonight marked the celebration of the Initiate's Transmission of Studies. Cheerfully crossing over to stand at her window Annuj ran her fingers through her thick auburn hair, tossing it about. She watched, as MoonCola, Spectrum's moon, begin it's assent beyond the towering crystal prisms. Violet blue, and magenta reflections from nearby crystals slowly begin to paint the landscape.

"It is just so intoxicating," she murmured

Her younger brother, Jasso, spoke from outside the door.

"Annuj, it will soon be time for your arrival at the ceremony. Are you ready?"

"Yes, Jasso, thank you. I will be ready to leave shortly. Tell Mother Hanna, and Father Ralla, I will be down soon."

Quickly refreshing herself, Annuj donned her attire. Standing before her mirror, she allowed for an extended glance at her appearance.

Hmmm, she considered; *dark-amber skin, a light cream colored gown, and an amber RobeCape of Ritual exquisitely embedded with Quin Lapisian blue lapis along the trim...*

Yes, I like this — so far!

She quickly completed her appearance adding a silver waist band which dangled from her slim waist. It embraced raw amethysts and rare sea-foam colored moonstones from the Sea of The Forgotten Place.

Continuing to linger, Annuj adjusted her thin head band and considered her choice of a complimentary shade of green eyelid blush enhanced by a dark caramel eye liner for her sparkling hazel eyes. Her lips glistened in a moist light amber lip color.

"Yes," she said to herself, dashing out the door.

Calla...

Calla, the chosen Initiate of Ebonisia, elegantly stood waiting by an open window enjoying the crisp cool breeze. For the ceremony she favored a soft, form-fitting sleeveless gown falling to her ankles. It was camel colored and accompanied by an ebonite waist sash inlaid with pure amber. On the hook beside the window hung her Ebonisian RobeCape of Ritual. Blended light ochre and violet eyeshades twinkled with glitter mysteriously adorning her bright honey colored eyes. For the moment she held her pure amber head band, having decided to put it on just before leaving.

Ah, there is Annuj coming down with her family. She has such beautiful long hair, I wonder if I should let mine grow long again? But, I like my hair short! Besides, it suits my preferred lifestyle just fine and it just feels good.

Curious, she turned to look at her reflection in a nearby mirror. Her short, sandy blonde hair shimmered in the light of MoonCola, now flooding in through an open window. *I am sure it undoubtably raises an eyebrow or two ... but that is alright, I enjoy it.*

A hint of a smile appeared.

Playfully, she shook her head allowing her hair to dance loosely about her face. She smiled at how earthy and natural it appeared in the mirror. Calla delighted in physical exercise — and it showed. Her alluring, velvety brown skin glowed. Calla smiled a confident smile.

At this moment of my life, she reflected, *my only passion is that of nurturing my new idea, "Stedics."*

Stedics was a combination of exercises she developed consisting of a continual flow of specific movements followed by a period of deep meditation.

I know it is truly beneficial for one's soul as well as body. It will become the thing to do. I just know it.

Bocc...

Meanwhile, Bocc, of Opalisia, having arrived early, sat on a cushioned couch just off the main hall with his Opalisian RobeCape of dark silver tossed rumpled beside him.

I am a poet, he thought, as he sat intently staring at his journal of empty thoughts and blank pages.

I am so anxious to begin journaling and creating poetry concerning our Wisdom Path Journey ... why isn't anything presenting itself. Maybe it is because I am concerned about my relationships — or lack of. Hmmm.

Perplexed, and furrowing his eyebrows, he considered...

I need to develop closer friendships. That has to be it!

Bocc was an emotive young man. Handsome, with a smoky blue complexion and a mind that always gave the impression of being in a distant world. His dark hair was tousled, falling loosely about his face and softly framing his very haunting pale blue eyes. Stretching his legs out, he leaned back into the soft cushions and cast a glance toward the ceiling...

Alright Bocc, your intention from now on is to concentrate on paying closer attention to what other people have to say! Just be present to anyones attempt in conversation. You can do this!

Then, with surprising conviction, he mentally stated...

I promise myself to focus on the conversations I will most certainly have with the other Initiates during this journey together!

He silently repeated it to himself again.

Out of the corner of his eye he glimpsed one of his fellow Initiates, Patto, at the bottom of the stairs. He gave a small wave — watching as Patto wandered over to an outside patio. Bocc noticed how Patto's pale features contrasted with the dark gray Ivorysian RobeCape he was wearing.

I hope Patto does all right out there in the desert. He is just not used to a lot of Mother SunneLavva.

Inevitably, Bocc's mind, wavered once again.

Someday I will teach others poetry. I can picture the classroom. It is located somewhere without distractions. It is large with huge open windows to accommodate gentle winds and it will have soft, comfy chairs to sit back in — to contemplate, or toss ideas around, and ...

Suddenly, Annuj and her family chatting nearby brought him back to reality. Sheepishly looking around, he noticed Calla standing across the room.

Now Calla does not have, or seem to allow any distractions. I must follow her example.

Patto...

Everyone liked Patto. He was good-humored and quite knowledgeable ... perhaps a little naive around the edges from spending so much time alone high in the mountainous areas of Ivorysia, but a totally delightful being.

Patto was the Initiate from Ivorysia.

"My passion is to become a StarAstron Seeker of the Heavens," he had stated. Thus he was a night person — literally. As a result, Patto's skin coloring was ivory, and his large black eyes were set in an orb of pale blue. Being rarely exposed to the MotherSunne, the officials in charge of the Wisdom Path Journey had slowly introduced him to varying amounts of sunlight and developed a special cream to help protect him during the journey ahead.

When he reached the bottom of the stairs, Patto noticed Bocc, and gave a small wave as he passed by. He headed for one of the small balconies outside the main room. They had all agreed that alone time before the ceremony would give them a last opportunity to reflect on the ceremonies to follow, so Patto chose to wait where he could view the canvas of his passion, the stars.

I can enjoy my enchanting stars from the balcony, he thought.

Leaning against the railing, Patto stood looking at distant stars.

Well, lets see ... it could be interesting to name the stars for the Initiates during our journey to come. That would be entertaining.

Pondering the extensive palette of stars overhead, he thought...

Let's see, maybe I can begin tonight.

"There", he exclaimed, being drawn to the 3rd star beyond MoonCola, rapidly exhibiting a bright awareness in the vast Heavens above.

"That star is most assuredly Calla's star. It sparkles brightly already and appears to dance about playfully. That would be Calla," he chuckled.

"It is now officially StarCalla."

He began considering just how he would determine each Initiate's star.

They probably will not all be so obvious as Calla's star — or maybe they will be? Hmmm, I wonder if I should I use a geometric equation with astrological factors built in? No, no, I'll just let my intuition, and the "One" guide me. He looked back to the stars.

Poona...

Poona, caregiver of Emeralsia quietly stood nearby Laurra, thinking of their journey together, and gazing at a far away spot only she could discern.

It has been quite a quest for us, Laurra. You have faced many challenges, alone. I wish I could have done more for you.

She shook her head in heartache remembering those unpredictable and precarious times.

"We all did our best," she murmured softly.

Suddenly, Poona sensed a warmth and softness replace her feelings of anxiety. She placed her hands, left over right upon her chest.

Oh, Goodness of All Things — Thank you! I now feel peaceful! I know there is so much yet to come, so much uncertainty. But, like always, we will do the best we can. Let us enjoy the memorable moments of tonight. Tomorrow we continue on the path.

She turned to look at Laurra, still on the small balcony and now bathed in moonlight.

Hmmm, because of her origins, Laurra is becoming taller in stature than the girls her age. She is also maturing into a lovely young woman, and in only a few short years. My, it has gone by so quickly and right before my very eyes.

She walked towards Laurra.

Earlier, Poona had adorned herself in her attire for the evening. Her shimmering silver RobeCape contained a small smattering of tiny emeralds sown in to appear as stars. Seven to be exact. A graphite gray gown snuggled close to her body, while a simple silver rope chain dangled down the front of her gown ending with a small moonstone. It was the custom of her Beings.

She had carefully dabbed a small application of blended lavender and fuchsia eyeshadow around her distinctively large, gray-blue eyes. The area around her eyes, being much lighter than her blue skin allowed for subtle attention. She had smiled, thinking,

These lighter areas are always a source of attraction to both men and women Beings alike. Perhaps it appears like a mask that does not hide, but alludes to a sense of mystery. I wonder?

Her evocative eyes had playfully twinkled at the thought.

She had then colored her soft white lips in a foamy fuchsia, before directing her attention to the distinctive symbolism of her Beings. Upon her left cheek, and indicative of stars, she placed 7 small silver and blue dabs of a rare ointment called Trolon. A larger orb, she placed above the stars, represented the moon.

Then, reaching down she carefully picked up her tiara. The tiara was simple, but elegant and embellished with a single Neptunian sea-foam moonstone. She lowered it gently onto her hair. It rested there sparkling and luminous in the dim evening light.

Her hair, a mixture of gray and silver was worn long as in the ancient ways of the SoulTouchers of her ancestry.

When she left her rooms to join Laurra and the Initiates in the lounge, she was astonished … light, striking her simple tiara, created a myriad of crystal reflections darting through the air, and onto the walls. Poona reflected …

It is said that Gems signify spiritual illumination and were objects of wonder and fascination to the ancient ones.

"I believe we carry on the tradition honorably," she pleasingly said.

Laurra…

Laurra stood on a balcony adjacent to that of Patto, using her alone time to soothe her concerns. She could see Patto nearby and inside she noticed Calla leaning against a mirror.

I look forward to knowing them all better, she thought.

She recalled the events and decisions made thus far in her young life.

To have finally arrived here at the threshold for the journey ahead has indeed been a long, and complicated odyssey in itself. Hopefully, the final part of my personal journey will evolve as the Ancients promised.

"Amazing," she murmured.

Laurra had chosen a simple charcoal gray gown, falling to just above her ankles, with silver sandals laced up her legs. A silver waist sash decorously dangled down to just above her knees with a single moonstone encrusted at it's end. Upon her thick gray and silver hair, which fell loosely to the middle of her slender back, rested a simple, delicate silver tiara inlaid with tiny moonstones from Neptuna, the city beneath the sea.

However, if one could have observed her gray-blue eyes, they would have seen starlight glistening on tears now caressing her cheeks. Tears remembering countless dreams dreamt, past burdens, and hopes of future joy.

Laurra whispered,

"And now I am actually about to attend the ceremony as an Initiate of Brightness."

Wiping away the tears, and placing her hands on each side of her face in wonder, a small smile appeared as she thankfully thought…

Poona did everything she could do … and we succeeded. Bless you, Poona, and thank you, Goodness of All Things.

She shivered, becoming aware of the cool evening breeze, and pulled her silver RobeCape tighter around her shoulders, her thoughts wandering.

A soft touch on her shoulder brought her back. It was Poona. Smiling at Poona thankfully, they embraced, with both expressing their joy in anticipation of the ceremony ahead. Poona, seeing Laurra's tears wondered...

Are they tears of happiness, or sadness?

Gently taking Laurra's arm they went back to Poona's suite where she carefully cleansed the trail of tears, and dabbed an application of the rare Trolon ointment on Laurra's cheek. It was indicative of the Moon and 7stars. Finally, she replaced Laurra's eye shadow with a very light lavender and fuchsia blend. Fresh fuchsia lip creme completed Laurra's unpretentious, but beautiful image.

Yes, she is growing tall, and has matured into a woman quickly, thought Poona.

"Laurra, it is now time."

Laurra took another long, and longing look from Poona's balcony at the Heavens that had now become a deep sea of endless color and stars.

She then turned toward her destiny.

Chapter 7

The Messenger, And Perchance The Answer

The HighPriestess XennaOne

Not far away, XennaOne, the HighPriestess of the Voice of One stood on a small intimate balcony watching the stars flicker.

Why is it, I wonder, that Beings look to the stars when happy, or when sad, when in love, or when not in love, when praying — or for any reason at all?

O course, XennaOne realized she was avoiding her true worry— that of feeling unusually anxious regarding the Ritual ceremony for the Initiates of Brightness later this evening. She considered this…

Perhaps the cause of my uneasiness is my niece, Annuj? Yes, that could be it. There are secrets and truths that must be revealed to her when she returns from her Wisdom Path Journey …

"By me!"

Annuj is a tonality. She is also not aware of many important things, including being my niece. She is not aware of her rightful lineage and a destiny that is preordained, if she should so choose. Irregardless, it is one that will be expected by the Beings of Amythesia when it is brought to light … and, in time, it must be. She must be prepared for that.

"She will be," she promised herself.

The destiny of our family ancestry is directly aligned with the destiny of Amythesia. In accordance with the right of succession, Annuj will become the next HighPriestess of the Voice of One should she agree …and if she is so inclined to accept, I forecast great promise of her. But, first, she must be informed of the truth — and, more than likely, by me. I am the reigning HighPriestess! Although, she considered, *her mother Junnuj or grandmother, Solannuj could certainly inform her.*

"It will indeed be interesting to see just how our destinies will play out," XennaOne uttered, as she created the symbolic sign of the All.

Her thoughts shifted to Laurra…

One so young, but so gifted … and of exceptional wisdom. She has been on an incredible journey thus far. In a way, Laurra is also a tonality. Yes, that is an interesting concept that also will be addressed at the proper time. Many burdens for those so young.

A soothing breeze suddenly enveloped her. Sensing it as a spiritual intervention, she spoke to the comforting winds…

"Ah, soft winds, are you perchance the Messenger with the answers of events foretold to come? Events predicted and promised? Events long etched in the annals of history and lore? We shall see."

Returning to the underlying source of her apprehension, she determined it was in fact the importance of her message to all the Initiates this evening.

I must convey, that while being selected as Initiates of Brightness by the Voice of One is indeed an honor, what is eminently more important are the covenants, the bonds, and the truths they will be creating and learning … and what the future impact of this opportunistic journey promises for all Beings. It will be their compassionate, and honest offerings upon returning that will be their true gift to all life everywhere. That is the true gift.

Turning her eyes to the heavens, XennaOne once again formed the symbol for the One, the All. She whispered…

"Oh, Goodness of All Things, please grant me clarity to reach these young people with my message. Guide my words to impress upon them the momentous significance of the thoughts I have shared with you tonight."

Turning to leave for the ceremony, she stopped.

How amusing of me for having "looked up" to the stars when conveying my thoughts to the One.

"Oh Goodness of All Things, it is me again. For eons we have known that all we need do is simply "seek within" to call upon you. The Kingdom — our Kingdom, is within."

Still, she thought, *at times it is good to also turn to the majesty of that which is without — also a part of all the One's creation.*

Raising her gaze to the majesty above, and thankful for the majesty within, she whispered…

"There are so many unknowns yet to unveil."

Chapter 8

May You See Through The Eyes Of All

The Ceremony

The celebration for the Initiates of Brightness Ritual was an event unlike any other, save for the anointing of the HighPriestess, which undoubtedly was the pinnacle and the capstone for the Beings of Amythesia.

An anointing did not occur often, perhaps only once in a Being's lifetime.

The Initiate's ceremony began as a social gathering. The Ritual Hall was practically overflowing with Beings from all the Quins, plus an ambassador from Neptuna. Everyone was chatting and engaging each other gleefully when a soft gong rang signaling the ceremony was about to commence. Everyone took their seats, after which the Initiates of Brightness, and Poona were ushered in and stood before their seats in front.

Shortly, soft melodic sounds of the "Harptonian" floated through the air emulating the sounds of Amythesian winds blowing throughout the Halls of the Spectrum. This was followed by "Long Trumpecons" heralding forth beautiful harmonic vibrations of celebration. An atmosphere of anticipation filled the Hall and all became quiet and anxious in expectation of that to come.

A second gong sounded softly and the HighPriestess XennaOne entered.

It was always said that XennaOne exuded an intoxicating aura … tonight was no exception. Even those aware of her bright countenance were almost breathless at the astonishing presence emanating from her this evening.

HighPriestess XennaOne had chosen to wear the thin, round, solid gold, "Symbol of the Exceptional" HaloDisc, which framed her head. Encircling the disc, were embedded raw crystals containing the colors of the 5Quins, Neptuna, and Spectrum. Her dark, reddish hair fell in thick waves before settling upon her shoulders. She wore a white, flowing Ritual Cape, gracefully cascading to the floor and emblazoned with crimson designs. Her ebony gown draped in soft casual folds to just below her ankles, while a crimson sash sparkling with gems encircled her waist, meeting in the middle and dangling down to her knees. Upon her feet were ebony sandals. On her arm she cradled the Amythesian "Scepter of the One," with 7 bands of raw crystals intertwined at the pinnacle. The base of the Scepter was a singular ball of precious emerald crystal. HighPriestess XennaOne's face illuminated goodness, integrity, compassion, and resolve.

She indicated for the Initiates to be seated.

Looking down from the podium, the HighPriestess XennaOne smiled softly at the Initiates of Brightness. Then, gazing over the assembly, she raised her arms to encompass them all, welcoming them as witnesses to the ritual they were about to experience.

"You honor us with your presence. It is my privilege to introduce, and present the exceptional Initiates of Brightness to you this evening."

Her warm, hazel-green eyes … eyes of wisdom, settled upon the Initiates now seated before her. XennaOne spoke.

"Initiates of Brightness, please stand and present yourself as I introduce you to those here tonight, and ultimately to all Amythesians whom you will represent."

"Annuj of Lapisia."

"Bocc of Opalisia."

"Calla of Ebonisia."

"Laurra of Emeralsia."

"Patto of Ivorysia"

"And, Poona of Emeralsia, as the caregiver for the Initiates during this journey."

A soft murmur drifted through the audience at the mention of a caregiver from Emeralsia. XennaOne sensing, and understanding the confusion held up her arms to them, quieting the murmur.

"Please, let me explain. I have exceptional news to share with you. New amendments to existing laws, which we felt were long antiquated, have recently been enacted allowing for the inclusion of a caregiver to accompany our Initiates. It is a precaution to any unforeseen accident, or illness, which could occur along their journey. In the future, a list of caregivers will be drawn up of viable and willing healers and distributed to each Quin for consideration. Our young Beings are our joy and our promise. This is an initial step allowing for some measure of safety for each of our chosen Initiates, now and in the future."

Considerable applause throughout the Hall erupted and XennaOne paused to allow for the show of enthusiasm before continuing.

"Also, my friends, I have more exciting revelations to share. After consideration, another amendment to an existing law will allow for more than one deserving Initiate from each Quin ... as well as Neptuna and Spectrum to be selected. As you are aware, Neptuna carries an immense responsibility for those of Amythesia, and like Spectrum, our Capital, it is long overdue that they, too, should be involved in the Initiates of Brightness selection process.

Thus, tonight, is the beginning of what we are calling the "Caregiver of Compassion" and the "Exemplary Deserving and Worthy" Initiates selection process."

"Yes," she happily said to yet another large round of applause brought forth by the announcement.

"While our youth are to be our future, we cannot predict the future, especially on such a journey as they have accepted to undertake. Yet, it is the Wisdom Path Journey, that will help create truths, bonds, and experiences they will share with us upon their return. These new amendments will fully take effect on the occasion of the next selection process in the various Quins, which, I thankfully say now include Spectrum and Neptuna."

"In addition, it has been offered for consideration, that an Academy for all deserving gifted ones of Amythesia be established here in Spectrum. I applaud the High Council of the Voice of One for their deliberations, their justness, and their vision in the preparation of these new amendments, extraordinary proposals, and future laws."

Once again, the people in attendance took to their feet, applauding the news, and roaring their approval to the Initiates of Brightness and the High Priestess before them.

HightPriestess XennaOne, and the Initiates all beamed.

After the applause had calmed down, HighPriestess XennaOne directed her gaze at all before her, and continued.

"Initiates of Brightness, you will be Ambassadors of Amythesia, and also Ambassadors of the One ... the Goodness of All that is ... All that has ever been ... and All that will ever be."

"You will represent all the ideals we believe in and choose to live by. You will also honor and respect the teachings that others may hold true, according to their experiences and traditions."

"Collectively, or perhaps individually, you will journey "your" Wisdom Path. You will be accompanied by four Guardians of Destiny along the way to the edge of the Carbonian Desert, where your journey will continue. Your journey may be long and perhaps oft times arduous. It will present you with beauty, with challenges, with introspection, with decisions, and perhaps even danger. There will be unusual sights to behold — perhaps unique new Beings to share with and new customs to learn from ... and respect."

XennaOne paused briefly to let the meaning of her words settle in. She slowly observed the room before settling on the faces of the Initiates again. *They are totally listening to my every word,* she thought. *Even Poona, who truly understands my message. Thank you, oh One, for your guidance.*

"The unknown! Therein lies the beauty, and the challenge. Familiarity should be balanced with discovery. Know that the journey will brighten you and temper you, but will inevitably awaken you ... and alter you all, forever."

"Let me also speak of emotions to be discovered and experienced on the Wisdom Path. Perhaps love, perhaps joy, maybe sadness, maybe fear.

At any time, should any emotion cause you undue distress — go to SilentMind. Listen to your thoughts. Consider its message... and then, when the thought no longer creates an anxiety, dispel it. You will become calm. It will have been a lesson needed to be learned."

"You will find that gifts, not yet known to you, are hidden away within the inner sanctum of your being. They will be revealed along this journey, coming to the light when needed — or when appropriate. At a point along the way you will all realize a bond developing between you. A bond you have not known before, but one that you can rely upon in the future. This bond you develop and share together will last all lifetimes that you choose."

"Trust and respect each other's gifts, and at all times, or whenever possible, collectively make decisions based upon compassion, integrity, trust, goodness, and the safety of all concerned. Have respect, appreciation and happiness for another's accomplishments for they will be yours also."

"While all Amythesians are highly enlightened beings, and all Amythesians have the opportunity to advance in the profession of their choice, it is those chosen as Initiates, those who possess and have exhibited unique and uncommon gifts which we acknowledge on this day. By accepting the "Star of Guidance" you assume this honor, this obligation, this covenant — and in so doing, you will honor us as Initiates of Brightness."

"As you journey on your Wisdom Path, know that all Amythesians anticipate your safe return and the promise of your Being, now and for all futures.

The Goodness of All Things allows for life to happen and be experienced. That includes all that life entails my young friends. The freedom to be — the good — the grievous — and the inevitable transition to the next Realm, which is the promise of the futures I speak of. But, always remember, we do not know how long we each have…here in this lifetime. That is up to life itself. In other words, make each moment count! It is a gift."

Raising her arms, and holding the High Scepter of the One aloft for all to see, HighPriestess XennaOne stated…

"Initiates of Brightness, because of the promise we sense, and the belief we have in each of you, the Voice of One, the Beings of all Amythesia, and I, HighPriestess XennaOne, present each of you with the Star of Guidance!

This is a beginning that has been gifted you. You are the Initiates of Brightness — the journey is yours — the results will be shared with us all. Allow your souls to guide you with compassion, see through the eyes of all, and feel through every heart. You will never return to us the same as before, our young friends. That is our blessing, and our gift to you — and so it shall be!"

HighPriestess XennaOne stepped back, and bowed to all before her.

The Spectrum Hall erupted in an explosion of applause and accolades for HighPriestess XennaOne's words of wisdom and guidance and for the Initiates of Brightness. The Initiates all stood, hugged, and turned to share the joy emanating from the well wishers cheering. XennaOne personally came down and gifted each Initiate with their Star of Guidance. Everyone began to encompass the small group offering happiness, best wishes, congratulations, and a safe but learned journey along their Wisdom Path.

XennaOne, retired back to the stage. She quietly watched, and gave a small but sincere thanks to the One. Then smiling without, and thankful within, the HighPriestess XennaOne departed.

magical moments are meant to be experienced

but, a few times in life...

meant to be caressed...

meant to be cherished...

meant to be put away...

we are meant to proceed

bocc

poet and Initiate of Brightness on the Wisdom Path Journey
Prismacia
UGT 20,872

Chapter 9

Huge Waves Began Their Undulations

The King of The Sea of the Forgotten Place

The Mother MoonLunna was full and empowering her influence on the sea below. Huge waves, beginning their undulation far out at sea, rapidly turned into roaring walls of force crashing into the sandy shores and cliff walls of the vast Carbonian Desert far above. It was an attempt, however vain, to reclaim the land it had lost throughout time.

Ignoring the extreme risk, giant Gattlings, long winged, long necked and large billed, flew frantically along the embattled shore. Each determined to catch what may be their only meal of the day in the sea creatures blown out of the water and onto the sands. A frenzy of fighting and feeding amongst the great birds generally accompanied their feast.

However, the Clammonoids, hardshell creatures with tiny spindly legs, normally found basking in the excessive sunlight found along the shore had long since burrowed deep into the sands. There, they could safely rest until the carnage above them had calmed and receded and the great Mother SunneLavva was shining once more.

It was during this time that Luxxor, the King of this sea called the Sea of the Forgotten Place, sat alone in the Temple of the Moon and 7Stars in the under world city of Neptuna. The Temple was his office and edifice of gratitude to their two great entities — the Moon, and a star cluster called 7Stars.

Long cloaked in myth, the two entities had been discovered depicted in mysterious pictographs found in the Temple and other structures in Neptuna.

It was believed that together, the Moon and 7Stars controlled much of the destiny of the Beings and their world, here at the bottom of the sea.

King Luxxor was aware of the ferocity of the surface waters above him, but here within the Dome of Life it was calm. Outside the Dome, he could see various sea creatures, glowing colorful shades of known and unknown colors.

They swam silently, unconcerned with the torrent above.

King Luxxor, considered patient, calm, fair, and wise could most often also be found with a wonderful sense of humor and wit. However, today, Luxxor's mind was preoccupied with a seemingly endless dilemma. Long, long ago, during a time of the Ancients, a protective Dome of Life had been created to encompass and protect this city of yore. During these distant times Neptuna resided on the black sands above. Somehow it sank — swallowed by the sea.

Sitting in his sanctuary he began chatting with himself. Sometimes hearing his voice helped in understanding his thoughts.

"Neptuna survives today due to the foresight, ingenuity and courage of those who came before. Remarkably they masterminded the incredible feat of bringing life back to their city — beneath the Sea of the Forgotten Place."

Shaking his head with an expression of admiration, he leaned back in his chair.

"Lets see," he said, with eyebrows raised.

"I have engaged Past Recallers, Historians and Ancientologists to search deep into what annals of history have survived to find answers to our beginnings. And we do have some promising clues! Including some ancient stone tablets and a small cache of intriguing, but undeciphered crystal sticks. Even behind my desk are some striking etchings and pictographs — even a fountain relief. But, once again we do not comprehend their message," he bemoaned, head in his hands.

Hmmm, he now thought, *an even greater mystery discovered during our search for the beginnings of Neptuna is one small notation, etched on a fragment of an ancient tablet.*

"We believe It indicates another far older city once existed in the Carbonian Desert. It too sank beneath the sands at a time beyond recollection. The unnamed authors of the tablet called it Netropia."

This discovery stuck in King Luxxor's mind, as he often wondered if there was any plausible connection between Neptuna, and this ancient city of Netropia.

"Can this city be found?"

Or am I simply an incurable romantic entertaining hopeful dreams towards the past, he mused.

King Luxxor, chuckled at himself and swiveled around to face the wall behind his desk. A beautiful relief called the Fountain of Life depicting a lovely woman with her hands cupped, as if offering a gift, returned his wistful gaze.

He gestured at the lovely lady.

"Do you think I am irrational, or perhaps obsessive" he asked?

"Hmmm, I am not sure I heard your answer."

"I am the latest in a line of successors continuing to preserve the life the ancient ones created — while coexisting with the present."

"We have succeeded!" he stated.

"Neptuna continues to thrive. So why am I concerned this obsession?"

He swiveled back around, closed his eyes, and contemplated on the positive and possible.

Here in Neptuna we take great care to ensure all life is full, and there are no needs by our Beings. Here also, on the floor of the sea, under the Dome of Life, in an ancient temple called the Podium lay the Pods of Amythesians — Beings who choose, or need, to rest in extended DreamState until awakened at an appointed time. After all had been considered, the Pods being here under the waters of the Sea of The Forgotten Place was selected as the safest place.

King Luxxor shook his head considering the immense technical and moral responsibility involved.

Individual crystal Pods protectively enclose a Being's Spirit or Soul, while other Pods, containing their physical bodies are ceaselessly monitored until the two are reunited once again.

"The protection of these Pods is a privilege, and commitment not withstanding any in Amythesia. We will never do less than our best — ever!"

At times, King Luxxor, fraught with anxiety regarding the extreme importance of this task would drift into moods of deep concern, but at this moment, an awareness of fulfillment flushed through his senses.

"We will always persist," he declared. "All things are possible."

This was his mood when Liluuc, his Queen came to find him, here in the Temple of the Moon and 7Stars. Luxxor looked up as Liluuc entered the Inner chamber of the Temple — the "Sanctuary of Luxxor," as she liked to call it.

His mood lifted even more when he saw her. He adored her.

"And, how is my Chosen One, Liluuc?"

"I feel better now that I have found you, Luxxor," the Queen replied. "I have come to speak of our children, Tunnis and Dolpho."

"What is it, Liluuc, is all well?"

"Yes, yes, but they sometimes ask of me things I cannot answer unless it is an answer of possibility, and not one of certainty."

"Such as, my Chosen One?"

"Well, for one, Luxxor, our lovely Dolpho is inquiring as to how it can be so tempestuous on the surface of our domain, and yet so calm here below?"

"Hmmm," murmured Luxxor, "good question."

"And, Tunnis, our son, and mirror image of you, my Chosen One ... only, well, more youthful," she said teasingly, "is beginning to find an attraction to the lovely girls here in the realm. You need to be aware of that," she said with a grin.

"Well, it makes me happy he appreciates the difference," Luxxor said, also grinning broadly, and recognizing Liluuc's wit and humor.

"Yes, true, my Chosen One, my King, this does indeed please me that he is beginning to notice the wiser and fairer sex. Those of strength and compassion, those of beauty and high ideals, those of wisdom, those ..."

Raising his hand and lifting his SeaSeptor high, Luxxor said charmingly...

"Enough my Chosen One, enough. I cannot, and will not, argue against strength, compassion, beauty, wisdom, and ideals. For to do so would be disrespectful of all that you are, my Liluuc, my Chosen One ... my Queen. However, I will give thought to this matter, and handle it accordingly at an appropriate time."

Rising, and walking over to her, he softly took her in his strong arms, and kissed her. Liluuc rested her head upon his chest, thankful for her Chosen One.

Chapter 10

They Entered The Translight Beam

We will never return the same

It was a glorious day! The Wisdom Path journey began with much pomp, enthusiasm and anticipation. The Initiates took great care regarding items to bring as the weight each would, or could carry was an issue.

Light, all weather tents were given out, but each Initiate was responsible for their required items. This included foot ware, loose bodysuits, head wraps, and toiletries — items which could be worn daily and cleansed as needed. They also opted to include light, rollable, casual Ritual wear, plus eyeshades, perfumes, and jewelry limited to a small pouch. After all, they determined, who knew whom they may encounter, or what event may present itself.

Patto also included a portable StarGazeer for viewing the stars along the way. He stated...

"It will aid in using the stars as a reference for our approximate location should the need present itself."

Bocc, chose to bring his personal crystal scribe to script his thoughts and poetry.

Calla stuffed in body tights for her daily exercises, while Annuj included an assortment of healing herbs she had concocted.

"I have Limaset for colds, Cayya for cuts, Lapisian Clay for bruising, and Silverdrop for infections, and many of these can be combined for almost any remedy," she informed them.

Given Laurra was still not at full strength, Bocc and Patto personally insisted on carrying her items until she became stronger. Laurra, sensing "no" was not an option, accepted their generous offer, giving both a big sincere hug.

Finally, the Initiates added food and water to initially sustain them.

Since they were entering the desert at the "time of rain," water, as well as some food could be replenished. They were prepared.

The night before, the Initiates had attended a "sending off" festivity with the HighPriestess XennaOne and Ambassadors from each of the Quins.

Each Initiate was presented with a beautiful Amythesian violet hand palm crystal featuring Ivorysian white crystal screens. It visually, and verbally allowed them to record their individual Wisdom Path journey and if needed, could be used as a transmitter to send and receive messages.

The appointed time arrived, and their journey began. The 4 Guardians of Destiny, the Initiates, and Poona the caretaker entered the Translight Beam Capsule and the small group left Spectrum. Lining the way, they noticed many well wishers raising their palms, in salute and gratitude.

Annuj intuitively sensed an uneasiness emulating from many well wishers. Hidden beneath their smiles, perhaps the citizens of the Quins, and of Spectrum were realizing what she was now coming to understand herself.

"We will never return the same Beings as before — never," she uttered!

The High Priestess XennaOne said exactly that during the ceremony. Our childhood and the youth of our lives will disappear … forever gone, except in memory.

"We will awaken to — what," she whispered?

Standing near Annuj, Laurra overheard, and whispered back.

"We will hopefully awaken and return with a new understanding of life, enlightenment, and other emotions perhaps not experienced before, Annuj.

Actually, a real possibility exists that some may not return — due to choice, or chance, or reason, or destiny. Except for our involvement, the path is an unknown!"

Annuj gazed into the eyes of Laurra realizing the truth of her words.

A flush of empathy suddenly inundated her being and she sought comfort and support. She remembered HighPriestess XennaOne's comment.

"Go to SilentMind and listen to your thoughts."

Annuj closed her eyes and mentally called on the One, within…

Oh compassionate One, calm our worries. Our youth, our childhoods, and perhaps our innocence may vanish somewhere along the path. Let it be that our spirits always remain youthful. Allow childlike ways to always be within our beckoning and grasp. May the promise of this journey be only the first episode guiding our thoughts and actions for the common good of not only our world, but also for that which lies beyond in the Heavens. Allow our epilogue to be written…So it is, So it shall be, So be it.

She reached out for Laurra's hand.

Chapter 11

He Noticed A Soft Glow Of Light

Tunis and Dolpho, the ancient passage

From his crystal cave overlooking the Sea of the Forgotten Place, BucchaSim watched the ongoing drama of storm verses sea and land. The strong sea smells and heavy mist carried by the winds stimulated him.

I am experiencing something tempestuous and intense ... so much grander than myself, he thought.

He was about to give thanks to Mother Nature and retreat back into his cozy home when he noticed a glow of light escaping from a small crack in the side of the cliff across, and just below his view.

It suddenly disappeared!

Nearby, and far up a long forgotten passageway inside of the mountain, Tunnis and Dolpho peered through a crack in the wall at the fury of the Sea of The Forgotten Place far below them.

"We should really speak of our discovery to father and mother," spoke Tunis.

"I know, I know," replied Dolpho, as she watched the firelite she held burn out. "But it is our secret, our discovery, Tunnis. I like having our secret place."

"Yes, but this could be of great importance to father. I mean, if we know about this secret passageway into Neptuna there could possibly be others who do also. It could prove to be important in other ways, too, Dolpho."

"Well, I do not think anyone else is aware of this passage, Tunnis. If a stranger had wandered down to Neptuna, and ventured in, surely someone, by now, would have noticed. After all, they would certainly be the color of their Quin and not the color of our Neptunian skin."

This somewhat pacified Tunnis, but still, he thought...

I still feel the right thing to do is to inform our father about this extraordinary discovery.

34

"Dolpho, we have been coming up here for some two weeks now, and have yet to venture further than this room. It must be the end of the passageway, although I do not know why it would just end, but, it apparently does. It is time to tell father, Dolpho!"

The passageway itself consisted of stairs cut out of a soft material they were not aware of, and was about five feet wide, and approximately eight feet high. The walls were fairly rough, except for occasional smooth areas with strange drawings and figures carved into them that neither Tunnis or Dolpho had ever seen before.

Tunnis took Dolpho's hand.

"We should return to Neptuna, Dolpho. It is getting colder and darker, and we do not have another firelite. Besides, this is much later than we have ever been out exploring before. You know father and mother are not going to be very happy and will definitely want to know where we have been. We may have no choice but to tell them of what we have found."

Inching their way down, Dolpho said...

"We need to come across another firelite, Tunnis. There just isn't enough light penetrating these small openings in the walls of the passage for us to see. Any light outside has been completely blocked by those storm clouds we noticed earlier, and you are right, it is getting darker."

"Here is one, Dolpho," Tunnis anxiously said, reaching up for another firelite in one of the holders placed sparingly along the passageway.

He attempted to light it. It did not light!

"It does not light, Tunnis! We will just have to move on until we come to another one, and I am getting cold! It will take us forever to reach Neptuna."

Tunnis and Dolpho clasped hands once again and slowly continued their descent down the dark, foreboding ancient pathway. Tunnis was cold too, and became somewhat anxious. In order to take their minds off off the situation they were in he continued trying to convince Dolpho that they should reveal their discovery to their father immediately upon returning tonight.

However, Dolpho's mind was elsewhere.

She had first sensed and then heard the sounds, confirming her apprehension. She took in a long breath and exhaled.

There are never any sounds, in here!

Turning to Tunnis, who had now become quiet, Dolpho whispered...

"There is something up there, behind us Tunnis — listen."

BucchaSim had seen the faint flickering light through the small crack in the wall of the mountain and had then seen it disappear. He reacted quickly as it came from an ancient passageway he discovered many years ago. The passage began beneath the Neptunian Sea of the Forgotten

Place and led up through the mountain side cliff to an ancient Ritual hall overlooking the sea below.

At least BuccaSim concluded it could have been a Ritual Hall. The hall opened up into a large adjoining cave, which opened into the vast Carbonian Desert. BucchaSim had made this adjoining cave his home. It was at the beginning and the end of both the sea and the desert.

He called it 'SeaCliff.'

It was far from everybody and everything, which is what he had needed these past several years. After discovering the cave and exploring the passageway, BucchaSim realized that no one had used it for centuries — if not longer. The first thing he undertook was creating a false wall separating his cave from the Ritual hall. If anyone, no matter how improbable the chance, came up through the passageway they would believe it ended at the Ritual hall.

As he quickly considered all possibilities, BucchaSim surmised...

Whoever was in the passageway was certainly from Neptuna, for how else could they have gotten in?

Grabbing a firelite, he lit it, quickly entered the Ritual hall, descended the stairs and followed the sounds of footsteps and scuffling below. Knowing the passageway well, and having the firelite, it took him little time to catch up to the sounds. He had not yet determined just why he was doing this. Maybe someone had discovered his home, or maybe he instinctively knew someone may be in danger and in need of help.

He was right.

As he drew nearer, he saw what appeared to be two young Beings standing in the dark, looking back up at him.

He called out to them.

"Hello there, please stop where you are and let me help. I am BucchaSim.

Do not be afraid. I live near here, and I know this place well. This passageway can be dangerous in the dark."

Tunnis and Dolpho glanced at each other and then up towards where the light shone and the voice came from. They were anxious, but not frightened, at least not of the man calling himself BuccaSim. Something about his voice gave them a sense of calm.

Approaching them, BuccaSim held the firelite before him, casting wild and mysterious shadows on the walls. They flinched at this and clasped hands a little tighter.

In a calming manner, he said,

"Well, judging from your Seafoam colored skin, I believe you must be of the sea world Neptuna."

"I am Dolpho, and, yes, we are."

"And, I am Tunnis, and we do live in Neptuna below. We accidentally discovered this passageway and have been exploring."

"Aha, I see," said BucchaSim. "Well, Tunnis and Dolpho, it is indeed a pleasure to meet you, even in such strange circumstances, but you must know it is extremely late to be out here in this dark passage. If your intention is to return to Neptuna tonight, I can assure you that by the time you get through the darkness and back to your home, it will be very, very late. I am sure your parents are going to be terribly worried by then — if not already."

Stroking his chin, BucchaSim said...

"I believe we have a situation here, that in my opinion will require you to spend the night at my humble abode above. If what little I understand about crystals is correct, you can contact your parents through what is called palm transmission via an amethyst crystal prism, of which I have many in my home. Surely, one will work, if you know how."

"We do," they both chimed in.

"I am not surprised. You young Beings are up on all the latest advances. Alright, in that case, Tunnis and Dolpho, if you have been missed, I am sure your parents are undoubtedly deeply concerned. We should return to my place quickly to reach them as soon as possible for their peace of mind."

"Tomorrow I will lead you back down, and all will be well."

Tunnis and Dolpho both thought to themselves...

Not with father it won't!

Agreeing to go with BucchaSim, they soon reached his abode and were surprised upon first being shown the secret way into his home.

"I understand now how we missed your secret door," said Tunnis.

"It looks just like part of the rock wall with a crack in it." Dolpho added.

"Amazing," they both replied simultaneously.

They looked admiringly at BucchaSim, who inwardly smiled at his craftsmanship.

Once inside, they found BucchaSim's home to be very warm, tidy, clean, and quite spacious. Many unusual and interesting things were lying about, arousing their curiosity and questions, but BucchaSim was insistent that they communicate with their parents immediately.

"They will be worried," he said.

Dolpho and Tunnis found the amethyst crystal prism needed to contact their father and mother and together they placed their palms onto the smooth surface. Once their palm code was activated, the screen became white for them to record verbally on.

Nervously, they announced themselves.

"Hello father and mother, this is Tunnis."

"And this is Dolpho," she chimed in.

"We are fine, and up on top of the mountain above Neptuna. We were exploring and it got dark, and a nice man called BucchaSim found us. He says the way down is to dangerous in the dark and that he will bring us down early tomorrow morning."

She looked over at Tunnis...

"It is me, Tunnis, father and mother. Dolpho and I are so sorry if we caused you to worry. Time just slipped away from us, but we have exciting news and want to tell you all about it."

Then, together, Dolpho and Tunnis said...

"We love you. Goodnight."

BucchaSim added to their message...

"It is unlikely that you are even aware of me, but I wish you to know your children are safe here in my home. I will personally see they are returned tomorrow before noon. I am called BucchaSim and live nearby where I spotted the young ones. Please rest assured they are well and safe, and will have a comfortable place to rest tonight."

He stepped back from the screen.

Tunnis and Dolpho removed their palms from the glowing crystal and waited to see if there would be a reply.

It came quickly!

It was a man's voice, and BucchaSim noticed he spoke with kindness and relief, but also with authority.

"We are greatly relieved to find you are safe, Tunnis and Dolpho. Your mother and I have been concerned to say the least. We will indeed have much to discuss tomorrow. I agree with the man, BucchaSim regarding staying there overnight. It is the wisest thing to do given the late hour and distance involved.

I am truly thankful BucchaSim, for the concern you have displayed for our children. It will be remembered. You must join us tomorrow as our guest for dinner ...and stay the night. You would honor me and my Chosen one."

"Tunnis and Dolpho, you must let me know just how you came to leave the Dome of Life so we can meet you there when you arrive back tomorrow. I will be most interested. We will await your transmission in the morning. Until then."

BucchaSim looked at Tunnis and Dolpho.

"I am quite sure they will be very interested in what you have to say tomorrow. However, I need to ask one very big favor of you — I would be indebted to you if you only speak of your discoveries to your father and mother. At this time I choose to be alone, here, in my home. I would not want hoards of people coming to explore just yet. Perhaps, we can say I live in a cave nearby, which is truthful."

Tunnis spoke up…

"I am sure our father will be thankful for your help, and he is very good at considering what is best for all concerned."

"I see," said BucchaSim, "then let me show you to your cots for the night. We will begin down when the light illuminates the passageway early in the morning."

Beneath the storm and beneath the Sea of The Forgotten Place, Luxxor turned to Liluuc and said…

"Since we now know our young ones are safe, my Queen, I just want to say, this better be good tomorrow when I speak with them!"

Liluuc smiled at Luxxor's attempt at humor. She knew he had been very worried. Liluuc sighed, also relieved that their children were safe.

"You know, Luxxor, knowing Tunnis and Dolpho are well and in good hands, I must say that I feel a tingle of excitement that they are so adventurous and courageous … just like their father, my Chosen One."

Luxxor's eyes twinkled.

"I also am pleased, my Queen, my Chosen One. I love you Liluuc."

"I love you too, Luxxor."

Chapter 12

The Sky Grew Ominous, The Winds Violent

Poona, a revelation in the translight beam

Poona stood silently within the Translight Beam, watching, as the small group of Initiates, and Guardians of Destiny, slowly glided over the Amythesian terrain. They were on their way to the edge of the vast Carbonian Desert still many, many miles to the East.

And they were in no hurry.

For a while they passed over large, flat, polished crystals, brought in from each of the 5 Quins. These were arranged in beautiful mosaic mandala patterns. Serpentine in fashion, the path meandered along for acres outside the city of Spectrum. Flourishing with plant life, flowers, and resting benches, it was similar to ancient images Poona had seen as a small child, and nostalgia began to swell within.

From her vantage point she identified TransStarPalmations — tall stalks with large translucent palm leaves sparkling like star dew in the early morning moisture; diminutive Garloonas of a fuchsia shade which were barely recognizable; Crystolamunns, delicate tiny blue and deep pink flowers planted between the flat mosaic crystals; and finally, in the collected menagerie she noticed Marbolica stalks of a milky green color. When all are grown in a tight moss grass they created a crystal path of beauty and fragrance.

A garden place, she considered, *offering harmony within human souls for all to share, whether entering or departing.*

Poona breathed in the fragrance.

The significance of this beauty is not lost on me. It is symbolic of the Universe, and representational of the harmonious majesty and beauty of the galactic Heavens above.

"As above, so below," Poona murmured.

A slight glow seemed to continually radiate from within Poona. Known

40

as a caregiver, she was also a soul-keeper — but spirituality is where Poona found her values of life.

We all have within us the capabilities to commune with the One, the All... to react to situations, to sense and feel the comfort or pain of those which we are here to help. We have but to offer compassion, relief and guidance as it is delivered to us from The One. I wonder why those ...

Thunder from afar abruptly awakened Poona from her dream thoughts and back to the Translight Beam and her journey.

Ah, The sky is growing darker, and even more ominous since our departure.

Far in the distance, Poona could see veils of rain pummeling the ground. She wondered of the conditions they would soon find in the Carbonian desert.

Although within the protective sphere of the Translight Beam, they were beginning to feel the force of occasional gale winds approaching from their destination. Strong and disturbing to most, but not to Poona.

This is a living experience. An opportunity to encounter an offering of nature — it excites me, she mused.

A side of Poona, as of yet unknown, was definitely more earthy and decidedly mystical. Storms, mysteries, space and periods of DeepSoul meditation intrigued her — and occasionally ... 'other things.'

She noticed Patto and his reaction to the distant storm. He was intently watching it with what he called his StarGazeer.

Rather antiquated, she considered, *but apparently it is adequate for a closer observation. He does not appear concerned by the storm we are approaching at all. Enchanting! I must get to know you better, Patto.*

Chapter 13

It's Especially Good To Know Your Prey, Son, But Most Often, It's Even Better To Be Lucky

The Prismaworm hunts

TerraSim sat crouched down near the end of a ridge with the strong Carbonian Desert winds howling around him. The worm was still lingering beneath and he was forced to remain still — no movement at all, until he felt the worm move on, or descend deeper. Any motion now on his part could be a fatal move.

He had been following a ridge in the sand, which a worm leaves when close to the surface. He instinctively sensed that the worm must have apparently descended and come back up at a prior point along the ridge — and was now coming up behind him.

These creatures are great hunters, he thought.

Clever.

Hmmm ... perhaps a second worm, possibly a young one was following it's mother. Which ever, or both, he surmised, *a worm has ceased it's movement almost directly below my position by the ridge, and is waiting.*

Not my best scenario!

TerraSim had been researching the worms of the Carbonian Desert for some time now in an attempt to see what benefits, if any, they could be used for.

Perhaps the meat from a worm would be edible, therefore benefiting Prismacians in a sustainable way such as a food source. Perhaps they could be trained. Who knows?

He had learned much throughout the years in regards to the worm's habitats, habits, and diet! To his dismay, irregardless of how rare that it occurred, Beings were always an accepted and apparently a prized addition to any worm's meal.

Thankfully, he considered, *at least there are very few Beings who venture through this immense desert.*

Those that did, and were unaided, or without an experienced guide, hopefully knew the risk they took and worms were only one of the dangers.

If he waited, he knew that sooner or later a movement would be detected elsewhere by the worm, or it would eventually tire, and move on. Given the dark gathering storm clouds, increasing velocity of the winds, and the veils of rain he saw descending further to the north, his other option, would be to wait until the rains pelted down on the graved sands of the desert creating noise and movement, thus confusing the worm below.

He did not have long to wait. A great Gattling, usually found closer to the sea, flew down and settled on the the top of the sandy, graveled ridge where he huddled silently below. It began pecking around searching for assorted sand bugs and small crawling creatures.

I can't believe this, TerraSim thought, *The chance of a Gattling landing this close to a Being is unheard of and its movements are going to encourage the worm to strike. I am way to close to the Gattling. If the worm strikes I may be it's meal! Oh, luck be with me!*

Except for the howling winds little was to be heard in the so-thought emptiness of the desert. The smallest of sounds rumbled below the sands.

The giant Gattling raised it's head, curious.

It began to look around.

TerraSim held his breath as he wondered if he or the Gattling, or both were to be a meal. Terrified, he slowly pulled into a tight ball and waited for the outcome. The Gattling's last act was indeed it's last, as a huge gaping mouth exploded from the sand, engulfing the Gattling, as if a flea. Apparently content with it's small morsel of a meal for the moment and possibly thinking the Gattling was the source of any movement it had sensed above, the worm plunged into the sand once again and moved on across the desert looking for it's next encounter, and meal.

TerraSim dared not move. He let out a long exhale of thank you, thank you!

A Prismacian worm, besides being a ferocious predator, was appallingly ghastly to see. To begin with, it was huge and had a very pale, whitish-blue transparent skin that looked as though it were connected every 3 or 4 feet by an inner circular wire. This allowed the worm to contract or expand rapidly thereby giving it the ability to explode out of the sand quickly and violently. It had sharp, pointy teeth and when it's mouth was agape there was a constant mucous saliva spittle accompanied by a nauseating foul smell.

In the name of One I have not found a good reason for their existence.

You would think there would have to be one though, he pondered, now sighing heavily and recovering from his close encounter.

Eventually he lay spread eagle out on the sands, still letting out gasps of thankfulness. He had broken out in a cold sweat, but now he felt the rains begin to fall upon him and the sand, cleansing the scene, and scent of this horrific moment.

TerraSim lay for a long time, his heart still pounding, replaying the moment of whether he or the bird was doomed.

What in One's name am I thinking about.

He then softly chuckled to himself.

What did I just think? In the past, I would have thought what in God's name, but I said in One's name. Ah ha, I must be becoming a Prismacian.

Smiling, he eventually came to one thought … how his father, BucchaSim had been right.

It's especially good to know your prey, son, but, most often, it's even better to be lucky.

He finally relaxed, thinking…

How could you ever catch one of these things anyway?

TerraSim shook his head. He knew, as an old Earth saying went… he had dodged another bullet.

Chapter 14

This Was An Important Person In Neptuna

BucchaSim and the King

By the time BucchaSim and his two guests descended the long passageway the next morning and finally reached the hidden entrance to Neptuna, it was near noon. The descent went smoothly, but longer than necessary due to Tunnis and Dolpho's curiosity regarding the various wall encryptions and BucchaSim's opinion of them.

"You must realize mine is only an uneducated and uninformed opinion," he had stated, but found they still listened intently.

Actually, he found the two of them to be quite lively, curious and interested in his views. Their enthusiasm and spirit became infectious. What they were not aware of, at this time, were the secrets he opted to keep to himself regarding other significant discoveries he had found.

Tunnis and Dolpho had verbally transmitted the time of their approximate arrival to their parents — and where their arrival would be. So, as they approached the secret entrance, they were greeted by the presence of Divine Guardians lining each side of the passage. Tunnis cast a glance at Dolpho as they walked by them and both wondered if this was a prelude to an unpleasant reception from their father.

Tunnis and Dolpho, followed by BucchaSim, entered the sub chamber beneath the Hall of Records and Antiquities and saw that their father, and mother, were waiting with several members of the High Council of Neptuna.

They slowly came to a stop as Luxxor and Liluuc came up to them, and warmly embraced them. Luxxor knelt down on one knee before them both and placing his hand upon his heart, softly said...

"Tunnis, Dolpho, your mother and I are so relieved you have returned to us safely. We have always respected your honesty, and both applaud your innovative spirit, your curiosity and your enthusiastic interest in exploration. Your mother and I fully encourage it. However, from now on, out of respect for your mother and me, you are to please inform us of any findings before you explore them further. Who knows, I may choose to include myself in on the adventure and we could all share in it together!"

Compassionately, he said...

"We will speak further of this tomorrow, after our guest has departed."

"And," he added, "regarding our guest, it is due time to meet him."

Rising, King Luxxor turned his attention to BucchaSim, who by this time had ascertained that this was an important person here in Neptuna. As Luxxor approached, BucchaSim was unsure exactly how to react, wondering...

Who is this man, and just what was proper protocol?

"Be yourself, just be yourself," he muttered under his breath.

King Luxxor stood before him. They were close in height, with Luxxor being somewhat taller. Looking at each other in the eyes, King Luxxor said...

"BucchaSim, you are most welcome, and have our undying gratitude." Gesturing for Liluuc to join them, he extended his hand in thanks and greeting.

"Allow me to introduce ourselves, BucchaSim. I am King Luxxor and this is Queen Liluuc — we are man and wife, father and mother. Many will say she is my better half, and I can hardly disagree."

Smiling, he looked lovingly at his wife.

I like this man, thought BucchaSim, grasping Luxxor's hand, and exchanging a mutually firm handshake.

Queen Liluuc, greeted BucchaSim. Her expression portraying a mother's love.

"We are indebted to you, BucchaSim, for watching after our children. We, as I am sure you have concluded by now, are the very relieved parents of Prince Tunnis, and Princess Dolpho."

BuccchaSim, his light blue eyes finding hers, bowed his head in respect.

"It is indeed my pleasure to have shared time with Tunnis and Dolpho — pardon me, I should say, the Prince and Princess, and to help them back safely. It is also a great honor to meet you, King Luxxor, and Queen Liluuc."

"BucchaSim is an unusual name," stated King Luxxor, "but one we are thankful to welcome here in Neptuna. Come, join us, as we are having a lunch prepared in our home nearby. I hope you will enjoy the views, and I am pleased we can share some time together. I am also interested in just where you live."

Having a little time before lunch, King Luxxor took BucchaSim on a quick tour of some nearby buildings he felt would be of interest to BucchaSim.

Queen Liluuc went on ahead to see to things. She rather liked that.

Of course, to BucchaSim, everything in Neptuna was of immense interest.

"This is an amazing feat of architecture and engineering. How did they ever get the Dome of Life I see, in place, King Luxxor?"

"To explain the Dome of Life adequately is for others to attempt, BucchaSim. I can struggle through it, acquainting you with the fringes of high mathematics, the engineering, and the absolute marvel of it all, but would lack sadly in any adequate depth of technical explanation."

BucchaSim smiled, understanding.

Gesturing to the Dome of Life, Luxxor grinned, saying...

"Excuse the pun, BucchaSim, but, 'to top it off' this was achieved many, many eons ago. Designed, fabricated and installed, when Neptuna resided above ground, near the edge of the Carbonian desert and overlooking the sea. Apparently, violent, strong winds blowing from the desert towards the Sea of the Forgotten Place became the accepted rule rather than the exception. The opposing sea winds were apparently no match for the turbulence on the desert. More and more Carbonite dust was pummeling the city and the demand and need for enough adequate, daily breathable air was truly becoming hazardous."

"Life or death, if you will."

"They predicted another 50 to 100 Prisma years for them to survive in the desert location with the existing conditions. Astounding everyone, the engineers completely exceeded all expectations and within 14 years the Dome of Life was installed. It was, and is, a marvel of our technology and determination, BucchaSim."

"Not only did it create a completely breathable habitat, but another astonishing and incredible aspect of the Dome was that it was flexible — thereby able to cope with devastating events that could occur such as Prisma quakes, high winds, and eventually, as it turns out, the strong underwater currents we face today. You see, BucchaSim, so many eons ago, when Neptuna sank to the floor of the sea, it basically sank intact."

"Our Beings had evacuated the city, but the Dome of Life still surrounded and protected Neptuna, only this time the air contained within the Dome helped protect from the pressures of the sea itself. The story goes that once it was determined that the city was basically intact — with some breathable air still inside the Dome, a plan to somehow inhabit it again, under the sea, was formulated."

"All the Beings agreed."

"Still, getting fresh air in as soon as possible, and then the inhabitants, became yet another feat of unbelievable ingenuity, and expediency. A story to be told at another time. Where they lived during these years is not known, as much was lost, hidden, or destroyed in the quake."

King Luxxor, stopped, and sat down on a nearby step. He unashamedly wiped tears from his eyes.

"Their courage under such conditions still touches my emotions, BucchaSim. It is so overwhelming."

BucchaSim, momentarily overcome by the courage and sheer willpower of the Neptunian Beings of so long ago, shook his head in awe, saying…

"They have my utmost respect, King Luxxor, as do you and the Beings of Neptuna today."

He too sat down, beside the King.

Later they reached the royal dwellings, which were set within a large white crystal, affording views of the extraordinary sea life which existed outside the Dome of Life. BucchaSim was taken by the crackled, sparkling pieces of emerald crystal separating the large, white ivory crystal slabs which made up the flooring of the dwelling, and in which, he found out, also contained the conduit for heat.

All of this apparently created out of an existing crystal? How did they accomplish that, he wondered, *especially under the Sea.*

A pleasing source of soft light emanated from within large amber crystals situated throughout, creating a warm ambiance which spread through every part of the Royal dwelling. The 'sparkling' BucchaSim noticed from the cracked emerald crystals beneath his feet continually glittered throughout the dwelling too.

This would be easy to get used to, thought BucchaSim. *Someday I will bring Junnuj here.*

The decor was minimal, but tasteful and very comfortable — both physically and visually. He assumed it was the womanly touch of Queen Liluuc, and perhaps, Princess Dolpho.

Later, over a very late lunch, Queen Liluuc described the spectacular feast spread out before them.

"We have roasted Gattling, small tender quibbs served with lobtal sauce, and 'for your greens' please try these various boiled sea grasses. The main course is a large, baked Solomon basted with an incredible spicy sauce of unknown origin."

"I am sure it will be as delicious as it looks. Queen Liluuc. I am honored, and I thank you all," spoke BucchaSim.

The King poured Queen Liluuc, BucchaSim, and himself each a crystal of Loctuum, further warming the spirits of all. He listened intently, as

Tunnis, and Dolpho carried on excited conversations about the wonderful old passage they had discovered, occasionally asking BucchaSim for clarification on things they were not sure of. At one point, Queen Liluuth, suggested to her Chosen One that it would indeed be a nice adventure to accompany Tunnis and Dolpho in further explorations of the ancient passageway. King Luxxor nodded his enthusiasm for the idea.

BucchaSim sat back and relaxed for the first time in a long time.

What a very pleasant, entertaining and informative experience this is.

I do like these people. I must divulge other secrets they are unaware of. They will probably be incredibly pertinent to Neptuna. I truly should have done it sooner. I now know this for a fact. After all, it is their history and their linage.

I will do it soon!

Chapter 15

She Whispered In The Night—He Did Not Hear

A matter of tears

Before leaving the next morning BucchaSim took the opportunity to explain to King Luxxor his situation regarding the cave where he lived.

"It is just beyond a Ritual Room at the top of the passage," he explained.

"I have disguised the entry very well, but the possibility of being discovered has always been a concern."

Thinking for a few moments on the solution needed at this time, King Luxxor said...

"Perhaps, for the moment, we need to keep your place, your secret, BucchaSim. As I see it, there is no need to make public that an unknown exit from Neptuna has been discovered and that there also exists an entrance in which to reach Neptuna from the ground above. It will be difficult as it is to explain your presence in all this. For the time being you will be kept out of the picture. We will busy ourselves with studying the passageway itself, and the Ritual Room.

Then, when we all feel the time is right, the rest can be revealed. If needed, we can explain why it had to remain a secret for a while. I think all will be placated in due time. Are you in agreement BucchaSim?"

BucchaSim nodded in agreement, inwardly struggling with guilt about not divulging 'other secrets' to King Luxxor at this time.

I know I should reveal all to King Luxxor, but the disclosures will come soon enough anyway. The next time we meet I will physically show it to him. Given all that has transpired, and in such a short time, the right opportunity between myself and King Luxxor has not materialized to carry on further conversations about secrets within the passage — and they are important secrets. I hope I am doing the right thing.

Up until now, I did not know for sure about the moral and ethical fiber of King Luxxor — now I do! He smiled, feeling better about his decision.

Shaking hands in parting and thanking each other, he offered up the possibility for another visit in the very near future. King Luxxor enthusiastically accepted.

BucchaSim was in no hurry. It took him some time before finally ascending the long ancient stairwell and reaching SeaCliff. Many things were going through his mind and his heart was heavy. He went directly to a small area of his home that gave him a view of the sea below. The darkening sky began to brood overhead.

I need to think some more, or perhaps I just need to clear my mind.

It has become clear that I have become — what? Perhaps envious of Luxxor and Liluuc, he considered? *What they have is something that has been taken from me. They share their lives with each other each day. They have their love and their children, while I am basically alone.*

That is it!

Sitting, he stared out.

"Oh, Goodness, I am feeling so sad at this moment."

Restless, BuccaSim stood again and leaned against the railing of the balcony. The sea, with it's waves rushing in and then out again, were disturbingly comforting.

The emotions I am experiencing now have surfaced many times before over these past several years. Oh, how I need answers.

He questioningly confronted the waves...

"Was there something I should have done differently?"

A muffled roar from the crashing waves made its way up to BuccaSim. He thought back.

Yes, I have been blessed by the love of a good companion and have a wonderful son that I care deeply for and love very much. He is gone ... exploring most of the time now, though. And my daughter! Oh, Goodness, I don't even know my own daughter. I don't even know what her name is now, or where she is. She has been gone since she was but a baby.

Putting his head back, he sighed deeply, crying out...

"But I long for my Junnuj to come home, to love and share my life with — to share the remaining time I have with."

What did we ever do to deserve this, he thought in anguish.

He finally slumped down into a chair and gazed blindly into the now dark sky for a long, long, time.

How did it go wrong? Maybe I just don't have the gifts of understanding or communication that is needed in a relationship. Maybe I should have become more involved in standing up to some inane political laws that are unjust. Maybe I needed to be firmer in my convictions. Maybe I should have said NO to the events that have separated Junnuj and I for so long. Maybe, maybe, maybe...

I am who I am though. I have always been true to who I am, and of what I can offer. Holding his head in his hands he visualized the one woman in his life that still touched him so deeply.

"1 miss you Junnuj," he whispered, tears welling in his eyes.

Shaking his head he thought of all the time they could have shared, knowing those times were gone — lost forever.

He lowered his head and cried.

Far away on the other side of the Carbonian Desert, there lay a small village named Oneness. It was near a place called 'Those of The Edge.'

A place where Beings went who chose to meditate, be alone — or both.

There, a woman shuddered, as the pain of sadness reached out to her from afar. She too, looked into the stars of her night, her eyes glistening with tears.

She knew! She knew the pain, and from whence it came.

She whispered into the night...

"The fault does not lie with you BucchaSim. There is no fault. There are destinies to be played out and Junnuj was destined to become The HighPriestess of the Voice of One. It was beyond your control, BucchaSim."

He did not hear.

He cried. He needed to cry.

'I cannot say I cannot live...

I cannot live without you

should you leave, I will live...

but less than ever before'

bocc

poet and Initiate of Brightness on the Wisdom Path Journey
Prismacia
UGT 20,872

Chapter 16

The Sky Wore A Heavy Shroud

The Carbonian Desert — Sheathed In Silence

Arriving at the edge of The Carbonian Desert near evening, the Guardians of Destiny, quiet as usual, helped the Initiates unload their belongings and then stood by watching. The small group of Initiates talked among themselves deciding what next to do. Before them, a barren terrain seemingly went on forever as undulating black sands extended to the horizon. It appeared mysterious and foreboding.

Above them the Heavens wore a heavy shroud of dark ominous clouds, that, judging from the wetness everywhere, had been sending down torrents of rain for days. The wind was blowing hard, but thankfully the black sand dust had been pummeled into submission, to heavily ladened with moisture to permeate the air.

Scattered intermittently, and as far as the eye could see, sparse groupings of large crystals, life long witnesses to this eternal desert, stood — sheathed in silence. They thrust upwards towards the dark Heavens in an attempt to break free of the black sand's grasp.

The Initiates, each in their own silence, stood in wonder.

Patto shivered. Gazing upward, he envisioned the Heavens and the glorious array of stars therein, somewhere beyond this dense blanket of clouds.

"Stars I have never seen before," he uttered quietly.

He glanced over at Poona and Laurra, standing nearby.

"I have always wished to journey to the stars, Poona. One day I will. The Carbonian Desert may not be the Heavens or the stars, but it is filling me with many mixed emotions. It is daunting and dangerous — and yet in some ways I find this desert to be beautiful and intriguingly awesome. It is like, somewhere out there is an answer — perhaps 'the' answer we Beings knowingly or unknowingly seek."

He shivered again.

"For some reason that sends a chill through me. It is a compelling thought, but, I wonder … do I really need, or even want to know the answer?"

Poona, appreciating Patto's sentiments, observed him in the dimming light.

She moved closer.

"What an unusual thing for you, or most anyone to say, Patto. But, I understand! The unknown 'is' alluring, offering it's own distinct form of seduction. It encourages, even entices one to 'enter at your own desire' — or risk!"

Poona's inquisitive eyes scanned the black desert and then back at Patto.

"As for me, Patto, yes … I choose to seek and to know the answers. I also choose my questions very carefully."

Patto noticed that even in the dimness of early evening and beneath dark cloud cover, Poona's eyes were sparkling.

"Yes, I agree, Poona, it is important to consider one's questions carefully.

I particularly like your comment, 'enter at your own desire, or risk.' Should we, at some point, discover that unknown place will you be my guide?"

Poona's eyes danced. Studying Patto she observed a handsome young man with apparent maturity, enthusiasm — and perhaps 'budding manhood' in his demeanor.

Hmmm, I do not detect the naivete' someone mentioned regarding Patto, she considered.

"It will be my pleasure, Patto."

Laurra walked over and stood close to Poona. Reaching out, Poona put her arm around her in a sheltering and reassuring manner, and softly whispered,

"We will make it across, Laurra. The path will become clear, and it will come to be!"

"Rest," she said to Laurra and Patto. "We need rest."

Sensing movement, they turned. The 4 Guardians of Destiny raised their hands in unison, bowed, and abruptly turned, reentering the Translight Beam.

"What are they doing? Where are they going?" Bocc asked.

"They are returning as instructed, Bocc," Annuj answered.

"The HighPriestess promised they would accompany us to the edge of The Carbonian Desert, which they have done. Now they are returning to Spectrum."

"This is our journey," she continued, "and, well, it begins. Tomorrow morning we will collect ourselves, look over the few maps of the desert that we brought and decide on our Path of Wisdom. Small areas with potable water from the storms will have collected in cavities of rocks that are said to be found along the way. Palmation Groves are also indicated scattered throughout the desert. The 'One' is providing already."

Poona leaned over and whispered to Patto...

"I see we have someone who is courageous enough to take control here in the initial phases of this adventurous journey."

Nodding affirmatively, he turned to smile at Poona.

Smiling back, she mused...

He is not afraid, but still has so much to learn ... but then, don't we all?

Why is it that young men seem to generally 'grow up' at a slower pace than young women? Interesting, she pondered.

The next morning indeed brought more of the inclement weather saturating this part of Amythesia. It was pouring. Huddling inside one tent, in obviously very tight quarters, the Initiates were partaking in a small breakfast of dried fruits, while discussing the pros and cons of waiting another day before continuing.

"It could be this way for weeks," stated Calla. "At least the temperature is bearable. In my opinion we should venture forth. I mean, this is the Wisdom Path Journey and what possible good is it to remain here?"

"It does not matter to me, indicated, Bocc. I can do either. The journey is to take as long as it will take, so, if we stay, I can write, and if we go forth I can take images on my palm prism. So either."

Patto added, "I can not study the stars here with the overcast sky anyway, and Calla is right — this weather could last for some time."

"The path is ours to create as we will," stated Laurra. "All our paths actually began a long time ago and has brought each of us to this point. My belief is we should move forward too. We all know that whether wet or dry, the sand poses a strenuous ordeal ahead. So, we may as well get on with it. Not only am I happy to be a part of this journey, I am anxious to continue. I do not feel waiting is the answer."

It was agreed.

After packing their tents, and studying their maps, they decided on an initial direction. Standing in the rain, they formed a circle and held hands. Each gave a blessing to their journey, after which a moment of SilentMind was taken. A communal hug brought their little ceremony to a close. The

Initiates gathered up their packs and headed out into the largest desert known in Amythesia — and into a storm.

During intermittent periods of torrid downpours, ample opportunity to chat among themselves presented itself as they plodded slowly through the wet, black sand. Calla, being in superlative condition, led the way, and rarely complaining or feeling the need to stop and rest, doggedly trudged on. This, however, eventually became a problem for the rest as they just were not able to continue without a break from time to time — especially Laurra.

At one point, Poona approached Calla and kindly stated...

"The object of this journey is not to get across the Carbonian Desert in one day, Calla. We are a group, needing to carry forth according to the strength of the weakest individual within our group. As caregiver, I see some are having difficulty with the pace."

Understanding, Calla unhesitatingly agreed and thanking Poona, apologized. Walking over to Laurra, and grasping her hand lovingly, Calla looked at them all and promised...

"I swear to remember the strengths of each within our group. This is our journey — together. There are many things in the desert to appreciate and to study that quite possibly may never have been examined before, at least by us. And, we may not get back this way again. We have absolutely no need to rush. I ask you all to forgive my exuberance, and especially you, Laurra."

Calla and Laurra embraced tenderly.

Everyone smiled, and huddling together, sat for a needed rest.

Chapter 17

TerraSim – An Unusual Name She Thought

TerraSim, a meeting on the sands

Three days later, and many miles on their trek into the desert sands TerraSim spotted them. TerraSim was still lingering in the same area of his 'encounter' with the Prismaworm and still in gratitude for the liberation of his life. Delirious with joy may be a good way to put it. He had not heard or seen any worms since.

They must have moved on to dustier and dryer pastures.

Except for his continuing research on the worms, that was fine with him.

Squatting on the side of a dunne and dressed in his undetectable black garb is when he first viewed them through his antiquated telescope.

"Hmmm, I make out maybe six Beings," he muttered. "Fortunately there is no rain at this time. I would never have seen them at this distance."

Interesting, they seem to be just ambling along and from what I can tell, they are heading towards — well, nothing that I can think of.

"I wonder if they are lost?"

He decided to hang around and watch for awhile.

If they are not acquainted with the inherent dangers of the desert, and it seems apparent to me they are not, then I need to be close … to help if needed — just to be sure.

As for the Initiates wandering through the sands, it had been a day now since the cramps had diminished and their legs had stopped aching. Except for daily rain storms, which could last several hours, all were in agreement they were doing quite well.

Bocc and Patto, began playfully bantering amongst themselves.

"We must be making progress, Patto, "I can not feel my legs, and can no longer see where we started."

"Well, Bocc, for that matter, I don't know which direction to even look to see where we started."

For some reason, this brought about chuckles which turned into full belly laughs by everyone. They stopped, fell to the sand laughing and began flailing about. It was silly, and it was intoxicating … and it was needed.

"The desert is playing with us," laughed Annuj, sitting up from rolling in the sands.

"You know, it is beginning to get dark," Bocc said. "Why not set up camp right here and now for the night."

TerraSim, only a short distance away at this point, observed the group suddenly begin falling to the ground, flailing their arms and legs. He became anxious and concerned that they had all contracted some form of sand delusions he was unaware of. But, as he continued watching, he could see they were laughing and slowly returning to normal…

What ever normal is, he thought. *Hmmm, they are starting to set up their camp for the evening. Curious,* he considered. *Odd even.*

He could now see there were six people, four young women and two young men and he could distinguish they were of various Quins.

What are they possibly doing here in this desert?

He was mystified.

Oh, he worried, *they are making way too much noise! Sooner or later the Prismaworms will pick up their sounds and vibrations.*

He shook his head at the ghastly possibility, knowing they were quite lucky the worms had not noticed them already.

Now that would be a situation, thought TerraSim, grimacing.

I will make contact early tomorrow and inform them of this danger — and other dangers to be aware of.

For the Initiates, in many ways the nights were the worst. First, it turned very cold at night and there were no stars, and no moonlight. Only heavy cloud cover and a howling wind. Although falling asleep came pretty easily after a day of trekking in the sand, the prospect of more of the same the next day became almost a nightmare … not the best feeling to fall asleep to.

However, this particular evening provided the unexpected. The shroud of clouds passed on, leaving them, at least for this moment, with one of the most beautiful sights they could have hoped for … a clear night in the desert with countless stars to look at and enjoy. They foraged for anything that would still burn and started a small campfire.

Gathering blankets to keep warm and thankfully sharing each other's body heat, everyone huddled around Patto. He had offered to share his considerable knowledge of the stars with them this beautiful evening.

"Stardew," exclaimed a passionate Patto to the group.

"That is my description of the billions of stars that hang suspended in the sky above you."

As he rummaged through his belongings to find his StarGazeer, Patto proceeded to explain the purpose of galaxies, stars, planets, and how each functioned. Eventually, they all excitedly took turns star gazing with his gazeer, with Patto informing them of what they were seeing.

"You are actually seeing distant galaxies and star clusters," he declared.

"Perhaps sights you have never even imagined before."

At one point, Patto, garnering everyone's attention proclaimed...

"Are you aware that it is 'guesstimated' that over 100 billion galaxies exist in the known Universe? Some speculate that if we take a cautious estimate of just 1 advanced civilization per galaxy, among the untold millions of possibilities, it would relate to a conservative evaluation of 100 billion advanced civilizations in the Universe! Realistically, this means we should have hundreds, or thousands — or millions of technologically advanced civilizations through out the Universe."

Patto smiled brightly.

"For those who are interested, I believe there are even more!"

Poona smiled inwardly gazing at 100 billion advanced civilizations above.

He is definitely in his element, thought Poona.

"Of course, we all are aware of some nearby star life, but, my fellow star seekers, on a much grander scale — we are not alone."

Everyone sat spellbound.

Were TerraSim present, he would have stated...

"You could have heard a worm burrowing," as the Initiates were all so engrossed in considering Patto's theory.

Many questions followed and the evening turned out to be an incredible gathering for the six of them. They warmly thanked Patto before retiring, each to their tents, for a well deserved rest under their warm blankets, and under the 100 billion civilizations above Prismacia.

The next morning brought a surprise. Emerging from their tents, they found SunneLavva shining brightly and the sky saturated in a cloudless, brilliant blue.

However, that was not the only surprise.

Sitting by the campfire, which he had just reignited, was a man. He smiled at them as the Initiates exchanged glances with each other.

Standing, he said...

"Hello, I am TerraSim."

Astonished to find someone in the middle of the desert and also in their camp, they initially just stood there looking at each other, and looking at him.

Annuj, spoke first.

"Hello, to you. I am Annuj and we that stand before you are the 'Initiates of Brightness' from the various Quins of Amythesia."

The Initiates all introduced themselves in turn.

TerraSim managed to suppress a smile as he picked up on the formality of their tones and actions, before saying...

"I am honored to meet you all. I see so few other Beings here, in, and around the desert. Actually, I have noticed you for a couple of days now and wondered of your destination. Of course, I was also curious as to who you were."

Looking at TerraSim, Poona thought...

What an unusual name. I must ask about that at a later time.

"TerraSim," Annuj said, "we could also be interested in why you have been noticing us for two days without making your presence known, at least until now. And, just how it is that you are here in the middle of the desert, alone. Is there a settlement nearby?"

The straight forward honesty and innocence of these Beings is definitely of the Amythesian area, realized, TerraSim.

He gestured warmly.

"Let us sit around the fire and warm ourselves from this early morning chill. I will answer your questions, Annuj, and speak to you all of other immediate, serious concerns you should be aware of. There are dangers here."

They huddled close near the fire.

Chapter 18

A Thought Was On His Mind —
Where Is TerraSim

Thoughts of BucchaSim

BucchaSim was once again on his balcony overlooking the sea, and squinting at the SunneLavva, which awakened the day, but not his. He, once again, had endured a troubled night, but this morning he awoke with a calmness not felt in a long time. A peacefulness now replaced his unhappiness. To his relief, the self contempt he had been feeling by blaming himself for all his problems was missing, and he realized ...

The need to blame others — is wrong.

After all, he considered, *everyone, does the best they can at the time. Obviously, there are times when Beings are just not up to the challenges within relationships, within societies, or within life ... change does happen. People can grow in different directions and this is usually accompanied by sadness to both parties involved. And, in my case, I felt I had no control over events taking place. In any event, I am thankful for my relationship with Junnuj and my family. And, it will not be long now that I will once again, and forever, be with my Junnuj.*

"I truly am not responsible for my current situation," BucchaSim stated, feeling a renewed sense of hope and expectation. Elated by this revelation, he lifted his arms to the Heavens. He breathed in deeply. His chest ballooned out, he felt lighter than air. Cheer filled him!

Strolling out beyond his home and into the desert, BucchaSim gazed to the horizons in all directions.

Hmmm, nothing but sand and some Gattlings soaring above in the distance. Where is our son, TerraSim? What has it been now, he thought...

Two weeks, three weeks?

A few more days and I go find him. I will give him that much time.

BucchaSim decided right then that he and TerraSim must learn to use the crystals to contact each other.

Tunnis and Dolpho are so young, but even they have a command over things I have just not been interested in.

"Well, that will change," he stated to himself determinedly.

Continuing to scour the desert landscape, he realized,

This has always been a dilemma, when to look after my son. My only son!

Wishing to waylay his concerns, he convincingly thought,

There is no doubt that TerraSim is knowledgeable of the desert. He knows the ways of Prismaworms, and the like.

BucchaSim shook his head. He did not find relief in the fact that TerraSim was, indeed, very capable in the ways of the desert. After all, anything can happen. Turning, he went back to his home, SeaCliff, overlooking the Sea of the Forgotten Place.

I like the name, the Sea of The Forgotten Place, he thought, *it is intriguing, and mysterious."*

He took a deep breath, reveling in his new found peace and considered what to do next.

I need to contact King Luxxor — soon! He must be informed him of the discoveries I have made in the ancient passageway. I must make arrangements to show him the locations as soon as possible. It is not good to keep this secret hidden from the King and the Beings of Neptuna any longer. After all, I have become a found man.

He chuckled to himself.

Chapter 19

An Undiscovered City Of Myth

TerraSim speaks

Squatting near the flames and occasionally stirring the ashes, TerraSim told his story to the small group huddled around the warmth of the fire burning before them.

He began with where he lived.

"I live at the edge of the desert and high above the Sea of the Forgotten Place. As long as I can remember this has been my home, which I share with my father, BucchaSim."

Poona pondered the names ...

BucchaSim, TerraSim, where do they get these names?

TerraSim then went on to inform the Initiates about the Carbonian Desert and the dangers it holds.

"Most dangers revolve around desert creatures, but obviously, also drought, and lack of food. However, both food and water can be found in the desert if you know where to look."

He prodded the fire.

Silently and respectfully the Initiates listened. They had all studied, and been informed of much of what to expect and were fully cognizant of situations that may occur unexpectedly. Remaining calm and calling on SilentMind would be the quality to rely on in most situations — if not all situations. They were, however, very interested in the creatures, as yet unseen, lurking in the desert, especially the giant worms they were told existed here.

Then, as if reading their minds, TerraSim, stood and gestured for them to be silent. Scanning the desert surrounding them, he quietly returned to his squatting position. He gazed into each captivated face. With a serious expression and in detail, he described the giant worms.

"To begin with, Prismaworms are extremely huge — except for the babies. The adults have sections of their bodies which can detach, becoming it's own Prismaworm — complete with developing another brain, mouth and so on. They are expert hunters! However, they have no eyes! Living under the sands, they rely solely on sound, or movement. Given the distance, even the smallest of sounds, or movements can be detected."

"Once you encounter one — and live to tell about it," he hesitated, again scrutinizing each mesmerized face, "you will understand completely. Always remember, the good thing is that if you remain alert you can usually tell when one is approaching. Unless it is already there and waiting on you!"

The Initiates's eyes opened just a little wider.

Bocc raised his hand and asked, "How is it, TerraSim, that we have not encountered one. We certainly have been parading along for the past few days?"

TerraSim lowered his head in thought.

"Well, my first instinct is rain. The rain has an effect of confusing the worms. It creates a lot of surface noise. Secondly, I truly feel luck could be involved. Perhaps the worms were at a feeding area far away from your path. There are many 'perhaps' to be considered. The good thing is you are here and you are all well."

Poona filed away a thought to be looked into at a later time.

Just how is it that the Initiates are in a desert full of extreme dangers we know so little about?

"Also," TerraSim continued, "there are swarms of flying Gattlings. They have razor sharp bills and claws to contend with, although they are usually found along the shore. As a rule, they generally shy away from Beings — we think!"

"Next," he continued, now totally involved in his narrative, "there are especially dangerous, and, due to their small size, generally undetectable, small burrowing Tailations. Their particular lethal weapon is the poisonous tip of it's tail!

Let me repeat — unfortunately they are normally undetectable, so 'ALWAYS' check your shoes and bags before slipping your feet or hands in or out. You can sometimes tell of their where-a-bouts by the tell tale funnel holes they dig in the sand. If you spot a cone shaped funnel in the sand — stay away! Generally they subsist on small bugs that crawl into the funnel. The 'meal to be' slips down the sides to where a Tailation awaits just under the surface. Not pleasant, my friends, for the little creatures who are to be dinner!"

The Initiates, spellbound by the informational narrative being given, started glancing about the sands around them.

TerraSim took the opportunity to throw another log onto the fire.

"For the moment, I will end this Carbonian survival course lecture with the 'Floating Death.' It can best be described as similar to a fog, or heavy mist, and is comprised of gas from deep in the Prismaterra that seeps up and lingers low to the ground."

The crackling of the fire was the only audible sound heard.

"It can be recognized by it's light olive green color, and, well," said TerraSim, "you do not want to get near enough to smell the scent of it. It can be lethal! The good news is the gas always surfaces near the center of the desert and not near any Being routes. There are only a few ways to reach Palmation rest areas anyway — except, of course for the 'newly discovered' path you have so kindly left in your wake!"

He smiled at the Initiates.

"It appears that somehow, through time, the small creatures and Prismaworms have become immune to the floating death. But, as for us Beings and other larger surface animals we need to be aware and watchful. At this particular time there is little or no need for concern because of the heavy rains, which disperse the gas into manageable levels. Besides, we are nowhere near the center of the desert."

"Oh," he exclaimed excitedly, "there is one more danger I do wish to mention. I speak of ravenous herds of wild 'Lurds'.

"Lurds," echoed Bocc?

"Yes, Bocc ... Lurds. They grow to a height of about our knees and generally roam the borders between the desert and the mountainous crystal regions. They have an obnoxious odor that will give them away from a distance and they will likely turn and scatter as you approach — unless, of course, they are hungry, or agitated!"

"Great," said Patto, sarcastically looking around at the others.

"However," TerraSim added, "Lurds are known to have notorious bad eyesight. That is a plus for us. And, lastly, never, NEVER, get between adult Lurds and their babies!"

TerraSim did not elaborate.

"That said, know that there are also many wonderful animate and inanimate things in the desert to be seen and experienced. Such as rock creatures we call 'Geodies.' They are interesting and cute and not dangerous at all. They look just like a rock, but with large eyes. And, you can hold them in your hands.

If one is fortunate you may discover fossils, from when the Carbonian Desert was apparently all under water — one huge sea. The Sea of the Forgotten Place is all that is left."

"Lastly, my friends, just to further peak your curiosity, it has been handed down through ancient myths that an undiscovered fabled city of riches, beyond comprehension, once sank beneath the sands of the Carbonian Desert. I do not speak of the great city of Neptuna, but of one even further into antiquity. It is said to be the home of the ancient ones."

He looked at them. His light blue eyes were twinkling and alive with life. Captivated by his stories and explanations, the Initiates asked many questions for the next hour or so, which TerraSim answered to their satisfaction. After awhile they all sat back, including TerraSim, and let out a collective breath.

Annuj spoke.

"We must decide what to do next. TerraSim, can you explain where we went wrong in reading our maps and perhaps guide us in a direction to find these Palmation rest groves? Also, TerraSim, with due respect for your concerns as to our being lost, please remember, this is 'our' Wisdom Path Journey. It is not necessary that we be on a particular path, or even have a specific direction or goal. Our path will unfold as it should and as dictated by the wisdom of the Goodness of All Things — the One."

Gesturing to Poona and the Initiates, Annuj added...

"We do not know of your obligations, TerraSim, but if you will allow me a moment to collectively discuss this matter with my friends, I have a thought. We may have an idea you would favor."

She paused, looking at him.

TerraSim, curious and once again taken by the presence of Annuj and the Initiates nodded affirmatively. After a few moments, they approached him.

He was throwing the last log onto the fire for that morning, as the chill had all but gone.

"TerraSim," spoke Annuj, "we all agree that your presence could very well be destined by the One. You have conducted yourself respectfully, offering advice in respect to our ultimate safety during this journey and we are grateful. It is an honor for us to ask if you will entertain the idea of accompanying our small group for whatever length of time you deem appropriate. We would welcome, and enjoy your company."

Surprised, TerraSim stood there for a moment. He looked out over the vast Carbonian Desert into the unknown, thinking.

He smiled. For some reason he felt honored.

Chapter 20

I Come With A 'Suggestive' Suggestion

Queen Liluuc of Neptuna

When he could not be found elsewhere, Queen Liluuc found Her Chosen One in the usual place — the Temple of the Moon and 7Stars, in his 'Sanctuary of Luxxor.'

King Luxxor had been mulling over several important issues regarding Neptuna and he found this to be a place of quiet and enlightenment where he could think clearly. Upmost on his mind at the moment ... the immense plumbing configuration located deep beneath Neptuna itself. Long ago, in the initial phases of recreating Neptuna under the sea, the thought of where to place this facility was conceived. It was agreed to place the plumbing plant beneath the city and it was located exactly fifty feet below Neptuna. Now, the undertaking of this enormous renovation weighed on King Luxxor's mind.

"My Chosen One," she said softly as she approached King Luxxor.

Greeting her in his usual manner, one of sincere thanks for her presence beside him, he pleasantly said...

"It is always my treat to have you visit, my Queen. However, it has been a trying day, Liluuc, so please excuse my rather focused mood."

Liluuc, answering in a beguiling manner, said...

"Yes, my King, I am aware of the exhausting responsibilities weighing on you at this time. I do, however, come with a, hmmm — somewhat 'suggestive suggestion,' my Chosen One. However, perhaps to risqué for your attention at this very trying time ... I just do not know ..."

Luxxor, with eyes now curious and sparkling, looked up from the confusing plans of plumbing configurations scattered before him and smilingly inquired...

"Just what 'suggestive suggestion' would that be, my Queen?

Liluuc leaned over and whispered her suggestion.

Luxxor listened and smiled.

Liluuc then said, "My Chosen One, my King, the SunneLavva is shining and the air is soft and warm. We need a quiet repose to spend an hour or two away, relaxing and being alone together."

Eyes twinkling, she blew him a kiss, "Trust me, Luxxor, it will be good for both of us! I promise!"

Luxxor chose not to refuse.

Later, they took the small Translight up through the crystal prism protruding above the now quieted waters of the Sea of The Forgotten Place. Liluuc continued to comfort Luxxor. Their destination, she informed him was obviously to be the Tower rooms high above Neptuna and high above the waters. She also informed the Divine Guardians that a small rest time was to be taken by the King and, short of a galactic emergency, there was to be no contact of any sort.

The entrance to the Translight was to be closed.

Reaching the small intimate room, Luxxor, very happy for the interlude offered by Liluuc, stood and gazed over the sea. Meanwhile, Liluuc busied herself with emptying the basket she had brought of hot oils, scented candles and fresh floral aroma sprays from her garden below. Also, not to be forgotten, Luxxor's favorite — a decanter of Loctuum, two goblets, and a selection of Luxxor's favorite foods.

Feeling more at ease already, Luxxor leisurely meandered over to recline on the soft day couch.

Liluuc lowered the filter shade so the SunneLavva would not be overbearing to them — they, of the underwater world, Neptuna.

Teasingly, she sprayed her 'Chosen One' with the essences of flowers, a dilution of Rosewater and Lavendrius, his favorite fragrances. She happily poured a Loctuum, his favorite drink. Then, after laying out some refreshments for them to munch on, she cuddled up next to him. Together they rested for a long time, sometimes quiet, but ofttimes in soft conversation. They spoke of their children, Tunnis and Dolpho, and how anxious and enthusiastic they were about their studies and teachers.

"Oh, Luxxor," she said, "they are growing up so quickly. Where is the time going?"

He only shook his head nostalgically.

They remarked about the adventurous discovery of the ancient passage, which was slowly being examined to more fully ascertain it's origin and how and why it came to be.

They chatted about the discoverer, BucchaSim, an adventurer, who needed his solitude, and who lived high above the passageway.

Luxxor, gazed into the eyes of his Queen, his beloved.

"I want to know this man better. I liked him and felt he liked me also. He seems an honorable man, Liluuc. I will send a message to BucchaSim soon.

Friends are always a welcome blessing, my Liluuc. One may have but a few, but one can never have to many."

The SunneLavva was beginning to dimmish now and Liluuc lit the scented candles. Then, after pouring another Loctuum for them, she snuggled up close once again. Liluuc could see that the layers of tiredness and strain were slowly falling away from him as the afternoon went on. Luxxor gently pulled her to him and kissed her. She held him tightly, and caressed her 'Chosen One' tenderly.

The day passed, and became night and they were not disturbed. Slowly, the small MoonCola of Amythesia crept into their vision. It was indeed magical.

The Translight remained closed until morning. The same Divine Guardians were at their posts when the King and his Queen returned. They would not leave until their King and Queen left.

The King and his Queen were refreshed.

'the horizon makes no promises...

come with me, and excite in those moments...

the unknown vanquishes the known...

if you are so inclined...'

bocc

poet and Initiate of Brightness on the Wisdom Path Journey
Prismacia
UGT 20,872

Chapter 21

Perhaps 'Cat-Astrophic' Would Be Fitting

The Sand Panther

Meanwhile, far out on the desert, with TerraSim guiding the way, the small group finished another days trek. They came to rest at one of the Palmation groves and were thankful for TerraSim's willingness to share his presence and knowledge with them — even if only for a little while.

TerraSim had taken Patto, Laurra and Calla off to show them where certain crystal shards could possibly be found, while Bocc, Annuj and Poona had opted to stay behind, setting up the tents near a small pool among the Palmation trees.

It was Bocc and Annuj who first heard the sound coming from just over a large dunne near the edge of the pool. Going over to investigate they were totally shocked and in disbelief at the sight of a gigantic beast — now standing right in front of them. All that they were told, and knew they should do, simply dissipated as they froze in the moment.

Instinctively, some control quickly came back to Annuj and she frantically wrestled with what to do in this incredible situation. Glancing over her shoulder, she saw Bocc was still by her side.

"Annuj," said Bocc, looking up. "This is the largest cat I have ever seen!"

"I can not disagree with your description, Bocc."

They were dwarfed and menaced by the beast's size, and it's intentions were unknown. She knew that to turn and run would be fruitless and besides, it would indicate their fear. Bocc and Annuj could not move, and the unbelievably massive black cat, did not move.

Throwing back it's head it gave forth a foreboding, deep, hollow roar, after which it began hissing and pawing at the sand. It's gaze was intense and unwavering — and this beast was huge.

"Do you see the size of it's claws, Annuj?"

"Yes, how could I miss them … do you see it's teeth!"

He could only nod yes.

"What do we do?"

Reaching inward, Annuj called silently to the One for the strength needed to ward off this immense animal. Bocc slowly inched forward, in order to place himself in front of Annuj, hoping to protect her or perhaps give her a chance to run. Sensing Bocc's approach, Annuj slowly placed her left hand upon his chest halting him and then, raising her right palm, faced the foe confronting them.

Hissing, it tilted it's head up and with teeth barred, let out yet another deep resonate roar, while continuing to paw at the sand in front of them. Concentrating, Annuj willed it to retreat and leave. Her raised palm began to pulse and slowly turn white. Energy was now being directed at the beast as it slowly edged closer. Suddenly, it dropped it's head, then looked up and then back at Annuj and Bocc. Strangely, it tilted it's head to one side — almost inquisitively.

It seems confused, the Power of Power is working, thought Annuj.

Just behind, on a small ridge above the unfolding scene and unbeknownst to Annuj and Bocc, Poona had raised both her palms and was sending forth intense, but controlled 'PalmPower' energy directives at the giant black cat.

Poona's palms glowed deeply as rapid pulses of power-energy bombarded the immense creature. She saw it begin to back off slowly and then, letting out one last bellowing roar, it turned slowly away, dazed and disorientated but otherwise apparently unhurt.

Poona lowered her hands and felt a slight uneasiness begin to overtake her. She had concentrated deeply in warding off this magnificent animal without harming it. She knew her nausea came from this concerted effort. She found a place to briefly sit down and return to calm.

Annuj, unaware of Poona, turned to Bocc who managed to say…

"I do not remember, whatever that was, as being something we were warned of by TerraSim."

Her heart pounding, Annuj, replied…

"No, no, I believe TerraSim left one out of his 'dangerous creatures to avoid,' list, Bocc."

She dropped to the ground with Bocc close behind.

She felt hot and sticky.

Now that it had ended, the realization of how dangerous the encounter could have been overwhelmed her. She noticed Bocc was perspiring and breathing heavily also. Laying back on the sand he turned to look at Annuj.

"Whatever you did, Annuj, you saved us."

"I am not so certain, Bocc. Something in me says it was not out to harm us. I am positive it was just a chance encounter and it seems to me that whatever that thing is called, it wished us no harm ... any more than we wished to harm it."

From above, Poona watched as Annuj and Bocc dropped to the ground, undoubtedly exhausted.

Annuj displayed great courage, and Bocc also, she considered. *In what must have seemed an eternity, and perhaps, to them, the possibility of a certain tragedy, they survived through courage and Goodness.*

In time, and with the guidance of the One, Annuj will learn to control PalmPower. She is indeed destined.

Poona looked out to the magnificent black cat, who, occasionally looking back, slowly walked off into the desert.

To perhaps it's home?

She felt a wave of compassion flow through her towards this creature.

Is it loneliness I feel for it? Does it have a companion to go to? Does it even have the capacity to experience love, compassion and fear?

"Of course it can," she said aloud. "All things living are gifted with life's emotions. All living things are sacred. Oh, if only we could have communicated somehow."

Poona continued watching until the cat disappeared into the distance. She consoled herself, being thankful that she only needed to frighten the beast off and not seriously injure it.

Rising, she slowly walked back down the path and listened to Annuj and Bocc as they excitedly shared their tale of encountering the giant cat.

For a while they all three sat there considering what had just transpired when Bocc said...

"You know what, it may sound odd to say this at this time, but I have always really favored cats!"

Annuj looked at Bocc, and then over at Poona before responding...

"Well, Bocc, I don't really think we can call that a cat — but perhaps CAT-astrophic would be a fitting description!"

All three of them looked at each other for a second and then burst out laughing.

A light moment was needed, thought Poona and she smiled thankfully for having been there to silently assure their safety.

They will never know of my involvement, she thought. *This was one of 'the unknowns' that can occur, but it was a good lesson for us all.*

She felt certain it knew of them before approaching. Certainly a cat of the desert would have sensed their presence here at the Palmation grove immediately.

74

I am sure that it was only presenting itself as formidable until it was sure of our intentions. Yes, she felt, *that has to be the answer.*

A little later, as the seven of them sat around the campfire, TerraSim, Calla, Laurra, and Patto intently listened to the story of the encounter with the extremely large cat. Darkness was settling in when all was finally told.

TerraSim sat silently for a few moments considering the story. He finally spoke, saying…

"It is my belief that you had an encounter with a giant sand panther. This is a rare encounter, as they are seldom seen and even I have never been close to one. It was probably here in search of water, as these pools are used by all life forms in the desert. I do not believe that you startled it, as much as it frightened you. And, I do not believe it's intentions were to harm you.

It is 'impossible' though, that it was not aware of your presence here. I have learned they have incredible eyesight, hearing and scent glands that would have detected you from quite a distance away.

As to why it confronted you … I have no clue."

"Perhaps a social call?"

They all grimaced at his attempt at humor.

"Ok, so, under the circumstances and you not knowing the ways of the sand panther, I will say you acted in a responsible, protective and brave manner. You are unhurt and from what I understand, the sand panther will undoubtably recover from it's injuries, if any. That said, Annuj, I must speak with you about this PalmPower and how it works. Also, just as a precaution, I will not leave the group from now on."

Poona smiled to herself and silently vowed…

I will remember the sand panther as a just and valiant warrior … and by the name 'PANTHEON' … 'All Gods to All Peoples!'

Poona then spoke…

"TerraSim, you have a vast knowledge of the desert. You must have been exploring this desert for a long time?"

"Yes, Poona, my knowledge comes from experience and from various nomadic peoples who are of the desert, or close by the fringe of it. For instance, I have learned much from Beings in a few isolated small villages on the extreme other side of the Carbonian Desert, where some go to get away and be alone."

"Actually," he continued, "there is one small village called 'Oneness' which has always been on my mind to someday return to. You see, I was born there but left very early on in my life. It is very Spiritual and artistic, from what I have been told. The homes are all built around various large crystals and colored by the glow emanating from the crystals that help form the abode. Cobalt Blue, soft white, lavender, and deep magenta crystals are numerous. There is a rather large oasis there also."

"Listen, I have a thought," he said. "It would be good for me to head towards my home by the sea tomorrow. We are only about two days away and I owe my father the consideration of knowing I am well. It will please me immensely if you will join me and be our guests at SeaCliff, our home. I also want to introduce you to my father, BucchaSim. The view will do you good, and you can rest there while deciding on the next direction of your journey."

"Who knows," he smiled, "perhaps you could all use a solid meal by then."

No one said no.

Chapter 22

Oneness

The black ebony sands were gravelly, but soft

Under the Mother MoonLunna the starlight of unknown thousands of stars twinkled on her RobeCape, a gift of Neptuna from long ago, but still, Solannuj shivered.

The desert looks, and feels unusually cold tonight — and indeed a desert can look cold, thought Solannuj, trembling.

Sitting on a stone carved by wind and water over countless eons of time, she reflected on how blessed she was to live here.

Oneness is almost as far away from everything as one can be, and still be within what is known as Amythesia. What lay beyond our majestic crystal mountain ranges, the horizons of the sea and that of the desert is truly immaterial to most of the Beings here. Except, of course, for some occasional curiosity, life for us of Oneness exist in and around this village.

Of course, she considered, *we realize that Beings, long lost in antiquity, settled here on the planet of Prismacia. This is believed. This is known. What is not known is 'why' they left.*

Solannuj gazed into the darkness with eyes of a life long lived. She shook her head in wonder and lay her head in her hands, drifting towards unknown paths.

These Beings of antiquity abandoned their future descendants, extraordinary mysterious sites, including Neptuna, and the lost, undiscovered city of Netropia — and for what, she again wondered?

It was so long ago, no one knows for sure who is a descendant of these Beings, or who were perhaps born here from others, travelers, also of long ago. Maybe even me, she reflected with raised eyebrows.

Obviously, the Beings of various Quins within Amythesia look different, but nobody ever questions why — or for that matter, cares why. We are all of Amythesia and all are Beings of Prismacia. We are all of the One. Nothing else is important.

There are so many memories, she reminisced, smiling warmly. *As a child I loved to sit outside during this time of the day, watching the twinkles of starlight cascading from gravel chip to gravel chip. And, I will never tire of seeing soft shades of moon glow white, cobalt blue, and deep magenta glowing from the round dome style homes here in Oneness.*

She looked down at the black ebony gravel under her feet.

Hmmm, Much different than that of the Carbonian Desert sands. Ours is larger and smoother in texture.

Closing her eyes, Solannuj felt the smooth texture, and soft edges under her feet.

Ummm, it still holds the warmth of Mother SunneLavva.

And, she thought, *I merely have to dip my bucket into the cold, clear stream meandering through our small village from a source high in the crystal mountains. Oh, but we are so fortunate. Plus, we have our natural hot pools nearby too.*

Solannuj smiled at the simple and natural things that bring pleasure to one's soul.

We enjoy them all here in this small area of Oneness. 'Here below, as above,' she reflected.

Scattered among the black gravel and crystals were the homes of those choosing to live in Oneness. They are Domes and created of a reflective and absorbent material providing comfort within through-out the year. The Domes were quite unique in that they were round, and incorporated large crystals, often of varying colors which not only illuminated the Dome from within, but also provided warmth. It was peaceful and inspiring.

Yes, Oneness, itself, was unique in many ways, but the landscapes surrounding Oneness were also as dangerous as they were unique and stunning.

Mountains and towering crystal monoliths with high harrowing trails encompassed them on one side, while the Carbonian Desert bordered them on the other. Far away lay The Sea of the Forgotten Place abutting the Carbonian Desert — and the unknown.

At the northern end of Oneness lay a rather large freshwater oasis with refreshing Palmation shade trees surrounding it. In ages past, several large crystals had tumbled into the tranquil pool giving one the opportunity to lay, somewhat submerged, while relaxing under the Mother SunneLavva, or the Mother MoonLunna.

Those choosing to call Oneness home were not only creatives and thinkers, but came from all walks of life, including Solannuj, formerly

SolannaOne, HighPriestess of the Voice Of One. Pellona, her companion and friend for countless years had followed.

The common denominator was their wish for peace, beauty, and privacy. All in all it was a place for those who chose to live a less involved life, in a quiet and beautiful Oasis, known as Oneness.

Solannuj 'was' at peace now, remembering many evenings thinking of her past, a frequent occurrence of hers for some time. Suddenly a twinge of nostalgia overcame her as her memories turned to her family, and children. For her, life had been a life of destiny, nothing else. She had followed in the steps of her mother, LannaOne, the first HighPriestess of the Voice of One, becoming SolannaOne, the second HighPriestess.

She marveled at being the mother of two lovely and gifted daughters, also HighPriestesses that continued the family succession to this very day.

Ah, Junnuj and Xennuj, even though I was not present for most of your childhood, how happy I am to be your mother. You have both done your very best and that is all one can ask.

It became noticeably cooler. Solannuj tightened her RobeCape.

"And now there is the young one, Annuj. The lovely and gifted Annuj," she murmured. Pensively, she whispered…

"Parley Luk … I wonder where 'you' are, Parley Luk? I knew you could not remain long, but…"

"Solannuj!"

Interrupting the profound deepness of her thoughts, Solannuj heard her name being called. Turning, she saw Pellona approaching, her faithful companion these many years. Pellona looked youthful beyond her years, and was absolutely dedicated to the former HighPriestess SolannaOne. They had been together since SolannaOne's 'Gifting of the Voice of One,' so long ago.

Watching Pellona approach, Solannuj considered…

Pellona may know more about me than I do myself.

"Yes, Pellona, what is it my dear."

"It is beginning to chill, Solannuj, so I have brought you a warm blanket. I have also thought about the vision sight you received, and shared with me last night."

Solannuj, was a gifted FutureVisionSeer, receiving visions of future happenings to come. Some calming, some disturbing.

"Yes" said Solannuj.

Pellona sat down, and was silent for a moment, her thoughts becoming lost in the dark empowering landscape extending out before her.

Solannuj allowed Pellona's thoughts to wander as they may.

Bringing herself back, Pellona continued…

79

"Since we will be receiving guests, I should prepare for their arrival. There is extra shopping to do, perhaps cleaning, and may I lay out your Ritual wear?"

"Not this time Pellona. We are now Beings of this quaint village. Oneness is our home, Pellona. This is who we are — and we are, as we are."

Turning to face Pellona, Solannuj added...

"I must say though, there is an anxiousness flooding my body and soul — of anticipation, and of longing ... and yet, at the same time, I sense promise emerging from this visit to come, Pellona."

She shivered again. Solannuj wondered...

Is it from the night's chill, or something else entirely?

Pellona noticing Solannuj shiver, said...

"Move here, close to me, Solannuj. We will share the blanket."

Scooting over, they huddled together in warmth under the blanket.

Solannuj whispered...

"Let us enjoy this together my friend, while we can. I fear there is still a storm to come our way."

Chapter 23

BucchaSim Sensed A Change Was Coming

A BucchaSim thought

BucchaSim knelt atop a jagged prism watching the steadily diminishing sea storm play out. The beauty of the power unleashed was mesmerizing to him. Now and then, light beams from the 'SunneLavva' filtered through scattered storm clouds. They highlighted multi-colored crystals reaching high out of the sea continually seeking the Heavens above. Their rainbow reflections darted to and fro across the turbulent waters, now beginning to calm.

A slight rain spray, along with the insistent fog-mist still lingered, harboring soft, intoxicating, aromatic scents of the deep waters below. BucchaSim knew that soon the fog-mist would intensify, creeping in and among the profound crystal monoliths, and hiding the sea and turmoil beneath.

His warm blue eyes, aged by time and stress, gently smiled as his gaze swept across the stunning vista here at his home 'SeaCliff,' high above the Sea of the Forgotten Place.

BucchaSim felt an intuitive sensation of expectancy begin to slowly pulse through his body.

I sense a change is coming, he thought, *but is it one of promise, or do I sense something foreboding?*

Quavering, he wondered…

Is it the cold or the premonition.

BucchaSim continued to watch and wonder as the storm fought for it's last gasps of dominance.

Irregardless, he thought, *a change is coming!*

Chapter 24

The Storm Had Nothing To Do With Weather At All

The RogueEmpire of CodL

Emperor CodL patrolled his command and control tower which was situated near the front of an enormous space station he called the 'RogueEmpireComplex.' As normal, he was agitated and in no mood for —anything!

CodL came from a planet plagued with the name 'Rogue.' It was situated in the star system Paradox, Galaxy 33, as it is known on this date 20,872 UGT (Universal Galactic Time). Among other things, CodL was a bandit and a good one. He was unscrupulous, uncaring and would do anything to further his Empire.

Looking out through a view screen at the blackness of space beyond, he said to no one in particular...

"The leader is CodL. I am the Emperor of all I want."

Never tiring of his self-serving rhetoric, he then blathered...

"Planets beg to pay tribute to CodL."

Pointing his finger around the control tower, he looked at the crew...

"My name alone makes strong men weak in their knees. No one is more ruthless than me! I have no conscious and even less patience."

He finished, and with squinting eyes looked around for any dissenting stares from the crew. A sinister smile crossed his face, but then disappeared, quickly replaced by a smoldering rage. Pacing slowly, now wanting to scream, he looked for someone to yell at.

"I am not in a bad mood," he spurt forth, "but, for anyone that is interested know that I AM in an UGLY mood!"

Once again his vile gaze swept around the room.

Shortly before, CodL was informed of the loss of his latest supply vessel, including prisoners and crew totaling eighty-five. It was struck by space debris that had resulted from a neutron dispersion of large asteroids, which he had ordered. It was in the vicinity of yet another illicit extraction of minerals and prisoners. He was angry, and he wanted to hurt somebody. He wanted retribution.

This had been a prized ship.

The crew can be replaced, he thought, *but replacing the ship will take a year or more, and all the minerals and prisoners are lost too. Someone must pay for this!*

CodL's Empire consisted of 2000 units. 10 specialists in command of 150 highly trained units each, with the remaining 500 or so consisting of engineers, scientists, and those in charge of maintaining and running his RogueEmpireComplex. Except for the engineers and scientists, who were basically prisoners, all had come from the dregs of life through out the galaxy of Rogue, including the mining planet of Trion.

CodL selected them well. They were tough, but considering their harsh backgrounds, they had become disciplined, especially when faced with the certainty of his punishments. The few scientist types that he put up with were only a necessity. He needed their minds. It galled him to need them at all.

To him, all people of intellect and all artists of any kind, were nothing more than worms and cowards, incapable of anything manly. If they became dispensable, they could quickly be fed to the deep dark holes of space and replaced.

However, CodL spared little regarding the quality of the tools of his trade. He demanded extremely high technological capabilities, including weaponry and his vessels had been acquired at any cost. As for the mineral drilling and extraction equipment, it was normally acquired through conquest, or outright theft.

He ruled his RogueEmpire from this huge space complex, now hovering in his home galaxy, Rogue. Sitting down heavily in the Master Control seat, he anguished over his thoughts — thoughts he was unable to overcome.

Looking at the clock, CodL grimaced. He waited impatiently for the worm, MorQ.

Don't be late, MorQ, he thought, simmering.

At that very moment, MorQ was standing just outside the entrance to Emperor CodL's command tower. He was nervous, very nervous. MorQ was a diminutive man and not one meant for the turmoil and stress he was forced to endure here. Glancing down at the stupid uniform he had to wear in accordance with his position as Chief Engineer/Scientist aboard the RogueEmpire, he could see the tell-tale signs of perspiration.

I'm sweating already! Oh please, please let this go well.

Taking out a handkerchief, he wiped his forehead, took a deep breath, opened the door and stepped into his personal horror and tormentor.

CodL slowly swiveled in his chair at the announced entrance of his chief scientist, MorQ, who had stopped just inside the doorway.

He grimaced again at his immense displeasure of having to deal with this worm, this little person. Just looking at him made his eyes twitch.

But, at this time, I need this annoying twerp.

Months before, MorQ had sent out 3 Spacial Rogue galaxy probes directed at specific planets deemed worthy of mineral analysis. They had arrived back yesterday and MorQ had requested a day to quickly analyze the samples, organize the visuals and formulate his impressions. He would then give his conclusions to the Emperor CodL. With CodL, there was no room for error.

CodL viewed MorQ disdainfully, then gestured for him to come forward.

Chief Engineer/Scientist, MorQ, approached to within four feet and removed the files from the brief he carried and prepared to deliver the results of their contents to Emperor CodL.

He gave CodL the obligatory bow.

"My Emperor CodL," he nervously began, "the reports are favorable, very favorable for Planet 8, in Galaxy 17."

Trying not to tremble, he scanned the reports he held and continued.

"The samples and visuals are promising, my Emperor, as they display the elements required for minerals of the type and quality we seek."

"However," MorQ added, "it would be an expensive and lengthly voyage to make, Emperor CodL, and ..."

CodL raised his fist. He was in no mood for how-evers. Not now or ever. Slamming his fist into the arm of the chair he glared at the scientist.

CodL stood.

He moved to within inches of MorQ's face. Trembling, MorQ dropped some of the papers and was definitely ready to faint or collapse — he just knew it.

He could smell, and feel CodL's breath — hot, rapid, rank.

But, in a surprisingly calm voice, CodL menacingly said...

"Never, NEVER, think you can tell me, Emperor CodL, whether or not the voyage is to expensive or to long, MorQ. That decision is for 'rulers and leaders, men of strength' to decide — of which YOU are neither!"

"And, MorQ, when you say 'WE' seek," remember this — there is no we!"

"We, as in you and I, do not seek, MorQ."

He blared out...

"I, CODL, SEEK!!! I CODL DISCOVER!!! I CODL COMMAND AND RULE!!!" … "ARE WE CLEAR!"

"Pick up the papers, MorQ."

MorQ was about to lose control, He felt his bowels about to relinquish everything. He fell to his knees to retrieve the dropped papers.

Turning his back to MorQ, CodL commanded…

"Now leave, and send me a detailed report by this evening."

MorQ did not hesitate, rising, he quickly turned to leave.

"And, MorQ," said CodL, quietly and mockingly — "just for me, your Commander, your Emperor … calculate the time needed to reach this Planet 8, in Galaxy 17, and include it in the findings."

"Don't forget to bow on your way out, MorQ."

He smirked, and turning to face MorQ, watched as his Chief Engineer/Scientist bowed, and backed towards the door trembling.

Exiting the door, MorQ thought…

My God, I am alive.

I need a bathroom.

Chapter 25

Can A Meek Man Seethe

MorQ seethed

Safely back in his small room, he went immediately to the bathroom.

Afterwards, MorQ poured himself a small drink. He felt tired, sad, frightened and very unhappy. Holding his head in his hands he wished he could cry. This was not his choice to be here working for this insane madman.

He then wondered...

Is 'insane madman' saying the same thing? Am I now repeating myself? Oh dear Heaven within, what am I going to do?

For the next two hours MorQ sat, staring out his porthole at the frigid expanse that had been his view for the past six years.

He thought, and he considered.

Then, slowly standing, he quietly stated to himself...

"I have made up my mind, once and for all."

I now begin the immediate implementation of the plan I have been working on for some time. Nothing could be worse than dying here in this cesspool, except continuing to exist here in this cesspool, and I will no longer live in such depravity.

MorQ, was miraculously energized and determined. He felt calculated anger pulsing through his veins. Suddenly he was no longer afraid. His fear had been supplanted by survival, and his will to truly live! Looking into the mirror, he realized...

I am angry at myself for allowing this to continue all these years. No More!

Sitting at his small desk he compiled all the results of his survey regarding Planet 8 to send to CodL.

I will not address CodL by the title Emperor anymore, he swore silently.

He is not worthy to be called Emperor, and never has been. It is all based on fear anyway.

MorQ purposefully enhanced the results of the survey from Planet 8 knowing it would make CodL anxious to send out a reconnaissance team. He would have the report delivered to CodL that evening.

"This will be my chance," he said to himself.

I will have a small window of opportunity, and I will have to be …

"Be what," he considered?

Very, very, lucky, he concluded.

I have never had such courage in my life, he thought to himself.

Fear and faith can account for incredible feats, or incredible stupidity!

MorQ knew he had at least a week, maybe a little less, before CodL could arrange for a reconnaissance ship to depart for Planet 8, Galaxy 17. However, he also knew that because of his previous planning, that was ample time for him to be ready.

I have been preparing my escape plans for some time, and now the opportunity presents itself.

He smiled nervously.

Nonetheless, being the scientist, he wanted to have all his i's dotted, and t's crossed. So, during the next two days MorQ thought out all possible avenues, the good and the bad, that his actions could lead to. Some were very unpleasing, so he spent extra time considering emergency contingencies for these.

His mind was racing.

I need 95% predictability of certainty in my plan, which also allows for any future circumstance beyond my control.

He had toyed with this idea and intention of escape before, but never with such bravado and never in real time! For nearly two years now he had discretely gone through the agonizing stealth of copying certain engineering and structural blueprints of the RogueEmpireComplex hoping beyond hope they may someday be put to good use.

"That day is here," he murmured. "This will work, or I will die."

I may be meek, MorQ thought, *but right now I am seething, so watch out!*

He stopped and pondered on that thought.

I am seething!

"What does that mean anyway," he asked himself?

Can a meek man seethe? I mean, CodL looks like he seethes — but me!

Looking at himself in a mirror, he said…

"It is a strange feeling to seeth, and not even know what it is I am doing."

Continuing to look into the mirror MorQ answered himself...

Oh, what do you think it means? You have unexpressed anger — you need to let it out, to vent — you need to be brave — you need courage — you...

He then thought...

But it could get me in big trouble.

"Good Heavens," he said aloud.

Chapter 26

A Spider's Web Is No Place To Be Caught

The 'Black Widow' comes

In the Galaxy of Crystola, a few planets away from Prismacia, hovered the Black Widow, a highly technical and offensively powered space craft. The explorer and owner of this vessel, LesterJonko, worked for the giant GemCraft Corporation. GemCraft was based on Earth III, but had it's fingers throughout the galaxy. He liked to call it the Gem 'Graft' Corporation, as their protocol and ethical decisions were at times quite suspect _ even for him.

Sitting alone in the 'Red Spot' Lounge and sipping his favorite libation, he was thinking…

I have been been doing exploratory work for GemCraft during the best part of my 47 years, and I can imagine nothing else as a replacement for being my own boss. I have enjoyed space travel, a very good income, almost total control, and, he smiled mischievously, *the opportunity for enhancement of my personal wealth through my very wise and ingenious supervision.*

His crew of 100 were experienced and always enjoyed the 'hard spirits' to help console their 'inner spirits' during the long three month intervals between a 'Deliverance'.

He laughed.

Heck, I enjoy the Deliverance as much as the men. A needed diversion.

'Deliverance' was a much anticipated perk they always looked forward to. It denoted the arrival of a troupe of women and men — entertainers/musicians, etc. who entertained the men during their leave time from the mineral digs on a planet or star. The 'ETC.' act was the highlight of the evenings, and the 'entertainment' — well, was entertaining! The Deliverance was sponsored by GemCraft for one week, every three months. Needless to say, security was high during this particular time.

It was also especially high, during and after gems were discovered and shuttled back to the Black Widow for cleaning and processing. If gems were found in your possession you were prosecuted and imprisoned. Simple as that.

However, while perusing through the nicer gems discovered, LesterJonko, occasionally found a unique stone he felt should be subject to his personal examination and it eventually and discreetly found it's way into a personal vault on Planet X. It was one of the perks he felt was owed him through his long devotion to the Corporation.

LesterJonko sat back in his chair looking out the wide view port. He was imagining the galaxies beyond, and contemplating his life.

I know I have made a few mistakes, but I am fair with my men. Of course, I am also tough on those stepping out of line. I run a tightly controlled crew, but my men respect me — some may even somewhat like me, but they also fear any repercussions should they get out of line. That was what mattered most to LesterJonko. Space was no place for the weak, particularly on board the Black Widow.

I love this ship, he thought, taking another sip. *She is built to last, has speed when needed and we have weathered many hard times together.*

A smile appeared on his face.

She is large, he considered, *which makes her somewhat vulnerable, but she is also equipped with glancing shields, which, when directed and angled correctly are capable of redirecting opposition fire back at an enemy. And, she has impressive firepower aboard to protect herself in most situations.*

"All in all, I cannot ask for more," he muttered to himself. "I love my Black Widow."

Raising his glass, and taking a big sip, he made a toast …

"And I thank you my son, FinnJonko, for many of the impressive improvements you have implemented over the past few years. Very well done indeed, my boy."

His son, FinnJonko had suggested smaller attack ships named 'Spiders,' resulting in the infamous 'Spider Webs.' The attack ships were small, sleek, piloted ships, easily maneuverable and equipped with extremely high powered neutron capabilities. He had also proposed 'Spider Webs,' which were to be used only in those situations when interrogation of their enemy may be needed, or if they did not want to destroy a vessel.

'Spider Webs' were capsules that when launched, would attach to an object, such as an enemy ship. Once attached, they were programmed to release a foam like substance that completely encompassed the ship — like a sponge web!

The occupants cannot see out, nor transmit, or receive transmissions. They are caught in the web of a Black Widow!

Not a place to be!

Thanks for all these, FinnJonko, he smiled, finishing his drink.

The mother ship, the 'Black Widow,' and all the craft, were matte black — very difficult to see during a firefight in space. There were 25 Spiders aboard at any given time and the number of Spider Webs was ten per Spider. The GemCraft Corporation took no chances when it came to protecting their investment and that of the Stockholders.

LesterJonko, seriously contemplating another cold libation at the 'Red Spot' Lounge on the lower underbelly of the Black Widow saw the color code for **'Important'** flash across his wrist screen. He swiftly went to a nearby monitor and entered the correct series of numbers known by himself, and his top advisors. This message was coded and from FinnJonko, his son.

Chapter 27

It Is Time To Come Back, JunnaOne ... It Is Time

The voice of a DreamState Pod machine

"It is time to come back, JunnaOne, it is time."

"It is time to come back, JunnaOne, it is time."

The sound was so soft, so very soft ... JunnaOne became aware.

I feel so very peaceful. I am in DreamState — the elixir of immortality, a state of blissful inaction and dreams. I have been in DreamState for four years now?

She attempted to open her eyes.

Of course I cannot open my eyes yet, as I am still only a cloud, a vapor, formless smoke, only energy floating around in a clear marbleized crystal DreamPod under the waters of the Sea of the Forgotten Place, in the city of Neptuna. Yes, I am in an ancient structure called the 'Podium,'um, um, um, um, JunnaOne drifted off and then quickly back again.

How apropos, she thought hazily. *I am in the 'POD'ium, exactly where all good 'Dream Pods' should be.*

She wanted to smile at her humor, but she could not smile yet, as she did not have her lips, but she felt sure her energy was glowing happily.

It feels so nice here, she softly whispered to herself ... *but I cannot whisper. So, I must be thinking. Oh, it feels so peaceful.*

JunnaOne drifted off again ...

"It is time to come back, JunnaOne, it is time. It is ti..."

This time JunnaOne opened her eyes. She floated.

Am I still a cloud?

No, I feel the presence of a body.

She began focusing on beautiful, evocative, soft glowing colors now floating above her.

Are they stars? Oh, am I hearing the soft sounds of Harptoniums gently floating among my senses? I remember them, how nice ... and is that sweet intrinsic essence of Crystolamunn fragrance wafting about? Oh, how I love that scent.

Here JunnaOne would lie, floating in a state of delirious ecstasy for the next twelve hours, as her physical body continued it's stimulation and movement and as her SoulMind, having reentered her body from her SoulPod, became acquainted with its true home once again.

Earlier, her coded SoulPod had been removed from it's water chamber, taken to her coded BodyChamber and placed at the crown of her head where the transmission of her soul to body had taken place.

For the past four years JunnaOne's physical body was continually monitored and stimulated with soft movement and organ activation for two hours, every four hours, every day. Also, her body was kept submerged in Ambergel, a substance created to keep the skin organ soft and supple. Dignity and care for those in DreamState was foremost.

This was the allotted time for JunnaOne's completion. The DreamState completions were always scheduled for the mornings, as the last thing needed at this time was more rest for the patient. However, what 'was' needed was time to readjust to being a 'Being' once again.

When the time was right, a TransLight beam quietly took JunnaOne to a lovely room high in one of the Prisms where a view of the sea awaited. Safety eye filters were placed on her before leaving the Podium and here in her room the filter shade was drawn down until a time her eyes were able to adjust.

It was necessary for someone to be near at this delicate time and given she was JunnaOne, a HighPriestess of the Voice of One — and given this was Neptuna, Queen Liluuc insisted it be her personal Queen's Princess in waiting, 'Lilonna,' who would have the honor of assisting JunnaOne during her recovery.

It was the custom for families of a PodSoul Being, to take their loved ones home once DreamState Completion recovery was finished, but in the case of HighPriestess JunnaOne, a special request had been made by SolannaOne, the matriarchal HighPriestess, and JunnaOne's mother! Her request was, when JunnaOne was ready, will they please do SolannaOne the honor of bringing her daughter home to her village, Oneness, at the edge of the Carbonian Desert. She herself had not the strength to be there for JunnaOne at such a needed and comforting time.

"JunnaOne has sacrificed much for Prismacia, and Neptuna," SolannaOne had said.

"I will be deeply indebted."

Chapter 28

And I, Junnuj, Will Champion These Causes

From this moment on

For a length of time, including physical rehabilitation, Lilonna attended to JunnaOne's every need. She was allowed the solitude and quiet time needed during this recuperative period to strengthen, reflect and recall.

One afternoon, JunnaOne, sat quietly, thinking. She had known, when going into DreamState that coming out might be harder on her than entering, but her powers of concentration and memory recall were already surprisingly clear.

She envisioned the last recollection of BucchaSim, her husband...

What a wonderful man, she remembered. *When can I return to him? Oh, how I wish to embrace him once again. I do not even know what my children look like. They were so young. Will they even know of me?*

"My children, TerraSim and Annuj, they will be grown now," she said to Lilonna, who was sitting nearby.

"I wonder if I am a grandmother," she questioned, a smile beginning to brighten a sad, but lovely face.

"Oh, so many questions," she said.

"I had so passionately not wanted to leave them, Lilonna, but, once again, at that point in time, I had no personal choice in the matter.

You are aware, that as the daughter of SolannaOne I was destined to become HighPriestess of the Voice of One since before birth. I had no voice in the expected succession — along with the commitment and responsibility it entailed. It was a forgone conclusion and never disputed."

"And that contemptible 'Law of Spectrum Initiative' they force upon Beings just isn't right," she declared. "There is no compassion involved at all. I wonder if anyone really thought about the consequences of their actions."

Lilonna's eyes widened at JunnaOne's strong tone of voice.

94

She, and Lilonna, sat in her quiet, dim room, as JunnaOne continued the completion of thought from what she remembered to the present.

After a significant lapse of time, JunnaOne raised her head, and gazing directly into the eyes of Lilonna, declared...

"Lilonna, from this moment on I wish to be only called Junnuj, my childhood name."

Lilonna's eyes warmed, as she softly said...

"Yes, Junnuj, so it will be."

Ideas and thoughts were now swiftly entering her mind and Junnuj suddenly exclaimed...

"I have a younger sister, Lilonna. Her name is Xennuj. I must know of her also! Did she follow and become the HighPriestess too?"

She paused, briefly looking out the window, and then back to Lionna.

"It seems my life was destined, until now," she said, lowering her eyes.

"Actually, I knew it would be. What I did 'not' expect, Lilonna, was falling in love with BucchaSim. He was my childhood friend and the young boy my mother, SolannaOne had taken in as one of her own. Of course, mother, being the HighPriestess of the Voice of One, was almost continually absent from me and Xennuj. We we were in the village of Oneness, in the desert, and mother was in Spectrum. During her long absences, we missed her so much, Lilonna."

Junnuj then stopped momentarily. She was smiling sweetly. Remembering.

Perhaps drifting off into a pleasant thought, considered Lilonna.

She waited for a few moments, before asking...

"Would you care for some tea, and a bite to eat, Junnuj?"

"Yes, thank you, Lilonna, that will be nice."

When Lilonna returned, Junnuj, took a sip of the mildly hot tea and thought again of her mother and how she never really knew her.

"Our CareOne keeper," she spoke, "was Carloona. She was a sincere woman and compassionate. Both Xennuj and I adored her," she said. "And, BucchaSim did too. However, BucchaSim kept quite a distance from Xennuj and me at first. But, eventually a bond grew between myself and BucchaSim — which became trust, and then affection, and then love."

She glanced at Lilonna imploringly.

"We loved each other so much, Lilonna."

"I am sure that love is still alive Junnuj, and for BucchaSim too."

Junnuj put her hands up to her face, and shook her head despondently.

"Everything we did, we did together. We were so happy. Then, as you can imagine, with two young people in love, one day I realized I was with child. I sensed — no, I knew it was a boy," she said grinning, and glancing at Lilonna, as if seeking acceptance, or understanding.

"When I informed my mother, SolannaOne, she was concerned, but told me she was not surprised. She left two days later for Spectrum."

Junnuj continued reminiscing.

"Oh, I so loved the young man, BucchaSim — my Starman. Were you aware, Lilonna, that he was a youth brought to Prismacia from far away and left here. There was no explanation, there was no one to seek out and find. So, since my mother had found BucchaSim, she felt it was destiny and a gift of The One."

Junnuj pausing, sipped more of the tea and sampled a piece of crumpet. Then, leaning back into the soft pillow on her chair, and with distant, remembering eyes, she went on.

"He said he thought he was twelve when mother found him roaming the desert near Oneness. A good age for my daughters, mother had said. She also stated that Xennuj and I spent to much time alone and that BucchaSim was a gift. We should all grow up and enjoy life together."

Lilonna saw tears beginning to appear in Junnuj's eyes.

"Our child is called TerraSim, Lilonna."

I wonder how he looks now.

"He must be very handsome."

Nodding in agreement, Lilonna added…

"I have no doubt, Junnuj."

"And then, two years after the birth of our son, we gifted my mother with a granddaughter we named, Annuj! Oh, what a beautiful baby."

"Do you see, Lilonna," she said, smiling briefly, "I am remembering all these wonderful things."

Lilonna smiled back tenderly.

"It was not long after that," she stated, "one year to be exact, that SolannaOne became physically incapacitated and to ill to remain as HighPriestess. By decree, the Council of the Voice of One, the people, and Neptuna agreed it must be me who would ascend to the position of the HighPriestess … as I was the next in line."

"Thus, my succession of Junnuj to JunnaOne, HighPriestess of the Voice of One took place when TerraSim was three, and Annuj was only one. It was the same year of the selections for the Law of Spectrum Initiative. Everything happened so quickly. We just had no control over anything."

"Trust me, Lilonna, when I say that BucchaSim and I were devastated. But, we truly believed SolannaOne would not be absent for long. We felt she would heal in a reasonable time. SolannaOne was to old to consider the Dreamstate and her condition was diagnosed as extreme fatigue. It was determined she would have an extended rest and then resume her position as SolannaOne, at which time I could return to my family. Oh, how destiny chose otherwise for me — for us," she reflected, gazing sorrowfully at Lilonna.

"I missed BucchaSim and my children so much. I desperately loved and wanted to share my life with them. That is all I ever truly wanted, Lilonna."

I hardly knew my children before leaving, and they did not know me at all. They still don't, Junnuj thought silently to herself.

Junnuj fell silent for a few minutes, turning to look at the sea and it's undulating waves, before turning back to Lilonna.

"Forgive me for being personal, Lilonna, but have you children of your own?"

"I have not been so blessed, Junnuj. Although that is my personal loss, or misfortune … or blessing, I have gone on to do things I am sure I would never have done were I a mother. It is as it is."

Junnuj, nodded understandingly.

"Yes, Lilonna, it is as it is."

"I did try, Lilonna. I endured for a few years, but each year I became more and more anguished from being away from those I loved. The emotional strain was far to much for me. My soul became so fragile. I felt so hopeless."

She shuddered, with tears now beginning to flow.

"We each have a physical and emotional limit, Lilonna and I could no longer endure the pain. Had I any courage left and my mental faculties intact, I would have done the unthinkable. I would have left with BucchaSim and the children. We would have gone away — anywhere! Even beyond where 'Those of the Edge' live. We all know there are lands and Beings beyond."

Lilonna nodded understandingly, thinking…

If Junnuj is ready, I want her to release these memories and emotions.

Turning back to the window, Junnuj did continue, recalling…

"When my strain finally became to much to bear any longer, it became obvious to even SolannaOne. She suggested, almost insisted, that I enter what is kindly called an Individual retreat, to be followed by, DreamState."

"Mother told me that Xennuj, my sister, and next in line of succession could become XennaOne, resuming my obligations until I recovered. Does this sound familiar, Lilonna?"

Junnuj paused and wiped her eyes.

The tears had now stopped.

"Lilonna, even in my tortured, emotional state when entering Individual Retreat, I knew that eventually, when I came out I would never assume the responsibilities of the HighPriestess again. Never. The only thing that made it possible for me to be here today is the love I carry for my family and that one day I would reunite with them again."

"My mother told me I was more gifted than any — and of great wisdom and resolve, but that I had become so very fragile ... to fragile for my position of HighPriestess. And the truth is, yes, I had! It was brought on by the loss of my family because of my ascension to the High Priestess of the Voice of One."

"I know that," Lilonna replied. "We all do."

Junnuj held her head in her hands and tears began to flow down her cheeks.

"Oh, One, she moaned, Oh, One, why did you abandon me, and why did I not have the courage to say no in he beginning?"

Lilonna rose quickly, and went to comfort her. Putting her arms round Junnuj, she held her gently and whispered...

"The tears are good Junnuj. You have needed this for a long time. Considering all you were forced to deal with, you always did the best you could do. Please cry now. Release all your sadness. Everyone of us is indebted for the extreme sacrifices you gave and I will overstep my position and say what happened to you was totally unfair."

"Those who decided your fate did not comprehend the total sacrifice and injustice you endured due to existing antiquated laws and traditions. Very, very few have given for their people what you have given, our dear Junnuj.

We must always remember that your life is just as precious — regardless of your position."

"We are 'all' of the One. And, as to your family, dear Junnuj, no matter the separation of the years, even now they wait for you. They look to the day they will embrace you and be a family again. I do believe this. I know it is easy to say, Junnuj, but love does and will endure all."

Junnuj cried for a long time with Lilonna never leaving her side. Eventually she lifted her swollen eyes to Lilonna and smiled. The tears had ceased flowing.

"I am feeling better now, but somewhat weary," she whispered.

"And, Lilonna, please know I am very sorry for your loss too."

Understanding, Lilonna closed her eyes. Small tears were forming.

Rising, she collected the dishes and slowly left.

Junnuj eased out of her chair and slowly walked over to the balcony.

She felt she was finally returning to Junnuj, the mother, the wife — a Being. She passionately determined to resurrect her strength of will and become whole once more, for evermore. She began to feel true hope for the future, for reconnecting and beginning from right here, right now.

I will it to be, and so it will be. Lilonna will help me with exercises, but I will begin my practice of meditation, and FutureSeer now.

Pulling over a pillow to the balcony and taking a seated position, Junnuj, with hands crossed over her heart, whispered...

"Oh, One, Goodness of All Things, at this very second I implore my vision as a FutureSeer."

Junnuj closed her eyes. Invoking the 'Sound of the Silent' — the OM, she became transformed ... altered! What she then envisioned amazed her ... It was BucchaSim. Somewhat older, but handsomely older!

His aging process must be slowing down due to acclimating to Prismacia's cycles, she thought. *Good to be from Earth III it seems.*

She liked this, and smiled.

Suddenly opening her eyes, she called out to Lilonna, who quickly appeared. Passionately, Junnuj stated...

"Lilonna, new laws will be presented to the Voice of One, replacing laws outdated, or that were just irrational to begin with."

Lilonna, now sitting on the couch, sat up, eyes wide.

"One law shall state that any HighPriestess of the Voice of One has the right to have, share and live their lives, with their families, during their time representing and presiding over the Voice of One and all Amythesians.

One law will state that the Law of Spectrum Initiative is nullified — permanently!

A law like this cannot be good if it brings pain and anguish to any involved.

Besides, tonality is being introduced and created naturally, through inner marriages and bondings among the Beings of Amythesia, and through Beings curious to live in other Prisms and Quins. All without the pain that accompanies, the Law of Spectrum Initiative."

"And," Junnuj continued, "all existing laws will be reviewed immediately by a collective of Beings to assure the inclusion, in any law, of compassion, truth, justice and goodness for all Beings everywhere — and I, Junnuj, will Champion these rights to be added as laws!"

Unknowingly, Junnuj had raised her right hand as did a HighPriestess when a proclamation was degreed.

Lilonna, listening and watching from the couch put her hands to her lips.

Now it was she with tears _ tears of joy.

Not only have I witnessed Junnuj release years of sadness, but I see her physical stamina returning. And, as importantly, Junnuj is now recognizing hope and determination also … her Spirit is lifting.

Opening her arms she rushed over to Junnuj, and they embraced.

'if love is just a dream...

then keep us all forever fast asleep...

but the joy of what you have come to feel...

is that what is happening, is real...'

bocc

poet and Initiate of Brightness on the Wisdom Path Journey
Prismacia
UGT 20,872

Chapter 29

And Profit Is The Deity

DrexL stood alone

DrexL was standing alone on the control deck. Dismissing the night-watch-in-charge, he personally assumed control of the RougeEmpire for the remainder of the evening.

It is late, he thought, *so this will be a quiet time. And, I need time to be alone with my thoughts.*

His gaze passed over the vastness of this endless place called the Heavens.

Endless, but hardly void, he knew, *imagining untouched worlds, and life forms, perhaps unlike anything known before.*

It was exhilarating for him, this mystery, these unknowns. He had come to realize that this was his preferred existence — here among the stars. It was unknown and far away from anything remotely related to his past. He had even taken to speaking with the Heavens as if they were his friends, which, to him, they were.

Lost in the astonishing Heavens stretched out before him, he whispered...

"Now, my silent friend, I must escape from CodL, consortiums and societal laws, whose only vile purpose is control, greed and power."

I'm close, he thought, *close in the attainment of my dream. I know that my opportunity, my chance, is near. I feel it!*

His contempt for CodL had grown profoundly over the past few years. So much so that, at times, it partially clouded his vision — exasperating him and leaving him to merely exist, in survival mode, here on this corrupt complex called the RogueEmpire.

The one thing CodL has done for me is to give me a different existence here on the Rogue. It is not necessarily better, just different, he considered. *But, he did not do it for me,* DrexL thought, *it was always for CodL.*

"At least I got out of the deep mining camps of Trion," he muttered, inconspicuously looking about the control deck, conscious of CodL's cloak and dagger surveillance devices hidden discreetly about the craft.

I guess I owed CodL something for that, he deliberated silently, *but I know I have long since paid back any debt of servitude due him. Trion, my home planet, offered nothing but a hard existence of laboring in the deep tunnels of the mining camps. It was run by Consortiums, where only the strongest survived, and 'Profit' was the only 'Deity.'*

He smirked, remembering when CodL had bought him and many others several years ago.

Actually, he considered, *nearly one forth of the crew aboard the RogueEmpire are from Trion. We were used to the harsh conditions of the mines. The RogueEmpire at least offered us a way out. In a twisted way, it offered an obscure feeling of freedom from the bondage and hardships we had experienced while in the mining camps. Basically, we were prisoners, and in many ways, still are,* he grimaced, thinking back to those years.

We exchanged our fear of mining gas, dust, deep tunnel collapse and any thought of a better existence, for the fear of CodL.

"How ironic is that," he said softly, shaking his head in disillusionment.

Although, he reminded himself, *several of the smarter, and hardened Trionites had become DarkCapes, Commanders of Units, consisting of 150 men. They were fearless of most anything.*

"And now, I am their Commander," DrexL muttered under his breath— "under the auspices of Emperor CodL, of course."

It was from this background that DrexL came. He was obviously no stranger to hard ways and hard times. With distant eyes, he momentarily flashed back to his father and brother, wondering if they were still slaving away in Trion.

Are they even still alive, he questioned?

Pulling himself back to the present, DrexL stepped back from the the view scape, looked around, and settled into the Control chair situated along side an array of levers and buttons. He wanted to shout...

I am not afraid of you CodL. I am as tough! I know of others who are not afraid either — and given the opportunity, we will escape this wretched situation.

"I count on that very fact," he confidently whispered.

High in a suite of rooms atop the RogueEmpireComplex sat CodL. He had watched as DrexL dismissed the on duty night-watch-in-charge.

"Staying on top of things, eh, DrexL," CodL said out loud.

"What's that ... what's that you're saying? You need to speak up, DrexL, I can't hear you."

I must consider getting some sort of lip reading device, he considered.

CodL shifted his weight, thought for a while, then walked to his bed.

A good man, that DrexL, he thought. *Always keeping an eye out.*

As he got under the covers, he once again looked back at the view screen and muttered to himself…

"I must remind DrexL about who 'THE' Commander and 'THE' Emperor here on The RogueEmpireComplex is!"

"A tough man, DrexL," he exclaimed.

He turned to sleep.

He left his view screen on … as always.

Chapter 30

Life, Death, Destiny ... In Just A Few Seconds

That was a huge Prismaworm

TerraSim had insisted they stick close together during their excursion back to his home at the edge of the Sea of the Forgotten Place and he told them why. As they trudged along, he explained characteristics about the Prismaworm they could not have known.

He informed them that the long, fairly straight mounds of sand stretching off into the distance are the trails, or wake, of a Prismaworm.

"Not that you would want to follow the trail of a Prismaworm," he stated, "but, if there is a gully where it ends, it means the worm has tunneled down and could have doubled back, or come up elsewhere."

"If there is no gully," he said, "it usually means the worm is still there, patiently lurking and waiting somewhere near, or at the end of the sand mound."

"And," he continued, "always remember, that for a worm, a group walking close together gives off the sound of a single person, while walking further apart from each other will give the sounds of several people and be more likely to attract the worm."

The Initiates, and Poona chose not to deliberate the issue and kept close together. As it turned out they were heard anyway and spent the better part of a morning huddled on the side of a worm mound as the worm lingered nearby waiting for movement. Outside of hoping for rain, whose repetitive sounds could confuse the worm, they were virtual captives waiting for a miracle, or for the worm to tire and move on — which, TerraSim had informed them earlier, was highly unlikely.

They were fortunate, as once again, two Giant Gattlings landed some distance away in hopes of finding lunch.

TerraSim whispered...

"Lunch, is probably in the form of Munkins ... small desert creatures that burrow around and live in these desolate and sparse surroundings."

The Gattlings began to scratch and claw at the sand in an effort to frighten the Munkins into the open. TerraSim had seen this drama unfold before and turned the group's attention to the Gattlings.

"Watch," he said softly, "although this will not be pleasant. I must say, I am sorry for the Gattlings, but at this moment it appears they are to be our saviors."

In anticipation of what they may witness, and hoping it would not be them, they all silently huddled together, hardly breathing. Bocc, nervously, and quietly pulled out his Palm Crystal Recorder in the hopes of capturing the scene about to unfold before them.

As before, the Giant Gattlings became aware of the danger below — it was probably a small sound. But, just as they raised their large wings in an effort to escape, the ground exploded and a grotesquely immense Prismaworm burst through the sand. With a gaping mouth it swallowed the birds and in a continuing motion dove back into the sands of the Carbonian Desert.

It was thunderous — it was shocking — it was terrifying — and it was quick!

TerraSim whispered...

"That is one version of life and death here in the desert. It can be instantaneous or it can be slow and agonizing."

The Initiates sat disquietly, staring at the now empty space where the carnage had taken place only a few yards from them. Looking at each other in concern, they now truly understood the possibility of how sudden any situation could change. Bocc still held the Palm Crystal Recorder in his shaking hand — unused.

"Thank you, TerraSim," said a breathless Annuj, and echoed by the rest.

"Life, death, destiny — all in such a few precious seconds," uttered Laurra. "It is humbling ... and frightening at the same time. We who choose to believe in the afterlife, where a soul gently transitions to the next higher level, must attempt to comprehend real life transitions that are not gentle at all. This was a harrowing example of just how quickly it can end, at this level — and not so gently!"

"Life can be fleeting."

TerraSim listened, captivated by Laurra's eloquence and calmness after such a distressing experience. Once again he silently wondered of this unusual group. Together they all clasped hands, closed their eyes, and gave thanks to the Giant Gattlings for their involuntary sacrifice

Later the Initiates would describe the Prismaworm as having the appearance of a massive invertebrate with a thin pinkish/white membrane covered in blotches of what looked like hair. It had been a brief moment, but terrifying.

Traveling in a tight group they made it back to SeaCliff on the morning of the third day. They were tired and hungry, but in one piece and with a new memorable respect for caution in the sands of the Carbonian Desert.

Here at the edge of the desert was the sea, with it's moisture laden air and a sense of peaceful deliverance. Peering over the edge of the cliff, they could see gentle waves caressing the shore of the Carbonian black sands far below.

In unison, they all turned to look at each other with a sense of gratitude. Each breathed a sigh of relief from surviving their trek across the desert that had been dangerously adventuresome and yet with extraordinary lessons, gratefully learned.

TerraSim turned their attention to a large rock and crystal formation. It was further away and along the edge of the cliff.

"That is home. That is SeaCliff, my friends."

"Oh, TerraSim, that is so unusual. It actually has rooms," asked Annuj?

"Can you see the sea from inside, TerraSim," chimed in Bocc?

Poona, also fascinated that someone chose to live within a rock and crystal structure, questioned...

"TerraSim, how is it that this assemblage of rocks and crystals came to be here at the edge of the cliff. Has part of the cliff fallen off during the past?"

"Well, yes, yes, and yes," answered TerraSim grinning. "What my father and I believe is that sometime in the far distant past perhaps an earthquake caused a large portion of the high cliff to fall into the sea. The remaining structure left open spaces that actually now look out over the sea itself. The crystals were a real gift though. As you are aware, they give off heat, and an amount of dim light, and for those inclined, they are spiritually illuminating as well!"

"And, they can be used for communicating," spoke Bocc.

"I believe crystals are aesthetically magnificent and hold many mysteries," said Laurra, thoughtfully.

And a few more wonderful things than that, my young friends, thought Poona.

"Yes, so true, Bocc. However, father and I are not up to speed with the latest innovations regarding communication."

"And, Laurra, I feel the very same thoughts as you."

"Also, remember this all used to be under water. It is possible some kind of an underwater disaster occurred. Who knows?

But, it is home! Come, I am anxious to introduce you to my father, BucchaSim."

As they got closer, he noticed the unusual craft sitting nearby.

Chapter 31

When We Are Lonely, Sometimes We Need To Be Alone

All things in their time

On the balcony overlooking the sea, BucchaSim, and King Luxxor were discussing the tomb and the passageway connecting Neptuna and SeaCliff.

"I can only apologize for keeping the discovery to myself, King Luxxor. I became totally obsessed with protecting SeaCliff and maintaining it's secret, and, well, I did not think things through responsibly. In retrospect, it was obvious that the significance of this passageway and the tomb within, could be of immense importance to the history of Neptuna and it's Beings. I knew that eventually I would inform you, but as it turns out, I have been in remiss."

BucchaSim looked up and into the eyes of King Luxxor.

"Personally, King Luxxor, I have been experiencing an extreme loss for some time now, and, at times, I am lonely and despondent beyond comprehension. I just have not been myself. I hope you and the Beings of Neptuna can accept my heartfelt apologies."

King Luxxor, looking closely at BucchaSim, saw a man of strong conviction and honesty, and he did appear tired — from worry, he assumed.

He thought for a moment before responding.

"I must express my anguish that such a discovery was kept hidden, BucchaSim. This tomb could be of our history — perhaps hiding long sought answers we have searched for since our beginnings here under the sea."

BucchaSim hung his head and nodded understandingly.

"But, at the same time," the King continued, placing his hand to his heart,

"I am sympathetic with your situation, BucchaSim — and while I feel it would have been right to have informed us immediately, nothing was damaged, nothing tarnished. As someone once said — all things in their time.

The past is just that, my new friend, it is past. In your situation, I may have handled it in the same manner as you have. Is it not an interesting phenomena, BucchaSim, how when we are lonely, sometimes we need to be alone!"

"We will go forward from this moment on" he finished, standing and offering his hand in friendship, and understanding.

BucchaSim, relieved, also stood and took King Luxxor's offered hand, clasped it warmly and they embraced in friendship, both knowing goodness was within them.

Sitting once again, King Luxxor expressed just how anxious he was to explore the tomb as soon as possible.

"Many things relating to Neptuna's antiquity were lost during the sinking of the city in centuries past," King Luxxor stated, "and this revelation, your discovery, will result in a momentous impact for the Beings of Neptuna. We have already initiated procedures to organize the exploration of the passageway, but now, with this new information, we can also include the even more extraordinary hidden tomb. My hope is that the tomb will prove to be of our ancient ancestors, BucchaSim. I can not find the words to describe my elation and excitement.

Can we begin tomorrow?"

As BucchaSim began to respond, he overheard a commotion at the entrance to his home. Hearing the voice of his son, he said instead…

"Please excuse me, King Luxxor. I believe I hear my son, TerraSim and I have been somewhat concerned about his extended absence. Allow me but a moment and it will be my pleasure and honor to introduce him to you."

As long as he could remember, only he, and his father were aware of SeaCliff, so TerraSim was taken back at the flying craft he had seen outside and the appearance of four men when he entered his home. However, he quickly ascertained they must be of the undersea city of Neptuna due to their distinctive coloring and clothing. Scanning the immediate area and looking for his father, his thoughts quickly turned to wondering what, if anything, was wrong.

TerraSim then saw his father gesturing and hurriedly moving in his direction from the balcony where a stately looking man sat. TerraSim intuitively felt all must be well.

BucchaSim, beaming in relief, came to the group standing by the entrance and embraced TerraSim.

"Son," he said grinning, his hands now upon TerraSim's shoulders, "you appear a little weather worn, but look great to my eyes. I was beginning to become concerned."

Happily, TerraSim replied…

"It is good to see you too father."

The Guardians, also relaxing, stood back.

"Is all well," TerraSim whispered, glancing at the Guardians.

"Yes, all is well. These are guests from Neptuna, the city beneath the sea. I have much to inform you of later, my son."

Turning to the Initiates, BucchaSim said…

"I see you have picked up a few friends along the way too, TerraSim."

"Yes father, I am happy to present my new friends, the Initiates of Brightness. This is Annuj, Calla, Laurra, Bocc and Patto. They are on their Wisdom Path Journey, and we were fortunate to meet in the desert.

"Yes, I am sure," replied BucchaSim.

And, this is Poona, father, the caregiver accompanying them, who is from Quin Emeralsia."

"It is indeed my pleasure to meet you all," BucchaSim said, sincerely embracing each in his friendly custom.

"However, introductions are not yet through. Please follow me. It is my esteem honor to introduce all of you to my neighbor and new friend, King Luxxor, King of Neptuna, the city beneath the Sea of the Forgotten Place.

"King Luxxor, allow me … this is my son, TerraSim, the Initiates of Brightness, and Poona, caregiver for the Initiates."

King Luxxor arose to greet them.

"TerraSim, it brings me pleasure to meet the son of my new friend, BucchaSim. Grasping him in an embrace, he smiled.

Then, embracing Poona and each Initiate, he added…

"I am well aware of the Initiates and the Wisdom Path Journey. However, I am not aware of a caregiver — although it makes good sense to me. I have always heartily supported the tradition and it's promise. I will soon be lobbying for the inclusion of an Initiate from Neptuna to be recognized and awarded the honor also. In my opinion, it is long past time."

Poona, listening in respect, offered…

"I agree, King Luxxor and from what I am aware, the merit, and worthiness of your Beings is far beyond argument and discussion in this matter. There could be no reasonable justification for any further delay were you to present your concerns to the High Council in Spectrum. But, King Luxxor, for your information, recently, HighPriestess XennaOne introduced the subject of Neptuna's involvement to the Council of the Voice of One. An amendment has been ratified and agreed upon already."

"It states that in the continuing process of selection for the Initiate of Brightness program, Neptuna will now have two selections, as will the other Quins — and also, Spectrum. I would assume you should be notified at any time.

We all are extremely pleased at this wise, and just decision.

As you aptly stated, King Luxxor — it is long past time."

"Why, thank you, Poona, I am practically speechless. At this moment I am filled with honor, and total joy. Since we speak of such a commendable program, forgive my attempt at humor — but sometimes I feel we Neptunians, being from 'under' the sea, are often 'over' looked!"

Everyone caught his meaning and his humor and while applauding his wit, understood the deeper feelings involved.

"I will so look forward to proclaiming the great news," stated King Luxxor.

"My, I am elated! I must send a crystal message to Queen, Liluuc — she will be ecstatic. So much good news, and in such a short while. My!"

He smiled brightly, as his new friend, BucchaSim embraced him in happiness. Turning to everyone gathered, King Luxxor, beamingly said…

"You may be interested to know that it has been Neptuna's honor to have accommodated Solannuj and Xennuj among others, during their Wisdom Path Journey — before they each eventually became a HighPriestess of the Voice of One. Junnuj, who became the HighPriestess JunnaOne, also was awarded the honor, but generously gifted it to another of the nominees. Being married with a young family, Junnuj deservedly, and understandably felt her place was with them."

King Luxxor did not notice BucchaSim flinch at the mention of Junnuj and neither did anyone else — except TerraSim.

Quickly understanding the pain his father could be experiencing, TerraSim decided to change the course of the conversation, and asked…

"King Luxxor, what is protocol for a visit to Neptuna, the city beneath the sea? I have always been intrigued by it's mystique."

Raising his arms, as if proclaiming a proclamation, King Luxxor said…

"Actually, TerraSim, being neighbors, you will be welcome anytime."

"And," gesturing to the Initiates and Poona, he added — "we will be honored should you choose to visit us as well, my new friends! As I stated, an exploration to Neptuna by the Initiates has been a tradition for some time now … and I wish it to continue."

Everyone thanked the King for his generous offer.

Yes, for sure, King Luxxor, Laurra and I will look forward to visiting Neptuna, Poona thought to herself.

TerraSim, added…

"Father, I believe our guests could use a little time to rest and cleanse. It has obviously been a long, and at times, an arduous trip full of adventures we can share later."

"Yes, of course," answered BucchaSim. "I will let you do the honors of showing these fine young Beings to their rooms. King Luxxor, and I will look forward to hearing all the details of their journey, over snacks and drinks. Shall we say approximately half an hour, and we will meet back here?"

"Perhaps I can entice King Luxxor to join me in the kitchen while I prepare some appetizers. I just happen to have a portion of Loctuum, for special occasions. This afternoon seems very special to me given the wonderful news of Neptuna's inclusion in the Initiates of Brightness selection.

BucchaSim and King Luxxor both smiled.

Later, after arranging themselves around a small table on large, soft pillows, the Initiates politely, but hungrily enjoyed appetizers, and listened.

Given King Luxxor's approval, BucchaSim informed everyone of recent events, including the unknown tomb he discovered in an unknown cliff passage many years before. The King thrillingly added details of his son and daughter who found the entrance and bravely explored this passage before BucchaSim's involvement with them and his eventual meeting King Luxxor.

"The disclosure of artifacts, scrolls, etchings, stelae on the walls, or any discovery, will create unparalleled joy and enthusiasm in Neptuna," King Luxxor stated enthusiastically. But, most importantly, it could provide us with beneficial information regarding our past."

The Initiates, all enthralled with the story and the upcoming exploration, expressed their extreme interest in helping King Luxxor and Neptuna in any way they could. King Luxxor, sensing the Initiates eagerness, glanced at BucchaSim and then back at the Initiates, saying...

"Allow BucchaSim and myself a moment to confer about a matter I have in mind my new young friends. We will be right back."

Upon their return BucchaSim asked...

"Perhaps the Initiates would like to participate tomorrow in an exploration we have planned. King Luxxor and I intend to explore the tomb in the morning and if you feel rested it would be our pleasure to have your company and input. However, it will be a long day, and ..."

All of the Initiates and Poona raised their hands in unison.

"YES !"

King Luxxor grinned brightly, as did BucchaSim.

"Wonderful," said BucchaSim, but are you sure?" The group just stared at him. "Alright, he said with a chuckle, tomorrow we go exploring."

"Now, if King Luxxor can stay for dinner I know he and I will both look forward to all the exciting details you choose to share with us tonight regarding your journey thus far."

King Luxxor arose to stand before them.

"BucchaSim, my new friends, thank you, but my family does in fact await me, and I have promised to be home to share the evening. And, as you can imagine, I am extremely excited to celebrate the promising news of our involvement in the Initiate's program. I have contacted my Queen and she is so very happy. I must leave shortly, or for sure I will be late. But, I will stay until you return for dinner to say my goodbyes."

"I am sure we can arrange for another time to be together to hear of your exploits. Perhaps in Neptuna," he gestured to the initiates? "I know my Queen would like that, as well as Tunnis and Dolpho, the explorers you heard about earlier. They are close to your age and would be thrilled."

Delighted, the Initiates expressed their eagerness to spend time in Neptuna at a later date, and retired to their rooms to prepare for dinner.

In respect to their host BucchaSim and to say goodbye to the King, they decided it would be proper if each put on their nice adornment for the evening meal. Annuj, Calla, Laurra and Poona wore simple, fitting gowns that fell to their ankles, with silver waist chains, the gem of their Quin as a clasp, and a small simple head band with matching earrings. Bocc and Patto dressed in simple body suits, the color of their Quins, and also wore their head bands

When they arrived back to the cozy sitting area, they found BucchaSim had the evening meal almost prepared.

"Ah," BucchaSim said, as he saw them approaching, "I was looking for some help. There are plates and utensils to put out, and a lovely tablecloth would be nice too."

King Luxxor, got up from his stool and once again offered his apologies that he unfortunately could not share dinner with them this evening.

"However, I would be remiss not to add how lovely you young women look, and how handsome you young men look, also. All this and 'gifted' too."

"Marvelous! I am indeed impressed."

Smiling, the King's eyes twinkled, and they all smiled back appreciating his sincere remarks.

"Now, I insist, my new friends — remember to consider adding Neptuna to your Wisdom Path Journey. Please allow myself, Liluuc, my Queen, Tunnis and Dolpho, and the Beings of Neptuna, the pleasure and honor of sharing our Neptunian hospitality with you."

"I will look forward to seeing you all tomorrow when we visit the Passage of Antiquity."

He paused, arched his eyebrows, smiled at them, and then to himself. "I believe I have just named it ..."

"The Passage of Antiquity! Hmmm, I like it."

"Now, I must leave. I am expected back soon."

He gave them each a farewell embrace, saying "Until later."

Shortly, BucchaSim, TerraSim, Poona and the Initiates sat enjoying a very nice meal with BucchaSim now listening intently, as each Initiate shared their version of the extraordinary adventure experienced thus far. Some of the tales even raised his eyebrows and he asked several related questions during their chat! He was definitely enthralled with the sand panther episode.

Tired, and well fed, they all slept soundly that evening, under the unending Heavens of Crystola, listening to the ever present winds and the relentless waves of the Sea of the Forgotten Place.

Chapter 32

And It Worked

A MorQ thought

Thus far, everything proceeded as MorQ had anticipated, and hoped.

As he assumed, after reviewing the altered survey reports, CodL quickly sent out orders to prepare the RogueReCon for launch in 7 days.

A little sooner than I expected, MorQ thought, *but within my parameters.*

For the next few days, MorQ purposefully went about his duties as Chief Engineer/Scientist normally, thankful that CodL had not seen fit to demean him further. Nonetheless, inwardly MorQ was a mess, becoming plagued with occasional bouts of nausea, an upset stomach, and a continuing apprehension that somehow he may be found out. After all, CodL did have eyes everywhere.

However, to his amazement, CodL was completely ignoring him, and putting no further demands on him.

He probably does not want to see me either, MorQ considered.

"Oh God I hope so," he exclaimed out loud!

Then, completely unanticipated by MorQ, CodL selected DrexL to command the RogueReCon for this mission. For MorQ, this was an unexpected gift from the Gods.

DrexL is Commander of the RogueRecon! DrexL may be tough, but he is also known to be wise in his judgement, and fair in his treatment of the men. He has always been professional and respectful to me, MorQ thought, *so, maybe it also could even prove beneficial later on.*

On the day before departure MorQ made appearances at various pre-selected locations on the RogueEmpire to be sure they noticed he was around. Then, he deduced, if they do not see me for a few days, or weeks, it should not arouse suspicion, as I will still be in their memories occasionally walking the halls.

I'm hardly seen much anyway, MorQ grimaced, *and most likely nobody cares. Besides, everyone considers me a recluse. My plan to steal aboard the RogueReCon during the evening meal when most activity is taking place in the cafeteria makes the most sense,* he concluded. *However,* if *I am seen prowling the corridors late at night, which is something I never do, it could definitely attract CodL's attention. I do not want that. I must be clever, and deceptive.*

The appointed evening arrived. MorQ felt squeamish.

Standing in the hall with his backpack, he thought, *I am right though, it is dinner hour, and there is nobody in sight. That will leave only a skeleton crew remaining. This is the best opportunity to execute my escape.*

He glanced around carefully.

"If, by chance I am seen, for all they know I am here for a reason," he whispered nervously, "and they would be right, I have a great reason for being here!"

With the stealth of a cat burglar, and being extremely careful to avoid sensors, and viewing screens, MorQ, traversed the corridors of the RougeRecon on his way to his destination — the escape pod on the lower level.

Thus far, he was fortunate to have not encountered anybody, but twice he just knew he heard a rustling noise or a voice down the hallway. In shear fear he began to sweat excessively, and heard himself repeating...

"Just get me there, just get me there."

"Oh Goodness, I'm losing it," he said to himself!"

Just calm down, MorQ. Take a few deep breaths, and pull yourself together! You are almost there. You can not stop.

Finally, MorQ found his way safely onto the lower decks where the storage, and escape Pod chutes were located. Sighing a breath of relief, he took a moment to calm himself and familiarize himself with his new surroundings. He knew things sometimes look different, or have been moved, from that seen on a blueprint.

As he anticipated, here on the lower decks the lights were kept on low voltage to preserve energy, and hopefully allowing him to stealth about unnoticed.

Alright, he thought, *I need to sequester myself in escape pod #1, located at escape hatch #1 of this vessel.*

Looking about, he said...

"That will be over there."

"God, as chilly as it is on this level, I'm still sweating!"

I feel wet and cold.

MorQ stopped in his tracks.

I am in a condition of anxiousness. I am nervous, and I am scared.

Taking several more deep breaths, MorQ muttered another invocation of "Please help me," and continued on.

Also figuring into his escape formula were the semi frigid conditions which would be present outside his pod. MorQ knew that the heating on this level was kept at an absolute minimum during the voyage. It was a normal policy to preserve energy where ever possible. So, to compensate, MorQ devised a hot-wiring system, which he went about implementing. He reconnected an auxiliary backup heat conducting coil, and redirected it to escape pod #1.

"If someone does come down here they will have to look hard to discover the wires I have hidden," he boasted to himself, taking a long look at his handiwork.

If I am dressed properly, he had considered, *there are several storage facilities nearby for water, and essential needs that I can get to, and back, unnoticed by the all seeing eyes of CodL's detectors. I expect no guests down here in this frigid place while in the deep Heavens.*

Seeing absolutely nothing glaring out at him, MorQ felt reasonably assured he would not be detected and entered what he expected to be his home for the foreseeable future.

"Home, sweet home," he said, now smiling.

"I will make this work," he said.

"This will work," he corrected himself.

"This is working," he gloated.

MorQ settled in.

Chapter 33

The Rogue Recon Slightly Quivered

DrexL, heading to deep space

DrexL was informed of his assignment to command the RogueReCon and could not have been happier, although he would never let CodL know it.

He would undoubtably pull me off as Commander if he was aware of the internal jubilation I am now feeling for the chance to get away from the RogueEmpireComplex — not to mention, CodL.

The days of meetings, discussions, expectations, and preparation came and went quickly and unaccountably with very few appearances by CodL.

A very odd and unusual phenomena, thought DrexL.

"The RogueReCon is ready," he stated.

"Anchoring systems have been released. Departure countdown commencing ... 7,6,5,4,3,2,1... ignition, and power."

The RogueRecon slightly quivered as it raised from the hard metallic surface and DrexL slowly positioned it in the Space Exit Chute. As with all exits, the departure chamber had been evacuated and the large craft exit door now opened unto the Heavens themselves.

DrexL, in the command tower, had the RogueRecon in manual mode and loved the feeling of exhilaration that came over him just before engaging Neutro thrust. He looked ahead, saturating his visual senses and his Soul in the innumerable stars twinkling and beckoning him forth.

Checking gauges one last time, he accepted the star's invitation gladly.

Neutros engaged, as he nudged gently forward on the rectangular shaped throttle, and the 'RogueRecon' slowly left the debarkation port of the RogueEmpire, slightly rolling to the right before Neutro thrusters were set at 75 percent.

Thus, DrexL, the crew, and, the sequestered MorQ, headed into the twinkling promise of the Heavens, leaving the RogueEmpireComplex and CodL behind.

A course plotted and engaged for Planet 8, Galaxy 17 in deep space was entered.

Farewell, CodL. You are a blight to civilization.

On board the RogueEmpire Complex, CodL watched. He had postponed approaching DrexL regarding his suspicions until another time. Actually, he was not sure his suspicions were justified.

Could I be paranoid, thought CodL?

Nevertheless, paranoid or not, I have placed a man aboard the RogueRecon that reports only to me. I now have my seeing, and reporting eyes on board.

An unusual occurrence then occurred — CodL smiled!

"Stay in line, and for your sake don't disappoint me, Drexl …

I'm watching you."

Chapter 34

Don't Tell Me Finn, Let Me Guess

You do remember he is an Emperor

FinnJonko stood at the space monitoring screen in the control station waiting for his father's response. They had the very latest military tested equipment on board — a fact that had to do with a political connection of his fathers on Earth5. It seemed this particular politician was obsessed with gems and women, and LesterJonko was seasoned enough to know how to please.

Whatever, thought FinnJonko, *at least we aboard the 'Black Widow' now have the ability to look deep into space, plus the capacity to receive high quality images and of all things, also receive sound echoes, or transmissions when possible. How that is accomplished is beyond me,* he thought, considering signaling his father once again.

I know a lot of things, but Interstellar Galactic Sound Retrieval and it's add on feature, Galactic Solar Wind Noise Reduction, leave me shaking my head in wonder.

He was contemplating just how it was all possible when the white light flashed, signaling his father's response.

"Yes, Finn, what gives up in the dizzying heights of the Control Tower?"

For a tough man, he can be amusing at times, thought FinnJonko, smiling.

"Well, father, the intelligence gathering units are sending in reports and we are in the process of receiving and interpreting them as we speak. I felt you would like to know that someone is snooping around this vicinity. Thus far, the photovisions received show they are Rogue Spacial Probes, among your favorite, I believe, father," he said jokingly. "Apparently CodL is interested in something around here. From the info received thus far we have deduced that these units, three to be exact, were exiting from

121

Planet 8, Galaxy 17 and heading towards a star system I understand you are familiar with."

"Don't tell me Finn, let me guess, the Paradox star system and could it possibly be Galaxy 33?"

"I see we are on the same page, father. Can I assume CodL is still wanted by StarForce, and that you, excuse me, we, are still interested in the bounty on his head?"

"Yep! Ever since that run in with TechStar Corporation on Planet Trion, he has been a marked man. Him and his self glorified, self serving, contemptuous, RogueEmpire."

Sarcastically, LesterJonko then said...

"You do remember he is an Emperor, right, Finn?"

"Yes."

"CodL's wanted through out the Galaxies already, but messing with a Company the size and power of TechStar is suicidal. The bounty on his head is undoubtably the size of his maniacal Ego — huge," exclaimed LesterJonko.

Finn smiled to himself. He knew without question his father would investigate this situation even if it takes time away from their previously planned endeavors.

"Signing off father, I will keep you updated."

"Right, and thanks, Finn."

Chapter 35

A Day In The Tombs Of A Wormhole

But, what about the scratches

BucchaSim, rising early to prepare for the days tomb exploration, was surprised to find breakfast almost ready for him as he entered the kitchen.

All the Initiates were present and milling around, with Poona as the selected 'chef' for the morning breakfast. Laurra, Calla and Bocc were on the balcony watching the sunlight beginning to skim across the waters on The Sea of the Forgotten Place, while Patto, and Annuj were setting the table.

Walking into the kitchen, BucchaSim found Poona putting the finishing embellishments on what appeared to be a mouthwatering huge plate of giant Gattling eggs and baked fish.

Those must be gattling eggs, and obviously enough for all, too, he judged.

He determined it had to be gattling eggs as he was out of the smaller, more delicate Troner Hen eggs as of a few days ago.

"Good morning, BucchaSim."

"Good morning to you, Poona. My, but this looks and smells absolutely delicious, and I do feel ravenous today."

"Well," replied Poona, "I will not be entering any culinary competitions any time soon, but eggs and fish are fairly simple, even for me."

Several things were running through his mind, and all were good with one being especially very special.

My Junnuj is soon to be out of DreamState. Soon you will be home, and we will make up for the time apart."

Oh One, what a beautiful day that will be," he softly said.

"Did you say something," asked Poona, smiling.

"Yes, I did, Poona. I said, Oh One, what a beautiful day."

"You are correct, BucchaSim — it is a beautiful day."

BucchaSim looked more closely at Poona.

She appears to glow a little, even in the light of day, he thought. *It must be the vitality of youth these days. I don't know what these young Beings are eating, but sign me up.*

He chuckled.

Laurra, entering from the direction of the balcony, smiled at BucchaSim.

"A beautiful good morning to you also, Laurra. How is the view from the balcony this morning?"

"Invigorating, and with a lot of promise thrown in," she said, her eyes sparkling.

Laurra helped Poona carry the breakfast out to the table where a single small flower had been placed in a vase at the center. Bocc, Calla, Annuj and Patto all came in and asked if they should awaken TerraSim.

"You can go check," said BucchaSim, "but my guess is he has already gone out for his morning walk along the beach. It is a ritual with him. He loves the sunrise, with it's smells and sounds of the water lapping up onto the shore during the early morning. He says it is like therapy from the One."

"He was definitely quiet" said Patto, "I did not hear a thing."

"Years on the desert avoiding Prismaworms," remarked BucchaSim.

That comment took on a life of it's own over breakfast, as one by one the Initiates once again presented their thoughts and feelings of the encounter they experienced while facing the dreaded Prismaworm.

"Well, not exactly facing the worm," Annuj admitted, "it was more like burrowing into the sand and praying to the One to save us, while hoping TerraSim really did have a definite sense of experience and survival from his years in the desert."

"It is easy to laugh about it now, but during the encounter it was terrifying," chimed in Bocc.

BucchaSim, excusing himself, went to check the light outside. Returning, he said..."

We best be heading out very soon. We need to hurry along in order to have a good full day in the tombs. Thanks so much for the breakfast everyone. Just leave the dishes in the kitchen, they can be cleaned later."

Smiling devilishly he added...

"If we are lucky, TerraSim will do the dishes when he comes home."

"Oh, don't forget to bring any personal items you feel you may need — just don't make your load to heavy. Meet you all at the back entrance in ten minutes."

Ten minutes later, all were assembled and anxious to start out.

"We will be on our own today," stated BucchaSim. "King Luxxor, who was supposed to join us, sent a crystal transmission stating his regrets. He has been detained for the entire day. He will however, see us at the tombs tomorrow at approximately noon — with hopes of seeing all of the ancient secrets he knows we will discover today!"

Sensing their disappointment he said...

"Now, let's go and find an ancient secret to gift our friend and King with tomorrow."

Everyone brightened up at this thought, and BucchaSim led them into the Ritual Room at the back of his home. The Initiates were still enamored, and fascinated at the skill, and ingenuity BucchaSim and TerraSim had possessed in creating the false wall separating his place from the Ritual Room. It was virtually impossible to discern from either side.

Entering the top of the passage they found there was enough light coming through the cracks in the side of the mountain to see clearly — but BucchaSim told them the passage will prove to become dimmer, and eventually quite dark as they traversed deeper and deeper into the depths of the mountain.

BucchaSim gave Patto and Bocc firelites to carry, which lighted the way for the rest — and the adventure began. As the small group proceeded along, erie shadows lurching and twitching about on the walls accompanied them thanks to the flickering flames. As they journeyed deeper, and closer to their goal, each became immersed in their own thoughts.

Will this be enlightening, or perhaps, a harrowing experience? Just what will we discover within the ancient tombs ahead — ancient treasure, hieroglyphics, sarcophagus, or perhaps, very little?

Bocc, in the back of the group was carefully holding a firelite, walking, and taking photovisions with his Palm Recorder of the evocative shadow formations cascading and flickering on the smooth walls of the passage. He suddenly had a thought, a question, and called out to BucchaSim.

"BucchaSim," he asked, "why did the ancients take the time and effort to smooth the walls, and ceiling so extraordinarily well? It would not have been necessary in a passage such as this."

"That is a very good question, Bocc, and I have some theories," he replied.

"They revolve around everyone's favorite subject and life form, the Prismaworm!"

"A Prismaworm," everyone exclaimed!

"Yes, a Prismaworm," answered BucchaSim. "Come, gather around and I will explain my theory. This will not take long, and I believe it is important. I have given a lot of thought to the passage, and why the ancients would have expended the energy to accomplish such a task, which to me was unnecessary. Then it came to me... like, how had I not thought of, or realized this before?"

He paused.

"Well," they all chimed in.

"Ok! You have noticed the smooth walls, but what about the scratches or abrasions that run haphazardly along the walls, and ceiling? Certainly those are not meant to be artistic enhancements, or some unknown form of writing!

Please, take a look."

The Initiates began to examine and study the markings.

"Yes," said Bocc, and then Calla. "We see what you are speaking of."

"I had not even paid much attention to them," said Annuj, adding, "They are not very deeply etched into the walls."

"No, they are not" answered, BucchaSim.

"Here is my theory. Are you ready?"

"YESSSS!"

Laughing, BucchaSim said...

"Alright, I'll be serious. After years of living in the desert, TerraSim, and I have had the opportunity to experience many things. Among them are the Prismaworms and more to the point, specifically their tunnels. We guesstimate a normal adult Prismaworm is approximately 10-12 feet in circumference and can be quite long. We found tunnels where worms had exited and very carefully mind you, explored a couple of these tunnels to measure the circumference. We found them to be right around that size."

"But," he continued, "the tunnel we are in is only around 6 to 8 feet in circumference. Why so much smaller? We came to the conclusion that this particular tunnel was created by a baby or young Prismaworm just going out on it's own.

Like learning to crawl — it was learning to burrow."

"As to the scratches in the walls, that was an enigma for us, but we finally came to an answer that satisfied us. A Prismaworm is covered with blotches of wiry hair. We believe the scratches come from the wiry hairs of a Prismaworm as it plows and slithers it's way through the desert sands — creating a tunnel at the same time."

"One last and very interesting fact is a Prismaworm is formed with connecting body sections, and it is believed that these sections can 'be' released or 'release themselves' from the main body, becoming a Prismaworm of it's own. We suppose this occurs in times of self preservation, but we are not really sure."

Everyone became silent, contemplating the plausibility of BucchaSim and TerraSim's analysis — but only for a moment.

Patto stepped forward, "In my opinion, you are to be complimented, for what you have deducted is very plausible and is certainly one possible solution to the mystery. It does, however, bring up another mystery for me and that is, why are the walls and ceiling and floor so hard? I mean this is sand and gravel here in the desert. Reasonably, one would expect the tunnel to fill in as the worm burrows through." Does, that sound reasonable, BucchaSim?"

"Also, what about the stairs," asked Laurra. "Where did they come from?"

"Alright, I will begin with Patto's very good question. The solidity of the tunnel was a real dilemma," answered BucchaSim."The lack of an answer to that question almost destroyed the basic foundation of our theory. It was TerraSim who finally figured it out and what a revelation it was — and is! His hypothesis came from an accident that garnered his curiosity.

He noticed that when enough pressure is exerted on the sand, it hardens. We tried hitting it with some large rocks and found it hardened even more. So, we theorized that the intense pressure exerted by a Prismaworm, pile-driving through the desert sands could, well let me rephrase that, 'will' harden the area it has passed through. We have actually discovered carbonite gravel that has solidified into 3 foot thick walls. The wiry hair abraded the walls as it was hardening from the pressure of the worm traveling through, leaving the markings we see today." He gestured at the walls revealed from the firelite."

"TerraSim and I, believe the ancient ones, having deduced these same facts, used the tunnels for their own needs. How they circumvented encountering the Prismaworms is their secret. We will probably never know. They are the ones who decided to create secret tombs in the tunnels. No one, who is at all aware of the worms, would go near a Prismaworm tunnel — let alone into one."

"So," asked Patto, "the passageway to, or from Neptuna is an ancient wormhole that somehow held together while dropping several hundred feet during the sinking of the Carbonian Desert into the Sea — including the city of Neptuna?"

"Yes, Patto."

"And, Laurra, we believe the stairs you inquired about were added in the tunnel after the wormhole sank, as they would not have been necessary when the tunnel was level. The tombs could have been put in before or after. We have yet to find out, but are leaning towards after. Sorry for this pun, but that is our conclusion in a wormhole."

A communal moan echoed through the tunnel.

BucchaSim shook his head and laughed.

"I have discussed this recently with King Luxxor and he is satisfied that with the facts we presently have, our findings are quite probable, at least until something turns up to prove otherwise."

During BucchaSim's account of the tunnel, they had slowly continued down towards the tomb they were to examine — the tomb that BucchaSim had discovered. Once again, silence, as they all considered the ramifications of BucchaSim's story. It's significance could be monumental considering all the possibilities of the many tunnels that could possibly exist and the discovery of the 'hardening of the sands' could have many useful purposes.

Bocc, still in the back, continued to capture unique photos of Calla and Annuj, who were directly in front of him. He decided he would artistically chronicle the journey they were all on with his Palm Recorder. Something within told him this was special and that he would need to write down his thoughts as quickly as possible, in prose, to accompany the images he was capturing thus far.

He then thought to himself...

I have actually been listening and involved thus far!

He grinned broadly.

Annuj was having some deeper thoughts herself ...

There is something about BucchaSim and TerraSim I can not put my finger on. It is almost as if I have known them in another lifetime. I need to bring up questions of just where they are from originally. When I have the chance, I would like to draw upon Past Recall — but in the meantime I will store these questions in QuietMind.

They finally came to some ancient relief drawings and writing on the wall.

"A stela" stated Poona. "From my studies in Paleography — ancient writing systems, she clarified. This one appears to go back unknown millennium. Usually they are upright stone slabs or columns that display inscriptions — they are also sometimes used as grave markers."

"From my research that is correct, Poona," said BucchaSim. "At least that is our thinking right now. We are hoping to find more discerning evidence that will link everything together. There are a couple more stelae yet to come."

Patto, found himself totally impressed with Poona's knowledge regarding the ancient stela.

I suppose Poona, being from Quin Emeralsia, those of Spirituality, has had the opportunity to study volumes of ancient texts on Spirituality, and Religions and their Ritualistic rites of life and death. Smiling, he thought, *I will definitely look forward to more time with Poona.*

They passed a second similar stela, and then came to a third.

BucchaSim stated...

"This is it. This is the tomb!"

They all stopped in their tracks.

We are finally here, was the composite thought among them. They looked, and although it appeared almost like the first two stelae in regards to the drawings and relief patterns, this one was much larger, almost reaching the floor of the passage.

BucchaSim asked Bocc to bring his firelite up to the stela. Looking at them, and then back to the ancient stone, he said...

"Do any of you see anything that catches your eye?"

"It is larger in height and width than the previous ones," said Laurra.

"Yes, good, what else?"

Now, all the Initiates, curious as to any differences, gathered in front and studied it carefully — looking at the etchings, the reliefs, anything unusual they could find that BucchaSim could be referring to. Perhaps something that may allow them to enter?

"Are we searching for a way into the tomb," asked Calla, anxiously?

"Is it alright to touch it, BucchaSim," asked Patto?

"Yes, and yes," he said, "but we need to put on gloves to protect the tomb first."

"Bocc, you have clean, soft, gloves in your pack," said BucchaSim. "Please hand them out to all."

"I do," asked Bocc?'

"Yes, I took the liberty of putting a few things we could use in your pack as mine is full of nourishment for us later."

"Oh, well, yes, of course," responded Bocc, who put his firelite into a wall holder on the opposite side of the tomb, and took off his backpack.

Finding the gloves, Bocc handed them out, and everyone began carefully feeling the stone. There were several carved reliefs covering the ancient stela, so it made sense that there could be a hidden latch to discover that would open the tomb.

Poona crouched near the bottom of the stela, more intent in trying to decipher the drawings and writings.

There was a good 15 minutes of prying around the edges, gently pushing this and that, and chatting about just what these drawings could mean, when Patto said excitedly...

"I have found something!"

And indeed he had! Near the bottom, he had noticed a relief depicting a woman with a headdress, and a waist gown. She stood on an artist's rendition of an apparent mound, or bowl, and looking down at what appeared to be ripples of water, like the sea.

"I believe it's here, under the part that is supposed to signify a mound. I think it is a lever," said Patto.

"Well done, Patto! Pull the lever forward towards you, but gently — we don't want to break it," BucchaSim softly said.

It became very quiet as Patto carefully grasped the lever with his right fingers, and pulled it slowly towards himself.

A heavy click echoed through the immediate passage, and also echoed into what must have been an open area behind the stela. Everyone, but BucchaSim, drew in a deep breath as the large stone slab slowly swung inward.

Standing to the side and slightly behind Annuj, Poona began to softly glow, and her eyes seemed to sparkle at the moment of entrance. They were about to enter an ancient place, possibly a tomb, or a place of Ritual — or both. Perhaps unknown treasures of history awaited. BucchaSim put the firelites inside for illumination, and the small group of archaeologists entered.

An overwhelming deluge of past promise, and future destiny swept over them. In time, time had become lost — now belonging to distant antiquity, and to those who would reclaim it. Untold thousands of years had gone by, with the history contained here resting solemnly, patiently. Apparently content to wait until the Universe felt ready to have this sacred chamber, and it's secrets rediscovered.

"I feel humbled," Poona whispered, raising her eyes and lifting her hands.

Kneeling, she quietly said, "If I may ..."

Somehow they all knew to kneel. Poona crossing her hands upon her chest, then offered...

"To the 'One' we give our thanks for the privilege bestowed upon us to enter, and have insight in this sacred and wondrous space.

May we respect, and honor the memories of those who came before us and may we be thankful for our place and our time in the vastness of your Celestial Universe. Oh One, may the silent acclaim of past Ages, past Beings, and 'the Goodness of All Things' forever be gratified, revered and honored."

Poona, lowering her head, and opening her eyes, arose.

Everyone arose. BucchaSim looked at Poona.

"Thank you, Poona. I personally have not heard a sentiment as worthy and heartfelt. It is we who are honored."

Turning to his youthful and budding Ancientologists, BucchaSim proclaimed...

"It is time for work to begin."

He issued instructions, and after pointing out the do's and do-nots, the

Initiates and Poona, enthusiastically began the search for secrets, and for perhaps, destiny.

Time went by, as they familiarized themselves with the hidden chamber, personally scrutinizing all the stelae, inscriptions, altars and pottery. What was initially found that captivated their curiosity the most were some small, seemingly unimportant Goddess figurines which appeared to be made out of crystal. There were about 100 of them, beautifully crafted, and all looking alike. Each figurine had a small slot in its back which garnered a great deal of curiosity.

Also found in the same area, but in a separate enclosure, were many 'z' shaped metal pieces, also with no apparent purpose. However, their function soon became obvious to Laurra, as she excitedly exclaimed...

"I think I have it! I believe these small metal 'z' pieces fit into the back of the Goddess relics — and I believe it is possible they become keys to open something. But," she said, "I have tried a few combinations, and it seems only a correct 'z' key will fit into a particular Goddess. I am still trying to find a 'z' that will fit the Goddess relic I am holding."

Everyone came over see what she was talking about. The five Initiates sat in a circle and began considering opinions as to how to figure out this puzzle.

Calla finally said...

"This could take forever, so how about this ... we each take twenty relics, and ten z pieces. We try to find if 2 fit together. If nothing fits, we then continue to keep the Goddesses we each possess, but pass on the z pieces that did not fit to the next person, who will do the same by passing theirs on. Effectively we should get this done in a short amount of time and see just which ones go together — if any!"

It did go quickly, and they found that only seven of the z's fit seven of the Goddesses.

"The rest must apparently be decoys to confuse Beings, or for some other use for which I have no explanation," said Patto.

On closer observation, Laurra found a minute star on the forehead of the seven Goddesses that fit the appropriate seven z's. They deduced that this star was to distinguish them from the others, thereby making it easier to locate them.

"Very clever," remarked BucchaSim, "and very well done, my new friends. I am impressed to say the least."

"But," added Laurra, "I have not seen any openings, like slots, where these little Goddesses, and 'z' keys might go."

As it turned out no one else had either, so a total exploration followed, with each person taking a section of the chamber. Now, the focus was on finding slots, or maybe another hidden chamber.

BucchaSim, totally enthralled, determined that if a hidden lever was used to enter this chamber then quite possibly that would be the method used to enter yet another chamber— if one existed. He concentrated on a stela at the end of the Chamber, and behind an altar.

Where you find one, you may find another, he rationalized.

Given he was specifically looking for a lever, it did not take long to find it and he excitedly shouted out...

"Everyone! I believe I have discovered a second lever. It's here, only it is above this stela, not below."

They all rushed over and he gave the lever a slow pull. Once again, as with the first stela, the second slowly swung inward and when a firelite was brought forth they peered in and witnessed another chamber, but much, much more magnificent.

BucchaSim, gathering them all together, said...

"This is extraordinary my young Ancientologists. I am overwhelmingly pleased and remarkably impressed with all your efforts and how well you rationalize situations. In one day we have discovered secrets that have been hidden from all Beings for thousands of years. I am extremely delighted for what we will present to King Luxxor tomorrow when he arrives. He will be jubilant, and personally, I am ecstatic!"

"Now I know we have just discovered another marvelous chamber whose contents, I have no doubt, will be astonishing. It is highly probable we will come across things we may never have seen. Plus, we are all excited and enthusiastic to continue, but our day has flown by.

We have yet to return home, and, as you know, that takes a while. If we leave now we should get back in time to eat and still enjoy the sunset, and, besides — I'm hungry! We have been so involved and distracted, I completely forgot to bring out the food I brought for us to share."

"Tonight we will have a nice dinner and enjoy our success. Tomorrow we will return and with our newly found secret chamber awaiting, we will see what awaits us. Come now, lets gather our things and head for home."

"Also, he then exclaimed, tomorrow we will have the distinct pleasure of King Luxxor's presence. It will be wonderful for him to share in what we have found."

Glancing around the room at each other, they each realized BucchaSim was correct. They were tired and hungry, and although their enthusiasm would have carried them further into the night, they understood and truly wanted for King Luxxor to be with them.

And, yes, they were hungry too.

Later, when they arrived at SeaCliff, they found TerraSim waiting and all the dishes from the morning were clean.

'the best, so far, by far...

not to be expected, or explained...

making memories, left and right...

without effort, or intention...'

bocc

poet and Initiate of Brightness on the Wisdom Path Journey
Prismacia
UGT 20,872

Chapter 36

Drexl Smiled At The Subterfuge

Nothing goes unnoticed, MorQ

DrexL was quietly thinking that one did not leave the RogueEmpire without CodL's permission, when he noticed the green incoming transmission button was blinking. He actually considered not answering, but reluctantly did so anyway.

CodL's image appeared larger than life on the view screen.

"He looks in a foul mood," he said to the control room crew, "so I guess things are normal back on the RogueEmpireComplex."

A chuckle came forth from his crew, who knew exactly what he meant. DrexL then turned on the sound transmission button, enabling all parties to hear each other.

"What is your progress, bearing, and situation, DrexL?"

It is not a question so much as a demand, thought DrexL.

"We are proceeding as planned Emperor CodL. We are actually a little ahead of schedule, and will arrive at Planet 8 earlier than expected. The RogueReCon has performed well and there have been no situations to resolve thus far."

DrexL was still addressing CodL as Emperor. Until he completely formulated his plan to escape and knew for sure that CodL's long reach would be useless, he would continue the deception.

CodL remained silent for a moment — just staring at the screen, as if trying to see into DrexL's mind. He then declared...

"We still have not found that perp, MorQ. You are sure you thoroughly searched the ReCon?"

"Yes, Emperor CodL, everything was searched completely, ventilation ducts, and all. Each level and individual departments therein checked clean. We even searched the unheated lower hold and escape area, although nothing could survive in that frigid place for long. If MorQ is on this vessel he is clinging to the outside."

CodL continued to stare into the screen glaringly.

Hmmm, I know, DrexL. I have already been informed of the search and am aware that MorQ was not found. My 'eyes' sent the message as soon as the search was completed.

Then, without another word, the screen went blank.

DrexL had to smile to himself at the subterfuge he was pulling on CodL, because at this very moment, up in his suite, MorQ was probably languishing on a soft couch and enjoying the comforts of his freedom — at least for the time being.

Thinking back to MorQ's attempt at devious intrigue, DrexL once again had to smile, remembering …

I had been monitoring the various levels and stations on the RogueReCon from my private quarters when I first spotted MorQ ambling about trying to look as though he fit in. His guile and deviousness left something to be desired, but, as it turns out, not his courage, thought DrexL.

I wonder, maybe MorQ's desperation motivated him … "Whatever," he muttered. *Actually, the cunning ingenuity MorQ put into devising his scheme of escape was impressive — and also the bravado of his follow through.*

"I don't blame you for wanting to escape, MorQ," DrexL said softly.

Then, chuckling to himself, he recalled the moment when he had decided it was time to confront MorQ.

MorQ had been peering out the porthole window of the pod he inhabited and then he opened the door. As he stepped onto the floor, he froze, remembered DrexL. *Oh, if I could only know what he was thinking. There I was, leaning against Escape Pod #2, across from him, with my arms folded. I looked straight into his eyes and said, "Good morning, MorQ. Have you been sleeping well?"*

MorQ was speechless. I am sure he was wondering how could this be. Everything had gone just perfectly — at least MorQ had thought so, imagined DrexL. *Then I said, "I must say, MorQ, it was very clever how you went about sequestering yourself in that pod — and with heat! I mean, hot wiring the escape pod for heat — very well done. But, MOrQ, always remember, nothing goes unnoticed, no matter what. Someone on Rogue is always watching. I learned that long ago, and you should have too. Do you agree?"*

MorQ somehow managed to sputter out a nervous "Yes," recalled DrexL, shaking his head.

"I suppose rations were to come from 'cold' storage," I then asked.

Obviously, MorQ did not catch my attempt at humor, as he just stood there, speechless. "Alright, I said, let's set it straight, MorQ. I personally saw most of what you were doing. For your comfort, it is our secret, as I was watching on my personal monitor in my suite. No one else knows — yet!"

MorQ just continued to gaze at me, still speechless.

I said, "Why is it that I have kept this little secret to myself, you may wonder? Let me answer that for you, MorQ. I believe it is quite likely you can help me in the very near future, and perhaps also in the long run. If you don't understand I will explain later, and assume you will agree to an offer I will present, as the alternative would be, well — GRAVE! A very descriptive word, don't you agree, MorQ?" He had nodded, probably wondering if this is any better than being on the *RogueEmpire*. DrexL had to chuckle at the memory.

"We are not being watched now, MorQ, as my cousin is in control and the monitor has been turned off for the present. You will come with me and stay in my personal suites. Much more comfortable than this, I can assure you. As I said, no one will know of this, and, MorQ, you must NOT leave my personal suites for any reason without my knowledge and consent. It could have dire consequences for both of us. Is that clear?"

"Yes, DrexL, it is clear," he had replied. And then, surprisingly, MorQ said to me, "DrexL, considering that you said it could have dire consequences for 'both' of us, in an odd way that sounds promising for me!"

I stood and looked at MorQ for a moment before saying, "I must admit, MorQ, I am impressed with both your intuition, your perception — and now, your foresight and courage." Then, looking MorQ in the eyes, I said, "There is more to you than meets the eye, and I have felt that for a while. I am beginning to believe we have a promising future ahead of us. Now, gather your belongings, and let's remove any traces of your being here. I have an elevator locked off just for us to return to my suite. It's cold down here."

DrexL was brought back from his thoughts, and quickly returned to the present by the sound of LugA, his cousin, coming towards him.

"Commander DrexL, if we continue on this course our detectors indicate we will possibly encounter a fairly severe spacial wind storm in the Corona Maxim sector of Galaxy 7.

"I don't care for massive spacial winds, they are too unpredictable. Take us under, as the stronger wind force rises, but avoid it at all cost."

"Yes, my Commander."

Chapter 37

The Ancientologists Return To SeaCliff

BucchaSim, would you like to chat

The return trip up the passageway began with much talk of the day's exploration and discussions about what tomorrow might hold. But eventually all went into their own private thoughts regarding the day's events.

They were also tired. With the exception of sounds from shuffling footsteps on the stairs, and some labored breathing, nothing was heard.

Bocc, who was bringing up the rear with one of the lamplights could hardly wait to scan through his images and wanted to ask Calla if she would be interested in seeing them too.

"So I will," he said aloud, but softly to himself.

Catching up to Calla, he proposed the idea to her.

"Oh, I will like that very much, Bocc. Why don't we meet later, after dinnertime, along the edge of the cliff overlooking the Sea. It will be relaxing, but remember to bring a blanket as it will be windy and chilly."

"That sounds great, Calla. Our photo viewers are lit by a soft light so we will be able to see my images even in the dim light."

Annuj was perplexed.

What is it about BucchaSim and his son, TerraSim that continues to puzzle me. Oh, I wish I could find the time to attempt PastReCall. We have been so occupied with the journey, the tunnel, the tombs — and like everyone else, I have been totally engrossed with our discoveries.

She determined that after dinner she would ask BucchaSim if he could share some private time with her.

That will be nice, irregardless, she thought, *and just maybe I can clear up whatever has been troubling me.*

Poona, walking along side Laurra, was concentrating on the tombs, and, as always, of Laurra's well being. Smiling, she pondered the significance and consequences regarding these discoveries, especially for the Neptunians.

Leaning over, she whispered...

"We all are special Beings with our own unique gifts, Laurra. Tomorrow, King Luxxor will join us, and, along with his fellow Neptunians, will begin a journey hopefully promising monumental disclosures and revelations regarding their ancient history and it's involvement in the history of Prismacia."

"Oh," she reveled, "that is such a pleasing and rewarding thought. And you, Laurra, are here to share in this joy — in ways not yet known or imagined!"

She gave Laura a small squeeze.

In the shadows of the firelite, Laurra echoed Poona's sentiment....

"Yes, in ways not yet known or imagined, Poona."

They looked into each other's eyes. Even in the shadows a faint glow emanated.

"Tonight, when we return, I plan to relax under the stars, Laurra. I will view TrinoniaX, the Solonius Cluster, Pleiad 11, and beyond. Such beautiful stars and clusters will still be as awesome, regardless of galaxy — or Dimension!"

Glancing ahead, Poona saw Patto's silhouette dancing upon the wall. She whispered again into Laurra's ear...

"I will be right back!"

Patto, was walking alone and concentrating deeply on Poona.

I am aware of what is happening, he considered. *I know what I am feeling, but I feel totally helpless to alter these thoughts. Poona is inspiring! She is spiritual! She is enlightened beyond comparison, and so very wise! She fills me with enthusiasm! And, you know what, Patto, you do not want to alter your thoughts.*

"I like these thoughts," he stated aloud.

He did not realize Poona had quietly joined him.

Poona softly asked...

"How are you doing Patto, and should I inquire about these thoughts you just mentioned?"

Startled, Patto stumbled slightly and looking up saw the subject of his current thoughts standing beside him.

"Oh, Poona, you surprised me. I'm sorry about my reaction, I was in deep thought ... and just confirming some realities I have been thinking about. This has truly been an amazing day and I have much on my mind as I am sure we all do. Actually, Poona, I am very happy to see you."

"And I you, Patto. So many wonderful discoveries in such a short time — and who knows what may come tomorrow. We should all rest well tonight."

"That is true, Poona, however I believe I am entering into excited exhaustion, right now," he replied, smiling ...

Because you are walking here beside me!

"It will be quite thrilling for King Luxxor tomorrow, too. I am very anxious to see his reaction to our discoveries."

"Yes, I am anxious for that also, Patto."

Looking at him warmly and lightly touching his arm, she said...

"I just wanted to say hello, but I should really get back to Laurra."

As she started back, she turned her eyes to his ...

"Perhaps we can see each other later?"

"I would like that, and will look forward to it, Poona." said an elated Patto."

Deep within, at the very least, I hope to have a lasting friendship with her, he thought. *Maybe one day I can go to her Quin, and we could visit ... just the two of us.*

He smiled at the possibility.

All things are possible!

BucchaSim, leading the way, was also elated at the results of their day in the tombs. His thoughts kept focusing on what a great group of young people he was involved with and how serendipitous that they should all come together like this — and at this time.

"And my Junnuj, my sweet Junnuj," he softly assured himself, "You will be home soon."

Your four years of Dreamstate has been a nightmare for me. But, those four years are to be over soon."

He mentally repeated it again, and again.

When they arrived back at SeaCliff it was still light, but fading to dusk. BucchaSim, gathering everyone around and announcing that all would contribute in making dinner, said they should meet in the kitchen in 30 minutes. When they arrived, BucchaSim and TerraSim were putting out the items for the meal.

"Ok" said BucchaSim, "as you can see we are blessed with the presence of none other than TerraSim tonight."

TerraSim gestured, bowed, while grinning brightly.

"He will be in charge of the healthy stuff, while I will undertake the preparation of the prized fish for this evening's banquet — also healthy!

Annuj, you will organize the table — with candles mind you, and put out water, for us to drink.

I will take Patto and Calla, as assistants … TerraSim, you get Poona, Laurra and Bocc. Let's have at it."

Surprisingly, in 45 minutes they were all feasting on a delicious meal and enjoying a wonderful conversation, mostly centered on informing TerraSim about their day and the breakthroughs they had made. Hungry Ancientologists that they were, the feast went quickly and soon they were all relaxing in the living area, each into their own thoughts, with a light sea breeze gently caressing them.

BucchaSim looking at the group before him, spoke.

"My friends, tomorrow promises to be an eventful day. TerraSim informs me that he will be joining us also — we are so blessed," he said grinning.

"I look forward to seeing you all in the morning — early! Enjoy your evening. As for me, it is time to retire. Goodnight, and sleep tight."

As BucchaSim turned to go, Annuj arose and walked over to him.

"BucchaSim, I would truly appreciate it if you would chat with me privately for a while before retiring. I have some questions, and it looks as though everyone is either going out for a stroll, or off to bed, so we have the opportunity to be alone."

BucchaSim smiled back at her.

"More than delighted, Annuj. It will be my pleasure."

Chapter 38

I Have Discovered Some Interesting Facts, Shall I Continue

Allow me to attempt PastReCall

Annuj and BucchaSim sat on the balcony overlooking the waves below.

From their vantage point they could still partially see the waves and the shore, but not the horizon far away. It had rapidly faded away into the evening fog.

BucchaSim was happy that Annuj asked to talk for awhile, as he sheltered suspicions regarding just who Annuj could possibly be. There just were not many in Amythesia named Annuj, maybe none — except for his daughter.

As he watched, he took note of her mannerisms, the obvious way she tilted her head, her laugh.

The soft, dark amber coloring of her skin was almost identical to that of Junnuj, and did not match the Spectrum of her Quin, meaning Annuj was most likely a 'tonality,' separated from her biological parents while still a baby. And, as with all tonalities, placed in a select family, per The Law of Spectrum Initiative, with neither family involved knowing of the other.

Then there are her eyes, her nose, and her hair. It just has to be Annuj.

He wanted to hold her tightly and could hardly restrain himself from shouting out loud.

I have not seen my daughter since she was one — but, is she aware of it?

He was contemplating how to reveal to Annuj that he felt he was her real father, when she asked him the question.

"Where are you from, BucchaSim? You and TerraSim have such unusual names."

He thought for a moment.

I must go about this slowly. We will both realize it together — I hope. But, maybe I am wrong!!! Maybe, just maybe, there is another Annuj. After all, this young woman has parents, and often those from different Quins have married outside their Quin creating lovely children of various skin colorations.

I must be very gentle, and very careful.

"I guess I can be called a Starman, Annuj. I was brought here when I was around 12 years of age from a planet named Earth III. I have no idea how, or why I was left here on Prismacia. I was roaming in the desert and eventually found and mothered by a woman who lived nearby in a small village called Oneness."

"I know it is strange Annuj ... regarding who, how and why. They plagued me for a long time, but like smoke in the winds, these questions have finally disappeared. It just does not matter anymore. What matters now is my son, and the return of my sweet wife, Junnuj. I long for the reuniting of our family."

"As to earth III, I can only recall some of my times there, but most is vague, or forgotten. For example, I do not remember my parents on earth, but I do remember being with a lot of boys my age. Most all my memories are from here —like the woman here on Prismacia, who took me in as her own. Her name is Solannuj. She was loving and warm with me, Annuj. Then, she became, SolannaOne, and I was told she had to leave. I, of course, now understand she was the HighPriestess of the Voice of One."

"In her absence, Solannuj provided us with a warm, compassionate woman named Carlonna, who cared for her daughters, Junnuj, and her younger sister, Xennuj, and me. It is my understanding SolannaOne, now Solannuj, has returned to live in Oneness," he said. "For what ever reason she has never attempted to contact me. I do not understand that, but it is what it is."

Hmmm, he speaks of Xennuj ... I wonder if it could be XennaOne? And, if so, her sister, Junnuj, would have been JunnaOne!

"I fell in love with Junnuj, and we eventually married. We had ... excuse me, Annuj, we 'have' two children."

Annuj listening intently, remained quiet for a moment. Lowering her head, she considered everything BucchaSim had said.

"BucchaSim, thank you for sharing a very touching story, but ... I feel, if it were me, not knowing my prior life would haunt me — but then, perhaps it would not. I am also not clear concerning your wife being away for so long."

Leaning forward, Annuj asked gently...

"BucchaSim, would you be willing to allow me to attempt PastReCall

142

and perhaps entreat Prism History from the crystal? It may possibly unearth some things that are relevant to you and others as well."

"Yes, Annuj, I will gladly allow you that. Quite frankly, I am extremely interested in what you may find. By the way, Annuj, your choosing of the word 'unearth' is quite apropos, don't you think," he said, grinning.

Slightly confused for a second, Annuj quickly grasped the significance of her choice of 'unearth' to describe her intentions, and the fact that BucchaSim was from Earth III.

"Yes, BucchaSim, I do. You have a nice sense of humor. I like that."

With warm eyes they looked at each other.

BucchaSim then settled back into his chair, the breeze from the sea below blowing gently on his face.

Annuj, collecting herself, asked BucchaSim to close his eyes, and totally relax, explaining to him what he could expect.

"All right," said Annuj, "I will be using a violet crystal prism, the correct color spectrum for past ReCall and Retrieval. We will see what Retrieval reveals."

"Ready?"

Opening his eyes, he replied, "Ready, Annuj."

"You may leave your eyes open if you choose, BucchaSim," Annuj said gently. Placing her one palm upon the smooth surface of the violet prism, she softly uttered "Earth III, SolannaOne, Junnuj and BucchaSim."

Then, placing her other hand upon his heart, she evoked words unknown to him.

Astonishingly, to BucchaSim, a glow appeared in the prism and what appeared to be pages of symbols and images scrolled by their eyes. Annuj was apparently searching files, or records. It was amazing to him how she could comprehend the information, as it moved so quickly.

BucchaSim waited.

After a while the information stopped and Annuj closed her eyes, becoming pensive for a few moments … reflecting on what she had just learned.

"I have discovered some interesting facts BucchaSim. It worries me that some may bother you. Shall I continue?" she said, opening her compelling eyes in search of his.

BucchaSim was concerned, but, looking at Annuj, realized just how this could affect her too.

She is young, but surprisingly mature, he thought. *Still, things of the past could possibly be revealed that may hurt her as well.*

"I will put my faith in the one you call the One. So, yes, please continue Annuj."

Annuj, sat gazing into BucchaSim's eyes.

He is a good Being, she thought.

She also now knew there was more.

"BucchaSim, it appears that after an exhausting search nothing could be found on Earth III regarding your parentage. I am sorry. What I did find, that is known, is as a child you were raised in a home with other young boys."

"How did I get here, to Prismacia," BucchaSim asked?

"Apparently, one day you were just gone — vanished! And then your history begins here on Prismacia in UGT 20,842, when Solannuj found you in the desert.

You were twelve."

"Yes, I was twelve years old."

"It also tells of your marriage to SolannaOne's daughter, Junnuj, in the year 20,852. She later became JunnaOne, HighPriestess of the Voice of One."

BucchaSim nodded.

"Apparently, after years of service, eight to be exact, she became ill — to ill to continue and voluntarily resigned from her position as HighPriestess, entering into a treatment program for two years. This was all a culmination from the emotional stress related to her position as HighPriestess. Later, it was determined, that for her long term health, she would be subsequently entered into DreamState for an additional four years. She will be out very, very soon.

Perhaps she already is, BucchaSim. JunnaOne may be in Completion now."

BucchaSim felt the tears beginning to swell in his eyes, but said...

"And..."

"And," Annuj answered, "in sub-notes it described her true condition, or illness as related to family concerns, namely the absence of her family for extended lengths of time. Long periods of time, BucchaSim. It gave reference to the fact that BucchaSim and Junnuj have two children. A son, TerraSim, born in 20,854, and... in 20,857, a daughter, named Annuj," she said haltingly.

Annuj and BucchaSim sat searching each other's eyes, before Annuj slowly continued with eyes also beginning to tear.

"The daughter, Annuj, was selected at age one to become a tonality under the Law of Spectrum Initiative, and taken to another home within Amythesia."

"My Name is Annuj," she said softly! "I am 15 years of age, and I am a Tonality."

Uncontrollable tears began to roll down BucchaSim's cheeks and he was not ashamed. He felt just the opposite. BucchaSim felt so grateful.

"I believe I am looking into the eyes of my child, my beautiful daughter who was taken away such a very long ago."

Annuj and BucchaSim, clasped hands and were silent for some time, gazing into each other's eyes, until she gently asked, "BucchaSim, may I please, for your sake, and for mine, attempt PastReCall?"

He nodded and Annuj moved closer, softly placing one palm upon his heart and the other upon his forehead. She went silent as PastReCall did just that … it recalled. He could hear Annuj softly uttering sounds and whispering more unusual words, but he understood nothing.

Several minutes went by and BucchaSim thought his heart would soon burst, either in elation, or in heartbreak — or both.

He had kept his eyes closed, but the tears did not cease.

When Annuj removed her hands and as he opened his eyes, he saw that Annuj also had tears, but they appeared to be tears of joy.

She was smiling tenderly at him — as a daughter.

"I felt and witnessed a beautiful love between you and Junnuj, which continues to this day, my father! I believe — no, I know you are my birth father.

You are my father, BucchaSim, and my birth Mother is Junnuj. The sadness I felt when you recalled JunnaOne being taken away and then when your daughter … when I, was taken away from you, was heartbreaking."

Annuj cradled her head in her hands and softly weeped for a moment. She then looked back at BucchaSim who wanted desperately to hug his daughter.

"I was placed with my parents, Ralla and Hanna … in Quin Lapesia. They are the parents I grew up with and will love always. I have a younger brother there too, named Jasso and I adore him. They are good people BucchaSim — father. I want you to know that."

"Ralla, and Hanna brought me up to believe in truth, values and Goodness. My parents will always be a beautiful and loving part of my life. And, will always be 'in' my life — always," Annuj tearfully added.

"When you meet them, and you will father, you will be happier for it."

BucchaSim, over taken by happiness and sadness nodded.

"I believe you Annuj and I would not want the relationship you have with the parents that raised you so beautifully to ever change. It would not be right."

Reaching out, he squeezed her hands gently.

"I am so happy they are such good people and were loving to you, Annuj. I just want for Junnuj and myself to have the chance to also be your family, in any way we can and to share some time together from this moment on. We never wanted to let you go — it was never our decision, Annuj. You are our daughter."

"We were devastated."

"I know Father, it was the Law of Spectrum Initiative and I was randomly selected. There is no choice, even for the High Priestess of the Voice of One."

"After seeing you and upon learning your name, I suspected, but I just was not sure, until now," BucchaSim said.

"I must say how much in love I found you and my mother to be," Annuj shared softly. You carry much in your heart, father. Much loss and pain, and yet, much hope and love."

BucchaSim and Annuj both stood, tears in their eyes and for the first time since Annuj was a baby BucchaSim held her in his arms ... and Annuj knowingly held her real father for the first time ever.

They held each other for a long time.

BucchaSim suddenly remembered TerraSim and looking at Annuj said...

"Wait here for just a moment, Annuj. I must go find TerraSim and tell him his sister is here. He may want to say hi," he excitedly said, with tears and a grin.

She smiled at him lovingly, her eyes glowing brightly.

"So, 'TerraSim of the Desert' is my big brother. How lucky can a young woman be."

BucchaSim dashed off, quickly finding TerraSim in his room.

"TerraSim, there is someone special I would like you to meet."

"Yes, father," replied TerraSim.

"Yes," said BucchaSim barely controlling his excitement.

"Your sister, Annuj!"

"My sister! Annuj is my little sister," TerraSim exclaimed!

"I could tell she was special but this is incredible! It's wonderful! Are you sure father, I mean..."

"We are both sure, TerraSim. Now come my son, and embrace your sister."

Later that evening after sharing tears, hugs and stories, the three of them were all emotionally drained and feeling the need for a good night's rest.

It was a very significant, emotional, and beautiful day for each of them.

After giving each other a big hug, a father and a brother walked Annuj to her room. At her door, she turned to BucchaSim and, with a twinkle in her eyes remarked...

"I do believe I have a true Starman, as my father. I could not be happier. I wish to share this tomorrow morning with my friends. It is such a blessing. They will be very happy for us. I know."

"Of course, Annuj. Finding each other, here at the edge of the Carbonian Desert and the Sea of the Forgotten Place, is truly a gift I will always remember — one we will thankfully and gratefully share.

It was dark when he lay down in bed. Turning towards the opening he called his 'portal to the stars,' he marveled at the the ever magnificent and mysterious night Heavens and the events of the day.

Except for the return of Junnuj, I would have never thought anything could overshadow the discoveries of this day ... except this discovery tonight of our daughter. She is such a wonderful young woman, he thought to himself laying there in the shadows of the Moon.

And then it came to him...

Being Junnuj's child, how else could she have possibly turned out — but beautiful, talented, full of enthusiasm ... and, truly good.

He smiled. *Junnuj will be so happy.*

BucchaSim was so happy.

He slept soundly and at peace.

Chapter 39

Our Paths Will Never Be Distant

Poona and Patto

Returning from such an eventful day at the tombs and after a wonderful dinner, Poona felt drawn to the night air and stars. After checking on Laurra, who indicated she was tired and chose to just stay in for the evening, Poona, selected a soft blanket to lay on and left SeaCliff, strolling over to find a spot under the incredible array of stars and moons through out the seeable Galaxy. Lying alone by the edge of the cliffs and above the Sea of the Forgotten Place, Poona knew that with all that had transpired lately she was in need of the peaceful calm of the stars. Wandering in her thoughts she reminisced.

Out there is my true home, but Prismacia is so unique and stunning in it's way, and holds so much more than is known, I wonder if ...

Surprisingly and happily she then noticed Patto coming her way.

"Poona," said Patto, "the stars are certainly breathtaking tonight. May I join you? You mentioned sharing some time tonight."

"Yes, please, Patto, I will like that."

They chatted briefly, but then remained silent for a long time ... just lying there, close to each other, imagining distant star systems, enjoying the solitude and wondering of each other's thoughts.

As they listened to the waves crash against the shore in their seemingly ancient rhythm, it was Patto that spoke first.

"Incredible, isn't it Poona? To realize we are just a speck — and just in our own galaxy. I often revel in wonder at that which awaits those with a spirit — a spirit with the courage to be curious. Those who are adventuresome, embracing all life forms — life that we know is out there!"

His gaze became intense.

"Sometimes I feel it is beyond mere Prismacian comprehension, but I want to go there Poona. I just don't know how — yet."

He rolled over on his side and smiled at her.

Poona, rolled over too, returning his smile.

"And, besides," he continued, "it is my wish to go with someone I care for who chooses to share this voyage to the stars with me. I guess I ask for a lot."

Patto looked at Poona who had remained quiet. She could sense he was about to say something of importance to her and waited.

"This is a little awkward for me Poona, but I have grown very fond of you.

When our Wisdom Path Journey is over and if we happen to go our separate ways, I wish you to know that I will miss you. I will miss your wisdom, your trust in that which is good, the total absolution you offer in the Goodness of all things and of how you introduce it into all that you do."

"I will also miss your smile, the softness you bring to all — and the happiness you bring to me. I will miss just seeing you and knowing you are near.

I do not require, or need, or hope for a response from you, Poona.

I just truly wanted to share how I am feeling."

Then Patto was silent.

Poona, was taken by the sincerity of Patto's remarks and his courage to speak his truths. She remained silent for awhile thinking of the significance of what Patto had said, and considering what to say in return.

She decided.

Gently scooting closer to Patto, she gazed warmly into his dark eyes.

"It is my belief, and more importantly, it is my desire, Patto, that our paths will never be so distant! At this moment in time, we share the Wisdom path together, but when this is finished you and I will be on separate paths, Patto. I have many obligations that take me far, far away, and you will be completing your StarAstron Seeker studies and who knows where that may take you. Perhaps to the stars themselves. At another time and place we will meet again Patto.

She then softly kissed him on his cheek.

"All things good are possible, Patto.

Poona stood and collected her blanket.

"I should go now Patto. It would be the right thing ... at this time."

Patto turned on his back, and under the entire Universe known to him, he repeated...

"It is all possible, all things good are possible," as Poona said. Filled with promise, Patto fell asleep, under his stars, with thoughts of Poona.

'I tried it, and it felt like a cloud...

I experienced it, and it warmed like the sun...

I loved it, and touched a rainbow...'

bocc

poet and Initiate of Brightness on the Wisdom Path Journey
Prismacia
UGT 20,872

Chapter 40

This Does Not Look Like A Woman In Distress

The King and Queen and Junnuj

As he viewed JunnaOne entering the room, King Luxxor thought…

This does not look like a woman in distress, or for that matter, straight out of four years in DreamState. She looks formidable. Thankfully she is healing well.

It is said that through-out it all, JunnaOne remains the most gifted HighPriestess of the Voice of One ever.

Continuing to watch her walk towards them he could see and feel the distinctive aura she projected. He sensed the authority she continued to emit, even after such unpleasant circumstances.

You have come a long way back, JunnaOne, he thought quietly to himself. *I sincerely hope you are now handling the pain beneath the surface caused by this experience.*

He felt a wave of sadness overcome him and he reached out and took Liluuc's hand. Looking over at him and experiencing similar emotions she understood and squeezed Luxxor's hand gently. They both recalled that JunnaOne's misfortune was caused by excessive long absences from her family.

I can certainly identify with that, she thought, looking at her Chosen One, King Luxxor. *I can not imagine being apart from my family for any length of time, let alone what JunnaOne had to endure.*

Odd, Luxxor considered, *Liluuc and I have come to know JunnaOne more during her 'Completion' here in Neptuna than during her reign of several years at Spectrum. I unfortunately never had the opportunity to meet her informally, only briefly at official functions where we had little opportunity to truly chat without interruption. How could that have been,* he thought? *Are we of Neptuna, or those of Spectrum that detached, or that busy? I could have reached out and invited JunnaOne here to Neptuna as our guest …*

152

that makes sense and it would have been the right thing to do. I must make it a point that whenever possible, to never let time and obligations negate the opportunity to share with another Being.

He, and Queen Liluuc stood to greet JunnaOne. During Junnuj's rehabilitation, Lilonna, King Luxxor and Queen Liluuc became close with JunnaOne. They joined her each day for short walks, which evolved into lunches and then dinners, allowing plenty of time to converse regarding the proceedings in Neptuna. However, JunnaOne had been very private regarding her family, asking that the subject not be broached.

They honored that.

JunnaOne walked up to King Luxxor and Queen Liluuc and they all gracefully bowed in respect to each other. After which they sat on the divan in the comfortable living area of the King and Queen's home.

JunnaOne, smiling at her new friends, opened with,

"King Luxxor, Queen Liluuc, from this time forward please address me as Junnuj, my true name and in fact, who I have always only wished to be. It is to be my name from this moment on. It is a realization I experienced while in Lilonna's care and I am now making it official."

"We will honor your wish, Junnuj and we may be called Luxxor and Liluuc, in private, or with close friends."

With sincere and bright expressions, they all leaned forward and touched hands.

"Luxxor, and Liluuc, oh, I like the way that sounds," Junnuj said cheerfully.

"It is my understanding that my sister, XennaOne, the HighPriestess, has acclimated to her position and is performing extremely well in my absence. I want you to be aware that it is my wish, my friends, that she continue as HighPriestess of the Voice of One — if she so desires. I will make that clear when addressing the Voice of One at a convenient time which will be sooner than later."

Then, in no uncertain terms she stated...

"Irregardless of XennaOne's decision to remain, or relinquish her position, there is zero possibility of my becoming the HighPriestess ever again."

Displaying a resolute calmness and strength of conviction, Junnuj sat back on the divan while waiting for a response. After the trials she had endured, to see this strength of character left Luxxor without any words for a brief moment. Looking at Liluuc, and then back at Junnuj, he responded.

"I am sure I also speak for Liluuc when I say, after what you have been through, the losses you and your family have endured, and the ensuing suffering following so many exasperating years of service to Amythesia, we do understand, Junnuj. Liluuc, and I are in total support of your wishes."

Liluuc, tearfully clasping on to Luxxor's hand, softly added...

"As a wife and a mother myself, Junnuj, I cannot fathom the pain you have endured. To have lasted as long as you did under such wretched circumstances demonstrates the strength of character you truly possess. Those years cannot be brought back, but, Junnuj, they must be forgiven, and, by moving on, from this moment on, you and your family will assuredly heal. There is much life ahead."

Junnuj, close to tears herself, reached inward to the One, silently asking for strength and compassion. Then, extending her hands to her friends, who lovingly and gently took them, Junnuj spoke more openly of her family than ever before.

"It is my hope to be a mother for my children, if that is still possible after so many years. I will be my husband's wife, without exception. We — excuse me, I should say, 'I' have much to catch up on, and my heart is in joy that soon we will be together again, and, this time — forever."

They continued their conversation involving Junnuj's situation with the High Council before moving into the dining area to have a small bite to eat. Luxxor had made some rumbling about an afternoon Loctuum, so Liluuc deemed it an appropriate time. Innocently enough, during one conversation, Luxxor mentioned recently meeting the Initiates of Brightness who were in the general area on their Wisdom Path Journey.

"They were quite intriguing and wished to help in a recent discovery of an ancient passage that leads to the surface," he said excitedly. "We obviously tell you this in the understanding of secrecy, as short lived as it may be, Junnuj."

She nodded affirmatively.

"It was our children, Prince Tunnis and Princess Dolpho, the latest and greatest explorers, who discovered this passage," offered Liluuc proudly.

Luxxor and Junnuj both chuckled at Liluuc's description of Tunnis and Dolpho as explorers.

"It is actually a cute story now, but at the time they were not to be found anywhere and we were quite worried as you can imagine," she added.

Then, remembering Junnuj's children, Liluuc quickly regretted her choice of words, but Luxxor, understanding, jumped in and quickly continued as if nothing was wrong.

"Our children, Tunnis and Dolpho, were exploring the passage and lost track of time," he said. "It became late, and dark and from nowhere a man came to their aid, taking them to the surface and his home nearby, which was at the top of the cliff and at the edge of the Carbonian Desert."

"A captivating story, please continue," Junnuj remarked, intrigued.

"Well, Tunnis and Dolpho contacted us by prism from his home to let us know of their safety and whereabouts and this man spoke to us instilling a sense of calm saying they had a safe place to sleep and that he would bring them safely home to us the next morning. He is an extraordinary man who has also shown us the location of an ancient tomb which he found, and which we have been studying."

"They display enormous potential in revealing lost segments of Neptuna's history, Junnuj," spoke Liluuc.

"Yes," said Luxxor, not only are we indebted to him, but he has become a fine and cherished friend of mine, and Liluuc's also."

Junnuj smiled, waiting to hear what happened next.

"He is called BucchaSim, and is my new friend," said Luxxor happily.

Junnuj suddenly put her hand to her mouth and became silent looking at them with imploring eyes. Luxxor and Liluuc both knew something had happened and intuitively sensed it was the name BucchaSim.

"What is it, Junnuj? What has happened?"

Junnuj looked at them, afraid to believe what she had just heard.

She said…

"BucchaSim? BucchaSim is my husband's name. Are you telling me he is near? That he is your friend?"

Luxxor and Liluuc looked at Junnuj, and then each at other in a mild shock.

Chapter 41

If You Agree To My Kingly Decision

All things ceased to exist around them

"BucchaSim is quite private ... he never said" ... Luxxor's voice trailed off as he struggled to find words to explain and console Junnuj.

Liluuc softly added...

"A young man, his son TerraSim, lives with him, Junnuj."

Junnuj looked at them with tearing eyes.

"It is my husband and my son. I suppose somehow I just expected for BucchaSim to appear. To walk through the door and take me home," Junnuj said, tears now running down her cheeks.

"He probably is not aware I have finished 'Completion,' and is waiting too."

It was evident to both Luxxor and Liluuc that seeing BucchaSim was the wish of Junnuj — her number one wish.

Luxxor, thought to himself...

Hmmm, BucchaSim and I have made plans for the Initiates to study the tomb tomorrow and I am to join them. Perhaps this is the opportune time for Junnuj to reunite with BucchaSim ... but I have pledged to SolannaOne to return Junnuj to Oneness when she is ready.

"Hmmm," he hummed to himself, thinking.

Junnuj and Liluuc both looked to Luxxor, anxious to hear his thoughts.

With a small clever smile appearing, he stated...

"Alright, listen — my agreement was to accompany you back to SolannaOne in Oneness when YOU," he emphasized, "are ready! That was my promise to SolannaOne, Junnuj."

Quickly understanding his implication, and idea, Junnuj slightly began to smile also, and asked...

"When 'I' am ready?"

"Yes, that is the key, Junnuj, when 'you' are ready. And, being King, in my opinion, I feel you will only be ready after you see BucchaSim. That is, of course, if you agree with my Kingly wisdom, and decision!"

Junnuj, tears flowing, jumped up, and running over to Luxxor, hugged him thankfully and adoringly.

With a slight flush in his cheeks, he added...

"I will send a palm prism transmission to SolannaOne immediately relaying that you are healing and improving daily — but, in our opinion, time is still needed for your Completion.

It was done.

Later, alone with Liluuc, he asked her opinion of his decision in reference to SolannaOne.

"What will they call this," he queried, "an act of omission?"

"Oh no my chosen one," said Liluuc, "they will say it was an undaunted act of sympathy, achieved through the compassionate wisdom of King Luxxor."

Luxxor could not help but love his Chosen one, his Queen.

The next morning, in the passageway to the tomb, King Luxxor, Queen Liluuc, and 4 guardians were keeping the pace slow for the benefit of Junnuj. However, given all she had been through, feeling tired never entered her mind. She desperately wished to just get there.

"Oh One, please," she whispered, "let it be. We are so very, very close!"

As they approached the chamber of the tomb in the ancient passageway, Junnuj, became more nervous by the moment. Her heart pounded in anxiousness, goosebumps appeared, and her knees felt as though they could collapse at any second. This was perhaps the most defining and longed for moment she had ever known. She had endured and sacrificed years waiting for this moment.

She closed her eyes. The tears were near.

Clinching the hand of Queen Liluuc, they entered.

BucchaSim was in the second hidden chamber with the Initiates working on deciphering some unusual symbols and also to hopefully find yet another secret latch, opening yet another hidden chamber, when Junnuj walked in accompanied by King Luxxor and Queen Liluuc.

BucchaSim simply stood and gazed at the only person he had truly wished to see for nearly 10 years. Now, his heart was pounding heavily, and tears were welling up in his eyes — which he refused to close for fear of her not being there when they reopened.

This is not a dream, not an illusion ... Junnuj is standing there, only a few feet away. Oh Goodness, she is truly back!

He could not take his eyes off of her.

She is radiant, she is elegant, and she is the most beautiful Being I have ever known.

At that moment there were no words he could possibly express for the joy he was feeling.

Gazing at BucchaSim, Junnuj was also spellbound, as if in a trance. Her heart had been breaking since she had been taken away some ten years ago, but it had never ceased loving BucchaSim. Never ceased missing him.

Now, standing across from him, so close, she was suddenly afraid.

How will he react after so long.

She was trembling and tears were flowing freely as she stood there waiting, anticipating, expecting, longing.

They both stepped forward in wonderment and then BucchaSim rushed to her arms, and held her tightly — and BucchaSim cried with Junnuj.

All things ceased to exist around them. It was only the two of them together once again and they both knew that this time — it was forever.

King Luxxor and Queen Liluuc turned and embraced, deeply moved at the outpouring of love and painfully cognizant of the terrible loss BucchaSim and Junnuj each had experienced — and they were honestly thankful it had not been them.

Annuj, Patto, Bocc, Calla, Laurra and Poona found themselves enveloped in a reunion of love as they never imagined. They just stood back, not saying a word, mesmerized by the touching scene unfolding before them.

TerraSim put his arm around Annuj to comfort her.

She realized what was happening and began to cry, and then sob. She looked up at him, tearfully whispering...

"This is my true mother and my true father, TerraSim."

Tenderly, BucchaSim looked into the swollen, but happy eyes of Junnuj, and softly said...

"Come Junnuj, I want you to meet our daughter, Annuj, and our son, TerraSim."

Junnuj put her hands to her face and looked over at the Initiates.

She knew immediately.

Annuj came forth, and then TerraSim — and the four of them hugged, weeping tears of joy and gratitude for this long awaited moment.

King Luxxor was the first to speak.

Wiping away tears, he said...

"I am sure Queen Liluuc shares the same sentiments as I do, my new friends. They are to invite you," he gestured to Poona, Calla, Laurra, Bocc and Patto, "to help with the exploration of the tomb through the remainder of the day, and to then return to Neptuna for the next several days, allowing myself, Queen Liluuc, and our fine children, Prince Tunnis, and Princess Dolpho to be your hosts. We have everything you could possibly need, and views you just will not find elsewhere. This is a Kingly decision, so a 'no' will not be accepted."

"I believe this fine family here before us needs some quality time together, alone, at their home, SeaCliff. BucchaSim, Junnuj, Annuj, TerraSim, we are all so very happy for you and we have been blessed to share in your loving joy on this glorious day."

BucchaSim and Junnuj came over to King Luxxor and Queen Liluuc and embraced them, with BucchaSim clasping hands with Luxxor in friendship.

"Thank you, our friends," they sincerely said to Luxxor and Liluuc.

The Initiates surrounded Annuj and TerraSim, offering thankful thoughts to them, with wishes for a beautiful reunion, and that they would hopefully see each other soon.

Then turning to the Initiates, BucchaSim smiled.

"I am happy you were here to share in our joy. You have all become very special to me. I, we — Junnuj, TerraSim, Annuj and I, will look forward to seeing you in the near future. You know where to find us. I must say, I am so overjoyed."

Taking Junnuj by her hand, he smiled, and tenderly said...

"Come Junnuj, let me take you to SeaCliff, your home."

"SeaCliff," she repeated.

"I love it already."

She put her arm around his waist, and waived goodbye, as they, and their children, TerraSim, and Annuj left for SeaCliff, for a family reunion ... long overdue.

'can tomorrow come to late, or to soon...

can the sun rise to early or to late...

can we spend to much time together, or to little..

can I love you to much, or not enough...'

bocc

poet and Initiate of Brightness on the Wisdom Path Journey
Prismacia
UGT 20,872

Chapter 42

Like Poetry, Queen Liluuc Said Softly

It was a mystery

Still emotionally energized by the touching, loving moments that unfolded before them earlier, King Luxxor, Queen Liluuc, Poona and the Initiates, plus 4 Divine Guardians remained in the tomb, trying to regain and focus their attention in understanding the purpose of the little intricate key-Goddesses.

After enlightening King Luxxor and Queen Liluuc on their discoveries from the preceding day, they stood there, perplexed as to what would be their next best move in solving this enigmatic puzzle.

Patto took the initiative.

"All right, as I see it, here is what we have. First, let me direct your view to the stairs at the back of the chamber. As we can see, on each side and in the front center are stairs leading up to what could be an altar. There are seven steps in each of the stairways."

Then, selecting one of the Goddess figurines, he held it up.

"We have seven Goddess relics, with accompanying keys that fit into slots in the back of each relic — and, on the wall behind the altar are numerous holes or slots haphazardly arranged within the ancient symbols. So, it makes sense to me there must be a relationship between the Goddess-keys and the wall of slots. It is also intriguing to me how the number seven seems to be involved quite often. Anyway, please offer your opinions, no matter how unusual they may sound. Sometimes that will spark a thought bringing us to an answer."

"I agree, Patto," Calla said emphatically. "We have Goddesses with slots, and keys ... and we have slots in the wall. It does appear obvious that we should try and see if anything fits!"

All concurred, and they immediately went about the task of finding correct key-relic combinations for various selected slots. Finally, when the last slot was filled with the correct combinations, it did in fact conform to a 7Star cluster.

"This must be connected to solving the mystery, said King Luxxor, so now what?"

They tried turning all the keys counterclockwise. Briefly there was a moment of elation as a distinctive click was heard, but nothing happened. No secret door opened, no stairwell moved aside revealing an ancient and forgotten secret — only the distinct sound of a click.

An exhale of frustration was audible in the ancient room.

"Let's look at this again" said Patto, beginning to show signs of exasperation. Resting his hands on top of his head, he remarked...

"The pattern of 7stars has to be an important element in this mysterious equation. It continues to reappear as a star cluster from which, it is believed, Beings visited here long ago."

"There is no question in our minds regarding that particular fact, Patto," said King Luxxor, his hand supporting his chin.

Patto nodded, and continued.

"We have discerned that the wall containing the special keyed slots have actually been fitted with correct keys ... so what are we not seeing," he said, shaking his head? "Is it something so obvious we are completely overlooking it?"

Everyone walked back down the stairs and turned to observe and contemplate the wall behind the altar.

Silence.

Laurra spoke.

"I feel we are close, Patto, and yes, there is apparently something we are not seeing. We know that each flight of stairs has seven steps, but I notice that in the center flight of stairs facing us as you ascend, there is a gemstone embedded in the front of each step. Could they have a purpose, or are they only decorative?"

"That is a good question," said an obviously intrigued Calla. "The gemstones could be an important part of the stairs we have overlooked."

Bocc quickly added...

"This may sound odd, but, the gemstones must be set in an opening, a hole, or a slot of some kind. Could there be a hole or slot behind a gemstone that a key could fit into?"

Eyebrows raised.

"Very good suggestions!" Patto said excitedly.

"And I have another suggestion which expands on these theories. Please stay with me on this, as I think I may need someone to explain what I am about to explain! Ok, here goes! By placing key-Goddess relics into slots on the wall we have created a visual of the 7stars symbol— the shape of a 7. I do not believe that is a coincidence.

It begins on the left, travels over to a point where the direction of the 7stars then turns downward, finally stopping at the bottom, completing the sign of the 7stars. From my vantage point it could be pointing, or leading our perception to the stairs. The top step?"

They all looked at each other. It made sense, kind of, and besides at this point it seemed their best option.

"A sound deduction," said King Luxxor.

Hustling back up the center set of stairs, King Luxxor was given the honor of prying out the gemstone on the top step, which came out quite easily.

There was no slot, no opening behind the gemstone!

They all stood back discouraged, feeling they were so close to the unraveling of this strange quandary. *What are we missing,* they all wondered? *This makes sense.*

"All right," said King Luxxor pacing the floor, "we are on to something. I know it. I feel it in my ancestors bones, and," suddenly beaming said, "I believe I have it! Consider this, as Patto said, the direction of the 7stars goes down towards the stairs below. That is it's intention. What it is meant to do.

We are absolutely correct on that. However, I believe the 7stars is pointing down to what symbolizes Neptuna, which is under the rest of the steps — at the bottom. Not the top step at at all. Don't you see? Neptuna is at the bottom of the sea, my friends. We need to try the bottom stair."

Everyone's eyes went wide in amazement. Could this be the answer?

Anxiousness permeated the chamber as intuitively they all felt King Luxxor was correct. Poona, now standing by Queen Liluuc, glowed. She was totally intrigued by the manner of deduction, and reasoning put forth in solving this trying riddle left by the ancients so long ago.

Poona spoke.

"I believe what we are viewing is indeed representational, and, as King Luxxor suggested, regarding Neptuna, it is not only symbolic of the 7stars, but it's intention, carefully devised, is pointedly suggestive of that which lies below — Neptuna! It is indeed a clever strategy to portray, or direct those who are worthy, towards the actual position 'beneath' the Celestial star cluster itself, and not 'within or just under' the cluster as we earlier believed. The gemstone in the center of the bottom stair is indeed a rational and plausible choice."

Everyone looked over at Poona.

"Like poetry," Queen Liluuc said softly to herself, gazing in admiration at Poona.

Without further delay, the gemstone was quickly pried out of it's encasement in the bottom step, and, sure enough, behind it was a slot. Shortly thereafter a key was found that fit the slot, and this time Queen Liluuc was chosen by King Luxxor to turn the key. It too was turned counterclockwise, and nothing happened.

A chorus of moans arose from the dusty, ancient ritual room.

"The Ancients were wise and clever" interjected Poona. Let us reverse, and try turning this one clockwise!"

Queen Liluuc did so. A loud, almost thunderous click blared forth as the stairs ever so slightly moved ajar.

Turning to Luxxor and smiling excitedly, she threw herself into his arms cheerfully. King Luxxor beaming his approval, summoned the Divine Guardians to push the stairs aside.

Realizing they were about to enter a chamber which had not witnessed light for untold centuries, the small group collectively held their breath.

Chapter 43

We Were Humbled

The small group entered

The 4 guardians King Luxxor summoned, were more than eager and with a little effort the stairs swiveled heavily to one side revealing an opening beneath the altar, which, like the other chambers, had not seen light or experienced life for unknown eons.

But they were wrong! As they peered in, a glow emanated from deep within the chamber!

"Oh, my Goodness," uttered Queen Liluuc.

Shielding the others, King Luxxor shouted…

"Hello in there."

Nothing answered, not even an echo.

"Guards," said King Luxxor, "go down and see just what it is creating this glow, and light any wall firelites you may find."

Slowly, the guards eased down the stairs and out of sight, their silhouettes becoming extended flickering shadows from the firelites they carried.

As the team of Ancientologists waited they could see more light begin to pour forth from the Chamber.

"The guards are lighting the wall firelites," said King Luxxor. "Apparently there is nothing to fear, but I cannot imagine what is glowing within."

One of the guards returned and looking at his King, stated…

"It is safe, my King, and if I may add …"

"Yes," said King Luxxor, "what is it you wish to say."

"It is beyond beautiful," the guard responded, and came to the top of the stairs to assist them in entering.

With King Luxxor leading the way, all entered and reaching the back of the chamber they could only stare — humbled and in great wonder at a sight they had never seen before.

Out of the dimness a phenomenon glowed silently.

Spiraling to a cathedral ceiling they could only vaguely make out, an immense silver crystal stood in quiet solitude before them. About a third of the way up and extending completely around the crystal were smooth angled facets, cut into the crystal and all exactly the same size.

Slowly, the small group walked around the crystal.

Laurra, taking Poona's hand whispered...

"Oh, Poona, we have witnessed crystals before, but this ... this is awesome. I am feeling a sense of gratitude and reverence towards what it possibly represents. It must be..."

"Yes, Laurra, this is one of the minor 'Crystals of Time' we have been told of — specifically, the Zodiac Crystal, because of the facets we see. Each facet represents one of the Zodiac's twelve original, ancient and equal signs. The facets were created to honor the ancient humans of Earth1. Their early exploration and fascination into astrology constitutes the foundation for astrology today through-out the Universe. And..."

"But, I count thirteen facets cut into this Crystal of Time," stated Laurra, quietly.

"True, Laurra, there are thirteen. You see, the great celestial sphere of the sun on Earth1 no longer signifies equal divisions of the 'signs' within modern constellations of today, as it did eons ago. Constellations have expanded and over ages the precession of the equinoxes can change. The ecliptic now passes through a thirteenth zodiac sign named Ophiuchus. Thus thirteen signs, thirteen facets."

Poona turned her gaze back to the crystal.

"The Crystals of Time continue in their odyssey, and purpose to those in the Heavens, Laurra."

Poona held Laurra tightly.

"The Zodiac Crystal has endured unknown ages of quiet solitude here in it's underground home. We are among the blessed who are fortunate, knowingly or unknowingly, to be in it's presence. Soon, a day will come to inform those of Neptuna of it's true purpose."

Slowly meandering around the ground surface of the crystal, a searing, slow moving stream of kaleidoscopic colors coalesced into one another forming subtle mosaic patterns and shades of a spectrum, yet unnamed.

"Oh," uttered Queen Liluuc.

"What exactly is this? It takes my breath away."

"I truly do not know, my Queen," answered King Luxxor.

Looking questioningly to Poona, Queen Liluuc asked...

"Are you aware of what this stream of colored liquid is, Poona? What is causing it to continually glow?"

Poona, reflecting for a moment answered.

"It is probable the glow comes from light transmitting through endless miles of fissures emanating from the core of hot molten, semifluid rock comprising the center of Prismacia, Queen Liluuc. And, from my knowledge, the flowing liquid you inquire about is liquid crystal.

As an example, consider its consistency to be like a gel you may rub on your skin — it is neither solid nor liquid, but exists somewhere in between. At certain extreme temperatures crystal will soften, or melt, evolving into what we see here today. This flow is not connected to the standing silver crystal, but comes from another source, perhaps much deeper … perhaps even the very core of Prismacia I referred to earlier."

"It is beautiful is it not?"

Queen Liluuc turned to King Luxxor who was also listening intently. She could tell he did not have a clue regarding Poona's explanation either.

"Regardless of whatever is causing the glow, Queen Liluuc, the liquid crystal stream consists of a spectrum, or a rainbow of colors. A very unique phenomenon, usually only spoken of and rarely seen," Poona said.

"It is curious that the individual colors within the crystal stream are in motion amongst themselves, as well as within the liquid stream that they flow in."

"As to the silver crystal rising from the depths, we can only speculate to it's height as we have no idea how much of the crystal lay buried. It has apparently remained unaltered in this hidden chamber for unknown ages.

It appears otherworldly, or perhaps even celestial appearing, don't you think?"

Poona pausing, let her words sink in and then asked...

"Would you like for me to continue with my thoughts of this inspiring, and possibly holy object?"

A soft chorus of, yes please, and positive nods answered her

She looked back to the mysterious crystal, a distant look in her eyes.

"The cut facets are totally foreign to any crystal ever seen. They are not natural on a crystal. They have been cut into this crystal to serve a purpose, or as an artistic embellishment, or both."

Poona turned to face them.

"What if one were to consider that the unusual facets we see were cut by ancient StarBeings, or perhaps ancient Beings of Prismacia? What could this purpose be?"

"Did this crystal grow here in this underground chamber — or was it transported here, long ago by some unknown force? Perhaps by unknown Beings — and, if so, from where, and for what reason?"

"To me, this crystal offers itself as a pageantry of symbolism and perhaps a requiem of history. For all one knows, an ancient script, unknown to you, is hidden within — just waiting."

Poona turned back to the crystal ... "So many questions."

They all listened, becoming lost in wonderings, and fantasies.

Everyone, and every thing was so very silent. An incomparable respect and an incomprehensible feeling of awe spread through the small group. No one wanted this extraordinary moment to end.

No one knew what to say.

Slowly, very slowly, they began to turn and look at one another, their eyes questioning and displaying the fascination and the mystery of this moment in time — this moment they were blessed in sharing.

King Luxxor spoke first, quietly saying...

"I am humbled. I am sure we are all humbled by the splendor of this magnificent and most noble creation. What this is, or its purpose simply defies definition and I honestly do not know what else to say — except to thank Poona for her informative explanations and possible scenarios ... all other words escape me."

"Our Priests of Spirituality in Neptuna," added Queen Liluuc, "believe they have deciphered stone tablets from long ago telling of Starmen from above and that a Silver Princess — Neptuna's 'Awaited One'— will come from the Moon and 7Stars to deliver us. And, now we have found a 'silver crystal' ... is there a connection maybe? Hopefully we will discover more answers here."

Her eyes scanned the mystery of the crystal standing before her.

"One thing that I have come to believe," said King Luxxor, "is that these chambers are not tombs as we suspected, but ritual chambers. We have not found the first sarcophagus indicating a place of burial. Everything thus far appears to revolve around ritual, or perhaps the study of the Heavens."

Unobserved, Poona closed her eyes and called on the One for guidance at this memorable time.

King Luxxor then offered words of closure.

"My friends, I feel we have just begun to discover what is concealed in this 'tomb of antiquity,' but the culmination and perhaps the reason we are here is actually this megalithic crystal — left for us to discover, to decipher and to learn from."

With eyes of astonishment, and admiration, Queen Liluuc, looking at her husband and the tired, but awe struck Initiates, offered a choice for them all.

"It has been a glorious day as no other day has ever been. We have shared many touching and heart rendering moments together here in these chambers ... now climaxed by a mysterious, awe inspiring silver crystal, the meaning and purpose of we have yet to grasp. I suggest we now go back to Neptuna, our home and simply relax. Some food, some rest, some time off and some reflection will do us all good."

All were exhausted — physically, mentally, and emotionally. They accepted happily, knowing they could, and would, continue the exploration into the history of the ancient Neptunians and of possible ancient StarBeings at another time.

But, now they needed to let this all settle in.

Now was a time to rest.

King Luxxor taking Queen Liluuc in hand, said quietly,

"Come, let us now go to Neptuna. We will have a light dinner and then each can take the evening for themselves. Tomorrow, we will begin to enjoy the offerings of our fine city, Neptuna. I guarantee you will see and experience things you have never seen before. I am happy we shared these memorable moments together. Thank you for all your efforts."

Taking a farewell look at the mystical transcendent silver crystal, and the continually glowing palette of colors in the flowing liquid crystal stream, they turned and left.

Chapter 44

The Slice Of Heaven Floated Before Them

Not my Red Spot Lounge, he implored

FinnJonko issued a message to his father LesterJonko that he should return to the Control station as the new innovative SpacialGram had finally been assembled and appeared to be working properly.

LesterJonko was where he normally was after his duty — at the 'RedSpot' Lounge having a cold libation, as he liked to put it.

He received the message, but continued to slowly finish his drink while considering the possibilities of the SpacialGram.

If this works as my associate on Earth5 indicates, we will be able to visually see what is happening in distant parts of Space, and in actual real time miniature!

He almost wanted to shout out loud, but laughed out loud instead.

This will be incredible. At least until the bad guys get them too!

He grimaced.

In the meantime kickbacks will be expected ... money or gems? I know my associates well — probably both this time, he decided. *This SpacialGram could be a deal maker, or deal breaker, but as long as it is mine, I have the first option and choice.*

He smiled, satisfied.

Arriving at the Control station LesterJonko stopped in his tracks. There, hovering before him, was the new SpacialGram.

It's floating, he thought. *Floating. Just hovering in mid air.*

FinnJonko looked at his father's startled expression, smiled and began explaining the vision floating before his father's eyes.

"Father, I present the SpacialGram, or, as I have named it, 'A slice of Heaven!' It is 12 inches deep, 36 inches wide, and 60 inches long. The slice of Heaven we are viewing right now, in real time, is showing the galaxy we

171

are currently in. It represents accurate size and distance relationships and is similar to a hologram, father, but greatly enhanced."

"It also indicates space anomalies occurring such as solar flares, spacial wind storms, asteroids, and meteor showers, and as you can easily see, they are occurring as we speak."

"Oh, yes, I almost forgot," Finn said earnestly, "if we project this infra-heat ray detector at the SpacialGram it will indicate the location of any craft in the selected area by sensing the heat produced from the craft or fleet of ships. They will appear as tiny red spots and their direction will be indicated."

"HMMM," sounded LesterJonko. "Red spots! Not my 'RedSpot lounge, I implore you Finn," he stated, jokingly! After all, the RedSpot lounge is my last vestige of refuge from this eternal search for security, riches, happiness … and finding the bad guys."

He grinned at Finn. Finn smiled back.

They both knew they had something special here in this SpacialGram, not to mention their vessel, the 'Black Widow' herself.

"Well, lets take a closer look at this modern marvel," said LesterJonko. "Show me the ropes, son."

FinnJonko silently thought…

He called me son. Interesting. Could father be mellowing?

"Alright father. Here we are, standing besides an actual miniaturized depiction produced by the formation of atoms in conjunction with the accompanying technology we introduced, and through specific coordinates entered.

In other words, a SpacialGram. Of course, if you like, father, we can call it, A slice of Heaven — as I suggested. Think on it."

LesterJonko just stared blankly at his son.

"Anyway," he continued, "it has the dimensions I stated earlier, and here it is, before your eyes, floating in mid air. The planets, or stars you see, are all proportionate in size relationship to the Heavens they are shown in. And, we can enter into any part of the Heavens we have coordinates for and create that particular slice of Heaven right before our eyes."

"Don't you think Slice of Heaven is a great name for this, father? I thought of it myself." LesterJonko looked over at his son, and drably replied…

"Yes Finn, it is a great name. The best I have ever heard. Can we get on with it now?"

"Ok. So, let us say we want to locate where the 3 spacial probes your old friend CodL recently sent out were coming from. We now have two choices. First, we spot them using the infra-heat ray detector. Then, considering the direction they are heading, allowing for the speed they are traveling and knowing the shortest possible route has been entered into their flight program, we can then enter this data into our computers. They will tell us precisely where they were coming from, and as importantly, where they could be going. I said 'could' be going, father, as there is no precise way to correctly determine their final objective other than sound logic ... or choice number two, which is to track them via the slice of Heaven and follow along until they reach their destination."

LesterJonko continued to view the hovering slice of Heaven, whose name Finn liked to take credit for. It's possibilities were beginning to grow on him.

This is remarkable. Absolutely astonishing. I can follow these spacial probes until I find CodL away from his Complex and in a vulnerable position. He is worth a great deal of reward to me and besides, he needs to be put away.

The Black Widow is ready.

"Finn, put a lock on the 3 spacial probes and let me know just where my old friend CodL is hiding out these days. I want to know the exact coordinates of his whereabouts and especially if he ventures out of his RogueEmpireComplex. His tenure is coming to an end, and soon."

LesterJonko looked at his son FinnJonko. He smiled, as a thought entered his mind.

"Come on Finn," he said, "you have done a great job. I'm buying you a libation of my choice at the RedSpot lounge in celebration. You know Finn," he added, "oft times when one thinks of a 'good' man they believe he may be a weak adversary. Not so! There is a magnitude of faith and determination pulsing through the hearts and souls of good men and women everywhere and there has been throughout all history. It continues to be so at this very moment, my son. Remember, Finn, the shadow may follow, or precede the Sunne, but it is only a shadow, and only exists because of the Sunne!"

Finn stood there momentarily surprised and caught off guard at his father's words. He was confused at the last statement by his father.

What did that mean, he thought? *And his father's offer to, what — share a drink with him! This was unusual, at best. But, a beginning,* he thought, grinning.

"You're on," he replied happily.

Chapter 45

A Crusty Place To Be

DrexL does not deserve this

The asteroid was crusty and lacking life, at least for life forms DrexL and his crew were aware of.

What would want to live here, anyway?

However, DrexL had looked at the asteroid as an opportunity.

"This is perfect," a worried DrexL, had said, ordering 1st Helmsman LugA to land three days before.

DrexL had been experiencing an uneasiness. There was nothing notable that would cause him to think this way, but intuition and the hair beginning to stand on the back of his neck left DrexL feeling something, or someone was watching, or maybe following — or waiting.

All instrumentation indicated otherwise, and, he could not pin down anybody in the crew he would not trust. But still, in his mind something was amiss.

The spacial wind storm in Galaxy 7 had proven to be more furious than originally expected and even though they were well beneath the wind's unpredictable corridor their craft had experienced minor damage from it's intensity.

This was a good excuse to settle and regroup for a few days.

A rest time was welcomed by all aboard the RogueRecon. It had been a long voyage thus far, made all the more difficult by being confined in a smaller craft than usual. Here, with specially equipped spacial suits they could explore, rest and take their minds off the tension of their voyage for a while.

For a couple of weeks now, extended colorations from Galaxy 17 had begun to starkly juxtapose into the darkness of deep space signaling their destination, Planet 8 in Galaxy 17 lay ahead. Any doubts of the unparalleled array of beauty from the stunning spectrum of colors they could expect were quickly expelled. DrexL had encountered many Galactic light 'phenominations' in his day, but Galaxy 17 was beginning to manifest itself as being more spectacular than any he had witnessed before.

As for MorQ, he continued to evade any detection, although DrexL found it difficult to believe any of the hand picked men aboard would have objected in any way to his presence. To a man they were from Trion and trusted by DrexL.

Together they shared a history and all were experienced, seasoned men in the Heavens and reliable in dangerous situations. Many were 'DarkCapes,' and once taken away from the influence of CodL and the harsh, senseless reality of the command he invoked, were good men.

Still, DrexL found himself considering options in how, and when to release the fact of MorQ's presence aboard the RogueRecon, and his personal involvement in the matter.

They will just have to accept my judgement and overall assessment of this particular situation, he decided. *It is not my approach as Commander to be anything but honest with those serving under me, but it is best to keep this under wraps given CodL's unrelenting pursuit. For the moment this will have to do.*

He frowned.

At least the truth will come to light, and it will come from me.

His mind suddenly flashed to 'Survival for Sinners,' and he smiled.

This game, 'Survival for Sinners,' that MorQ and I have taken up playing is an intriguing, but taxing game. I must be careful tonight, though. He is turning into a skilled and apt adversary. Who would have thought that MorQ and I would be so engrossed in a multi-dimensional game consisting of a Hologram in five levels.

Hmmm, there are many options to be considered. It is a mentally challenging game. I must decide ... do I choose the option to press my InnerSpace button allowing me access to certain inner thoughts and characteristics of MorQ's personality that he has programmed in?

I only get one opportunity!

YES!!! I need to do that when I return to my stateroom, he decided. *I can then decide which are applicable and truthful, and, how I can use them to benefit my sublimation of his total empire by implementing them into the Hologram level of my choice. YES!*

MorQ, of course, will do the same to me if I let down my guard. Hmmm.

He smiled again, anxious for the climatic ending he hoped for later.

The asteroid had a circumference of approximately 600 miles and was mainly barren. They had amusedly dubbed it 'A Piece of Crust.'

Some of the men traversed a few miles in various directions, but turned up nothing of consequence. However, the time relaxing was paying off for all of them as the stress of space flight, the unknown dangers found therein and the ever present tension of CodL's influence weighed heavily on their minds.

Throughout the voyage DrexL continued communication with the RogueEmpire but had recently been transmitting fewer and fewer reports of anything meaningful to CodL. He knew this would undoubtably enrage CodL, arousing his suspicions. DrexL also had no doubts that plans and actions were in progress, or already implemented, to apprehend him.

Perhaps this is the intuition I am experiencing ... he wondered.

Chief Communications officer and DarkCape, Salamar sat at the dinner table contemplating his uncertain future. He was under an obligation through unspoken loyalties to honor the commands of Emperor CodL, whether he agreed with the orders or not. On their last communication CodL had insisted, in no uncertain terms, that he once again do a thorough and complete search of the Recon for MorQ.

He did, and as before he had found not a trace. The only place Salamar had not looked was DrexL's private quarters and he knew MorQ could not be hiding there without DrexL's knowledge and permission.

Salamar had received the rank of Chief Communication's Officer and DarkCape through extreme hardships, and was proud of his achievements. However, it was not lost on him that CodL was losing control of his abilities to lead.

I am no longer sure how Emperor CodL will respond to any situation, given his mood at any particular moment. He is completely unpredictable and unstable in my opinion, thought Salamar. *Perhaps when we reach Planet 8, I will simply disappear, and find a place off by myself, living out the remainder of this life alone. No pressures, no commands.*

He realized a tiny smile had appeared on his face.

On the other hand, I respect DrexL, he considered, and had been repulsed, when ordered by CodL, under threat, to spy aboard the RogueRecon, reporting back via a special CodePass known only to CodL and himself.

Commander DrexL is tough, but fair, and always one to weigh all possibilities and hear all sides of the story before making decisions, he thought.

Salamar had been in Commander DrexL's command for only a short time, but during that time had developed a true admiration and respect for him. It actually began back on Trion when DrexL helped him and others free themselves from their bondage in the mines. Now, he was not happy and was becoming physically ill from having to spy on someone he respected.

"It is not what I am about. It is not in my character to do this, and Commander DrexL does not deserve this," Salamar murmured. "Maybe I should approach DrexL, disclose the situation, and explain how it came to be."

"Yes," he emphatically stated.

"That is exactly what I will do, no matter the consequences."

Salamar, immediately felt a wave of exhilaration sweep through him.

I feel no remorse in aborting my secretive assignment for the lunatic CodL — in fact I feel free.

He felt a weight of anxiety immediately vanish.

"I will not be returning to CodL and the RogueEmpire, irregardless of the result of my actions."

Rising from his uneaten dinner, Salamar headed for the control deck to seek out Commander DrexL. *I must live with 'my truth', and with 'myself,'* he thought.

An hour or so later, CodL received a private CodePass message aboard the RogueEmpire, from Salamar. It read...

Emperor Codl...experienced severe Spacial wind storm... normal tests aboard RogueRecon detected Neutron Thruster entry malfunctions, making it impossible to enter even a normal gravitational field...thus, we have sat down on an isolated, un-atmospheric asteroid to remedy the situation. It may take a few days to a few weeks, according to the engineers. Until they get into the Thruster cavity they will not know of the repairs needed, or the time required to repair the malfunction. it appears there will be a delay in reaching our destination...will keep you updated...Chief Communications Officer...Salamar...codeword 'worm.'

DrexL looked at Salamar after he had sent the message to CodL and smiled.

"Thank you Salamar. I believe we have perhaps gained some valuable time in respect to any pursuit by CodL. It is good to have you aboard and in my command. I do sympathize with the situation you were in and I certainly empathize with the inner turmoil you were experiencing. You have done the right thing, Salamar. I do not feel any animosity towards you for the part you played in CodL's scheme. You were following orders from CodL. However, I do respect your rationalization of the situation and the resolve and courage you exhibited in coming forward."

DrexL offered forth his hand, saying...

"Salamar, you will retain the rank of Chief Communications Officer here on the RogueRecon and I am pleased at what will be an open and honest relationship between us. We, or rather you, will continue to CodePass information to CodL as we feel is in our best interests. I feel it is now time to inform the crew of our situation, Salamar. I will make an announcement immediately of my intentions to leave CodL's RogueEmpire and give everyone the opportunity to make their decision.

I will offer them the choice of their loyalties. If any wish to stay with CodL, a way will be found to send them back. For the rest of us, it is time to begin our lives anew. After that, the first order of business will be to rename our ship.

The RogueRecon does not cut it for me anymore."

"I agree Commander DrexL," replied Salamar, accepting the hand outstretched before him with his own.

"Good, Salamar, I am pleased."

"Chief Salamar, after I have presented my intentions, arrange a meeting to entertain names for our vessel submitted from the crew who choose to remain."

Chief Communications Officer, Salamar smiled and took in a breath of fresh air.

"Yes Sir, Commander DrexL!"

Chapter 46

Dancing Silhouettes Of The Deep

Within the Domes of Life

It did not take long for the Initiates to acclimate to life in Neptuna. Their rooms were nicely appointed, with each having extraordinary views of the never ending undersea promenade of curious sea beings, exotic underwater plant life, and rays of deep dream like colors filtering through undersea crystals in the mysterious world of Neptuna.

They spent their first few days lounging, eating, and ofttimes just sitting together going over past events, rekindling their collective enthusiasm for the secrets yet to be discovered in the hidden tomb chambers and continuing to establish the friendships created thus far.

However, after a few nights of sound sleep, many very nice meals, and the celebrity status given to them by all Neptunians, they were soon very willing participants in a grand Neptunian tour offered by King Luxxor and Queen Liluuc, which included, more often than not, the charming Prince Tunnis.

Unfortunately, the renovation of the water and plumbing systems were still ongoing leaving King Luxxor no choice but to spend ample time with the structural engineering architects and related geologists regarding the immense project.

This left the matter of the tours in the capable hands of Queen Liluuc, who enthusiastically went about organizing visits to varying sites and destinations that had special significance for Neptuna.

She was careful to not overwhelm the Initiates with to much to soon and provided adequate answers to the myriad of questions asked by her curious guests.

What 'she' did not know, she sent Prince Tunnis to find out.

One such question was where did the immense blocks of stone come from since the original city was located in a desert with no apparent quarry anywhere near. Queen Liluuc had stated …

"Often we just take for granted what we see, what we walk on, or what we have always known, and honestly I have never entertained a question about it — until now! It is a very good question which deserves looking into. Tunnis will research that, won't you, Tunnis?!"

During the tours they visited the Podium, and were informed of it's significance and importance for all the souls of Amythesia. Witnessing first hand the large number of SoulPods being carefully watched and controlled, the Initiates were amazed at the Podium's capacity, and the organizational, and technological skill involved in this complex facility. The degree of responsibility for the care of these Souls was unascertainable, and monumental. They were rightfully impressed.

They toured the council chambers of the Wise, were intrigued by the Museum of Antiquities, and more than curious in the unusual Temple of Legend and Fable. Queen Liluuc informed them that in Neptunian's opinion there is much truth to be ascertained from legends and fables of antiquity.

In all these structures they found the integrity and dignity of both buildings and past occupants carefully and respectfully retained.

The Initiates became truly impressed with the accomplishments of these fine Neptunian Beings, and with the sense of achievement and even pride that they rightfully radiated. Where ever they went, they experienced happy and friendly Beings. Living here in Neptuna beneath the waters of the Sea of the Forgotten Place seemed to be a choice and an agreeable life for all they encountered.

And the food!!! To an Initiate they could hardly wait until the next course. Between them they developed a guessing game of just what it was they were eating and enjoying so much, asking specifically to not be told until they had given their guesses. This gave great pleasure to Tunnis and Dolpho who accompanied them for much of their visit.

Also, during this time, the Initiates became quite endearing to King Luxxor and Queen Liluuc. They, themselves, quickly became invigorated by their presence, their enthusiasm, and their unceasing curiosity. Days passed by as fleeting as thoughts — here for a second, and then gone the next.

It was during one of King Luxxor's 'need to be there' staff meetings that Queen Liluuc, Laurra, Calla, Dolpho, and Poona planned to meet Tunnis at the Temple of the Moon and 7Stars for a girls time out together. Tunnis insisted he accompany them as the token male escort, which all found amusing and endearing and of course happily accepted.

Laurra, stood with her eyes closed and hands pressed gently against the inner surface of the clear Dome of Life. She felt the coolness of the waters beyond pressing back ... as if in answer.

Slightly opening her eyes to the undersea world before her, she said...

"I feel spellbound, Poona ... by the dazzling sights here in the Sea of the Forgotten Place and in this incredible Dome of Life surrounding us."

Opening her eyes a little wider, she added,

"Tunnis and Dolpho secretly told me they believe the Sea of the Forgotten Place holds many more mysterious and intriguing relics of history than has been found thus far. Actually, so do I," she murmured to herself. "If this entire city of Neptuna sank, then imagine what may be buried in the surrounding areas. It only makes sense."

She glanced over at Queen Liluuc and Dolpho, sitting on a bench nearby, listening intently to something Calla was explaining.

Her eyes glistened.

"I am anxious to experience the Temple of the Moon and 7Stars, Poona."

Poona put her arm around Laurra and snuggled her in close.

"Yes, in some ways it will be the pinnacle of our stay in Neptuna, Laurra, at least at this time."

Laurra nodded, and rested her head on Poona's shoulder.

They waited for Tunnis to join them.

Outside the Dome of Life, the constantly changing colors and movement were extraordinary. Laurra and Poona stood mesmerized, watching, as darting little sea fish swam alongside gliding, slow moving large sea mammals. All appeared as flickering, intensely flashy vivacious colors. This was due to light from the Sunne or Moon filtering down, reaching deeper into the waters of Neptuna and cascading off the effervescent scales of the small animated fish bodies.

Sea grasses sensually danced in rhythm and unison with the sea fish in the ever changing currents. All were illuminated by the same sources of light and cast curious and ofttimes bizarre shadows as they moved to and fro.

"Oh, Poona, this is such an erotic and choreographed dance. The small, zestful little fish seemingly enter and exit at the grasses cue. It is like a dream."

"You seem to be feeling better each day, Laurra. I believe Completion is near and you are very close to being fully healed. It has been exasperating for me to be near you and yet, at times, unable to offer assistance to ease the pain you were experiencing. It has taken precious time, Laurra, but you have persevered."

"I have persevered, because I have a destiny — one I have chosen,

Poona. And just think, here we are in the Dome of Life, under the Sea of the Forgotten Place, friends with the King and Queen and I am an Initiate of Brightness. It is almost overwhelming!"

"Yes, Laurra, all things considered, it has gone well," smiled Poona, with eyes twinkling. "And, you seem happy here, Laurra."

Laurra turned, and met Poona's eyes.

"I am, Poona."

Clasping hands, they strolled over to Queen Liluuc, Dolpho and Calla. Queen Liluuc, offering a warm smile, asked...

"Are you enjoying our enchanting, never ending spectacle?"

Poona nodded, saying...

"I do not know how to stop watching, Queen Liluuc."

Laurra, once again gazing at the dance, commented...

"See the tall, willowy, sea grasses, Queen Liluuc? When they happen to be in front of a glowing crystal it appears as if they become 'dancing silhouettes of the deep,' choreographed by the currents of the sea."

Poona smiled tenderly at the visual Laurra had described.

"A sensitive reflection, Laurra," said Queen Liluuc. "You will find, that in time, the movement you are noticing become as the clouds and blowing sands on the surface of Prismacia. It is just the way it is. We always appreciate the dances and artistry of these colorful reflections, but it no longer becomes a distraction. We all realize this, but count on it being there for us when we need it. Actually, when we are away I miss it very much."

Each slipped into their own thoughts and they all turned back to the mysterious underwater world waiting patiently for Tunnis to arrive.

Laurra's thoughts drifted in an unusual direction. The sensuality of the provocative, ever present colored lights flickering and dancing about somehow lured her into a reflection of personal questions and longings.

"So sensual," she said, beneath her breath, eyes distant as if expecting to discover an answer to longings she was aware of, but had yet to experience. She slowly drifted deeper into these thoughts.

"Laurra, hello", said Tunnis, as he walked up to stand beside her.

Everyone smiled when Tunnis appeared. He was such a personable and enchanting young man, and always cheerful. They enjoyed his company and wit.

"Hello Mother. Hello Poona, Dolpho, Calla," he followed.

"My apologies for being a little late, but I lost track of time while researching the origins of massive stone blocks in Nepuna." He grinned broadly.

Everyone got his humor and returned his smiles. However, it did not slip by Queen Liluuc that Tunnis had addressed Laurra first.

She filed the thought away to be considered later.

"This morning, now that we are all present," Queen Liluuc then said, casually glancing at Tunnis, "is to take you to the Sanctuary of Luxxor, which is within the Temple of the Moon and 7Stars. As we approach the Temple, please note that at one time it sat by a large Ivory crystal and a blue crystal. Both were later incorporated into part of the structure itself, lending to the extraordinary architecture trend which is found through out Neptuna."

Arriving at the entrance to the Temple of the Moon and 7Stars, she said profoundly...

"The Sanctuary of Luxxor is in this ancient structure. It is where my Chosen One comes to be alone when he needs to contemplate important matters. When we ascend these steps we enter into the past, the present, and the promise of the future — I give you the Sanctuary of Luxxor, within the Temple of The Moon and 7Stars."

The Temple itself was small, two floors with only a few rooms per floor, but once inside they found the interior to be cozy, and obviously quite ancient. The very fact that it was so old influenced their thoughts, leading them to visions of secrets, concealed passages, and hidden messages within the 'as of yet' indecipherable letters and figures on all the walls.

"Intrigue, and mystery abound," whispered Laurra to Princess Dolpho walking along side of her. "Very ancient mystery."

"Oh, yes, Laurra, it truly does. As a child I came here often, and to this day I still believe there are answers here to mysteries we are aware of ... and hidden mysteries yet to be discovered. I sometimes feel like my father does too. He becomes quite a romantic in regards to his thoughts about the past, she confided."

"As we explore about," Queen Llluuc said, "you will find there are two balconies in the rear looking upon the Dome of Life, and beyond — to the dancing silhouettes you so aptly named, Laurra," she pleasingly commented.

Slowly leading them to King Luxxor's study, the Queen said...

"Quite honestly, we have not deciphered the vast majority of the inscriptions and reliefs found here. As in most of the structures, they are of a nature we are not familiar with. However, our linguists, Ancientologists, and AstroHeavens engineers continue in their pursuit of answers. What we do believe, however, is that what we are seeing is not a worship of Deities, but rather symbols and messages etched on stone, used in controlling their destiny and now, hopefully, perchance our destiny."

Everyone remained silent.

Continuing, Queen Liluuc, stated...

"Also, as my Chosen One, King Luxxor spoke of in the hidden chambers discovered recently, one ancient myth foretells of a wise, noble and compassionate Empress of Goodness, who will usher in the Silver Princess of the Moon and 7Stars. She has been mentioned in myth and folklore throughout our history. This event will herald in an era of promise that Neptuna has long awaited. Thus far we have all been blessed with High Priestesses of the Voice of One who have all helped shape the destiny of Amythesia, including that of Neptuna. We live and continue forward on faith."

"Do you have any idea of the age of Neptuna," asked Calla?

"And," added Poona, "of the actual original inhabitants of Neptuna? After the discoveries in the Passage of Antiquity, it appears they were obviously highly knowledgeable in the formation of the stars, their cycles, and most likely, the Heavens beyond?"

Queen Liluuc nodded and responded...

"We can only speculate as to Neptuna's age, but have nothing accurate to work with, so we just say, it is ancient — very ancient, and possibly the second community to exist here on Prismacia. Remember, this city was once above the sea, in the desert high above. As to the founders and original inhabitants, we have found many markings resembling star systems, but as you are aware, we have not deciphered all of these markings and we do not fully understand their impact, or if there is any message in reference to the Neptuna we live in today."

Poona, studied the reliefs and markings on the walls surrounding them.

"These reliefs are obviously extremely old, as the stars and planets today no longer reside in the appointed quadrants depicted. Constellations have shifted ... at least as I can make them out."

"Actually," said Queen Liluuc, "you are correct. According to our AstroHeavens engineers, what we think is the Moon and 7Stars Cluster shown in the reliefs, appears in a different quadrant of the sky today than where they are indicated being as depicted in the wall reliefs we are viewing."

"Yes," said Poona, "and we now know that some of the celestial events only take place every 50,000 or so years," quickly adding, "as I have been informed of through past studies."

Laurra turned to them, her mind quickly calculating the time frames mentioned and said inquisitively...

"Do you realize how long ago the ancients must have begun to track the stars, notice changes, and consider movements in star patterns? And then, just to get to where we are today, they would have needed to continually track the stars every 50,000 years over hundreds of thousands of years to realize and record that this event only occurred every 50,000 years! Why, it is astounding !"

"What you theorize is absolutely true, Laurra" said Poona. "It is not only astounding, but breathtakingly phenomenal."

"Just how far back do Beings actually go," questioned Calla.

Laurra added, "It would seem the universe, and galaxies as we know them, have been evolving with rhythmic cycles for more unknown millennia than can be fathomed. One could assume ... possibly hundreds of millions of years."

Poona nodded, "A very good assumption, Laurra, and, in my mind, I will not speculate, but state assuredly, that, as you calculated, someone has in fact been intelligently tracking and charting such activities for hundreds of thousands of years — if not more!"

For a moment everyone stood, silent, considering Laurra, and Poona's astonishing revelations.

Princess Dolpho, smiling, and with a twinkle in her eyes, said...

"We should be thankful to be among the improvements. I know I am !"

Everyone laughed and applauded her, for introducing a touch of humor into such overwhelming considerations.

Calla, then serious, expressed...

"But, I believe that which we have been discussing is all true. I intuitively feel it. We, as a species, have been here a very long time. More than some may want to admit to."

Prince Tunnis, who had been listening intently, said...

"I also believe that, Calla — completely. It only makes sense!"

Queen Liluuc looked at her young son and smiled warmly.

"Well," the Queen then said, 'we will obviously need some answers to these questions before we can conclusively state them as facts. Tunnis, you will have some research to do tonight!"

Everyone, including Tunnis laughed.

"So, for the moment, let us move on," said the Queen.

Gesturing to a striking relief behind King Luxxor's desk, the Queen informed them...

"This is a representation of our beloved Moon and 7Stars. Once again, we have no idea what it means to convey, or if it means anything at all. It may just be decorative, but it is our belief, that in addition to being decorative, the ancients rarely did anything that was without purpose."

She pointed to another relief affixed to the wall.

"We simply call this the Fountain of Life. It is a fountain relief, consisting of a woman with long hair, a crown of small stars and wearing a long gown with a thin sash clasped around the waist hanging down in front ... similar to the style worn today. As you can see, the clasp is hollowed out into the wall and has six irregular sides. Also, she appears to be smiling and her delicate hands are cupped and slightly protruding forth as if meant to hold an object of some kind."

"Yes, it does give one that impression, Queen Liluuc, said Poona.

Swirling her fingers in the air, Liluuc continued...

"Circling her head are depictions of the moon in it's phases, with the full moon centered and partly behind her head. The crescents at the beginning and end of the cycle are not reliefs but were cut out creating openings into the wall. And, finally, portrayed beyond the full moon — is a cluster of 7Stars."

Queen Liluuc stepped back giving all an opportunity to study the reliefs for a few moments.

"If you go to the wall and look from the side at the profile of the relief, you will see how beautiful she is," said Queen Liluuc. "She stands out one foot exactly, and while presenting an illusion of elegance, she is ever so sensual and to many, almost evocative."

"Is it possible she could be representational of the Silver Princess we await, mother," asked Dolpho?

"Why, Dolpho, that is a consideration we have wondered about often. She does have the small band of stars about her head. Seven to be exact. So, yes, it is a consideration that must not be dismissed."

Queen Liluuc paused, gazing at the ancient sculpture for a moment, her eyes distant.

Laurra, turning to Poona, whispered...

"The moon relief behind her head is very much like the HaloDisc 'Symbol of Excellence' that HighPriestess XennaOne wore behind her head at our ceremony. Surely someone must have noticed the similarity."

"Well," replied Poona, "as is known, the tradition is very ancient, but you are correct, Laurra. The similarity is too coincidental to disregard, or dismiss as irrelevant."

Queen Liluuc, having returned from her thoughts, was about to add that the fountain was non functioning, when a beaming King Luxxor entered, followed by two Royal Divine Guardians carrying two trays of tantalizing varieties of sea fish, with assorted other goodies and beverages for all.

"I do apologize for my unannounced intrusion," he said, "but I was informed of your whereabouts and thought it best to bring you some nourishment. The day is moving right along and, well, I thought perhaps you may be famished?"

King Luxxor, smiled at them, looking very happy.

Quickly deciding not to diminish the caring gesture of her Chosen

One by informing him that she had indeed given lunch forethought, Queen Liluuc said...

"My Chosen One, to what, or whom, do we owe the pleasure of your company and thank you so much for the very caring thought of this excellent food for our guests? As you can see, my King, we are well and your son, Prince Tunnis, is doing a masterful job of watching over us."

"I come, My Queen, My Chosen One, to share great news with you and with our new friends, of course."

Raising his hands in thanks, he gleefully and thankfully stated...

"We have completed the final plans for the water and plumbing project, and it is anticipated to be finished in a much shorter time frame than expected. It is a time for celebration."

"Also," he said, turning to Tunnis, "I wish to compliment my son, for the admirable job he is doing in seeing over the welfare of all our lovely guests.

I am envious, my son — well done."

Tunnis lit up in a huge grin, as he said...

"It is my pleasure, father."

Queen Liluuc eyes twinkled.

I am sure it is, my son, as she glanced at an unsuspecting Laurra.

As the conversation shifted to between King Luxxor and Tunnis, Queen Liluuc, quietly whispered into one of the Divine Guardians ears. He bowed ever so slightly and unnoticed, slipped away for only a moment to arrange to cancel Queen Liluuc's array of snacks which were being prepared for a short time later. He returned, his absence being totally unnoticed, except for Queen Liluuc who, ever so slightly, bowed her head in thanks.

Later, as they were leaving the Sanctuary of Luxxor Poona took one more glance at the Fountain of Life. Her thoughts became briefly distant.

Laurra, also glancing at the Fountain, looked over to Poona.

They smiled brightly before turning to leave.

Chapter 47

The Reflection Did Not Flinch

The 'DarkCape' heard the moan

CodL sat alone in his personal command tower debating his next move. It was obvious he had to make one. The real question was when.

DrexL has become arrogant and insufferable, but is to far away to order back at this time and this mission must be completed. And, Salamar! He doesn't have the strength of character to handle himself, let alone DrexL, or the rest of the DarkCapes aboard the RogueRecon.

Lumbering over to his space view portal he became fixated on his reflection in the view window.

He boastfully confronted his alter ego — the one looking back at him…

"I am strong — I am no one to mess with — all fear CodL!"

"It is my name, above all others, that all fear through out the galaxies!"

"I have built an Empire!"

Now obsessed by his reflection, CodL scowled at the irony in which the unenlightened always used unsavory remarks to repudiate his vast exploits.

"I am the true Master … Monarch … and the Emperor!" he shouted fanatically — now scowling at his reflection, which puffed out it's chest and scowled back at him.

"That's a strength of character others would die for," he said. "literally!"

However, there are no others. Only impostors, and they are all foul and nauseating. Their's is a blandness in what they called style.

"It is I who set the standard and the few others who futilely try to imitate or emulate are left wallowing in my contempt. They have all felt my wrath."

He smirked, staring once more at the image in the reflection.

CodL then closed his eyes, but his reflection remained, imprinted on the retina of his memory. However, it was not only the imprint of his reflection that remained but also that of his life that he now envisioned.

He held his head back, letting out a long mournful moan.

The DarkCape, FaLN, stationed outside CodL's tower room heard the moan, but paid it no attention. He had heard it before, and had learned the hard way not to intrude on Emperor CodL — despite any circumstances.

"Let it be, my only responsibility is to keep others out," he murmured, shutting out the moanful sounds from within CodL's tower room.

"What is it," CodL cried out to himself.

"What is wrong with me!"

Try as he might, he could not vanquish the tortured memories of a long ago time— beginning in his childhood. These thoughts had haunted him throughout his entire existence.

"This existence they call life."

He smirked.

"Life," he mournfully said. "The only life I have been able to have is by struggle alone. Where were they when I was young? For that matter, 'who' were they when I was young?"

"There was no one, just like now."

He turned back to the window reflection.

"Who are you!"

The reflection did not flinch. It only looked back in mockery at his agony.

CodL fell to his knees, head in hands, and tears fell for the first time in a long, long, time.

"I need something — no, I need somebody, anybody," he sobbed.

"But, there is no one, because "I" am my only one.

Standing, he wiped his eyes.

No way for an Emperor to be, he thought.

He checked his reflection in the window.

It was still there.

Just like the memories.

'expectations...

fragile creatures...

broken by a brief moment...

of an off hand word...'

'someone breaks it, you fix it'

bocc

poet and Initiate of Brightness on the Wisdom Path Journey
Prismacia
UGT 20,872

Chapter 48

The Days And Nights Were Tender

Junnuj

Junnuj became more radiant and happy by the day.

Being with her family here at SeaCliff, together for the first time in so many years gave Junnuj a new lease on life. Rarely did her smile leave her face except for the few moments when she remembered her past and it's recurring memories of separation.

However, these memories were retreating rapidly, thanks to her new and loving environment. She was at a loss for words at how unhappy memories could be erased so quickly by love.

Weeks flew by as the four of them became acquainted as a family and with the exception of her marriage to BucchaSim, and the births of their children, for the first time in her adult life, Junnuj was truly happy.

Today, she sat along the edge of the cliff overlooking the sea, thinking.

I could sit for hours, just watching the interactions between them ... and the similarities, well, *it is obvious we are a family.*

She closed her eyes, remembering the time she was so in love and first experiencing her life with BucchaSim.

How I used to tease him about his name, she chuckled, a smile lighting up her face. *And, all those fond memories of my life in 'Oneness' so many years ago — when we were young.*

"But, that was then, and this is our life now," she quietly said.

Junnuj was so happy. The ease, the comfort, and the joy of being together as a family was transforming.

Hugging herself, Junnuj thought...

Love has woven itself seamlessly into our lives and I am so joyful.

Junnuj took in a deep clean breath of sea air.

She gazed up at the colorful and beautiful Heavens and closed her eyes once again. These were moments when Junnuj felt she could not possibly handle any more joy and the tears shed were now tears of happiness and love.

TerraSim and Annuj were absolutely wonderful to her. BucchaSim enthusiastically encouraged her to spend as much time as she needed with them, knowing it would help her heal the wounds of a mother's separation from her children, her family.

She asked them what they liked, who were their friends, what were their plans, is there a significant other, and were they happy. She often inquired about Ralla and Hanna, and Jasso, Annuj's family in Lapesia, and smiled happily when Annuj spoke so lovingly of them.

And, BucchaSim! It was as if they were meeting for the first time. She felt love ... absent for so long in her life.

BucchaSim told her of his loneliness and sadness in being without her. He spoke of his life with TerraSim and how he only recently came to discover Annuj is their daughter. He spoke of the home he created and named SeaCliff, and of his discovery of the secret hidden tunnel leading to Neptuna.

Junnuj listened intently, soaking up every word.

They often walked hand in hand along the long deserted coastline of the Sea of the Forgotten Place, stopping from time to time to just sit and gaze out, and at each other — still hand in hand.

During one of these walks together, BucchaSim took Junnuj in his arms and spoke softly... "I knew beyond the shadow of a doubt we would someday share SeaCliff together, Junnuj. I always believed I would someday gather you in my arms, and whisper that we will never be parted again.

Ever!

Chapter 49

The Deepness Of Endlessness

There is a Destiny — it is just not pre-destined

Annuj was sitting on the balcony at SeaCliff. The hour was late and the others had said good night, retiring for the evening.

She sat there, alone, looking into the darkness, and pondered.

It is very obvious why BucchaSim chose this place for his home ...

the Sea of the Forgotten Place on one side, and the vast Carbonian Desert on the other. It is perfect for him.

Hmmm, Perhaps the deepness of endlessness as seen from here and the radiance of the Heaven's color in the darkness enhances the dreamy array even more. Perhaps it is the isolation — that of knowing you are totally alone — here at SeaCliff, under the 'pomp' of such an endless display of stars stretching on to endlessness itself, and beyond ... if 'beyond endlessness' is indeed possible?

"How is it to be endless, I wonder?"

"Colors without names exist here in our world," she said softly.

I wonder ... what does it look like, viewed from out there, deep in the Heavens, and looking back at Prismacia? I have never felt a longing to explore the other worlds that exist — but for the opportunity to see my world from out there, from the Heavens, well maybe!

Her thoughts then turned to reminiscing over the past few weeks together.

"I can see the similarities between me and my 'new' family." "My father, BucchaSim, is strong, and caring ... qualities TerraSim, my brother, also comes by easily. They are definitely men of honor, true to their word and their deeds. They would help anybody. It makes me feel good."

And, my mother, she pondered. *It is difficult to fully fathom the anguish and complete absence of hope she must have felt given her position as* the HighPriestess of the Voice of One. Deep within all she truly desired in this life was to be a wife, and a mother.

Annuj trembled slightly. *Those responsibilities, traditions, and laws kept my mother from the family she loved so dearly ...* "and from me!"

Her strength of character during such stress was deserving of complete respect and understanding given the situation. It was she who Beings turned to, but who could she to turn to? I remember that at one point while walking with my mother, Junnuj, looked at me. She said...

"Annuj, you are capable of anything, all things are possible. Remember, you are a PastRecaller, a Seer, a Mystic, and you are of healing. There is fairness in your wisdom and actions, but, perhaps most importantly, Annuj, you are one of compassion. I realize I bestow many accolades upon you, my daughter, but I also believe you will receive these accolades in the manner intended."

Annuj remembered when Junnuj confided in her how she personally intended to lead the movement to change these very traditions and laws.

Mother said...

"It will be a movement creating 'freedom of choice,' so that no one else will go through the same trials I endured, should they choose otherwise!"

"My mother felt obligated to continue the family honor and tradition and the expectations of the Beings of Amythesia.

"It was not her choice!"

"How sad."

"Oh, Oneness," she whispered, "please, please help me be there for my mother during this time of healing. Thank you for her return to our lives, my life! Thank you for both of my families. I am blessed."

"I believe I have a destiny, but ... it will be my choice."

"It is not always pre-destined ... I must remember the distinction."

Nevertheless, each of us are 'living' a destiny at this very moment.

"Has it been our choice," she asked, looking to the stars?

I, myself, am in line to become the HighPriestess of the Voice of One.

Annuj reflected out loud ...

"HighPriestess XennaOne is my aunt."

"Former HighPriestess JunnaOne is my mother."

"Former HighPriestess SolannaOne is my grandmother."

"Former HighPriestess LannaOne was my great grandmother
I would be called, HighPriestess AnnaOne of the Voice of One."

She put her feet up upon the railing of the balcony and thought about that.

'when does the stream become a river...

'like' turn to 'love'...

'want' turn to 'need'...

'soon' turn to 'now'...

'where is the moment, and who decides'

bocc

poet and Initiate of Brightness on the Wisdom Path Journey
Prismacia
UGT 20,872

Chapter 50

Annuj, You Must Become As A Sleuth

Yes, she exclaimed, I see them now

TerraSim and Annuj spent many hours together becoming brother and sister. Annuj even mentioned to TerraSim…

"You will be a wonderful role model for my younger brother Jasso, TerraSim, and I look forward to introducing you."

"I will like that very much," TerraSim responded.

One day while they were roaming near SeaCliff, TerraSim whispered to Annuj…

"Do you see those rocks over there, by the yellow crystal Annuj?

Glancing over, she saw a large yellow crystal and … looking back at TerraSim questioningly, whispered…

"Yes, but why are we whispering, TerraSim?"

He gestured to the ground.

"At the base of the large crystal, among the larger rocks, there are a few very small rocks lying about in a grouping."

"Yes," she replied, "I see some small rocks lying about at the base … so why are we whispering"

"I have a surprise for you, my little sister," he teased, his eyes sparkling happily.

"But, we must approach soundlessly," he said looking at Annuj seriously.

"That is why we are whispering."

"Why?"

"It is for you to discover," TerraSim said. "You, Annuj, must become as a sleuth, deduce from a myriad of clues and bring your findings to the light!"

Annuj chuckled and smiling broadly, played along, pretending to sneak up on the unsuspecting tiny stones and their mystery.

Suddenly, Annuj let out a scream, and began hopping up and down, as the rocks began to scurry about her feet.

"See," he said, "they heard you coming."

"What heard me coming," Annuj said, looking at the scampering little rocks, and then back at TerraSim, wide eyed.

With tears in his eyes, TerraSim was belly laughing from seeing Annuj's reaction.

"I have played a trick on you Annuj. These little things only look like rocks. They are disguised as a rock to protect them from predators, but they really are small living beings called Geodies.

Remember, back in the desert with the Initiates, I spoke of them once. Go ahead, pick one up. Geodies are quite friendly and are actually cute. They have large eyes, and appear to be smiling all the time."

TerraSim grinned.

"Are you playing another trick on me, TerraSim!"

"No, Annuj. They are absolutely harmless, I promise you. This time I am not kidding. Go ahead, Annuj, pick one out as a pet for your own if you like."

While TerraSim continued to inform her about Geodies, Annuj knelt down and began looking around at the little rocks, which seemed calm once again.

"Geodies exist mostly in the desert," he said, "capturing moisture from the sea air, and larger crystals."

"Moisture from the crystals?"

"Yes, generally they congregate at the base of crystals to share the warmth it gives off during the cold nights, then after a cold night when the Sunne once again heats up the crystals, condensation forms and trickles down where they can catch it on their lips and little tongues. Apparently, they really do not need much to survive, Annuj. I mean, what does a rock need to eat?"

Looking incredulously at TerraSim, Annuj calmly replied...

"I don't know TerraSim ... gravel?!"

"Pebbles?!"

TerraSim laughed at the thought.

Annuj stood up and walked towards TerraSim. He noticed she was gently cupping a rock, and was smiling brightly.

"SHE will be my companion," Annuj said.

"She?" inquired TerraSim.

"Yes, SHE."

"What will you call her, asked TerraSim?"

Annuj looked at her brother, in disbelief, and again said ... "SHE!"

"SHE?"

"Yes, her name is 'SHE.' I adore her. Thank you so much TerraSim."

Annuj took her brother by the arm, saying...

"Come, let us go back to SeaCliff. I want to share 'SHE' with mother and father, and create a pile of sand for it's living space. Do you think SHE will want a small crystal too? My little, beautiful, new pet rock. Look, TerraSim, 'SHE' is smiling! Do you think 'SHE' looks alluring?"

TerraSim raised his eyes, and arms towards the Heavens and exclaimed...

"Sisters!"

Chapter 51

He Would Draw The Line In The Crusty Sand

Emperor CodL

CodL ordered the major deep space exploratory and combat vessel RogueEmpire Warrior I prepared for departure in Emergency Class Level 1 time. It was done, and the following morning at precisely 4AM they departed the RogueEmpire's Complex following their coordinates to Galaxy 17, Planet 8.

CodL had alternative motives too. He hoped to intercept RogueRecon and DrexL before they reached their destination of Planet 8. It was his fervent desire that the RogueRecon and Drexl would still be stuck on the asteroid they told him about.

Sitting in the 'Emperor's' chair of his command tower, he fumed.

I, Emperor CodL, will draw the line in the crusty sand there. It is time to have it out with DrexL and any who choose to stand with him. I curse the day he was created.

CodL considered the manpower enlisted aboard; *4 Specialists, each in charge of 150 units and all trained DarkCapes; A staff of 150 working aboard the huge vessel ... Oh yes,* he thought, *and 2 scientists, although it disgusts me to have them along. However, their knowledge has proven valuable before — even though they are worms!*

This also leaves a sizable fighting force left behind on the RogueEmpireComplex to defend it against anyone foolish enough to attempt their own demise while I am away. I have more than enough forces to cope with DrexL and anything else that may lay ahead.

The RogueEmperor Warrior I is not only an extremely larger craft than that of the RogueRecon, but much more powerful, and faster. I will make up valuable time, and be there before DrexL knows what has happened.

He attempted a grin, but settled for a smirk.

The past few weeks had been miserable for CodL. He did not know what DrexL was up to and his diminishing correspondence irritated him even more.

A complete lack of respect for the most feared warrior in space, he thought, angrily. *If it were not for Salamar I would have no knowledge what so ever of the activities of DrexL's mission, but even Salamar is now sending pointless messages. And, where is that little worm MorQ? It makes my skin crawl thinking that he could have slithered away. It just was not possible. Unless....*

"Unless he is aboard the RogueRecon," he said disgustedly, "with or without the knowledge of DrexL and Salamar."

"I have to know," he bellowed to the walls of his command tower!

CodL, still haunted nightly by visions and memories of a past time, had now recently begun to have visions appear occasionally during the days. The frequency of these intrusions troubled him, and he could not be seen by the crew in this state.

He had taken to sitting for long periods of time in his private quarters trying to understand the visions and haunting nightmares occurring. They had always lingered in his subconscious, but for some time now they fought to encompass his daily thoughts, and they were succeeding, leaving him feeling defenseless and near the edge of control — and sanity!

"I have fought and beaten stronger opponents than you," he ranted once again to no one listening, except the trusted DarkCape, FaLN, outside his door.

Of course, unknown to CodL, it was definitely his ego in control and more apt at this kind of turmoil. It could and would inflict the most damage whenever possible. CodL had been feeding his 'ego-self' most of his life and his ego was more than up to the challenge.

Perhaps it was confused though? Because to take down CodL, was in effect to take down itself! Should CodL not survive, the ego would perish also!

The ego knew that it's battle was to keep CodL in complete submission, but still in control of his false securities.

This is what 'I' do, the ego thought. *CodL, has no idea what I have in mind.*

Perhaps it is time to pull back a bit and give CodL a breather. Let him get his strength back for the battles ahead. Then I can hit him again when he is comfortable and relaxed after another victory.

The ego smiled at it's strategy, and retreated into the recesses of CodL's thoughts, to keep watch over CodL — it's friend, it's enemy, and it's victim.

'It' did not stray to far though.

Chapter 52

We Will Host Our Hosts Said Bocc

Laurra stood before them

Time had absolutely flown by for the Initiates in Neptuna. They were completely rested and had been shown the Neptuna many would never experience.

One evening, when all were lounging within a cozy room watching the ongoing sea adventure swim by, Laurra surprisingly stood before them, saying...

"I have something to bring up for discussion."

Turning to Laurra, they all waited attentively, curious to hear what she wanted to discuss.

"As we are all aware," Laurra began, "we have been here for some time now, resting, exploring, happily becoming better acquainted with each other and with our wonderful hosts. I realize our Wisdom Path Journey has no definitive time restraints and we are free to continue, or to return as we each individually see fit — but, I believe the journey and it's varied encounters, including it's trials, as well as it's good times are intended to help us to bond, to trust, and to become a family of friends. The Wisdom Path is to share all that accompanies a journey of this magnitude."

"Personally, I feel most fortunate that I was allowed to become an Initiate and speaking for myself, I can say that I have experienced many emotions and feel love for each of you. But I know there is more, my friends. I know my Path continues."

"Annuj is not with us at this time to offer her input. She has gone off on an unexpected path of her own choosing and we all wish her the very best. It too is part of her individual journey."

"I believe the time has arrived, at least for me, to continue my Wisdom Path Journey. I understand we have all expressed intentions to explore the Tombs again, which I feel can also be a possibility for those who choose to do so at this time. I have also considered the thought that perhaps we could go separate ways, meeting up at an agreed upon time and location. This could allow for some personal time and perhaps varied personal experiences to share later during our reunion. I now offer this up for discussion."

"I am open to suggestions," she said, returning to her seat.

For a moment everyone remained quiet, all considering their own feelings regarding Laurra's comments, and somewhat surprised. But, as they each began to look around their small group, bright, enthusiastic, and energetic smiles were appearing from them all.

"Thank you, Laurra," spoke Calla.

"Being here in Neptuna has been absolutely fulfilling and a much needed rest, but I too have been anticipating our next destination. I am beginning to feel antsy."

Standing, Bocc added...

"And I also. Calla. But, I have an additional thought. If we all agree, I propose we give a farewell party for our hosts to offer our thanks and well wishes for the hospitality afforded us. They have been so generous."

"Well put, Bocc," said Patto, sitting between Poona and Laurra.

"I totally agree. Given the overall purpose of our journey, I too am inclined to be on our way, and yes, Bocc, let us 'host our hosts' who have given so much of their time and love."

Poona had remained silent, waiting to hear the opinions given by the Initiates, but finally asked...

"Is there a direction, or destination we can all agree on? We will also need to inform Annuj of these thoughts, and our ensuing intentions, so she may consider joining us, or not. She could very well wish to spend more time at SeaCliff with her family. I could certainly understand if she did."

Poona then stood, and in an authoritative, but quiet voice, said,

"Another important point to consider is my position as Caregiver for 'all' the Initiates involved in this journey. While I may understand and respect your thoughts on various paths for a period of time, please remember I was selected to be here for all of you in case of any need. Mental, emotional, or physical. If we decide to separate for a short time, for your own personal journey, that is assuredly permitted."

"I must, however, have your solemn promise that immediate contact with me be initiated should any problem or crisis occur that would require my assistance. We all have our Palm Recorders and there are the natural crystal transmissions that will always be available. Trust me, I will find a means of reaching you — and quickly. This is imperative to my agreeing to what you, as individual Initiates, or as a group decide to do — and have a right to do."

There was a silence of thoughts.

Each Initiate reflected on how they would like to experience their path at this time, keeping Poona's considerations and involvement in mind.

Poona turned and looked at Laurra sitting quietly next to her.

"Laurra, is all well, you appear tired?"

"Yes Poona, I do feel somewhat tired, but I believe it may be the anxiousness and promise of the continuing journey that is affecting me just now. I feel, no, I 'know' I am continuing to improve, Poona. Thank you for asking though."

"Trust me, all is well."

"Alright," Poona said, "feeling apprehensive.

I must continue watching Laurra closely. Perhaps the healing still continues, or perhaps this trek is taking more of a toll on Laurra than considered!

They reached a decision to give themselves the evening to weigh their choices. As individuals, each would consider their wishes and then meet early to discuss their options and decide on a plan.

The morning came and over a fine breakfast they shared the scenarios that each Initiate indicated would fulfill this part of their journey for them as an individual. After all was said and various options offered for consideration, it was decided to split up for a short while, reuniting at Oneness.

Patto, Laurra, and Poona indicated they wished to visit the tomb once more and then explore the westerly side of the Carbonian Desert, along an ancient trading route long since abandoned and rarely used.

It would be an easier route for Laurra, thought Poona, *given the surface should be packed hard from past use, and the prospect of encountering a Prismaworm was highly unlikely. But then, maybe not,* she reconsidered. *In this desert who knows.*

Bocc, and Calla opted to explore along the coast and then cut across a short expanse of the Carbonian Desert to the east, bringing them to Oneness.

Patto offered...

"It makes sense if we travel up through the tunnel, past the ancient tombs we want to revisit, and arrive at SeaCliff. We can visit with Annuj, and from there we can go our separate ways. We must contact Annuj today to give her time to choose between the different routes, or her own Path ... that is, of course, if she is indeed ready to venture forth yet."

Calla asked for a moment to consider, with Bocc, whether they would prefer to begin from the shore, right above Neptuna, and venture up the coast from there, rather than going through the tunnel again.

Bocc agreed with Calla to start along the coast here.

Except for Annuj, all was decided.

All the Initiates were happy and satisfied with their choices. They could look forward to sharing their journeys and hearing of the other's adventures when they all arrived in Oneness.

It was agreed.

Laurra, being the initial initiator, was selected to contact King Luxxor and Queen Liluuc, informing them of their plans and of their departure date in three days ... and of the 'thank you' party the Initiates wished to provide for them.

Bocc was selected to coordinate the farewell party for the King and Queen and family in two days hence.

Chapter 53

You May Not Be Aware, My Chosen One ... But

Queen Liliuuc In The King and Queen's Chambers

The party was held 2 days later and it left the hosts and their hosts laughing and crying in happiness. All agreed this should be an annual event.

King Luxxor informed them that he would accompany the Initiates, Patto and Laurra and Caregiver Poona, to what they were now calling, the Tomb of the Silver Crystal — within the Tomb of Antiquity — within the Passage of Antiquity, where they could have a last visit before saying their farewells until another time.

Poona, and Laurra had asked King Luxxor for the opportunity to once again visit this special place in order to experience and honor the marvels enclosed within, perhaps for the last time. This pleased King Luxxor very much.

Pride was not an emotion King Luxxor generally felt comfortable with, or felt was beneficial, as it often revolved around personal glory, but in this case, with discoveries of such magnitude in the Tomb of Antiquity, he believed it to be a Neptunian honor.

King Luxxor, however, now had one last request to consider before the group departed for the tomb and their continuing Wisdom Path Journey. It was a decision that weighed upon his mind. His son Tunnis asked if he would be allowed to join the Initiates as they continued to Oneness.

"I have asked the Initiates," Tunnis had excitedly said, "and they conveyed there is nothing saying it was forbidden, and that, yes, they would welcome my company, father ... should you and mother agree."

"My son," he said, "I am sure the Initiates are as happy as I am that you wish to accompany them to Oneness. Of course, this is a decision I wish to include your Mother in, as I am sure you can understand. We will speak in the morning."

King Luxxor could think of no reason for Tunnis not to join them. Tunnis was a part of most activities the Initiates were involved in and he felt they honestly would welcome his son's company. He realized that were it not for Tunnis and Dolpho, they would not even be aware of the passage and all that has followed since it's disclosure.

"This will be our sons first time away for any length of time," he said later, while speaking with his Chosen One, Liluuc in their private chambers.

"What is your impression, Liluuc? As for me, I have no reservation at all. The Initiates are remarkable, good, bright Beings, and I like them."

Queen Liluuc, who had been looking down at the scenic quaint little streets below, thought for a moment and then walking over, snuggled up beside Luxxor.

She laid her head upon his shoulder and sighed.

"Oh Luxxor, our little one is growing up and sometimes I feel it is way to fast. Of course, I am sure it is nothing more than a mother's love for her son and not wanting the moment to come when he will leave the nest, but nevertheless..."

Luxxor put his arm around Liluuc, consoling her.

"I do understand, Liluuc and I too have similar feelings from time to time. We have never been apart from our children for long, my Chosen One. Ever! Actually, in my case, Liluuc, our little Dolpho is the center of my concern."

"Dolpho is not a little girl anymore, my Chosen One. She has become a lovely young woman. Oh, they make me so happy."

"I know, my Queen, but as a father, I believe that it is good when his son matures and becomes a man — his own man. A man who goes out into a world of his own choosing and begins his life. Normally, in that scenario, I would include the expression, 'hopefully with the good values he has learned along the way,' but my Chosen One, with you as his mother, I have never had to worry about our children knowing values."

He smiled lovingly.

"However, you know Liluuc, a father always worries about his little girl ... who she will meet and fall in love with. I want everything to be wonderful for her as well."

They were quiet for a short time, reflecting on their words and aspirations for their children, Tunnis and Dolpho.

Liluuc, rolled her eyes up to Luxxors.

"You may not be aware, my Chosen One, but Tunnis is definitely showing an interest in Laurra."

Luxxor sat back and looked at Liluuc with wide, amused eyes.

"He is?"

"Yes, Luxxor, he most definitely is, and this is his mother telling you so. Who could tell better than me?"

Her eyes were beginning to twinkle and mist up simultaneously.

"Well," exclaimed Luxxor, "I will say this, Tunnis certainly has good taste.

Laurra is lovely, and bright ... and a tad mysterious, if I may say. His good taste in women must have come from me!"

He grinned mischievously — "As I chose you!"

Beaming back, Liluuc softly said...

"Oh, Luxxor, Tunnis has become a young man and right before our very eyes."

"Then, I now understand completely," Luxxor replied. "Of course he wanted to accompany them. He may not see Laurra for some time, and, well, if it were me, and if it were you in the same situation, I would certainly want to share as much time as possible with you too."

Queen Liluuc, eyes now tearing, whispered...

"Oh, Luxxor, I knew you would understand and be happy that our son is, well ... coming of age. You are so wise."

Then, not skipping a beat, Liluuc continued...

"You are also so very tender, nostalgic, sentimental, softhearted ... and romantic, my Chosen One."

Gazing at Luxxor playfully she kittenishly purred...

"Allow me to pour us a Loctuum and we will celebrate our joy."

"My one desire, Liluuc, is that our children are as unbelievably blessed as I have been. I love you."

Then, sitting back, he reflected.

"So, Tunnis is enchanted by the lovely Laurra, Hmmm!"

"Yes, my Chosen One, he definitely is."

She looked playfully at Luxxor.

"Do you have any thoughts or suggestions for celebrating, my King?"

She handed him his Loctuum, her eyes smiling mischievously.

"Definitely," he said, raising his glass to hers.

Their glasses clinked as they met.

Much later Liluuc whispered in Luxxor's ear...

"You know, my Chosen One, it may be the time to have a father and son chat about ... well, you know, life, and how it all begins — the birds and the bees — the you's and the me's!"

King Luxxor's eyes opened wide as he considered his Chosen One's suggestion.

"Oh my," he said, "I must do it tomorrow. Tunnis leaves in two days."

"Oh, my !"

Chapter 54

Are All The 'Baby Spiders' At The Ready

FinnJonko

FinnJonko paced the floor, walking in circles around the 'Slice of Heaven.'

There were two separate situations being shown that needed attention and he was determining which deserved their actions first. The answer was actually relatively simple, as one situation was still a week or so off before any confrontation could be a possibility, while the other situation was fairly close by, involving a craft sitting on an asteroid.

And, for what possible reason — stranded, or waiting, he considered? *We know that three Rogue Spacial Probes were detected recently in this general vicinity,* Finn considered. *We have also been tracking craft #1 for a few weeks now, and know it to be a RogueRecon craft due to its size. For some inexplicable reason it has landed on an asteroid, and has remained there ever since.*

The other situation, Craft #2, is definitely from the RogueEmpireComplex, he surmised, *and substantially larger ... possibly a Warrior series ship that CodL was known to have.*

FinnJonko knew that if CodL himself was in command it was a formidable ship and there would be considerable DarkCape forces aboard for whatever illegal activity he had in mind. He was not yet convinced of a connection between the two Rogue crafts however, although it was not uncommon for a smaller precursor vessel, like a RogueScout, or Rogue Recon ship to precede a main vessel.

They had prepared for this possible encounter for some time and it now appeared as though LesterJonko may be getting his wish ... to catch, and to stop the tyrant CodL once and for all.

FinnJonko knew where to reach his father. It was after his shift and where else would he be other than his favorite 'Spot' on board the 'Black

Widow' — the 'Red Spot.' Sure enough, LesterJonko was just finishing his second libation when the message from his son came through.

Quickly arriving back at the Control Center, LesterJonko briskly walked over to the SpacialGram hovering about three feet from the floor. What he saw was two SpacialGrams side by side indicating 2 different 'Slices of Heaven' for them to view simultaneously.

"Father," said FinnJonko, looking up from some notes he had prepared.

"Son," answered LesterJonko, more than anxious to hear the latest regarding what he knew would involve CodL.

"What do we have?"

"We have created two areas of interest that hover here before you, father.

While initially concentrating on the RogueRecon scouting craft that has been sitting on an asteroid for some time now, we decided to create the area in which CodL uses for his home base, The RogueEmpireComplex, to see if there was any unusual activity. CodL is on the left as you are viewing the SpacialGram.

We activated the infra heat ray detectors and found what we believe to be a large RogueWarrior Ship heading in the general direction of the Rogue scout craft. It is possibly a week away as it has much more powerful deep space thrust capacities than their scout crafts and is catching up quickly. It seems unusual to us that they would send such a powerful ship to help out a disabled craft, if indeed it is disabled."

"Is there anything else going on that arouses any suspicions," LesterJonko asked.

"Well, we have noticed higher than normal heat levels along the edges of specific areas in and around the galaxy including Planet 8 of Galaxy17, but, curiously enough, there is nothing we could detect physically to allow for, or explain the elevated heat levels."

"So, perhaps it is only an anomaly, father."

"Perhaps, son, but perhaps not. Keep a close eye on Planet 8. It seems to have aroused the curiosity of my friend CodL and that concerns me."

"Are all the 'Baby Spiders' at the ready?"

"Yes, we completely went over each and every 'Spider' since discovering the goings on involving CodL."

"They are ready!"

"Good, son … good."

Chapter 55

King Luxxor's Version Of The Facts Of Life

Tunnis and Dolpho leaned forward with eyes wide

"So my son, you are becoming quite the young man. You. have certainly demonstrated good judgement, a chivalrous manner and if I may add, a sense of interest in the fairer sex."

Tunnis sat, gazing at his father, waiting.

With no response offered by his son, King Luxxor, pacing back and forth before Tunnis, albeit somewhat more nervously, continued.

Hmmm, Leading the people of Neptuna is one thing, but explaining how fishes create minnows is quite another. My brow is wet, and my lips are dry!

Odd combination, he mused. *I will rue the day I promised my Chosen One that I would take care of this matter.*

He pressed on.

"My son, love and commitment should be the precursor to a deeper involvement and enjoyment of two Beings. The gifts two consenting Beings offer the other, beyond that which naturally comes with friendship of course, are beautiful and decidedly more personal. It is an attraction you will recognize, my son, as being, well, different from feelings for a friend ... as it will ignite certain emotions ... perhaps not experienced before."

King Luxxor paused. He turned to face out the window and wiped his brow and wet his very dry lips. Turning back he looked for any reaction from his son, but Tunnis just continued to sit there, looking at him.

Feigning a cough, King Luxxor took a deep breath.

"You see, my son, both you and your sister Dolpho have reached an age of maturity where your mother and I feel it is necessary ... well, maybe not necessary, but needed — no, that isn't it either," he stammered.

Tunnis then spoke...

213

"Father, does the subject you speak of involve babies, and the differences between men and women Beings?"

King Luxxor stood before Tunnis, considering his response.

He uttered, "Well…"

Tunnis, gazing intently, but smiling within, decided to end the pain his father was obviously experiencing.

"Father, please be aware that only recently Dolpho and I have discussed this very subject. So you, father, as always, are very astute in regards to your timing in broaching this discussion. I assure you we are both emotionally mature and capable in understanding the whys, the whens, and the hows of your concerns. Actually, father, Dolpho is just outside your Sanctuary, and at your beckon will happily join us."

King Luxxor, had not moved, and standing with his hands clasped behind his back, rocked back and forth on his feet continuing to feel bewildered and somewhat embarrassed.

"My son, since you and Dolpho are already showing an interest of that which I speak, I can think of no reason to not include your sister."

Turning to open the door, he silently prayed…

Since both are apparently expressing an interest, perhaps my task — no, my obligation, he corrected himself, *will hopefully be less arduous than I have envisioned and fretted over.*

Opening the door he glanced out and spied Dolpho, who was sitting nearby, looking, well, very much like a young woman.

"Please come in my daughter, and join us."

"Yes, father, thank you," Dolpho responded, entering and sitting beside Tunnis.

Oh where is my Chosen One when I need her, King Luxxor wishfully pondered.

Seating himself at his desk, but feeling that was not correct, arose, and stood behind his desk, attempting to come across as one in control of his thoughts.

He began, "Dolpho, it occurs to me to inquire if you would like your mother, the Queen, to be in attendance?"

"No father, I am quite comfortable," Dolpho replied, crossing one leg over the other, and looking expectantly at him with her large, and King Luxxor now noticed, intoxicating eyes.

"I see," said King Luxxor. "Well then, here we are."

"Yes, father, here we are," they harmoniously responded.

"Yes, indeed," he uttered.

"Well Dolpho, as I was saying to your brother Tunnis, your mother and

I feel you are both emotionally mature and have demonstrated sensitivities worthy of a young adult entering adulthood … such as it is," he stuttered.

"It is not uncommon at this time in one's life that one begins to notice and perhaps become curious of certain 'things' you had not noticed before, or at least become aware of these 'things' in a different way."

"By 'things', are you referring to the differences between a man and a woman, father," asked Dolpho?

"Yes, my Princess, I am," he said, wiping his brow once again.

"Does it seem unusually warm within the Dome of Life to you, today," he inquired.

"No, I am quite comfortable," answered Tunnis.

"I, also, father," said Dolpho.

"I see. Perhaps my robe is just a little heavy for the occasion."

King Luxxor sat down at his desk and regarded his children … his young maturing adult Beings. Taking his robe off from around his shoulders, King Luxxor leaned back in his chair, touching the tips of his fingers together and with as relaxed a voice as he could muster, said…

"You see, my children, there comes a time when Beings can become attracted to each other in ways beyond friendship. You just cannot wait to be with the other and never want to be without the other. When this occurs, and after a length of time, most Beings generally choose to create a bond together, a bond which lasts for their lifetimes. This bond is that of becoming a couple, like your mother, and I, you see."

Pausing, he smiled at the thought of Liluuc, his Chosen One, the Queen, but quickly brought himself back into the moment at hand and continued.

"We bond for reasons that include love, respect, creating a family, working together to make a better life for your family, and so on and so on."

Looking at them, he asked, "So far, so good?"

Both Tunnis and Dolpho smiled, nodding yes.

King Luxxor feeling more comfortable and confident by the moment felt rejuvenated.

"Good, Tunnis, Dolpho. I knew you would be receptive and grasp my message and intent."

"The family I speak of is when a man and a woman become a husband and wife, joining to share their lives together and generally to create a family."

Gesturing aimlessly and gazing at the ceiling of his Sanctuary, King Luxxor professed…

"We were all babies at one time."

Tunnis and Dolpho looked at each other with playful eyes and smiles.

"Creating a baby together with your Chosen One is one of the ultimate joys and gifts you will ever encounter. It certainly has been for your mother and me."

"Yes," he smiled, "a happiness that will change your lives forever. Falling in love and creating a tiny Being will come to you naturally, my young ones. No lessons, or experience is required."

King Luxxor rested his hands in front of him on the desk and feeling quite satisfied with his message and delivery, looked at his budding adults.

"Do you understand, and do you have any questions, or comments?"

Tunnis and Dolpho, cast a glance at each other.

"Father, thank you so much. I think Dolpho and I understand exactly what you mean. After all, we have had such exemplary examples for all our lives."

With twinkling eyes he looked at his sister.

"Is this not correct, Dolpho?"

"Yes, yes indeed, father," Dolpho replied. "Somehow, I believe Tunnis and I will be able to figure it out. We truly understand your concern, and mothers.

We sincerely thank you, father. You are being most helpful, and considerate.

King Luxxor standing, breathed in a huge sigh of relief and motioning for his son and daughter to come to him, embraced them in love.

Unbeknownst to King Luxxor, Tunnis, or Dolpho, Queen Liluuc had sequestered herself nearby and was listening in. She radiated approval and happiness. Quietly moving away, she strolled back to the Royal Suite, sat down, actually poured herself a small Loctuum and softly said…

"I do so love my Chosen One, and our children."

Chapter 56

Yogga, A Most Delightful Being

XennaOne

HighPriestess XennaOne sat across from her mother, Solannuj, former HighPriestess SolannaOne. They had stopped to rest on this small bluff enclosed on three sides by a beautiful array of green crystals.

Both agreed that the green colors of the crystals were soothingly peaceful and that this would be a perfect spot. It also afforded a slight view of the area below, where Oneness, their destination, awaited.

Later in the day the winds would begin their transformation from warm, to chilling, and oft times relentless, but, at this time it was mid afternoon, soft breezes were gently blowing to and fro against their exposed faces, lightly ruffling the gowns they wore.

It felt good.

They were returning from a most interesting encounter with a rather plump man named Yogga. Both had walked in silence ... each in her own thoughts. Solannuj was truly thankful for her daughter's presence here with her. She was still recovering and regaining her strength back, but at one point her energy had been so low she could not even be there for her oldest daughter Junnuj when she came out of DreamState. This saddened her immensely, rekindling regretful memories of an earlier time when she had also not been there for her children.

I was the HighPriestess, and in Spectrum, she thought, *but both Junnuj and Xennuj were so young and needing a mother ... and a father.*

Solannuj shook her head in sadness at the memory.

Letting it go she looked over at her daughter.

"I still require rest occasionally. Especially when at these higher altitudes, Xennuj. Just getting a little older I guess."

Xennuj, leaning comfortably against the warmth of a sea green crystal, nodded her head in understanding.

"Where did you ever hear of this man called Yogga, mother?"

"Casual chatter," replied Solannuj.

"Yogga was mentioned recently during a conversation I overheard at the reflective pool near the edge of Oneness. Some friends were discussing him and his form of enlightenment methods. It seems they had just returned from a visit with the man and were excited about his ideas, and curious mannerisms."

"I thought you may be curious too ... I was."

"How did they find out about him?"

"I am not sure, Xennuj, but apparently, out of nowhere, here was this unusual man, living high up the mountain and issuing forth a new approach to enlightenment while sitting in a crevice of crystals."

Xennuj chuckled at the vision.

Solannuj smiled humorously back at her daughter.

"He sounded intriguing, Xennuj and as there is little to do here in Oneness other than meditate, reflect, or be an artist, the chance to explore any interesting opportunity presenting itself becomes almost irresistible."

"And," she continued...

"I wished to enjoy this experience with you, the HighPriestess XennaOne, as my companion," she said winking at her daughter.

"You were coming home for a brief visit anyway and since I did not want to make the exhausting trek to his simple abode alone, I decided to drag you along!"

"Thanks, mother!"

They both laughed.

Oh, mother, thought, Xennuj, *it's moments like these that we lost — moments of feeling totally relaxed, unburdened by responsibilities and at ease with someone you love. Moments we all missed when we were young!*

"Just so you know, mother, for my part, I personally found the experience to be satisfying and intriguing. However, his ideas seem considerably less advanced in their development than what we are accustomed to in Spectrum.

So, what did you feel, or experience, mother?"

"As I see it, Xennuj, here he is, this rather plump man who calls himself Yogga. He is professing an ideology and advocating for what he describes is a new form of enlightenment requiring the practice of spiritual discipline, meditation, correct breathing, and body postures. Of course, I'm practically out of breath thinking about it!"

Stretching her legs out in front of her, Solannuj leaned back against a warm crystal herself, adding...

"Actually, Xennuj... I believe it is possible this is a very old practice being resurrected once again and that in itself could be an extremely good thing. As far as I am concerned, Yogga turned out to be a compelling man and I find his practice and methods to be invigorating. It certainly has my blood flowing."

"I will admit, Yogga is indeed an amusing and captivating individual. He definitely advocates more of a physical form of meditation and posturing than we practice today. Still, in a way, I too found it rewarding, and I would do it again. I suppose that constitutes a positive review of my experience today, mother."

"Well, I must agree with you that Yogga is quite a delightful person. It is mysterious though, is it not, that we have never heard of him before? Apparently he is not known in Spectrum, Xennuj, or you would be aware of him. Where could he possibly have come from?"

Xennuj shook her head implying she did not know.

"I will look into it, mother. Perhaps he is from the lands beyond. If he is of Amythesia, a 'Clarification of Being' will be registered. The further we get out of the Quins there are obviously many things we are not aware of."

They lapsed into silence for a short while, quietly putting the experiences and thoughts of this day into a quiet place to call on later when needed.

Both were enjoying sharing this little respite, breathing in the crisp, cool crystal mountain air, and resting in their thoughts.

"We must leave soon, mother, before cooler winds set in.

"Just a little longer, Xennuj. I treasure these moments."

Cupping her chin in her hands, Xennuj shared a thought...

"You know, mother, as a child, I can remember coming here with you and Junnuj. We used to come quite frequently to this area. I always looked forward to it, and still do. Do you recall we once visited the cave Yogga meditates and teaches in today?"

Smiling, Solannuj reflected back to those days long past.

"Oh, yes, I remember it well, my daughter. Were you aware, that my mother, Lannuj, your grandmother, used to teach me wonderful things here, also?

She and I would 'SilentMind' for long periods of time, and then, while I continued to meditate, your grandmother would inform me of 'Things Past', and of the 'Wisdom of the Ancients', and of 'Healing of the Ancients.'

Wonderful things, Xennuj.

I honored, and passed them on to you and your sister, Junnuj ... once in the very cave we were in today."

"Ah, I do remember ... the 'Wisdom of the Ancients,' and 'Healing of the Ancients' were my favorites."

"You carried on the tradition well, mother."

"Your grandmother, LannaOne, became the very first HighPriestess from our family lineage," said Solannuj.

"Yes, I recall the stories you used to tell us. As you are aware I have researched grandmother LannaOne in the 'Clarification of Being' files in Spectrum. Grandmother was indeed the initiator of many good things in Amythesia."

Suddenly, Xennuj reentered the formality her position and title denoted.

It was the HighPriestess XennaOne who now continued the conversation.

Rising, XennaOne moved over and knelt in front of her mother.

Gently clasping Solannuj's hands in hers, she softly looked at her mother.

"You taught and shared as well as you could, mother, but we have paid a heavy price … health wise, as a family, and in upholding the stresses that accompany the position of HighPriestess of the Voice of One. I speak particularly of my sister, Junnuj, and, of course, you, mother."

Solannuj, looking downcast, nodded her agreement, recognizing it was XennaOne, the HighPriestess now speaking.

"I had so hoped to see Junnuj during my visit," XennaOne said sadly, "but, as you will understand, I must return to my responsibilities in Spectrum soon and she needed time with her family."

"I have been informed Annuj has joined them."

"I have missed my sister so, but am so very elated that she has been released from Completion. I intend to visit her as soon as possible. Responsibilities will be put aside and have to wait for a while. The 'One' knows our dear Junnuj certainly has had to wait."

"Yes, Junnuj must have quality time to bond once again with her husband, BucchaSim, and her children. Ample time must be given for their reunion. It is an occasion of happiness and of great love," stated Solannuj.

"I am sure, mother," XennaOne said, agreeing, "but, it is my belief that Amythesia and the 'Voice of One' owe JunnaOne an immense debt of gratitude and acknowledgment for her effort. She performed magnificently as HighPriestess of Amythesia under exasperating and deplorable archaic laws that even you were forced to adhere to. Our family has suffered extreme sacrifices while administering the position of the HighPriestess of the Voice of One … and mother, I swear these issues will be resolved."

Solannuj sat quietly, in awe of her daughter's obvious determination and in reverence for her daughter, Junnuj.

Standing, in preparation to depart, XennaOne added…

"Additionally, mother, I was continually informed regarding my sister Junnuj's reentry and my understanding is that when her SoulMind reentered her body following DreamState, Junnuj responded very quickly. Her resolve to continue never faltered, and her hopelessness vanished. She must have willed it away … through love."

"Her readjustment to 'Being' was assisted by Lilonna, Queen Liluuc's personal Courtier in Waiting, XennaOne."

"Yes, we are exceptionally indebted to Lilonna, King Luxxor, Queen Liluuc, and those of Neptuna, mother."

"Yes, XennaOne, we are indeed."

"One final certainty I wish to share with you, mother…"

"And that is, XennaOne…"

"I will personally speak with Junnuj regarding the initiation of legal documents to be presented to the Council of the Voice of One for immediate amendments rectifying the situations we have just discussed. I will also personally fight for outright deletions pertaining to laws outdated or archaic — laws we, and others, have personally experienced as a family! Never again will unusual, and extreme sacrifices of 'health and family' play such a damaging role in the life of any HighPriestess of the Voice of One.

"I promise you," stated XennaOne defiantly!

Chapter 57

Until We Meet Again

King Luxxor watched for some time

King Luxxor, Tunnis, Poona, Laurra, and Patto, plus four Divine Guardians set out early for the Tomb of the Silver Crystal. The early morning chill brought some discomfort, but King Luxxor hardly noticed. He was consumed … somewhere between anxious and excited regarding his son Tunnis and the adventure that awaited him.

Tunnis has never been gone for the amount of time this journey to Oneness will take. I have a father's concern, he realized. *Everything will go according to plan,* he thought. *Everything will be fine. What an opportunity for a young man.*

He chuckled to himself … *the elation Tunnis had shown when he and Liluuc expressed their joy in agreeing to his adventure, and how...*

"We have arrived, our King."

The Divine Guardians had stopped just ahead and indicated they had arrived at the tomb. King Luxxor could hardly believe it.

I must have been totally engrossed, he considered, *which means I have been unduly rude to my guests this morning.*

"I do apologize, my friends," he said. "I have been negligent in my attentiveness, and deep into my own thoughts, and on this, your day of departure."

"I am sorry."

"Please, King Luxxor, no need," said Poona. "We have all been into our personal thoughts. Our journey is now leading us towards new directions which means we are departing the wonderful hospitality and friendship that you and Queen Liluuc, and all of Neptuna have extended to us. There are mixed emotions about leaving for each of us and we are all experiencing these feelings … happiness and yet sadness."

"Yes," said King Luxxor …"it has obviously been an especially wonderful time for us as well. You have become friends, sharing as a part of our family, and will definitely always remain a part of our extended family, for which we are grateful."

"None of us wishes for it to end, King Luxxor," added Laurra.

"So, I propose we do not allow for it to end. Let us say it is only a small pause until we meet again."

King Luxxor, smiled warmly.

The Divine Guardians opened the Chamber and lit the firelites within. In the receding darkness the heat and light from the flames brought inviting warmth. They made their way directly to the Tomb of the Crystal beyond the Ritual chamber rooms. The chill from their long and cold early morning trek quickly disappeared as the heat from the molten liquid crystal stream permeated the entire crystal area.

Peering at this sacred spot, Poona experienced the same awe and spiritual presence as before. No words were needed or spoken. Everyone else felt the aura of this presence too … a profound, but comforting presence.

King Luxxor ushered in his son Tunnis, and together they marveled at the silver crystal.

"Oh my, father. This is unlike any crystal I have ever seen."

"Yes, Tunnis, I agree. A feeling was offered that perhaps it was brought here for a reason."

"What could that be," asked Tunnis looking up at his father.

"We just do not know, my son. Crystals are amazing objects. It could be symbolic, or meant as a communication of some sort. Perhaps it contains messages meant for us. And, it could be just what we see, a beautiful silver crystal."

"If there is a hidden meaning it is for us to discover. For me, my son, if nothing else, it is a spiritually inspiring piece."

Tunnis's eyes widened.

"We will discover it's meaning, father."

King Luxxor smiled and hugged his son close to his side.

Forming a small semi circle they sat before the the glowing silver crystal, watching in reverence.

King Luxxor invited the 4 Guardians to join.

The glow emitted from the stream of liquid colors flowing by reflected off of the crystal and flickered onto the irregular walls. A total sense of wonderment consumed them all as the silver crystal continued to emit a sense of timeless mystery, as if asking …

"What is my purpose, and what is yours … How did I come to exist …

Am I to fulfill your dreams, your fantasies, your truths ... Or, is it just that I am ... and, that you are?"

They sat for some time, before Laurra arose and walked up to the crystal.

Placing her hands and cheek upon it's warm surface, she uttered...

"I believe I can feel the pulsating glow."

In turn they each followed and did the same, sharing in it's personal message to each of them.

Finally, all knew it was time to say their goodbyes to the crystal. In their own private thoughts before departing they knew that on this morning they were given a gift. A gift to take into their worlds ... to share.

As two Divine Guardians, the Initiates, Poona and Tunnis walked further up the tunnel passage towards SeaCliff and their ensuing journey, King Luxxor stood and watched.

The flickering light of the firelites faded and they were no longer visible.

Only then did he and the remaining Guardians turn to go back home.

Chapter 58

Openings In The Cliff

There is no bird dung

Bocc and Calla departed the same time as the others had left for the Tomb of the Crystal. they were transported to the surface where they began their personal journey along The Sea of The Forgotten Place.

Sharing warm days, and brisk nights, they meandered along on their chosen Wisdom Path. They were blessed with glorious skies, soft, warm breezes and the salty smells of the sea.

It was exhilarating.

They lost track of time.

Once, in the distance, they witnessed dark and foreboding storm clouds preparing to assail the Carbonian desert lying to the South and the East. Thankful they were far removed. Pausing, they offered thoughts of safety for those who chose to follow the desert path.

Bocc, often secluded himself for long periods of time writing and recording his thoughts, occasionally sharing a poem, or a thought with Calla when she became lonely.

In general, Calla was content in exercising, and exploring during Bocc's quiet times. During one of these moments, while lounging on the shore, she noticed what appeared to be three narrow openings in the side of the cliff. Huge slabs of stone had apparently broken free from the cliff face and cascaded to the sandy shore below, revealing openings once hidden.

They were located high above on the the face of the cliffs, and she could see no way of reaching them. Continuing to focus on these, she became mesmerized and her imagination took flight as to their purpose.

The openings do not seem exceptionally large from where I am studying them, she considered. *They could possibly be nothing more than crevices in the rock formed eons ago. But, they are so compelling. Are they sending me a message?*

Calla slipped deeper into her imagination …

Could it be that in a long ago forgotten time, before part of the land had sunk beneath The Sea of the Forgotten Place, these openings were indeed passageways created by some great race of Beings? Perhaps a part of some fantastic corridor system of an ancient city. Maybe at one time they were part of an above ground ancient city, she theorized. *Of course, the openings could be nothing more than natural nests for birds …*

"and nests for large birds, too," she said aloud while looking at the sky for signs of Gattlings.

No, she finally affirmed in her mind, *it is the uniformity of shape and size of the 3 openings that guide my instincts.*

Calla stood and put her hands on her hips. She stared intently, as she talked to herself.

"I am sure that their true and original purpose must have been passages. Or, maybe worm holes. Yes, that could be a real possibility too. But no _ They are not the same shape as a worm hole, Calla. They must be part of some ancient civilization, long forgotten like the Ritual rooms we recently explored in the worm tunnels."

Calla then began struggling with the name of the city they were told about. It was lost long ago, covered and hidden by the ever changing sands of the Carbonian Desert. It was supposedly the city that came long before Neptuna.

It is a huge desert, she thought. *Is it even remotely possible I could stumble across a city so long lost, and so long searched for. Could it be that these three openings have only recently surfaced,* she surmised. *Surely they would have been noticed by fishermen, or travelers before now.*

Calla ran up the shore to find Bocc.

Involved in a lengthy bit of prose, Bocc was not pleased, and unhappy about the interruption. But upon listening to Calla, and seeing her enthusiasm and eagerness, he put aside his initial reaction and patiently followed her back to the mysterious passages she described.

"They are probably nothing more than a nesting place for all the birds we see," said Bocc, studying the openings above.

"I thought of that, but…"

"Calla, seriously, what else could they be? Look how far up on the face of the cliff they are. Actually, they would be easier to access from on top of the cliff than from down here."

"Yes, I agree. It will be a formidable climb, but I believe they were not meant to be entered from either down here or from on top. I am sure, Bocc, that they are passages and I have no idea where the surface entrance could be."

"Yes it would be, Calla, and — wait a second, did you just say 'WILL' be a formidable climb?"

Calla smiling excitedly, looked at Bocc with expectation, and quickly said,

"Bocc, just imagine what secrets could be hidden there."

"Well, yes, I can imagine, Calla. A lot of birds, and bird dung," he said, with a smile beginning to form.

"No doubt, my clever but unimaginative poet, but what if ..."

Calla's eyes smiled mischievously and provocatively as she let her question fall away into the ethereal Heavens, leaving it to Bocc's curiosity.

Sitting back, they watched intently for a while as Gattling birds continued to enter and leave, repeating the pattern time and time again. They noticed that once in a while a little head would pop out looking around curiously.

"I have to concede, Calla, they do have uniform shapes which in itself is unusual for three distinct rock openings."

"You know, Bocc, it is very possible these have not been visible before. Look at the base of the cliff. There are large chunks of stone laying piled up on the sand. They must have fallen off revealing the openings."

"I am beginning to believe it is possible, Calla."

"Dare we," she asked.

"Dare we not," he replied, jumping up and reaching out to pull her to her feet. They scurried nearer the cliff base and determined the distance up to the openings to be at 100 feet or more.

"I see no way up from here. No path or footholds at all."

"I do recall a crevice about a mile or so back that might gain us access to the top," offered Calla.

Tilting his head back, and casting his sight to the Heavens above, Bocc jumped upon a nearby rock, proclaiming...

"If it is possible to achieve the openings in the cliff confronting us, let us get on with braving the dangers of the vast unknown, let us go where, hopefully, no worm has gone before ... and decided to stay," he grinned, turning to look at Calla.

"Let us go back and see," he replied, standing posed as a poet on a pillar, arms pointing forward, and eyes appearing lost in a distant trance.

Calla stood looking at Bocc with her hands on her hips, shaking her head.

The climb up the crevice, and then to where the openings loomed beneath them took almost 3 hours. They were both perspiring even though the breeze from the sea was constantly blowing. It had been an invigorating climb to the top.

After cooling off and having a bite to eat, they began to tackle the problem of how to access the openings.

"Well," Bocc stated, "they look to be about 20 feet below where we are standing."

Calla, peered cautiously over the edge.

"The sea appears so vast from up here, and hardly a sound is heard from the waves rushing in far below. I can only hear the cackle of the Gattlings and the slight hum of the breeze blowing the desert sand around."

"Don't pay to much heed to the birds," Bocc stated.

"It is probably only a warning for us to stay away."

"And if we don't stay away?"

"Then, being large Gattlings, they will undoubtably scoop you up and deposit you out in the middle of the Sea," he said, breaking into a large smile.

"Funny!" Calla replied, grinning!

"How do we get down there. It is pretty sheer and we don't have any rope."

They sat, exploring the few options available but decided all were to dangerous given their circumstance.

"Maybe we have not thought of all the options, Bocc. Perhaps there is an entrance up here. Remember how BucchaSim found the entrance to the worm tunnel from the cave he made his home? He was on a cliff too, and, well …"

She shrugged, as if saying why can't we find one too?

"Great suggestion, Calla, let's look around. There are a few crystal clusters jutting up, and, who knows, maybe an entrance too." he said, smiling brightly.

Only 30 minutes later Calla shrieked, and called out to Bocc who was a short distance away examining a patch of amber crystals.

"What did you find?"

"There is an opening between these crystals, Bocc. It's small, but maybe…"

Lowering himself to the ground, he attempted to peer into a small opening only slightly larger than his hand.

"This is about the size of a Geoddie," he said.

"Maybe this is where all the Geoddies come from." Grimacing, he stuck his arm in up to his elbow. Turning back to Calla he said…

"The bad news is — it is pretty small. The good news is I believe it is a void and there is a slight draft blowing out meaning another opening somewhere, Calla … perhaps the entrances you found!"

Calla, bubbling over in excitement, fell to her knees and they

228

immediately began to enlarge the opening by clearing away the sand and loose crystal chips. Finally they created an opening large enough for them to snuggly slip through one at a time.

Bocc selected a couple of medium size stones and tossed one in.

They heard it hit something solid.

"There is apparently solid footing in there, but I can't see a thing," he said.

He looked at Calla, and gestured, saying…

"You can go first Calla. I have heard tell that a gentleman should always open the door for the lady to enter first. I realize in this case it is only a hole, but still, ladies first …"

Calla cast a look at Bocc with a 'you got to be kidding me' expression.'

"I believe you have just as much right to go first as me, Bocc — but, thank you, I will now enter the dark, and unknown abyss … first!"

"No Calla, I was only kidding around," exclaimed Bocc, beginning to feel bad about his joke.

"Well, I was not, and in I go."

Calla squeezed, and slithered into the opening … and disappeared.

Bocc, anxiously waited before Calla called out

"It gets larger about 10 feet in, Bocc. My eyes are slowly adjusting to the darkness, but it is large enough to where I can crawl now. I just wish we had one of those firelites."

Bocc squirmed through the opening and caught up quickly.

"Lets go slow, Calla, we must make sure we can turn around if we need to get out of here. I certainly don't want to get stuck in what might be a wormhole with a worm coming at me!"

Calla's eyes widened at the mention of a wormhole, but she said…

"It's remarkably smooth in here, Bocc. I believe we could have discovered something crafted by the hands of Beings, not worms."

Crawling slowly, Bocc answered…

"So far it's only a small tunnel which could be natural, or created by hand, or maybe small worms once played here. But you are right, Calla, so far there are no scratchings like we found in the larger tunnel."

"I feel the draft more strongly now and the passage continues to get larger, Bocc. It just has to be the tunnel from the openings we saw."

Bocc stopped crawling.

Rising to his feet, he said, "Guess what, Calla?"

"What, Bocc?"

"Three things … first, I can see you, so that means we are near a light source of some kind. Second, as you can see it appears we can now stand."

"And the third thing," she smiling asked?'

"NO BIRD DUNG ... YET!"

Calla threw back her head in laughter.

Bosc and Calla both sat down, delightfully exhausted, and rested against the warm wall of the small tunnel.

"You know it is to late to return to the shore. It may be warmer in this tunnel than down on the sands with the cold evening winds howling about," Calla said.

"Well, I believe we brought enough supplies and blankets in my pack for just such an emergency," responded Bocc.

They spent a cool night cuddled together for warmth, awaking just before dawn with the arrival of the Mother SunneLavva.

After eating a little of the remaining food they had brought with them, Calla and Bocc ventured further before reaching a 'T' in the passageway. It was obvious from the sound, and the light, plus the newly discovered accumulated bird dung, that the openings to the sea were to their right.

"The unknown openings we saw are that way, Bocc."

"Yes, Calla, but the passage to our left is the real unknown and mysterious way. It appears to lead even deeper under the sands of the Carbonian Desert.

But, it is really dark that way!"

"We should have firelites, and more provisions to explore further."

"Oh, but I do wish to continue, Bocc," Calla sadly exclaimed. Looking at Calla, and then glancing down the inky dark tunnel, Bocc turned to Calla...

"Alright, Calla, me too, but we will go slowly. This could lead to an abyss!"

"An abyss!"

Calla's face suddenly went pale!

Inching their way deeper into the unknown darkness their eyes eventually adjusted and they were actually able to see each other and things nearby.

They began to feel more at ease.

Hours passed. With the light available they examined walls, and slowly shuffled their way farther in. On occasion they discovered what could be a marking on the wall, but in the murkiness nothing was definite.

Finally, Bocc said...

"We will have to be patient, Calla. Lets head back to the shore and let King Luxxor know of our discovery when we reach Oneness. He will certainly want to help and if what we feel is correct, it is truly the people of Neptuna who should rightfully be doing most of this."

"Given the hour and the time needed to retrace our steps, it will be some time after nightfall before we can reach the shore campsite, Bocc."

"Hmmm, you are right. Why don't we make our way back to the high cliff openings you first discovered from below. We can settle in for another evening."

Calla agreed ... secretly smiling mischievously.

The return went quickly. They pulled out the blankets and supplies and suddenly feeling famished, quickly finished off the remaining food and most of the water before settling back to view the setting Mother SunneLavva — soon to relinquish her spot in the Heavens.

"The Gattlings have apparently abandoned this spot, at least until the intruders have gone or have been vanquished," stated Bocc.

"Intruders," questioned, Calla?

"Yes ... us, Calla!"

"Oh!"

The sky did not materialize into what they expected It rapidly turned to a dark gray. A gathering breeze filled with salty moisture blew into their faces as they watched the waves grow in intensity. The sky formed ominous, quickly moving clouds blowing in from the west.

"This looks extremely foreboding, Calla. I am glad we are here, high above the sea, and not on the shore."

Cuddling closer together for warmth, they listened to the wind continue to intensify, now accompanied by huge, guttural belches of thunder that they felt for sure would dislodge the very walls of the passage. It signaled impending danger was approaching.

The shore below was experiencing obvious manifestations of extreme upheaval. Gusts of moisture, and sand ladened wind reaching all the way to the top of the cliffs was stinging their faces, relentless against all within it's path. Squinting and guarding their eyes from the howling wind and sand they witnessed the whitecaps becoming fiercer. The ferocity of the approaching storm came closer and closer.

They watched, as the last remaining Gattlings that were still on the shore snatched up whatever fish and crustaceans that were being tossed about and quickly retreated to the safety of the cliff caves.

But not theirs.

"Oh Goodness, can it possibly become worse," yelled Calla, above the noise. However, Bocc was totally enthralled in the unfolding drama of the storm's brute aggressiveness. He reveled at nature's beautiful and natural display of power. Holding Calla tightly, Bocc, ever the poet, stated...

"This is the Sea of the Forgotten Place in all it's fury, Calla. We are captivated captives of this moment in time. Let us appreciate our good fortune!"

She snuggled even closer and speaking loudly, now struggling to be heard, expressed...

"This excites me, Bocc. I have only heard about something of this magnitude. A hard rain is all we ever experienced in my Quin Ebonisia."

Eye squinting streaks of white lightning then preceded loud claps of preposterous thunder rising to a boisterous crescendo that seemed to shake the cliffs themselves.

"Why do I hear thunder sometimes, but not see the lightning," Calla asked.

"The lightning can be within the clouds, and not always visible," Bocc replied loudly. Although it is probable you will see the clouds light up. These lightning bolts and thunder could awaken a Dreampod Being."

Calla thought back to the temple in Neptuna, housing and protecting those souls that were in Dreamstate.

Oh, I do trust that the pods are protected from a storm such as this.

She then expressed her concern to Bocc.

"I am sure they are, Calla. King Luxxor stated that all contingencies had been explored, taken under consideration and plans of action put in place."

"How interesting and unusual it must be to awaken after years of Dreamstate, and reenter a totally different existence from that which you departed," she softly said in Bocc's ear.

Bocc nodded, and holding Calla tightly, they became quiet, continuing to watch in awe, as the approaching storm was almost upon them, and becoming more extensive in scope. Then with the sand, and rain blowing in from the storm raging outside, Calla turned to Bocc, and gazing into his eyes, passionately kissed him. Bocc looked at Calla, puzzled.

"And, that was for," he asked, speaking above the storm.

"That was for me, Bocc, and the unbridled passion you spoke of earlier," Calla said emphatically. "And, for what it is worth — I enjoyed it!"

"Calla, this moment is forever locked in a special place of my heart. I want you to know I truly look to the pleasures we will share together that are yet to come."

"You are such a poetic romantic, Bocc. I do like that."

Nuzzling even closer, Calla looked deep into Bocc's eyes and whispered...

"I look forward to those pleasures too, Bocc ... starting now!"

She lay back.

The storm raged on in it's beauty and unbridled passion.

When they awoke it was still early. The morning light was washing away the lingering effects of the storm that had passed by sometime in the night.

It had left a freshness in the air, which Bocc breathed in deeply.

Smiling warmly, he embraced Calla who was just opening her sleepy eyes.

"Wake up sleepyhead," he said. "I have something to share with you."

"Already," she responded, her eyes twinkling.

"I was very happy sharing last night!"

Bocc smiled and poked her playfully.

"I wanted to share with you that Patto secretly told me of a star he named after you, Calla. He said 'StarCalla' is energy and brightness. I agree that is a great description, for you, Calla...but I would like to add, 'one that pulsates an evocative and inviting glow," he whispered, charmingly.

Calla blushed happily.

Putting her hands behind Bocc's head, and looking into his opalesque eyes, she said...

"Interestingly enough Bocc, Patto secretly told me of a distant star honoring you. It is in a constellation he has named Boccma! He says its main star, StarBocc, is mysterious in its ways and that all the other stars seem to cluster around it sharing in the warmth it gives off."

Bocc's eyes closed. He uttered...

"Boccma, StarBocc. It sounds distant, as in another world, Calla."

"That will be you, Bocc," Calla said, echoing his previous words and softly smiling. Embracing each other tenderly, suddenly Calla jumped back and shrieked!

"What! What is it Calla," Bocc exclaimed, looking around?

"NETROPIA! NETROPIA," she shouted to Bocc, the echo reverberating off the walls into a chorus of Netropias.

"The name of the sunken city beneath the sands is Netropia!"

Chapter 59

The Place Of Dust

The dust storm howled

The dust storm, came up rapidly and was steadily increasing in strength. Patto, Poona, Tunnis and Laurra, slowly inched their way across the barren dust flats rightfully known as, 'The Place of Dust.' They could only anticipate the footing underneath as the maddening dust swirling torrentially about them made visibility virtually impossible. They eventually needed to pull their robes up over their noses in order to catch and retain what oxygen there was left in this punished place. Poona, turned to Patto indicating that it was best to stop, and wait out the storm.

"I am concerned this is far to taxing for Laurra, Patto, and it has become a precarious situation for us all," she yelled.

Patto agreed, deciding that continuing on would be insane.

Then, the unforeseen occurred. Poona stepped into a 'dust sink void.' Loosing her balance, she fell, striking her head on a hard object hidden by the storm, and the dust. Patto, partially seeing the fall, attempted to throw his body under Poona, but only accomplished losing whatever sight of her he had. He did however, hear Poona hitting what must have been stone below and the moan that followed … and then, except for the howling wind, her silence.

Quickly making his way back onto his feet, he became confused and lost track of where Poona had fallen. The cyclonic swirls of dust blowing feverishly, and biting into his now exposed face had turned him around. He began frantically searching for Poona, who, he knew had to be near.

He managed to grasp on to Laurra and Tunnis and hurriedly explained what had happened. Holding on to one another's hands, they began to grope around in the swirling wind and dust to find Poona.

Finally, in what seemed a lifetime, Patto felt her ankle and then pulled himself over to shield her as best he could. She was not responding to his calls and he realized she was unconscious.

Gathering Poona gently in his arms he could make out that her head was bleeding. Covering her face once again from the heavy, stinging dust, Patto sat there and rocked Poona protectively, tears welling up in his eyes.

What can I do, he thought, *what can I do.*

Tunnis and Laurra fought their way through the swirling wind and dust to the other side of Poona and then together, Patto, and Tunnis, on their knees, spread their robes forming a make shift tent above Poona, shielding her as best as they could.

Laurra, herself weak from the exertion put forth in battling the storm, sat, and gently placed Poona's head in her lap. Then, placing one hand on Poona's wound, she instinctively went deep within her soul calling upon the healing powers of the One, the Goodness of All Things.

"Oh Goodness of All Things, Oneness .. that which is within all, I call within to you, for Poona. I call the One within Poona, also. I thank you for this healing. In your way, and time, release the healing energy within Poona, for her sake, and ours. We are of spirituality, and we believe in your healing ways. Please heal! We are of faith, we believe. Please heal! We trust in the power of the One within all things.

Laurra sat, confirming it over and over, and over.

For Patto and Tunnis there was absolutely nothing they could do but wait and trust that Laurra's invocation would be answered ... and that the storm would play itself out soon.

After what seemed an eternity to them, the fury began to cease, the harsh wind ended abruptly and all that remained was a light swirling dust.

Except for the gentle, soft whispers offered by Laurra, all became quiet.

Patto and Tunnis stood, shook off their robes, and looked around desperately in an attempt to see anything in the aftermath of the subsiding storm.

The strange thing was the abnormal lack of sound when one would have expected the howling to continue for a while as the storm dissipated.

"It has become unnaturally quiet ... so very quiet," Patto said.

"Strange, as the calm usually comes before the storm."

Then it began.

At first Patto thought it to be 'after swirls' blowing the dust around near the ground, almost like water boiling and bubbling under foam.

But then came the ugly sounds.

Hollow, raspy, coughing sounds, accompanying the swirls of 'boiling foam dust' slowly ebbed its way towards them.

"There is something living and hidden beneath the dust clouds, Tunnis. It's moving in our direction. Can you hear the sounds?

Several somethings, he thought.

His skin prickled and a cold sweat broke out on his body.

He turned to Poona. She was still unconscious, with her head upon Laurra's lap. Kneeling down, he softly touched her cheek. Looking over at Laurra, he smiled at her, as she continued to whisper her words to the One, the Goodness of All Things.

Tunnis now aware of the sounds, leaned over and whispered...

"What can we do, Patto? Do you know what this is?"

Patto had been wondering about that too.

"No, Tunnis," he said quietly, but we need to move towards the sounds and away from Poona and Laurra. Perhaps, if we put distance between us, Poona and Laurra may not be noticed and our barrier will somehow protect them."

Standing, Patto began to move away from Poona and Laurra.

"We must distract whatever that is out there."

Tunnis was frightened.

I have never been in a compromising situation, he thought, *but somehow I do not feel all is lost.*

Gently touching Laurra's hair, and cheek, and taking a hopeful look at Poona, he immediately turned to go stand bravely beside Patto.

Together we will face whatever danger is approaching and somehow, 'Goodness' willing, we will all come through this alive.

Walking a distance away they stood between Poona and Laurra and the approaching hollow coughs beneath the dust.

They waited silently.

Except for the approaching menace, It was all so quiet.

Curious, Patto considered, *in a situation where the chance of my death is indeed such a distinct probability ... I do not feel that frightened.*

He looked at Tunnis, standing next to him, and, reaching out, placed his hand confidently on the young man's shoulder, silently thinking to himself...

He may be youthful, but I believe he does understand the serious situation we are in. I have even more respect and admiration for this brave young man from Neptuna.

Although an optimist, Patto was much more in touch with the realities of life than Tunnis. Realizing the severity of this situation and the lack of resources with which to protect themselves, his only thought, as they waited for the unseen terror he knew to be immanent, was...

to divert and draw the adversary away from Poona and Laurra so that they might somehow survive.

"We have to believe — Goodness be with us."

The hollow caustic coughing, now accompanied by a rancid odor, grew in intensity as the threatening swirls became more erratic, and ominous than before ... and much closer!

Patto, had a brief thought to send Tunnis back to protect Poona and Laurra while he would make noises and run in the opposite direction to distract whatever this was approaching.

Then the totally unexpected occurred.

Patto and Tunnis suddenly jerked in astonishment, surprise and fear when an extremely large, dark form slashed through the higher layers of dust, leaping with such force that it landed between the sickening noises and where Patto and Tunnis were standing. Patto, trying to make sense of what was happening, could vaguely distinguish a massive black form standing in a swirling cloud of dust. He heard hissing and snarling in the bubbling dust. It was menacing and terrifying, and made his skin crawl.

"Tunnis, this would be a good time to return and be with Poona and Laurra."

With eyes of wonder, Tunnis nodded his approval.

As they turned, a brief, sudden silence emanated from the swirling dust, and then many high pitch screams and snorts of fear. The swirling, boiling dust quickly became a cyclone of retreat accompanied by raspy, hollow coughing sounds until you could hear them no more. The surrounding dust was enraged, turning into a landscape of thick dust clouds.

They could see absolutely nothing in front of them. After a short while there was only complete, and utter silence.

Laurra gently released Poona to the ground and stood, slightly shaking, and very frightened ... for Poona mostly. She had no idea what had just happened, but knew something bad had been in the dust.

She saw Patto and Tunnis quickly returning to them. Patto rushing to Poona's side, knelt beside her and held her hand.

He was still listening, sweating, and watching.

He could no longer see the large form, but sensed a presence.

The presence of what though, he wondered.?

Gently releasing Poona's hand he stood, completely quiet and hardly breathing. He indicated to Tunnis and Laurra to be silent also.

Ever so slowly they watched the dust settle. Small beams of Mother MoonLunna's light began filtering through the floating dust that remained creating an atmosphere of extraordinary beauty.

"A beautiful kaleidoscope of dust," he finally said. "Certainly nothing I could have imagined just a few moments ago. Nothing appears to be here any longer."

"I can not understand what just happened, Patto," said Tunnis.

"Nor can I, my friend. Perhaps the One intervened?!"

His attention hurried back to Poona. Laurra had once again cradled Poona's head in her lap. Bending down, Patto felt her pulse. It felt and sounded strong to him and the bleeding had thankfully ceased. He intuitively felt her returning to them.

Again, Patto stood, and listening intently for some time, still heard nothing.

He shook his head attempting to comprehend what had just taken place.

It is beginning to get warm, Patto thought, *Odd, to be this warm after such a storm, and getting late into the evening. It should be cooling off.*

Suddenly, a warm forceful breeze blew down heavily across his shoulders and back.

He froze.

How strange, he thought to himself, *a hot breeze — and I'm getting cold chills! My knees feel weak!* Reassuring himself, he then thought, *That is not so surprising considering the turmoil and fear I am experiencing right now.*

Then Patto realized…

There is something behind me. Something very large. Something so large that it is breathing down on me.

His mind began to race even more than before. He could make out Poona laying close by him and so wanted to protect her, but, what could he do against whatever it was behind him, and…

Whatever is breathing heavily behind me is also, strangely enough, probably responsible for saving our lives earlier from the hollow coughing creatures beneath the boiling dust.

Patto ever so slowly turned around to face the unknown.

He was facing a huge pair of legs, attached to a huger Cat! Looking up he gazed into enormous icy blue eyes. The creature stood there, defiant, yet surprisingly unthreatening.

"Nice cat!" he whispered.

Patto slowly turned to Tunnis and Laurra.

He quietly said, "Do not move."

Tunnis and Laurra sat wide eyed, also gazing unbelievably at the towering physical presence before them.

"Do not worry, Patto," Tunnis whispered back, "we will not move."

For a very, very, very, brief second Patto almost had to chuckle at the reply from Tunnis.

The Cat towering over Patto must have been ten feet tall at the shoulders, and was powerfully sinewy and graceful in it's appearance. Patto could only stand there in awe, powerless to do anything ... even if he knew what to do, which he did not.

The Cat cocked it's head as if studying Patto and then slowly lowered it's head. Using it's nose it pushed Patto gently aside. Of course Patto had almost become ill when he saw the large head coming towards him, but was now confused at it's intentions, and gentle manner.

The Cat softly and quietly moved over to where Poona lay. It nuzzled Poona ever so gently ... and then it studied her, turning it's head.

Apparently in contemplation, thought Patto, who now plopped down on the ground amazed at the unbelievable spectacle unfolding before him.

Extending it's large pink tongue, it ever so gently, somehow licked the wound on Poona's head.

Patto, Tunnis and Laurra watching in amazement and wonder, witnessed the wound heal almost immediately ... and then disappear.

Had he been standing he would have collapsed. As it was, he simply crawled over to Poona, and taking her from Laurra, cradled her in his arms, crying tears of joy and relief and wonder. Tunnis and Laurra did the same.

Poona opened her eyes. For a brief moment they remained cloudy, but quickly became amazingly clear and aware.

"Patto..."

"Poona..."

"Patto, what has happened?"

"Oh, Poona," said Patto, between tears, and rocking her gently...

"I am so thankful you are back." He then explained what had happened since her fall and her resulting unconsciousness. Poona remained quiet, thinking within. She then turned her head and looked at Laurra, resting against Tunnis, at her feet.

"Laurra, this storm must have been quite an exertion for you. You appear somewhat pale. I am so sorry, Laurra, I should have stopped long before we did."

Patto replied...

"She was concentrating on your faith in the Oneness to help in your recovery, Poona. Tunnis has hardly left her side except to stand with me earlier as I explained."

Patto then pointed over her shoulder to where the Cat now sat looking down at them. It had seen Poona and the other three struggling in the storm. It sensed the upcoming danger that they were about to encounter.

The Cat was also thinking within. **I remember you, from the oasis. You were valiant and fair. I remember. I would not have harmed you.**

It was never intended. I was only curious. Now I know … your name is Poona.

It knew this, and remembered. It remembered Poona and her compassion. Poona looked over, and immediately understood. Poona murmured…

"It is Pantheon."

The Sand Panther blinked it's icy blue eyes … **Pantheon, yes. I like the name, Pantheon.**

"Pantheon," said Patto quizzically?

'Yes," said Poona. "This is the the Sand Panther, from the encounter at the oasis a while back. Remember, it was Annuj and Bocc who came face to face with the Cat. It was a frightening situation, but no one felt it actually meant any harm."

"TerraSim indicated they were rarely seen," said Patto.

"I remember," replied Poona.

"I named it 'Pantheon." It is an extremely ancient word meaning, 'A Place of All Gods to All peoples.' In those few moments at the oasis I saw that Pantheon was magnificent and valiant. It had shown restraint and even approached what I felt was wisdom, as all living things possess," she said.

"I silently wished to communicate with it. It seems now I have my chance."

Pantheon lowered it's head, and stretched out on the settling dust. It's very large icy blue eyes looking into Poona's. A sound resembling a purr came forth.

Do you understand my intention?

Instinctively, Poona nodded.

"I do not know why, but I just had a thought! I believe I understand Pantheon's intention."

"We are to climb onto Pantheon's back. Pantheon will take us to safety."

Chapter 60

Entering The Valley Of Stone

I will call it 'Pantheon'

Poona knew it was still one or two days to their destination of Oneness, but felt uplifted by the presence of a vibrant glow. Floating and caressing the walls of the white canyon in the distance ahead the group witnessed the emerging shadows of early morning light rippling across the surfaces of stone, like shadows undulating across the bottom of a stream bed.

The shadows preceded the welcoming gift of morning's warmth, soon to follow.

It was called the 'Valley of Stone.'

Even though It was the time of Dawn, surprisingly, Patto and Poona were not tired. The ground beneath them was moist and cool and a bed of frost still lingered, as yet untouched by the rising of The Mother SunneLavva.

Patto could see Mother MoonLunna still clinging to her position on the horizon, as the fading darkness of the night was quickly vaporizing before the approaching Sunne.

It would soon slip away for another day.

Patto, gazing into the endless eternity above, suddenly became intrigued at a thought that came to him. He glanced at Poona, walking slowly beside him, and then back at Pantheon, who was a short distance behind them.

"Poona, I have just come up with an idea, a revelation and I am very excited about it. I wish to share it with you. I would like to know your feelings in regards to it."

Curious, Poona smiled at Patto's enlivened enthusiasm.

"And what idea would that be, Patto?"

"Well, as you are aware, I am naming stars after all the Initiates while

241

on this journey. But now, a wonderful thought occurred to me to also name the vast Skyscape of the Heavens, which envelops all the stars.

I choose to name it after none other than… Pantheon! You told me the name Pantheon meant a place for 'All Gods of All Peoples,' and has it's origin from a very ancient people. It seems appropriate, don't you think?"

Poona gazed warmly at Patto, once again taken by his loving, kind nature, and consideration for all life — irregardless.

"Patto, that is a heartwarming tribute to bestow on Pantheon. Somehow I feel he will understand and be delighted.

"Pantheon, of the Heavens" … "So it is, so it shall be!"

She then hugged, and kissed Patto on the cheek.

This took him by surprise, and he felt his cheeks become flushed. They both looked back at Pantheon, who, in turn, looked back at them with a curious and inquisitive expression on his noble face.

Resting comfortably on Pantheon's back, Laurra was visibly appearing to be feeling better, and Tunnis was walking along side Pantheon.

All seemed well.

Laurra, had been daydreaming, reliving the Wisdom Path Journey, when suddenly she looked down to Tunnis.

"Tunnis, I think I know the name of those beasts in the dust. I believe they were Lurds! TerraSim once told us about several dangerous creatures of the desert and Lurds definitely is one of them. They fit in quite well with the experience we all just endured. We did not actually see them, but the odor, and the sounds are exactly like he explained."

Tunnis lit up brightly.

"Lurds! Yes!"

"I must tell, Patto, and Poona when we stop."

As for Patto, he was happy. As a matter of fact, he could not imagine being in a better space at this time. Poona was once again herself, as if nothing had happened to her at all.

She healed so quickly. It is almost amazing. Between Laurra's faith healing, Pantheon's healing licks, and the compassion of the One, we were spared an unknown fate.

And the storm, dangerous as it was, has given me more than it took. I came face to face with my vulnerabilities, and with extreme fears, but am elated to have overcome these fears in moments of such uncertain circumstances, and menacing times. I also witnessed exceptional courage from a fine young man and new friend, Tunnis.

Resting both hands on his head and looking at the sky, Patto let out a deep sigh of thanks. He felt as if both his awareness and love of life were bursting forth in thankfulness.

I am a part of it all, he rejoiced.

Poona, also enjoying some time alone with her personal thoughts, walked along reflecting on Patto's description of Pantheon's dramatic appearance and involvement with the menacing beasts beneath the dust swirls.

I now know of the heroic efforts and compassion for my well being by Tunnis and Patto ... as well as Laurra's healing offerings to the One.

She turned and looked back. "And, of course, our new companion, Pantheon."

"Oh, I am so fortunate and privileged being with these four noble and courageous companions," she uttered softly.

And, Tunnis, *hmmm, It will be promising,* she concluded, *thinking of him innocently mentioning his thoughts on the possibility of a surface community for Neptuna, built close by the edge of the sea.* "Which will," he had stated, "once again establish the original Neptunian idea of a city on the sands of The Carbonian Desert. The underwater city will also remain for those choosing it as their home and will continue to safeguard the 'Pods,' as before, besides developing extensive underwater farming, creating a food supply for Neptunians, and those of all Amythesia."

It was impressive, these ambitious ideas of the young man, the Prince from Neptuna. She looked forward to how it all played out in time.

He is a bright young man, she thought, *and honorable.*

They continued walking until the beginning, of the end, of the light of day.

Poona was now contemplating on the inner talk of her inner world, while watching Mother SunnaLavva slowly ebb into a world of darkness, once again relinquishing her sovereignty to Mother MoonLunna.

The never ending circle.

Like the Heavens, my inner truths embrace both darkness and light, all being dependent on circumstances and truths. Hmmm, my inner truths. My secretive, personal space where the luminaries of light and the mysteries of darkness are known only to me ... and only I can objectively and without prejudice, justify or summon either source should I deem it necessary.

Glancing at Patto, still walking close by her, she felt a sense of rightness.

It feels good having Patto, here so close to me, she acknowledged.

A thought suddenly came out of nowhere ...

I wonder about the possibility of a relationship with Patto! Poona chuckled at another humorous thought, *he may be out of my 'REALM' of possibilities!*

Perhaps somewhere in the future. We live rather far apart!

She shook her head, smiling.

Poona was anxious to reach Oneness, which was on the other side of the Valley of Stone and less than a day's walk away. She consoled herself, knowing they would be there tomorrow and anticipated the events that would come together there … for many!

However, in the meantime her stomach was proclaiming it's need for nourishment.

"Patto," she said, "am I the only one who is hungry?"

"Are you jesting with me, I am starving, Poona. I still have some supplies from Neptuna and from BucchaSim, but we are almost at the Valley and once there I am sure we can find some embellishments to create some sort of concoction. Hopefully we will find some water too. Ours is getting low."

Poona smiled.

"Well, I hope there are a lot of plants and vegetation for Pantheon's sake."

"And, a large pond to drink from," smiled Patto.

Turning to let Tunnis and Laura know they would be stopping for the night, he heard Tunnis call out…

"Patto, they were Lurds. Laurra remembered that those things in the dust were Lurds!"

He turned to Poona, eyebrows raised.

They both broke into smiles.

Chapter 61

Time Off For Sad Behavior

Can you envision my vision

The King sat in his Sanctuary, the Temple of The Moon and 7Stars reflecting on how happy he should be ...

I have the most extraordinary, devoted, intelligent, woman as my beautiful Queen ... my family is kind, compassionate and enthusiastic — sometimes they are a little headstrong, but in such a wonderful and delightful manner. And, after all, that is just part of Being.

"They undoubtedly get it from me," he said, chuckling.

"Let's see, where was I ... Oh, yes..."

We live in the stunningly exotic, and extremely ancient city of Neptuna, with it's Dome of Life, it's beautiful and devoted Beings, it's incredible underwater sea creatures, ancient structures full of myth and history ... all ours to enjoy at anytime! Ah, my list just goes on and on, he reflected.

"So, what is making me so blue," he uttered to the lady in the 'Fountain of Life' situated on the wall behind his desk?

Oh, I do so miss my son Tunnis, he knew, leaning back in his chair, gazing at the ceiling, decorated in paintings and reliefs so old they had no record of origin. *However, I also realize how important this adventure is for my son and how valuable of an experience it will be in his life to come.*

He turned his attention to the ancient water sculpture on the wall, the 'Fountain of Life.' He studied it almost longingly.

So feminine, so mysterious, and so wanting to be understood. How baffling and marvelous you are.

Swiveling his chair in a circle and continuing to ramble about, he thought of the relationship between Tunnis and Laurra, or for that matter if there even was one.

"I feel there is much more to Laurra than meets the eye, "he confided to the Lady of the Fountain. *Laurra is bright, and quite lovely, but there is something else, and I can not put my finger on it.*

"Hmmm _ what could it be," he asked the Fountain of Life? "You are not going to tell me, are you?"

Realizing he would not get an answer to any of his concerns Luxxor swiveled back to his desk and randomly selected a scroll to pick up and study.

And this is the mood, in which Queen Liluuc found King Luxxor, in his Sanctuary beneath the Dome of Life attempting to act as though he was intently working on revisions to remodel some historical site, or another plumbing project.

He appears weary, and somewhat sad, she mused, standing, as yet unobserved, in the entry to his study. *This is so unlike Luxxor,* his wife, friend, Queen, and mother of their children, knew. *My Chosen One is missing his son, Tunnis. This is his drama,* she determined.

Provocatively positioning herself in the entrance to his Sanctuary, she sultrily announced herself.

"My Chosen One…"

King Luxxor raised his eyes to the familiar and always enticing voice of his beloved.

"Yes, my Queen," he answered, raising his eyebrows at her appearance.

"My King, I feel time off for 'sad behavior' is just what you need," the Queen responded with red, pouting lips.

Luxxor sat back, eyebrows raised, as Liluuc appeared to float into his study, her soft gown caressing and clinging to her body. The fluidity of her movements, tantalizing and capturing his attention, brought to an end, at least momentarily, his contemplation of blue and forlorn feelings.

"I have fantasized nights alone in the Tower rooms of the Royal Chambers, high above the Sea of the Forgotten Place, my Chosen One. Just you, and just me," she softly whispered into his ear, gracefully gliding by, but stopping to wipe a dust web of neglect from the evocative sculpture depicting the divine feminine on the wall behind his desk.

Attempting a provocative pirouette, which she managed quite gracefully, Liluuc turned back to Luxxor.

"Can you envision my vision, my Chosen One?"

King Luxxor turned to follow his Queen's sensual dance around the room with growing expectations to where this was leading.

"I am certain we do not need an excuse or a reason, my Chosen One — and if we do then I suggest we seriously consider your position as King, my King," she suggested, lowering her eyes tauntingly!

"My Queen," he responded, "just to satisfy my curiosity, is there an alternative reason, other than your concern regarding my 'obviously obvious' discontent brought on by the extended absence of our son, Tunnis?"

"Yes, my King, that is it exactly. An alternative reason! Am I so transparent, my Chosen One!?"

She rolled her eyes seductively.

"You have once again demonstrated your astute wisdom in deciphering my novice attempt of deceptive persuasion. However, my love, I am secretly hoping my performance, and future performances," she said evocatively, raising her eyebrows, and revealing her mischievous eyes, "will not only entice, but give promise to, perhaps 'lifting' your, uh, spirits, if you will excuse my pun, my King."

She bowed teasingly.

"Let me envision, if you will," Queen Liluuc said, continuing her alluring circulation of his study and wiping away a dust bunny here and there as she went.

"I will peel your grapes, pour your beloved Loctuum, massage your concerns away, using, of course, only the finest herbal body oils and exotic scented floral fragrances available. Including, my Chosen One, Sandalus, and your favorite, the essence of Garloonias. I remember how you love the Garloonia's color of fusia, and it's sensual fragrance."

"Also, as an especially special addition, my Love, a rare and complete Lapisian Clay body mask ... and rub!"

Queen Liluuc, erotically raising one eyebrow, glanced over at King Luxxor, and said...

"Yes, I will do all these things for you my King."

Despite the conflict Luxxor was experiencing between the blues brought on by the absence of Tunnis, and the happiness for his son's opportunity to join the Wisdom Path journey to Oneness, Luxxor could not help but grin broadly.

He then broke into hearty laughter. Rising, he snuggled Queen Liluuc in his arms.

"You know, my Queen, I can not refuse such a reasonable request from my Chosen One ... and, in all honesty, I probably have earned it."

His Queen then poked him in the chest!

Holding her in his arms, he said...

"It is, after all, the responsibility of the King to keep ALL the people happy, and if peeling my grapes will make my Queen happy how can I refuse?"

"Oh," Queen Liluuc continued, "I also have a surprise gift for you if you will but grant me the liberty to bestow upon you, my esteem, my gratitude, and my generosity, in the form of this gift." Her smiled glowed.

"And that is," he asked inquiringly?

"Ah, I will reveal the surprise later my King. Much later tonight, after the needed and deserved respite I have envisioned for you," she said.

And, it was indeed much later that evening, after the Translite ride up to the Tower rooms, the Loctuum, the ritualistic peeling of the grape, the massage, and the rare and complete Lapisian body mask, after ... after everything, that his Chosen One, Liluuc whispered in his ear ..."Are you ready?"

"Ready! Ready!? Are you serious, my Love. I'm exhausted. I can barely move! I need just a little more time, I..."

"My King, I will consider that a compliment, but I mean are you ready for my surprise gift?"

"Oh, oh, yes, my Queen."

"Well, my Chosen One, I have arranged for you, myself and Dolpho to journey to Oneness for a needed Holiday, and to bring our son Tunnis back home to Neptuna when he completes his arduous trek with the Wisdom Path Initiates to Oneness."

Luxxor sat up, and with the moon glow of Mother MoonLunna softly filling the room, he looked lovingly at Liluuc laying beside him.

"Oh, my Queen, mother of our children, this is a journey together I will welcome. A gift unsurpassed! You are wonderful and thoughtful, my Chosen One."

"As are you, my King, my Chosen One ... as are you."

'how easy it is to skip that long sought after stone

on a quiet pond...

what a different story when it comes to a rolling surf...'

'you provide the stone...

i'll come up with a pond'

bocc

poet and Initiate of Brightness on the Wisdom Path Journey
Prismacia
UGT 20,872

Chapter 62

Laurra Has Grown

Laurra reflects

Laurra was laying near the edge of a fallen amber crystal, half submerged in the oasis pool. She became intoxicated by the constant movement of shimmering light from the setting SunneLavva as it sparkled across the surface of the water, unknowingly casting flickering shadows playing on and about her body.

Oh, I feel peaceful, she thought, looking out at the magnificent crystal prism range forming the mountainous area abutting Oneness.

Laurra discovered this isolated little cove shortly after reaching Oneness and liked to think it was her secret spot ... to rest, reflect, and share with her personal spark of the Source.

Lazily glancing around she noticed Pantheon in the distance. He too contentedly laying on his back and resting in the shade under a grove of tall Palmation trees.

"You appear so relaxed. Not a care in the Heavens, huh, Pantheon."

Oh, Goodness of All Things, she thought, sighing, as she lay upon the crystal soaking in it's warmth, *it certainly has been an arduous and compelling experience thus far, but now I am here in Oneness. Solannuj, and Pellona, my charming hosts, are wonderful, and I now feel complete.*

Laurra closed her eyes and reflected back on the adventures she and the Initiates shared with Solannuj and Pellona.

They were completely captivated by our stories in traversing the Carbonian Desert ... especially the Place of Dust, complete with it's tales of dread, and woes ... oh, and heroism.

She smiled tenderly.

And, Pantheon! Everyone is still in awe. Of course, everyone was understandably standoffish when first introduced to Pantheon.

Laurra chuckled at how It had taken encouragement from them all to get Solannuj and Pellona up on Pantheon's back for a short ride down to the oasis.

It was only when Tunnis volunteered to join them, she remembered, *that they finally relented, climbing ever so hesitantly on to the massive neck of the great beast.*

She shook her head in delight at the vision of them struggling to get up on on Pantheon's back and then laughed some more.

Then it took just as much coaxing to get them off! They were totally enjoying the extraordinary experience so much they were not ready for it to end.

Especially Pellona, who was laughing so hard she had tears flowing down her cheeks, which, in turn caused Solannuj to begin laughing, and then everyone joined in the fun, including me.

She suddenly wondered, *Maybe Pantheon was smiling too — in his way.*

Pantheon now had celebrity status in the quaint village of Oneness and when not the main attraction, he could be found sunne bathing himself at the far end of the oasis, which he had adopted as his unofficial home.

Her eyes were twinkled happily at the thought.

She shifted her position on the long horizontal crystal half submerged in the pool. The Mother SunneLavva returned to her thoughts.

Hmmm, the Sunne is still shedding it's warmth. I have some time before the approach of the evening chill.

I will just remove my wrap and stretch out on the crystal for a little longer, bathing in these final comforting rays of the day ... allowing it to softly caress my total Being.

I feel good, Mother SunneLavva, she gratefully thought. *My time of the 'Maturity Immersion' is now complete, and I am truly thankful the difficult and dangerous times are now behind me. I am feeling whole, Oh One.*

Laurra, marveled at the significance of this thought, this transformation.

After several months, I remember gasping at my obvious change when I first looked into the mirror. And then, each year I witnessed myself quickly leaving my childhood further and further behind for a destiny I had willingly accepted.

I will never have the childhood most beings take for granted.

Her mind, quickly determined the sequence of events from when she and Poona arrived in Amythesia up through her transformation.

The Wise Ones determined that my physical development should accelerate nearly three times faster, each year, here on Prismacia. However, it could not be ascertained or guaranteed that my mental and emotional development would actually manifest in a similar way.

"Therein was the dilemma," she acknowledged aloud, suddenly sitting up, and shaking her head in wonder. "It was imperative that my physical body be compatible with that of my mental and emotional development."

Poona was not immune from the physical effects either. She regularly entered nearby Starlites to immerse herself in a 'cell growth regression chamber.' It had been carefully set up to control her growth patterns while on Prismacia. It was not always pleasant for Poona either, she grimaced.

"And, here I am, on Prismacia. A young woman, who at this precise time in all history, awaits to create her destiny," she softly spoke.

She abruptly felt a chill. *Hmmm, yes, it is that time.* She shivered.

As she prepared to leave, Laurra kneeled and cast a glance at her reflection in the oasis pool. It revealed a lovely and mature young woman of seventeen.

Laura's thoughts dreamily drifted to Tunnis. Her eyes softened and she whispered...

"What am I to do with you, my sweet Tunnis, you who would be my champion? What am I to do?"

And,'my' hopes and dreams ... what of them?

"Someday I will fulfill them too," she affirmed, crossing her hands in the symbolic gesture.

"All things unfold as their destiny allows, and, being it is my destiny ... it will unfold as I allow."

This brought a smile to her face.

The vastness of the Eastern Heavens darkened, quickly swathing the lands all the way to the western horizon. Night time was upon the small oasis village of Oneness.

Walking along the path back to Oneness, Laura witnessed Twinklings appearing in the surrounding desert — thousands of feather light 'thistle balls' of desert dust, carried along by soft winds. They were dancing about the Palmation Grove oasis pools, sparkling, and glistening in the moon and emerging star light. Often disappearing into the darkness, before launching into yet another dance, on another breeze ... creating a fantasy world within a fantasy world.

Not unlike Neptuna's dancing silhouettes of the deep, thought Laurra.

'play with the wind...

toy with the stars...

romp with the sand...'

'but ... do not jest with my heart'

bocc

poet and Initiate of Brightness on the Wisdom Path Journey
Prismacia
UGT 20,872

Chapter 63

They Appear To Be Out For A Morning's Crawl

An exciting sighting

There was an exalting and joyous atmosphere at King Luxxor and Queen Liluuc's abode as final preparations were put in place for their departure the very next morning. It was early in the evening and King Luxxor was enjoying his favorite beverage, a Loctuum, as he packed the last item of clothing he felt may be needed during their excursion to Oneness to collect their son Tunnis.

King Luxxor was still in awe of his Chosen One's thoughtful gift and in high spirits.

They heard from Tunnis only a few days before, via his Palm Recorder. He, Laurra, Patto and Poona arrived in Oneness accompanied by 'Pantheon,' Tunnis had said … leaving the King and the Queen to wonder as to who or what 'Pantheon' was, or is.

Tunnis then said that he had exciting experiences to tell them, but refused to elaborate, wanting to share with them in person. This was teasingly tantalizing to both the King's and Queen's curious natures leaving them more anxious than ever to see their son. Queen Liluuc inquired as to how Laurra was feeling and was happy to hear she had improved greatly during the last few weeks. It appeared that Tunnis was watching after her well being, along with her 'caregiver' Poona, of course.

Queen Liluuc did not miss the fact that her son was being quite the caring friend in watching out for Laurra!

Dolpho approached her father, King Luxxor and asked…

"Will it be possible to take the desert-seashore route to Oneness, father? I am really curious to see a Prismacian worm."

"A Prismacian worm," her Father remarked, with a twinkle in his eyes. "Well, I see no reason, to not see, if we can see, these creatures of the sands. I would actually like to see one myself ... all these years and I have never had a sighting."

"It is a big desert Father."

Queen Liluuc was informed of a SeaStorm brewing and made arrangements for she and the King to spend the evening in the Tower room of the crystal prism overlooking the Sea. It could be a spectacular sight from their vantage point.

Just in case they overslept, she left instructions for her personal 'Courtier In Waiting', Lilonna, to awaken them before dawn, as an early start was wanted by the King.

The evening went wonderfully, and sometime during the deep darkness of the night, they did indeed witness an incredible SeaStorm.

Propped up on large puffy pillows, they witnessed the dramatic storm unfold in all it's splendor. Heavy thunder, echoing across the Heavens followed jagged streaks of lightning that cut through the night, revealing the secrets of even the most dense, impenetrable darkness.

Accompanying all this were strong gale force winds, and a torrential downpour which were in total control of the Heavens for most of the night.

Early the next morning, Lilonna awakened them and they could see that the SeaStorm had thankfully passed leaving an approaching dawn.

A promising, beautiful, clear and crisp, day for their journey lay ahead.

King Luxxor, Queen Liluuc, Dolpho, Lilonna, two Divine Guardians, two SeaLand Pilots, several Royal bags, plus other King, Queen, and Princess things, were loaded aboard. Nestled within his pocket was a gift for Prince Tunnis from he and his Queen, for having completed the arduous journey from Neptuna to Oneness in stellar fashion! The Royal family chose not to diminish their pride in this feat of courage by their son, Tunnis.

The highly anticipated moment came and the submerged flying craft SeaLand took off from beneath the 'Sea of the Forgotten Place,' bursting forth from the now tranquil waters.

They set their course to explore the cliff sands high above the shore and waters below, anticipating an approximate flying time of five hours to Oneness. This was allowing time to view Prismacian worms should, as King Luxxor put it, they happen to be soaking in a little of the Mother SunneLavva's rays.

About halfway into their flight, Dolpho, ever on the watch, was the first to notice them. They appeared on the edge of a sand cliff just ahead of the SeaLand craft.

Dolpho exclaimed, "Look, up ahead!"

King Luxxor responded, "Have you spotted a worm, Dolpho?"

"No Father, but I think that is Bocc and Calla down there."

King Luxxor, who was at the controls at the time, slowed the craft down and maneuvered a slow circle around the area to get a better view.

"Dolpho, you have the eyes of a Gattling looking for it's only meal of the day."

"We will land nearby and see if they have any needs."

Calla and Bocc had left the tunnels and ventured out to the sand's edge to discuss their strategy regarding their continuation to Oneness.

Realizing considerable time was spent in and around the cave and tunnels, it was apparent to them that they may have to cut across country, which, although more dangerous, certainly shortened the distance to Oneness. They had scanned the shore below and realized their belongings were undoubtably long gone, snatched by the sea.

"It's important we reach Oneness as soon as possible," Bocc was telling Calla when a dot in the sky caught his eye. Calla noticed it also, and as they watched, they realized it was becoming larger by the second.

As the dot got closer, they saw it was a craft descending in a large swooping circle. It finally settled in the sands a short distance away.

Dolpho quickly exited the SeaLand and rushed over to Calla and Bocc who were walking towards them smiling, but curious.

Dolpho embraced them warmly.

"Oh, she said, I can not believe we ran into you out here in the middle of nowhere."

Queen Liluuc commented to King Luxxor, "It seems Dolpho has taken up an affinity with the Initiates, my Chosen One."

"Yes," he replied, "perhaps one day Dolpho also will be selected as an Initiate. A truly Honorable Honor."

"Indeed," smiled the Queen, "Indeed."

Hand in hand, they strolled across the sand to greet Bocc and Calla.

"Our good friends, Bocc and Calla," began the King, "it appears we were meant to spend yet more time together. I trust all is well?"

"Oh, yes," both chimed in, smiling at each other. "Except many of our things were blown away during the storm last night," added Calla.

"We were just deciding on our path to meet up with the other Initiates in Oneness," she said.

"We became somewhat sidetracked here, and before we knew it days had past leaving us dreadfully behind in our time frame to reach Oneness."

"However," she added, "It was definitely time well spent."

"Well, we actually happen to not only be going in the direction of Oneness, but 'to' Oneness, my young friends," stated King Luxxor. "We will be pleased to offer you accommodations should you choose to join us for a splendid ride in the SeaLand."

"At no charge," grinned Dolpho.

"Yes, and the views from our view ports are remarkable," added Queen Liluuth.

Bocc and Calla looked at each other, and shrugging their shoulders in the gesture of why not, we will love to, both said "yes" simultaneously.

After all had boarded and seated themselves, Lilonna, the Queen's attendant, brought in refreshments for all to enjoy.

Queen Liluuc asked Lilonna to join them, and patted the seat next to her.

It was only a short time, before Bocc, looking out his view port excitedly exclaimed...

"There, there! A Prismacian worm!"

"Where," Dolpho almost screamed, as she scanned the desert below.

Everyone quickly moved to the left of the cabin where Bocc was sitting and peered out at the passing scene below. Thankfully, the Pilots, having been informed of the Prismacian worm infatuation, slowed, and dropping lower, tilted the craft to the left, allowing all an unobstructed view of the sands beneath the craft.

And, there it was, or better said, there 'they' were! A large Prismacian worm and what must have been a small baby worm wiggling alongside.

They were both just undulating along slowly.

"My," said Queen Liluuc, "They appear to be out for a morning's crawl."

"What an exciting sighting!"

"An exciting sighting! I like that my Chosen one," said the King. "I see some of Bocc's influence in words and poetry are rubbing off on you."

Bocc grinned broadly.

Queen Liluuc smiled ... everyone grinned happily.

As the event of 'the worms' faded into the distance, Bocc turned to them, and said excitedly...

"King Luxxor, Calla has extraordinary news, especially for you ... another discovery! It is Calla's discovery, so she should be the one to explain."

King Luxxor's curiosity peaked.

"I am anxious to hear about what you speak, Calla. You have our complete attention, please begin."

An hour or so later, The King, Queen, Dolpho, and Lilonna, sat back, practically speechless at the news.

"It may prove to be the discovery of Netropia itself," he said in amazement, taking the hand of his Queen and squeezing it gently.

"I assure you, that when we return to Neptuna, I will convene a special council to discuss an imminent Royal Directive for the exploration of these caves and tunnels you speak of, Calla."

Queen Liluuc looked at King Luxxor and sensing his approval, added...

"I want you to know that I personally have thought about the difference you, and your fellow Initiates, and, of course, Poona, have made since being in our lives. I have become aware of a fresh, youthful, energetic, and enthusiastic interest in our lovely and unusual city of Neptuna. An energy, and enthusiasm I have not lost, but perhaps taken for granted somewhere along the way.

This new energy, this wonderful enthusiasm, which you have helped rekindle, is a 'spark for life' for all of us," the Queen stated energetically.

"I am sure I speak for all when I say to you, thank you from deep within our hearts. I feel unfathomable promise pertaining to Neptuna's history — and as importantly, if not more so, to Neptuna's present and future.

We are indebted to you," she concluded, her eyes soft, sincere, and beginning to tear.

"Neptuna's King Luxxor, my Chosen One, and my King," she said, taking up his hand and kissing it lightly, "is a most honorable King, and Being. I assure you that what you have initiated will not be forgotten."

"In conclusion," she added, "while I am aware of my responsibilities as the Queen, and am happy for what that entails, I wish to make it clear that as a mother, and a wife, the only spark for life I truly need and desire, is that of my Chosen One, and our lovely children, Tunnis and Dolpho.

I am, and will forever be grateful."

King Luxxor sat there, a little rosy from the compliments coming from his Queen, but more joyful in the thought and meaning behind the words spoken by his Chosen One.

Liluuc. I love you too, my Queen.

Chapter 64

It All Seems So Right, So What Is Wrong

The wind continued to listen

It was a time when time seemed as though it ceased to be ... and a time when Annuj felt she had always been a part of this family.

Junnuj, her birth mother, BucchaSim, her birth father, and TerraSim, her older sibling brother.

It all seems so right, she thought.

I am happy being with them, here at this time in our lives, sharing stories, some joyful, some not so pleasant but nevertheless all now bringing us together. Everything seems as it should be!

So, what is wrong? Why are my feelings so heavy, when I should be overjoyed?

Annuj was leaning against the warmth of her favorite crystal, which also helped shield her from the constant winds from the sea. However, somehow the strong winds still managed to circumvent the large crystal allowing cool breezes to flutter wisps of her hair to and fro. Annuj pulled her shawl tighter around her body, as she was not yet used to the constant cooler winds here along the coastal areas.

Her thoughts flashed back to the Sea of the Forgotten Place, the hospitable people and their city deep beneath the surface waters. She felt that the sea's name was indeed haunting, offering a tinge of mystery, but somehow heavy-hearted, or perhaps sad too.

Closing her eyes, Annuj, lay back, sinking softly into SilentMind in hopes of seeking an answer for her uneasiness.

I am experiencing anxiety. Something is right beneath the surface, something sad, and it is wanting out.

Suddenly, Annuj opened her eyes wide! Sitting forward, she exclaimed...

"Of course! I've known it all along, but have been so caught up in these beautiful present moments to remember my cherished past moments as well."

The winds listened as they continued their whirling dances.

"I am missing my family back home … my mother Hanna, my father Ralla, and my little brother, Jasso. All there in Quin Lapisia, the place of my youth.

Oh, I miss you, I miss you so very much."

Annuj, placed her hands on each side of her head and spoke hurriedly to the desert sands stretched out before her.

"I must speak of my quandary to mother Junnuj and father BucchaSim. I choose both families as my own, because they are," she exclaimed aloud, arms extended as if to embrace the winds that had now picked up momentum. This difficult situation is through no fault of either family and I am so blessed to have them both."

She sat for awhile trying to put the pieces of this trying, but beautiful puzzle together, speaking aloud to add clarity to her thoughts.

"Perhaps we can arrange to have Ralla, Hanna and Jasso visit us here at SeaCliff," she considered. "Yes, it will be a great awayness for them and both families can meet — and become friends. I just know they will."

The wind continued to listen, and occasionally howled — but to no avail. Annuj shut out everything but her hopeful wishes.

"Maybe my Aunt, the HighPriestess XennaOne, will arrange passage. If not to SeaCliff, then to Oneness. I need to be there soon anyway. It is time for me to rejoin our small Wisdom Path Journey and I do so want to complete it with them. Oneness, what a wonderful place for a first reunion of my two families."

As Annuj settled back against the crystal again an unexpected and sudden wave of emotion flowed through her being.

It was of sadness.

Once again speaking to the winds, Annuj tenderly and tearfully uttered…

"It will be ending soon, our Wisdom Path Journey, our camaraderie, our companionship — this extremely special time in our lives.

As a FutureSeer I feel it intuitively.

It is coming soon."

Chapter 65

I Intend To Use A Little Pull

A getaway, and a loving stay

Annuj ran through the sands arriving breathless at SeaCliff. She found TerraSim and Junnuj preparing an exquisite fish TerraSim had managed to catch that morning.

Junnuj was sharing her secret recipe with TerraSim who was listening intently. BucchaSim was still cleaning out the sandy residue from the previous night's main attraction, an exceptionally fierce sea storm, accompanied by an incredible light and sound show for them all to experience.

Junnuj looked up, greeting Annuj, as she hurried into the kitchen.

"How was your walk, Annuj," she asked, while cutting into the delicacy before her.

"Fine, mother," Annuj replied, still considering how to broach the anxiety she was feeling between her two families and her new sad awareness of impending endings regarding the Wisdom Path Journey.

It is both a time for beginnings and a time for endings.

Junnuj intuitively sensing the feeling immediately, walked over to her daughter.

"What is it honey," she asked, putting her arm around Annuj, and embracing her. "I can tell you are not the same as when you left this morning and I have sensed you struggling lately. We are all here for you, my daughter, please, understand, there is nothing — absolutely nothing we cannot resolve together through love and honesty."

TerraSim, sensing his mother's concern, put aside preparing the fish and he too moved closer to his sister.

BucchaSim, also overhearing the conversation came into the kitchen.

"Hi Hon," he softly said. "What is it? What can we do for you?"

Annuj, who thought she knew exactly how she would bring it up, then broke down and cried, with both her mother and father, and brother comforting her. Much later, after all had been revealed, they sat around the comfort room. The Sunne warmed them, somehow helping reassure them all. They listened compassionately and truly understood the honest and sincere feelings Annuj was experiencing.

"You are a compassionate and extraordinary young Being, Annuj," said Junnuj. "Of course you would feel this way. The reality of learning you have two families is understandably something that will take time to work out.

Ralla, and Hanna actually raised you, and were ... excuse me Annuj, I meant to say, 'are' your parents. Jasso is in truth, also your brother, and now, if that were not enough, you are also anticipating the upcoming closure of the Wisdom Path Journey.

However, your new friends, that are so meaningful to you, will continue, as will your memories, Annuj. Life, as we know it, consists of beginnings, and endings, and everything in between ... achievements, friends, compassion, dreams, sadness, joy, love — everything!

And, if we are fortunate, we are the 'Creator' of our lives.

I should have realized the complexity of this and what awkward circumstances it could bring to a sensitive young Being like you."

"Annuj, know that your father, like myself and your brother, understand.

We have been so caught up in becoming the family we were not allowed to be long ago that we were just not seeing what was so obvious.

This is a precious time we have been gifted, of sharing, and loving and planning dreams together for what may come. Something we, as a family were denied in what seems like ages ago."

"I feel Ralla and Hanna are truly compassionate Beings to unquestioningly understand what it means for us to get to know one another — but at the same time wanting you there to share with them. The family who gratefully raised you and sacrificed for you so you could become the fine Being we are all so very happy for today."

Lovingly embracing Annuj, Junnuj went on to say...

"We will, of course, invite Ralla, Hanna and Jasso here to SeaCliff, or Oneness if you prefer. Yes, Oneness. Then you could be with the Initiates once again. Your father, and I will personally invite them for a getaway and a loving stay."

How does that sound to you, Annuj?"

"Oh, mother, it makes me very happy," Annuj said, beaming.

Junnuj smiled. "It is also important, Annuj, that you share what remaining time together you have on this journey with your new friends, the Initiates, and Poona.

Time with those we care for is precious, my dear."

Sitting back with a small mischievous smile on her face, Junnuj said...
"It just so happens, Annuj, that I have a sister and you have an aunt,
who is none other than XennaOne, the HighPriestess of the Voice of One!
To phrase it bluntly, my dear, I intend to use a little pull!"
Annuj turned bright with joy!

'why is it that we remember those loves lost,

or never achieved...

more than we do those summer days,

of holding hands...

nights of tender conversation, of perfect loving...

'why can we not have it all'

bocc

poet and Initiate of Brightness on the Wisdom Path Journey
Prismacia
UGT 20,872

Chapter 66

One More Time With Yogga

What is a mustard seed

"While I may emit a projection of such, please know, my young friends, that I am not a Profit, nor am I a Savior. As it turns out, I am, surprisingly enough, an elation to myself. Somehow, someway, a benevolence was bestowed upon me, along with a glimmer of enlightenment, allowing me the opportunity to follow my bliss — to become what you see, and will experience today. I hope what you encounter nourishes your soul, delivering you to a better place within, and closer to your true source."

Annuj looked at Poona.

"There is such an innocent mastery in his manner, and in his thought and truth. Or, is it innocent arrogance," she questioned? Poona, slowly began to revel in the belief that, here, in Annuj, was another source of a wondrous beginning.

"My intuition, and initial feeling is 'simplistic,' Annuj. But, yes, innocent mastery describes him well."

Calla raised her hand.

"Yogga, please accept this question as a question of curiosity only and meaning no disrespect. I am curious as to your age. Would you mind telling us how old you are?"

"Well, let me see, Miss Calla, I really have not given thought to it. But, I was obviously born, as I do not sit here before you as an aberration or figment of your, or my, imagination. Would someone please pinch me to make sure."

Yogga laughed heartily at this, as he looked at all the Initiates and attendees, who only looked at each other curiously.

"Ok," he then said, "so, let me calculate. Hmmm, the date of my birth, in what I like to describe as the 'Universal Galactic Level of Consciousness,' happened on UGLOC 20,743."

266

"Hmmm," he mumbled once more, gazing up towards the ceiling.

"Why, that makes you approximately 129 years of age," Patto stated.

"Wonderful," Yogga said, his eyes twinkling. "Yes indeed! Well, my friends, you see, time and age in and of themselves do not exist. We created time to help manage our lives Miss Calla, which also led to that noun we label as 'age'. Does this answer your question suitably?"

Everyone sat quietly, but nodding affirmatively.

Bocc, rising, then stood before Yogga.

"Why is it Yogga, that you choose, or need to be in a lofty secluded place, such as this crystal mountain cave, to honor and channel your God. Could you not be on the busiest corner in Spectrum and still be able to meditate, thereby connecting to your Source, while also connecting with many more Beings to enlighten?"

Yogga smiled softly, and then laughed heartily once again.

"Master Bocc," he finally said, "once again, forgive my laughter. In no way is it meant to disrespect your ernest inquiry. To answer your question, yes I could — but you, Master Bocc, you could not, at least, not yet. One must cultivate discipline in order to control distraction, Master Bocc."

"Also, in reference to your usage of the term God, I find that you may suggest I channel God, or the One, or perhaps the Source. Please know Master Bocc, that it is all of the former that has in some way created the spirituality within my soul which I channel and share. I believe in the Goodness of All Things, and the Oneness of All. I believe in a beginning Source. These truths have always existed within me, and are as much a part of me as I am a part of all things that ever were, or that will ever be."

"My 'One,' or your 'God,' or the 'Source' are referenced and referred to by many names and by many tongues. When they become an enlightened truth within you, you will understand that everything has but one Source, and all things are part of the One."

"My new friends, I share what I believe to be my truths, from my personal enlightenment — through experiences and thought. You may agree or disagree, as your own experiences lead you to believe, but I am hopeful you may ponder what I offer and that you may find something helpful. I will be happy for that. We are all blessed, my friends."

"By making this trip, enduring your sacrifices, as arduous and taxing as they have been, you demonstrate to me, and more importantly to yourselves, the significance of your journey. This is your individual pilgrimage, and within it may come a chance discovery of your truth although I rather doubt there is any 'chance' involved. You see, Master Bocc, and fellow friends, this is your personal need at this time. To discover your truth, your inner peace, your spirituality, your One, and your Oneness within."

Yogga smiled softly again, then stood and moved into a stretching position. He looked and saw their quizzed stares, and explained.

"I have found that remaining in a sitting position for to long a time is, well, bad for my posture, and, quite frankly, just becomes uncomfortable. So, if I occasionally engage in various stretching movements and meditate for extended lengths of time, it becomes a disciplined meditation.

I need to engage, and hold these positions while meditating on the reason I am here in the first place. And why I am standing in such an awkward manner, you may ask?"

The Initiates, and attendees once again looked at each other quizzically.

"Listen carefully, my young friends ... an enlightened being once said, if one has faith the size of a mustard seed, then one truly could move mountains!"

Yogga closed his eyes, and still smiling, said...

"I can do this!"

Placing one foot on the inner thigh of his opposite leg and raising both arms high above his head with palms placed together, he stood there unwavering on one leg, apparently deep within his inner space.

Suddenly opening his eyes, he said...

"This is tree position! It isn't always easy!"

He then closed his eyes.

Poona could hardly believe what she was witnessing.

This is a transforming moment ... the transformation of a thought into a movement, that will take root and evolve, once again establishing itself in time — as it had long before.

I have just witnessed the innocent beginning and return of a belief that originated long, long ago on Earth I. Perhaps millions of years ago and all without knowing of it's past. Incredible.

Smiling softly, Poona felt her heart racing.

Bocc, Calla, Annuj, and Patto still sat enthralled by the wise and loving nature of Yogga, who, while remaining in his position of the tree, was mentally far away in some distant and beautiful place.

Poona heard Calla ask Bocc, "What is a mustard seed?"

She chuckled softly and smiled brightly, dwelling on what this meant. The Initiates were not aware of Poona's fulfilling moment, as they too were part of the new beginning, each in their own way and time.

Laurra is here too, thought Poona. *I know it. She will impart and share these thoughts and revelations to Tunnis at the right time. I sense her presence with VisionShare, and she is just as thrilled as I am.*

Laurra 'was' there. She was still resting in Oneness, but as long as

Poona's VisionShare was enabled she could share from afar. The vision slowly faded and Laurra knew that meant Poona had disengaged.

Laurra felt the extreme satisfaction of hopes and beliefs being rewarded. She sensed the thoughts from Poona regarding Tunnis, and nodded, lovingly.

Tunnis had left with his family a few nights before.

It was a wonderful delight, having King Luxxor, Queen Liluuc and Princess Dolpho here for a short stay. I will miss them. I was sad to see Tunnis and his family depart.

Placing her hands on her chest, left over right, and thumb to thumb, she formed the symbolic triangle of the All. Lowering her head, Laurra softly said goodnight to the creative and compassionate Source from the very beginning.

She closed her eyes.

I am feeling so much more complete.

It will be soon!

Chapter 67

The Black Widow Prepares To Share Tea

An encounter on a dusty piece of crust

A ways off, far from the happiness, solitude, and simplicities of Oneness, a drama was beginning to unfold. It was on an unlikely arena — an asteroid they had named, 'A dusty piece of crust.'

DrexL, and the crew of their vessel, now proudly called the Peaceful Voyageur, thanks to an overwhelming vote by the crew, sat waiting for the time to feel right to venture further away from the clutches of CodL. Actually, they were in the midsts of determining their destination when the word came to them.

Salamar approached DrexL indicating he had important news to relay.

"Yes," said DrexL, "what is it Salamar?"

"Champion DrexL, another ship has been sighted and it is making landing preparations nearby. We had not noticed it earlier, as it approached from behind the asteroid Sir, thus blocking our sensors."

"Have we been contacted, and do we know who we are about to entertain as our guests," asked DrexL?

"As of yet we have not been contacted, Sir, but all indications from the viewing tower are consistent with a craft we have all heard of ... that would be the 'Black Widow,' Sir."

DrexL signaled a pause to the meeting and stood. They headed to their posts, with DrexL and Salamar joining the crew on duty in the Control Center of the Peaceful Voyager.

"I am quite familiar with the reputation of this craft, the Black Widow and it's Commander, one LesterJonko," said DrexL.

"They are known to have exceptional capabilities in regards to scientific equipment, including an extremely sophisticated surveillance SpacialGram, which I have only heard about."

"If needed, do we have any indication of their firepower, Sir?"

"Salamar, I understand it is unique and awesome, provided by some giant space corporation from somewhere. Sorry to be so vague. Let us trust that we are not the object of it's scrutiny, or intention to harm."

"Indeed," answered, Salamar.

The Black Widow, sitting down a little ways off from DrexL, immediately sent 3 Spiders to the surface a short distance away. Inside the Black Widow, FinnJonko was scouring the surrounding landscape.

"What a barren and ill fortuned place! I can think of only two reasons to be here. One, you don't want to be found, two, you have craft repairs. Oh, and a third — you are not in your right mind!"

LesterJonko nodding in agreement, stated...

"If the third reason is accurate, then CodL is in there, but according to our present information, we don't believe he is."

Addressing his chief pilot, LesterJonko asked...

"Are all our players in place and at the ready?"

"They are in place, and ready, Sir."

"Alright, lets do it. What we want to know is, who is in there, and why they are here in the first place."

Looking at his son, and the attending crew, he stated...

"Let's find out."

Contact them, see if a meeting is in the realm of possibility, and if so, set it up. We need to see of their intentions and take care of this situation before CodL, and his main craft arrive on the scene."

Meanwhile, the Peaceful Voyageur was monitoring the Black Widow and it's infamous Spiders. DrexL knew the Peaceful Voyager was not equipped to withstand the superior capabilities of the Black Widow should it initiate hostile actions.

So, DrexL waited.

The wait was short, as the message came soon after the Black Widow sat down.

"She is opening communications, Champion DrexL," stated LugA.

"The Commander, LesterJonko, is requesting a meeting, and indicates it is important."

"Answer them, LugA and ask what his requirements and intentions are."

"LesterJonko, has been in pursuit of the RogueEmpire — mainly CodL, and it has been on his agenda for some time now," DrexL stated to LugA.

"Sir, the reply I have received is a rather odd invitation for you."

"What is that," asked DrexL, suspiciously, but curiously?

"Well, Sir, they, that is, LesterJonko has invited you, and a party of your choosing, to join him aboard the Black Widow for..."

"For what," asked DrexL?

271

"For tea, Sir. For tea."

"Tea?!"

"Yes, Sir, for tea."

DrexL smiled. His uneasiness dissipated.

"That is quite hospitable of him." "So," he added, "it appears we are to be the guests rather than the hosts. Send back our reply that I gladly accept, and stipulate a request for 'green tea.' Add that there will be four attending, and that we look forward to sipping a fine tea together. Sign it Commander DrexL of the Peaceful Voyageur."

"Yes, Sir," grinned LugA.

FinnJonko received the reply to their invitation, and chuckled as he read it.

"It seems like pretty decent folk aboard the vessel they are calling the Peaceful Voyageur. An unusual name for a RogueEmpire Vessel."

The Commander, DrexL, has indicated he would like green tea, father.

LesterJonko, looked at his son, then laughed.

"It appears we will have to rummage through the cupboards, Finn."

Chapter 68

Remaining Neutral Was Not On Her Agenda

Let it be, Mulon— Ginesthoi

Having confirmed Laurra's health as excellent, Poona excused herself from any activities or subsequent spontaneous events, exclaiming she needed to have some time to herself.

"Perhaps one or two days," she said, "in order to reflect on my experiences while crossing the vast Place of Dust."

Which is absolutely true, she thought.

Walking through the gravel near the Pool of Oneness. she noticed Pantheon lounging in the shade of the trees. He turned and quizzically looked her way as she disappeared behind a large dunne.

Magnificent Being!

Poona was now Princess Poona, the Emerald Empress of The Moon and 7Stars. Well aware, and well informed of the situation occurring on the asteroid between the groups they of Topaz were monitoring. Analyzing the details as they were relayed to her, she determined that at this particular time a situation was developing which required her to make an appearance.

It is time to lay some ground rules I have been considering for some time.

Empress Poona, intuitively sensing the urgency of the moment, prepared to respond to any actions being considered by those on the asteroid, or elsewhere. Being recently informed of the imminent arrival of CodL and his RogueEmpireWarrior I fighting ship, she considered...

CodL seems to be in a hurry, no doubt with a mission in mind.

Walking further into the dunnes, she also considered the connection of the three crafts here in this Galaxy, all at the same time.

There is the Black Widow, with Commander LesterJonko, an opportunist working for Corporations on Earth and known to be somewhat unscrupulous, but considered a fair person — a smaller reconnoissance craft known as a RogueRecon, which had been dispatched some time ago from CodL's Empire and believed Championed by DrexL — and finally, the approaching arrival of the RogueEmpire Warrior I, a major combat vessel with untold 'Dark Capes' aboard, and commanded by CodL. There is no possibility the three crafts being here together is an innocent encounter of fate. No, I sense an immediate danger for Prismacia.

She, and those of Topaz always knew that there would be those who came searching — searching for ores, plunder, enslavement … seeking to exploit.

And, Prismacia was a jewel.

Where ever it was in the known Universe, when a situation began unfolding in a way deemed detrimental for all Beings involved, or destruction of ancient knowledge was obvious, the Wise Ones of Topaz intervened. Situations were altered where they felt circumstances required their involvement.

However, at times, she considered, *they allowed the ways of life and the Heavens to play out the scenarios to their ultimate ends, feeling that some events are immanent in life, and should be allowed to occur — good or otherwise.* She remembered, they had stated…

It is the way of all existence.

This concerned Empress Poona. She did not agree with this concept, or any ideology that she felt lacked compassion. Inwardly, she always questioned, and at times, participated in augmentation with the Wise Ones of Topaz about doing nothing for 'some' in need of help, while at other times immediately sanctioning the aid of victims in a similar situation.

All people deserve to be offered assistance and hope, she thought, looking around. *But in this case we are here on Prismacia, a planet that houses the recorded history of all Beings in all time … not to mention beginnings long thought lost forever are surfacing once again.*

"*But, Goodness,*" Empress Poona spoke, "*If we of Topaz are truly being guided and enlightened by the One, then we can not sit back and judge who will be helped and who we allow to be left to the will of fate, or power. We must aid all that we possibly can.*"

I wonder if that is Heavenly possible. It is a colossal, and staggering responsibility, she considered. She shook her head at the thought.

Empress Poona then avowed, "*In my mind, if at all possible, I will always offer aid to all who lay in the way of peril. Remaining neutral to atrocities, or injustice, will never be an option. One day, when face to face, or Spirit to Spirit, with the One, I will bring this up for discussion.*"

Lifting her eyes to the Heavens, she took in a deep breath.

Empress Poona, now having entered into the black sands of the adjacent Carbonian Desert, finally sat down and waited.

The softly glowing Emerald Starburst silently appeared.

As she entered, CrownStarBeing Mulon greeted the Emerald Empress respectfully, and informed her of the latest developments. She sat, listening.

Then she went to her suite to prepare herself spiritually, and physically for the encounter ahead.

After a short meditation, Empress Poona went about selecting her attire for the occasion. The fabric of the simple pure white gown she chose was exotic and rare, originating from Plaieton, one of the 7Stars in her galaxy of Topaz.

It was of delicate bufur, which had been shorn from a high desert life Being called Simubu.

White symbolizes purity and truth, and is the pure non color from which all colors have their origin. On the other hand, she considered, *my robe will be green as green represents calming, and trust, and also is the color that contains all colors.*

Poona then sat down before her vision view and artfully applied soft, subtle colors for her eyes, face, and lips, giving special attention to enhancing the eyes.

They illuminate the Soul, she recalled!

Reaching for her head band, and gathering up the Scepter of The Moon and 7Stars which she nestled against her arm completing the aura, Empress Poona stood, and gave one last look.

"My skin is softly glowing ... it is done," she said, thinking...

Image is not everything, but it can be significantly instrumental in representing and achieving one's goals.

Shortly, CrownStarBeing Mulon approached.

"We have arrived, my Empress. We are on the asteroid, and are prepared to transbeam you aboard the Black Widow where Commanders LesterJonko and DrexL are having tea."

Empress Poona looked at Mulon curiously, and echo'd, *"Tea?"*

Nodding affirmatively, CrownStarBeing Mulon smiled.

She too then smiled, saying...

"Perhaps some semblance of a civilized mind may be in attendance after all, Mulon."

Bowing her head, she placed her hands over her heart, left over right, thumbs up and touching. She called on the One.

"Oh, Goodness of All Things, I ask for your guidance,

clarity, and compassion. And, also understanding — I need to understand."

A radiant glow appeared, and the Starlites danced about her.
The Emerald Empress of The Moon and 7Stars,
Princess Poona, was ready.
"Let it be, Mulon ... Ginesthoi."

Chapter 69

Tea Was Served

They were just getting up ... when

DrexL, LugA, Salamar, and MorQ boarded the Black Widow. Greeted by Commander LesterJonko and his son Finn, a brief, period of formalities ensued resulting in an understanding that their mutual positions regarding CodL and his RogueEmpire were on the same page.

Lester and his son Finn found their guests surprisingly pleasant and unthreatening and happily began showing them around the Black Widow.

Arriving at the Control Center, Finn gave a brief demonstration of the SpacialGram's capabilities to their visitor's amazement. LugA, MorQ, and Salamar just stood, shaking their heads while DrexL, hands on his hips, watched in awe as 'actual time' happenings were seen — as they were occurring.

"Slices of the Heavens in miniature," he stated.

"What will they come up with next?"

"It would seem reasonable that other layers of the Heavens could float above and below, or before and behind, allowing for somewhat of a 3-dimensional Spacialgram," MorQ said. "Of course, I would need to study up on the specific diagrams to determine if it is physically feasible to stack Spacialgram layers. It sounds intriguing though."

"A sound deduction and suggestion, Mr. MorQ," said Finn. "I will look forward to discussing the probabilities later if you like. I am sure someone, somewhere, is working on all we speak of, and more."

"I am Chief Engineer and Scientist, Finn," stated MorQ, "but, I prefer, and answer to just MorQ."

"You got it ... MorQ," smiled Finn.

Second on the highlights of the tour were the Spider webs.

"We have all heard of these," said DrexL. "Webs of doom, I've been informed."

"Well," answered LesterJonko, "I will agree you do not want these wrapping up your vessel."

Ushering them towards a lift, LesterJonko said…

"Come, let us retire to the Red Spot Lounge, where, I have been informed, tea, that is, 'green tea,' is awaiting our arrival."

"Tell me, Commander DrexL, how is it you have disengaged yourself and your crew from CodL," questioned LesterJonko?

"I honestly feel the vast majority of my crew, and myself have harbored these thoughts of separation from CodL for a long time," DrexL replied.

Then looking over at MorQ, he said, "But MorQ is just a stowaway!"

Everybody, including MorQ laughed.

"The obvious, difficult part," DrexL continued, "was how, and when, and whom to trust. As things continued to deteriorate on The RogueEmpireComplex, it became increasingly evident that something had to be done. CodL was spiraling out of control almost to the point of madness. Actually, I truly believe he has attained that level. My one and only advantage was that most of the men in CodL's command were from my home planet of Trion. A mining planet, if you are not aware, Commander LesterJonko."

"I am aware, Commander DrexL, and I see we have arrived at the Red Spot. Please be seated," he said, gesturing to a table with a large view port, and an assortment of snacks to embellish the preferred libation of choice, green tea.

Taking their seats, he added…

"I would like to suggest we drop the formalities. Please call me Lester or LesterJonko."

Smiling, DrexL extended his hand, and echoed the sentiment. "I too, will like that, LesterJonko."

They shook hands, after which everybody shook hands, and a second wave of awkwardness was vanquished from the scene.

For nearly three hours everyone shared their encounters and stories regarding CodL … and Lester's fascinating vessel, the Black Widow.

Sitting back in his seat, FinnJonko looked around at the faces of the men who had either endured the prison of being in CodL's command, or had endured his wrath, or both.

"An end must be brought to this situation," he said. "I do not know what brings such evil to our lives, but it must end, and soon."

"I can guarantee that CodL is not far behind, said DrexL. You see, unbeknownst to CodL, Salamar, supposedly aboard my ship as a spy for CodL, has been secretly sending him false messages about our whereabouts. Salamar feels the same way as I about the terrible conditions

CodL enforces on everyone. He approached me and told me of the subterfuge CodL had demanded from him."

"I have great respect for you, Salamar," DrexL said, looking kindly at his new friend.

We owe a huge debt to you. You put yourself on the line for not only your ideals, but also for me and for all the men aboard the Peaceful Voyager. It will never be forgotten."

"Without question," LesterJonko said, "it is a pretty well known fact I have been scouring the Heavens for CodL, and, if you're right about him being on his way, maybe this is the web he might just fly into."

They were just getting up when the vision materialized.

Chapter 70

The Emerald Empress Visits A Black Widow

Forgive my intrusion, gentlemen

They were half out of their seats when the aberration began to manifest before them. The men gathered on the Black Widow froze momentarily in place, unable to fathom just what was occurring before them.

It began as constantly moving, twinkling starlites, within a mist. Then slowly, Princess Poona, the Emerald Empress of Topaz, materialized. The starlites, of blue, white and magenta colors, moved slowly, encompassing her completely.

She appeared wondrous and other worldly!

The scene unfolding before their eyes was one of controlled mastery, including knowledge, power and technical advances certainly beyond their understanding. Only in their imagination could they have conjured up this scenario.

The mist and starlites lingered, but when the vision within the mist presented itself to them, they saw that of a young woman, totally captivating, radiating sovereignty, command and beauty! All they could do at this moment was to look on in awe. An immediate feeling that the vision meant no threat to them prevailed, but they could not comprehend what was occurring, or why.

Peering through the mist and starlites, Empress Poona, smiled softly, but remained silent for a few moments, studying the men. They waited and wondered.

Lester and FinnJonko looked at each other, quickly ascertaining that no alert, or alarm from the Control Center had preceded this appearance. In fact, as they came to find out, the Spacialgram had not scanned or picked up on any indication of nearby, or distant spacecraft at all.

FinnJonko judged her height to be around six feet.

Tall for a woman Being. And, he realized, *she is of a coloration I am not aware of. She obviously is formidable,* he continued thinking, *but at the same time, there is a softness about her.*

"Incredible," he uttered under his breath, to his father.

Empress Poona's simplistic gown of pure white softly caressed her form exquisitely. With sensual folds extending to her ankles, the contrast emphasized the blue shade of her skin pigmentation. She had accented her gown with a waist sash of emerald green, encrusted with small opalescent moonstones.

The men noticed she seemed to be faintly glowing in a minute pulsating fashion enhanced by the ever moving twinkling mist.

Known for it's spiritual illumination, a delicate small headband inlayed with tiny blue, magenta, and white polished gems rested regally upon her head.

Thick silver and gray hair cascaded down below Empress Poona's shoulders.

Over her gown, and draping to the floor, she wore a robe cape of emerald green. The cape's tall collar extended up to the middle of her head accenting her slender neck and was also trimmed wth ancient opals.

Large, light grey-blue eyes, accentuated in pale magenta eye shadow and a sparse silver sparkle wash projected truth and command. Upon her left cheek and neck, Empress Poona had applied rare Trolon, signifying the symbol designating the Moon and 7Stars. Finally, cradled in her arms, she held the 'Scepter' designating the Moon & 7Stars of Topaz.

The men were speechless. To a man their hearts were pounding in awe and anticipation — and bewilderment.

When the Emerald Empress, Poona spoke, it was eloquently, resiliently, and forthright. They could, but listen.

"Forgive my intrusion gentlemen and the unusual dramatic fashion in which I join you — unannounced.

But, let me assure you, at times, there are times, when time is of the essence, and gentlemen ... we are all here at this time with a common purpose."

Princess Poona, slightly bowing her head, gestured to them.

"I now choose to answer the curiosities you must all be wondering and speculating about — as to who I am, what am I, and why am I here. To begin with, I am that, that I am ... Princess Poona, the Emerald Empress of the Moon and 7 Stars.

I represent the Beings of a group of worlds that peacefully co-inhabit our galaxy known as Topaz. It is a galaxy and world I highly doubt you are familiar with, gentlemen."

"Topaz is quite close, but for those who are not yet capable,

it is an improbable and, quite frankly, an insurmountable distance away. Topaz, and those of Topaz are generally unknown, especially in your dimension. It is our choice," she stated with resolve, "to remain undiscovered, gentlemen."

"Generally, in normal circumstances, I would greet other Beings without the mist cloud, and 'Clinamen starlites' you see twinkling about me. But, you see, this is also my Being Shield."

Gesturing with open arms to the gently moving mist and starlites continuing to encompass her, she explained.

"Together they protect me during my transbeam ... as I materialize, and as I completely emerge into my Being body. For your curiosity, the starlites you see enveloping me, gentlemen, are millions of tiny atoms in a perpetual swerving motion. Because of this motion, nature is altered, creating an impenetrable fabric.

As you can see, this fabric, or Being Shield includes the appearance of mist, or fog. Along with the Clinamen starlites it assures that absolutely nothing will pass through the barrier it collectively creates."

Smiling, she continued.

"It is actually an interesting story how this came to be, gentlemen. The Clinamen were named by a poet from many, many eons ago named Lucretius. He was from the Planet known as Earth 1. His was only a theory, mind you, but, as we discovered in our research, a very sound theory that we enhanced to what I have described and what you see today. For what it is worth, Lucretius also felt that the Gods were indifferent in regards to their creation, which would be you, and me, and everything that is. However, we of Topaz believe, from our experience, that Lucretius was incorrect on that point!"

She smiled, glancing at each of those present.

LesterJonko, FinnJonko, DrexL, LugA, MorQ, Salamar, and several 'men of arms' all continued to stand, mesmerized and baffled by the astonishing eloquence of the oration given by Princess Poona, the Emerald Empress of Topaz.

This is not a SpacialGram, thought LesterJonko, shaking his head in wonder. He then noticed that the Being Shield had vanished and he had not even noticed it had dissipated. *Intriguing,* he thought.

"Now, gentlemen," Empress Poona continued...

"*I will address why I am here. It is paramount that we discuss a matter of utmost importance. There is an immediate and clear danger rapidly approaching those of us gathered here and others yet to be disclosed.*

This is urgent, but gentlemen, let me assure you that we of Topaz have taken care to see that matters, at this point, do not get further out of hand."

Poignantly, she said...

"*This danger involves none other than the object of your discussions today — namely, CodL, and his intentions.*"

This bit of news shocked the group back to some semblance of reality. They looked at each other inquisitively thinking …

How does she know?

"You are aware of our conversations, here on the Black Widow, Empress Poona," asked FinnJonko?

"*We, of the Moon and 7Stars, are not ones to eavesdrop on your private conversations, Mr...?*"

"My apologies, Empress Poona, allow me to introduce myself, and those of our gathering. I am FinnJonko, the son of LesterJonko who Commands of the Black Widow." He then directed her attention to each of the others in turn as he introduced them. Empress Poona lowered her head in respect and softly bowed to the men before her.

"*It is indeed a blessing gifted to me to make your acquaintance,*" she said, slightly cocking her head to one side and smiling.

"*Accept my apologies for not exchanging introductions earlier. You are being most accommodating and patient, given the circumstance of my uninvited arrival. I thank you all.*

As I was saying, we are not ones to eavesdrop. So to answer your inquiry and concern, FinnJonko … no!"

"*From what we have ascertained, and given the occurrences that have taken place in the last several weeks, the area became clear where the paths of all parties could, and would converge. It only became a matter of when.*

As to the subject of any conversation taking place here on the Black Widow, it was an obvious deduction. It could be none other than CodL, given the impending confrontation between he, and either the Black Widow, and or DrexL of the RogueRecon craft.

We of the Moon and 7Stars felt discretion was not an

option at this time. *The other, yet unnamed disclosure I had mentioned earlier, which is of utmost importance, is our 'particular, and primary' interest ... the planet Prismacia."*

"My pardon, Empress Poona," interrupted DrexL, "but I must inform you that there has been a consensus of opinion from the crew aboard my craft and it is now proudly known as the "Peaceful Voyageur."

"Well," a smiling Empress Poona said, *"a welcome change that I find quite appealing. The Peaceful Voyageur it is!"*

"Empress Poona," asked DrexL...

"what is the importance of Prismacia,"?

"Commander, to be blunt and completely open, Prismacia is one of only three places in the entire Heavens that shelters the recorded accumulative memories of all recorded time. That fact alone will always be enough to confirm our presence, but there are other vital components that, in their own way, will have a profound effect on civilization as we know it to be ... and become. They will be protected!"

"If what I am understanding is correct," DrexL responded, "we call Prismacia Planet 8 of Galaxy 17, and it is indeed in CodL's sights."

"It is as Divine Providence degrees then — that we are here, together, at this time."

Princess Poona turned to LesterJonko.

"Commander LesterJonko, I suggest we move on to the Control Center and initiate the SpacialGram you have on board. If you bring forth the particular section of the Heavens we are now in, including Prismacia, or Planet 8 of Galaxy 17 as you are familiar with, I will explain my visit. Included will be what we of the Moon and 7Stars have decided is a plausible scenario for all the participants involved, and what we intend to do, and will do, gentlemen."

"It is our ardent hope that upon hearing our intention, you will see it's potential and offer your support and blessings ... irregardless of any prior considerations or plans you may have forged. I will also expand on the priceless value of Prismacia and why it will be protected at all costs."

Chapter 71

I Can Not Know The Outcome, Only The Intent

I understand green tea is good for you

Walking to the Control Center, each man contemplated the recent events, considering questions and attempting to comprehend the bizarre situation in which they were now entangled. Salamar, summoning up his courage, walked up along side Empress Poona.

"Empress Poona, if I may ask, why is Prismacia so special that the sum total of all knowledge is kept there?"

"And, Empress Poona," asked LugA, who had joined them, "if the value to all Beings it represents is irreplaceable, should not Prismacia be better protected, given all the unknowns that could possibly occur?"

Empress Poona, stopped and smiled politely.

"Empress Poona," said MorQ, "you stated there were three locations that this knowledge is stored in. Maybe there are precautions we are unaware of in place. I personally believe, given the importance of these planets, there is."

Empress Poona warmly contemplated the three men before her.

"Very reasonable questions and observations, gentleman. As the evening progresses I hope to satisfactorily answer these questions and even more for you."

When they arrived at the Control Center, FinnJonko immediately entered into the SpacialGram the coordinates for their sector, and that of Planet 8.

Looking at Empress Poona, he said...

"For my own curiosity, and the future security of our craft, I have to ask ... how were you aware of the SpacialGram aboard the Black Widow, Empress Poona?"

"Before a situation such as this encounter, FinnJonko, when one enters an unfamiliar place, we of the Moon and 7Stars

285

employ what we call a 'Blue Radiant Scan.' It is necessary to acquaint ourselves with the 'unknown entity' in question, and any 'not' in question — for safety concerns! We noticed the SpacialGram."

All nodded affirmatively, inwardly mulling over just what is a Blue Radiant Scan, before turning to the slices of Heaven Empress Poona had requested.

Pausing, Empress Poona then gathered everyone's attention.

"Gentlemen, please understand there are times it is necessary for me to be Empress Poona, The Emerald Empress, as I represent not only the Beings of Topaz, but the myriad of others who cannot represent themselves. They need, and depend on my voice.

But, LesterJonko, as Commander of this fine vessel, the Black Widow, it is my wish that we now address each other less formally. Please address me as Princess Poona and let us all speak openly, and candidly."

"Agreed," said LesterJonko with the others nodding their approval.

Princess Poona slightly raised her Scepter, and smiling thoughtfully, addressed them again...

"However, gentlemen, please be aware that there may be times during our conversations when I involuntarily lapse back into the persona of Empress Poona.

Often, you see, Empress Poona speaks from a different podium than Princess Poona. Understand that it is not to elevate, or separate my station as an Empress, but to emphasize and express clearly to you, from within my Soul, certain truths, that 'we of Topaz,' have found throughout our experiences in the Heavens of our existence. And gentlemen, our presence within the Heavens is vast."

"So, Princess Poona," spoke FinnJonko, while gesturing to the hovering SpacialGram, "what you see before you is the live time Slice of Heaven we are now occupying. Just so you are not confused, a 'Slice of Heaven' is the name I have christened the SpacialGram," smiled FinnJonko.

Princess Poona smiled. LesterJonko shook his head. The others nodded.

"And this is the Slice of Heaven where Planet 8, or Prismacia, is located," he said pointing to a colorful area of the SpacialGram.

"Using this infra-heat ray detector, we can seek out heat emitting objects, from large planets, to space craft, to small probes, to meteors, etc. The SpacialGram is capable of enlarging an area in question so even small objects like this asteroid we are now on can be seen and examined."

"How about demonstrating by showing a couple of crafts sitting on this crusty old asteroid," asked, LesterJonko, grinning?

DrexL smiled too, and turned to FinnJonko for his reply.

"No problem, father," looking over and raising an eyebrow.

Everyone watched as FinnJonko set the coordinates, adjusted the zoom attachment, and activated the infra-heat ray detector directing it at the floating Heavens before them. Just as he had promised, two tiny red dots appeared on the asteroid they now inhabited. But also, completely surrounding the dots they surprisingly saw something resembling a vapory cloud.

Pointing to the cloud, Princess Poona stated, "For your information, that will be a contingent of the Moon and 7Stars, and a protective barrier not unlike the mist and fog that surrounded me."

"Poona, if I may ask an inquiry," said DrexL. He then smiled, saying, "I apologize, I mean, Princess Poona."

"Yes, of course."

"In due respect Princess Poona, you might understand my confusion and questioning of why you are here, if, at least in my mind, you and the Beings of the Moon and 7Stars have already decided on a plan of action that will take place with or without our approval."

Reverting back to the Emerald Empress as predicted, she looked assuredly into their eyes.

"Yes DrexL, your question is worthy of asking and worthy of an answer. You see, after many offerings of possibilities were spoken of among the Elders and the Wise Ones, the very problem you speak of remained a conundrum. We always pursue what we ascertain is the 'appropriate action' to take in each individual circumstance where we feel the need to intercede. And, unfailingly, gentlemen, the added inclusion of those deemed essential is always considered. Let me clarify that the 'appropriate actions' I speak of are guided by our faith in the Goodness of All Things."

"When bad things happen, and they unfortunately do, it is our true belief that Goodness will always overcome evil.

In special instances like this one, allowances to make a decision beforehand are deemed necessary for the sake of expediency. It is a critical situation, gentlemen, apparently spiraling out of control.

CodL was readying his forces to battle you that stand before me, with Prismacia possibly hanging in the balance.

We felt the outcome would be favorable to you, but the loss of precious lives would be extreme on both sides. And, however unlikely, if by chance CodL would somehow be victorious, his ultimate goal, and present focus would lay vulnerable before him."

"And, that focus is Prismacia," asked LesterJonko?

"Yes, gentlemen … Prismacia."

"You see," Princess Poona continued, slipping back into the informal, "nothing was presenting itself to us as a credible or persuasive alternative. From what we could discern, the Black Widow and the RogueRecon — pardon me, the Peaceful Voyageur, and those in command, were gearing up for a confrontation with the inevitable conclusion of suffering, loss of precious lives and eventual revenge or retaliation. It could be termed Goodness against Evil. But, as you certainly know, DrexL, there are many, many Beings under the influence of CodL who are, when given the chance, good Beings. Beings that, afforded the opportunity, could contribute in a positive way."

DrexL, nodded affirmatively, his mind drifting off to the Triton mining colonies, and then the EmpireComplex. He knew many men and women who fit the image Princess Poona described.

"We, also could not guarantee that CodL, in an act of deviousness, would not bypass the encounter with you altogether and attempt to assault Prismacia first. Obviously, he would have us to deal with, but, as I stated, it was a conundrum, and we must always entertain the possibility of an unexpected scenario."

"This is why, gentlemen," … Princess Poona stopped, smiled, and looking at the men standing around her, said, "may I be allowed to address you as my new friends?"

Everyone smiled, and shook their heads yes.

"Thank you all," she sincerely replied.

"Then, to continue, my new friends, this is why we expedited all facets of our involvement to come up with what we know to be a good and potentially great solution. One with hopefully no loss of lives. We are aware there is no absolute certainty or guarantee that a conclusion we deem as favorable will indeed succeed, but we believe our intention deserves a chance." Princess Poona transformed to The Emerald Princess once again.

"Lastly, my friends, there is Prismacia. Prismacia, simply put, is the beginning, once again, of an evolution of Beings

free from tyranny, greed, and all that accompanies such. It is, at present, a world of goodness, innocence, compassion, and learning. Yes, accidents happen. People do pass on to the next level. People can be sad, and fearful — perhaps even questioning life or why unfortunate situations occur. Being 'Beings' they make mistakes, including leaders and wise ones. They may create laws that in time, are deemed unfair, or insensitive ... but always they have elevated themselves to overcome any inequitable decisions, or misfortunes."

"Those of Prismacia are happy to help each other attain that which makes the other happy. All of which envelopes the purpose of life itself and is inherently natural to Beings through out the Heavens. Just imagine — life without the debilitating dark energy of hate, or anger, or jealousy, or greed, my friends — emotions that have seemingly always found their way into the existence of Beings."

"Those of Prismacia are a 'renaissance,' if you will, of a blueprint of life that somehow went astray long, long ago. They represent a new beginning, one that repeats itself from our very Source.

In addition, as I have also mentioned, Prismacia is one of the hallowed places in all the Heavens where the stories of 'All Things' are secured within certain sacred crystals, found through-out the lands and seas. It is the unknowing guardian, and it's people the unknowing custodians of the History of Time itself. As the guardian of All Things past and present, Prismacia's destiny is crucial. As I have stated, there has been a complete lack of hostilities during Prismacia's existence. Natural disasters always remain a concern, but Prismacia must, and will be protected. It must be allowed to continue it's growth and to flourish. For the sake of all, Prismacia and it's inhabitants are the hope for all Beings present, and those yet to be."

With glistening eyes, Empress Poona paused. The men all stood, silently.

"LesterJonko, FinnJonko, DrexL, Luga, Salamar, MorQ, you need look no further to discover that which you search and long for. Perhaps you will choose to be an intricate part of this new beginning I speak of. You would be welcomed."

Concluding, Empress Poona added...

"To the best of our abilities, we will never let an outside

influence destroy the history and the promise of all Beings of the Heavens. Never! For the Goodness of All Things, and for those voices I yield to, and those I protect, I do so promise."

Lowering her head, Empress Poona placed her hands, left over right upon her heart, with her thumbs pointed up and touching.

"My new friends, very soon I will have an extended visit with Commander CodL. Hopefully it will aid in encouraging and administering his return from the depressive anger, rage, and loneliness that has eaten away at his Soul for all these many years — actually, his entire existence. Please respect that I can not know the exact outcome, my friends, only my intent. With that said, I must now prepare to introduce myself to our current concern ... CodL."

"Get to know each other for another month or so, my friends. I understand green tea is good for you."

Softly raising her arms, the Climanen starlites and mist of her Being Shield resumed their journey around her Heavenly presence, and Empress Poona simply dissolved in a million tiny twinklings.

Chapter 72

Time Apart From Each Other

Poona sat there and could hardly believe it

Tonight, they had chosen the oasis pool for their gathering, and meal. The Initiate's normal evening meal together included discussing anything that was on anybody's mind. Patto, attired in the traditional silver robe and desert clothing of his Quin, stood before the Initiates, now all reunited, here at Oneness.

All were rested and had spent many memorable hours together sharing the journeys, and stories each had encountered on their chosen paths.

Patto had been struggling most of the day with how, or even if, to present a suggestion that in some ways he was not totally in favor of himself. However, he did feel it could be a vital addition to the Wisdom Path Journey they were all sharing. As he put his thoughts together, his gaze found Poona, and lingered for an instant, before he began.

"My friends, I have a suggestion to offer you. I choose to bring up the possibility of what I am calling 'personal aloneness and development time' for each of us. What I mean is, time apart from each other to reflect on our Wisdom Path Journey thus far. I realize we have each had ample opportunity throughout our journey to seek personal clarity, and at various times, we have each sought opinions or counsel from within our group. We have also recently taken alternative paths in different groups — but never alone. Through trust we have all come to rely on each other, and the bond we have created among ourselves has become strong. However, in my opinion, we have not taken adequate time to be by one's self, to rely on just ourselves, and explore personal aloneness that is inherent in being a Being."

Looking around at the Initiates, Patto then commented...

"Quite honestly, I have apprehensions about what I am suggesting. This is something I have never been inclined to attempt. While I am often

291

alone during my observance of the stars, my mind is busy with all the related aspects of my research — not the same as what I now present to you."

"I am open to discussion, but I am suggesting a time frame of one to two months, which will definitely be a challenge. It is quite a significant amount of time to be with yourself, and no others. It may not be easy. I doubt that it will be. But, I sincerely believe this to be as important as any of our other objectives during our Wisdom Path Journey, and, importantly, I must add that at any time, should one feel the need to return, they should do so.

And, at any time, should one need to communicate with Poona, due to illness, or emergency, it is imperative that they do so immediately. We can set up a 'check in' each evening through the crystal prisms found every where, or our personal crystal Palm Recorders. It will be known that we are all well. I am not sure if what I bring up for consideration would be condoned by the Voice of One — but, it is our journey and it truly is our path to decide. So, I have introduced my thoughts. Should you have a similar feeling, or should you be opposed, please offer it now if you so choose."

Everyone was silent for a moment before Bocc arose.

"This could be a daunting decision for those of us who are not sure, Patto. I suggest we take this evening to continue discussing it, and then dwell on your suggestion until we meet over breakfast in the morning. We can then share our feelings. Some may approve, some may not."

Everyone nodded in approval.

Poona sat there, hardly believing the way things were working out for her.

Thank you Goodness of All Things, she silently projected to The One.

She had been mulling over different ideas on how to excuse herself, once again, for what would be a considerable length of time away in order to accomplish the essential, and formidable task which lay ahead with CodL. And now Patto had come up with the perfect solution.

Well, not perfect, but it will do!

As difficult as it may be, she had calculated a month or a little more, given unknowns, should hopefully be adequate for what lies ahead with CodL.

Either it will come to be in that time, or it will not, she determined.

Poona then stood to address them.

"My friends, I do not want to influence anyone, but I choose to make my decision now, as I believe this to be a sound idea.

As Patto mentioned, aloneness is not easy, especially for an extended length of time. It can however, be potentially beneficial for one's being. As you are all aware, I recently asked to be excused for two days for personal reasons. I needed time away, and although it was for only two days, it helped me to strengthen and unify situations I needed to clarify. I choose to now go into a space I believe will be rewarding and fulfilling, not only for me, but hopefully to benefit everyone's future in some way.

Should the morning bring an agreement between us, I will begin my personal time away immediately following breakfast. But, by no means will I be further away than a communication. I give you my word. I am your Caregiver, and will be accessible. As Patto suggested, a communications connection will be set up via the crystal Palm Recorders, or crystal prisms."

Then, smiling at Solannuj, who hosted their meal, she added...

"With Solannuj's help this will be arranged. All will be expected to comply by checking in each day at a specific time. Should anything occur emotionally or physically, you are to contact her at once, and either she, or I, will take the measures needed to help you. Whatever your decisions, I wish you a continued rewarding Path, my friends. We will not always physically be around for each other, and perhaps a part of this journey should be to personally examine, and strengthen that very aspect of life ... feeling connected to a comforting strength, a source within our very souls — even when we are alone."

Turning to leave, she inwardly and briefly reverted to Princess Poona, the Emerald Empress. She looked back over her shoulder...

"If one believes, even as a mustard seed, are we ever truly alone?"

Early the next morning, after breakfast, and a unanimous decision for 'aloneness time,' Princess Poona entered the Emerald Starburst. It was a short distance away from Oneness in the nearby mountains, and hidden from any view by a large cluster of violet crystals.

Her mission began.

Chapter 73

I Know Your Name And I Know Your Nightmares

The encounter occurs

DregO anxiously approached Emperor CodL, bowed, and then kneeled.

"My Emperor, there is an extreme situation requiring your interpretation immediately."

CodL looked at him oddly.

What is this idiot going on about, he thought.

"Well, don't just kneel there. Tell me what you mean, and quickly."

"My Emperor, something has placed itself in front of the RogueEmpire Warrior I preventing us from moving. We cannot budge, your Excellency."

CodL sat there, totally confused and astounded.

His eyes became wild.

"Are you telling me, your Emperor, that the RougeEmpire Warrior I cannot move! This is ludicrous ... almost laughable. Why are we not laughing, DregO?"

Rising, Codl hurriedly pushed DregO aside and rushed to the Control Center. What he saw through the view screen astonished him. Hovering in front of them were 7 bright lights, Starbursts, with hundreds, if not thousands of small twinkling lights moving in and around them.

"Like star-flies," he murmured to himself.

DregO informed him the Starbursts were calculated to be approximately 45 feet high by 60 feet wide and 120 feet deep.

"The Starbursts are in the shape of an ancient symbol I once saw, my Emperor," DregO stated, while looking at the extraordinary scene. "But," he continued, "these are different in that they are glowing in white, magenta, and blue colors. We have determined these colors to be an energy field similar to electricity, which is constantly moving among them."

"I can see that DregO," CodL responded indignantly.

Considering his alternatives, CodL commanded…

"Move forward through them."

"As I said before, we cannot, our Emperor," DregO managed to say, fully cognizant of CodL's response.

"WE CANNOT?" CodL screamed, looking insanely back at DregO ?!

Grabbing the control lever from the chief pilot, TragL, CodL thrust it forward.

A slight jar and then nothing. The same result in reverse.

"Turn on the Nero thrusters, full power," he yelled.

"We have, Emperor CodL. We have tried, but to no avail Sir," pleaded TragL.

"Nothing we have tried responds, your Immanence," DregO offered nervously.

CodL looked at the crew standing around him.

What do I have here, he thought. *Are they all born from the same pathetic idiotic parentage?!*

Turning his attention back to the view screen, CodL hastily calculated his next command.

"Then blast them with the Neuro bursts, full force. I will play around no longer," CodL yelled. "They are like sitting ducks out there. Shoot them out of the Heavens, and out of the way. Destroy them, whoever, and whatever they are."

Then quickly turning to the crew once again, he added…

"Have they attempted to contact us."

"No Sir," said DregO.

"THEN BLAST 'EM! Here, I'll do the honors," CodL yelled.

Setting the sights, he sent a full force Neuro burst towards one of the Starbursts. The shot flashed forth towards it's target, and disappeared into the Starburst's light field. Nothing!

Nothing happened at all!

CodL was in shock, appalled, disbelieving. He was now perspiring with spittle slowly dribbling out of the corners of his frowning mouth. Nausea began churning in his stomach.

This is something I have never experienced, or even ever heard about in the whole of the known Universe, he frantically thought. *What kind of barrier field could possibly just eradicate or negate a full force Neuro burst?*

He sent a second shot, experiencing the same result.

Then came the Voice. So very soft, but so very clear, and so very compelling. The voice of a woman …

"CodL…"

"Yes CodL, I know your name…

*I know your thoughts ... I know your intentions,
and, CodL ... I know your nightmares."*

CodL stepped back, wavering.

*How can this be. We have no women aboard RogueEmpire Warrior I.
They were left at the RogueEmpire Complex. I am sure no one in their right
mind would consider doing this to me. To CodL, The Emperor!*

However, this was the only reasonable answer to what he had just
heard.

*Someone on board wants to assume power, and control, and has
arranged this elaborate, but stupid plan to confuse, and attempt to frighten
me ... Me, 'The Great CodL',* he thought, elevating his chin to reflect his
superiority.

*Someone has smuggled a woman on board! But how did she know of
my nightmares? How could she possibly have known?*

*This voice may have assumed my intentions, but never could it know
of my inner demons and fears which reveal themselves nightly in my
nightmares.*

Never!

He gathered himself.

*I must look in control and in command. My men are all watching how I
handle this situation. And this voice ... especially this voice, and whoever
else is involved must realize 'I' am in charge.*

DREXL suddenly came to his mind !

Could it be Drexl, he thought, quickly scanning the surrounding area
for any sign of his participation.

CodL was still perspiring and his mind was now becoming vague and
cloudy. Nothing was clear for him. Nothing decisive. Nothing seemed real.

I have worked myself into a state of confusion _ and delirium, he
realized. *I must appear confident and levelheaded.* Closing his eyes he
composed his frightened mind for a second. He looked up.

"Show yourself, you who are speaking. From what part of the Warrior
do you communicate with me? Step out and face me like a man — or,
realizing he was speaking to the voice of a woman, like whatever you are,"
he stammered!

There was silence.

Everyone just stood or sat in place. The breathing was shallow and
silent, so as not to miss a sound.

No one moved.

Then the vision appeared ... materializing out of nothing.

A communal 'gasp' released from all.

Slowly, the extraordinary vision manifested before them. It was a woman, and she was, without question, supreme! They had never witnessed anything of this improbable grandeur and splendor involving another Being ... anywhere! And, the power she emanated was just as breathtaking, as it was misunderstood by CodL and his men. They would come to understand that the power that was hers, was the greater power — that of Goodness, Compassion and Love. Now standing before them, having fully materialized, she continued to be surrounded by the slowly moving, tiny starlites. They were swimming around her in a recurring and eternal ritual.

Of what, they wondered?

Afraid to move, the men gazed at her. She appeared young, but wise, and astute. She looked to be a study in confidence, perception, and enlightenment. Every man there now understood that the one in total control of this situation was this manifestation before them. It was not those of the RogueEmpire Warrior I ... and it was not CodL.

She radiated absolute calm, no fear. For this encounter, Princess Poona had substituted her robe/cape of emerald green for one of brilliant white.

'White being the color indicating purity and truth, from which all colors have their origin,' she had discerned.

The young woman before them softly glowed. Her head was covered by the same lustrous fabric as her gown, also white. It came down to just above the eyebrows. A silver, silk, waist sash adorned the white gown worn beneath the robe, and a single gem, of iridescent colors, dangled from it's center.

A tiara encrusted with raw gems sat on her head and in her arms she cradled a Scepter with 7 intertwining slim bands, each with a star in the center.

Her eyes, they noticed, were encompassed in pale magenta, with hints of silvery blue sparkles. They were eyes of integrity, wisdom, and intelligence ... strong in conviction, but projecting absolute compassion. Along the side of her neck and cheek they saw a symbol. It was the sacred Topazian symbol indicating the Moon and 7Stars.

She remained silent. Observing. Contemplating. Giving them time to wonder.

CodL, and his men, still speechless, were attempting to put some sense into this exasperating scenario, when the vision spoke ...

"I am Princess Poona, the Emerald Empress of the Moon and 7Stars. I am here on behalf of the 7Stars, and of those who live and abide in this Universe of Beings. We are those that

adhere to the right to live their lives in 'fair, compassionate and just' ways ... in the ways of the Goodness of All Things.

My intrusion into your lives is required at this time for that of which I speak — the 'Goodness of All Things.

Therefore, apologies for this interruption are not warranted, but please accept our gift of friendship to you all."

Bowing her head and placing her hands upon her heart, she created the symbolic gesture of the All. Then, lifting her eyes, she gazed deeply, but softly, at all before her.

"At this time I respectfully choose to be alone with CodL. We have matters to discuss, and come to terms with.

I, the Emerald Empress, Princess Poona, and those sharing our beliefs in the Universe of the All, thank you for your understanding and timely compliance to my request.

Please, you will now leave."

Chapter 74

The Beginning Of The Beginning

The Empress Poona on the Rogue Warrior

Empress Poona looked at the crew and then at CodL. He stood before her, confused and slightly numb at the proceedings unfolding before him.

The crew looked at each other, at Empress Poona, and then to CodL, who was unresponsive, standing speechless before the vision.

DregO and TragL glanced at each other, left their posts and exited. The 12 other crew members in the Control Center at the time followed close behind. No one looked back. The door closed.

CodL, then simply surrendered, and dropped to his knees. His head laid back and he placed his hands on the sides of his head. He was in deep anguish and his resolve had completely vanished. He had struggled for to long. This moment of self-condemnation would wait no longer.

Princess Poona, her compassion literally pulsing from the true immanence she represented, moved to where CodL sat, hunched over in agony. She knelt in front of him, and laying her Scepter in the folds of her gown, placed her hands on CodL's head. She looked deeply into his eyes and spoke, softly and compassionately ...

"CodL, at this very moment you may be feeling that so much is lost in regards to your life and that all is over.

Not so!

You have unfortunately played out a script that you were forced to memorize as a child. One that has led you to anguish and sadness. This anguish is the pangs of conscience that Beings experience relating to guilt.

Guilt promotes fear, CodL. Fear plays out in many ways.

Past deeds, words, thoughts ... all that accompanies emotions of misconduct, wreck havoc on the soul, before the joy of what we can still save and still accomplish is realized.

You feel that it is to late ... once again, CodL, not so!"

"When you reach this point of exultation, this joy — and you will, CodL, know that the past will be just that ... something to reflect on, to remember, to learn from — but, the Past."

Then, placing her hands upon CodL's head, Princess Poona, closing her eyes, softly uttered...

"The pain in you is real, CodL, but the author, the creator of this pain is of someone else, whose pain was of someone else, and on, and on ... and on.

You were young, and innocent, and so very vulnerable, CodL.

These were adults, molding you ... a child.

Their mold was flawed, and you had no chance.

As the child within you grew, you did not know better, and continued the cycle.

Someone has to say ... the pain stops here.

You are strong enough to be that man, that someone, CodL."

His tears were flowing, and his anguish was uncontainable. CodL let out a sorrowful moan, hiding his head in his hands in sorrow and shame.

"What you fear CodL is that of the unknown.

What you fear is love, and yet you seek that which you fear, love.

You never knew love as a child, but you have sought it desperately as a young man, and as an adult.

Your recurring nightmares are sad reenactments of this painful loss. The loss of never having experienced love and the resulting despair of not knowing what to do.

You had no one to speak with. You had no friends."

"CodL, sometimes our path is chosen for us, and sometimes we choose our path poorly. It is, unfortunately, not an uncommon occurrence, but for you, CodL, it can end here. Now! It must, CodL!"

"Should you choose this path, this pilgrimage that I now offer, I will join you and help in your transition, and transformation. I am here to help, and to be with you during this time. I offer it freely, and in joy ... if it be your wish, CodL."

"This can be the beginning of the 'Beginning' for you, CodL. The satisfaction of helping others, for no reason other than

to help them, will bring unimaginable joy and respect, for you and all others. Trust Me when I say that you will find such inner illumination, and spiritual reward through simple acts of goodness towards all things, that there will come a time when you will even love and respect a rock! It too is a part of all creation, and everything that exists is due its love and respect. Everything is a part of the Whole, the Oneness of All Things, CodL."

"Remember, CodL, none of us can be the brightest star of all the stars. It is only through unification and togetherness that we create the brightest star ever. That star is Goodness, CodL. That Star is The Oneness of us All. That Star is The Goodness of All Things."

"All Beings enter life with a tiny spark of the Creator, the Source, within their Being. That spark is within you, and, simply put, needs to be reignited.

Before the Beginning, there was The Oneness, CodL.

Together, as 'One', in 'Goodness, there is nothing we cannot, and will not accomplish.

Join me on this pilgrimage CodL."

Poona then helped CodL up. Together they walked over to two chairs with a viewport looking into the Heavens.

"CodL," she said softly, "I insist that formalities be dismissed. We must speak together as one would talk normally with a companion. The only requirements are that we be honest and that the change we are seeking is the change wanted. And," Princess Poona concluded, "that we are both to listen carefully, and respectfully to what the other is saying."

For weeks, together, Poona and CodL walked the decks of the RogueEmpire Warrior I, talking, listening, silently thinking. Except for sleeping they were together constantly. All eyes from the crew were on them as they would pass by. No one knew what to think as CodL had never been seen, or experienced, in this manner before. Ever !

There were many moments in his Tower retreat, after speaking of a situation or hearing offerings from Poona regarding explanations of his life, when CodL would simply curl up as a child, and cry.

"Princess Poona," he said, one day, "I have never admitted this to anyone, ever, but I feel frightened. I'm scared."

Poona looked at him and his swollen eyes.

Eyes sad from years of sadness, she knew.

She saw a man pleading to be extricated of his past. A man desiring

301

compassion, and kindness, and gentle ways. A sense of empathy softly flushed through her being.

"CodL, I cannot resurrect, and undo certain wrongs committed — for you or anyone. However, a 'new' life of Goodness can be achieved. Slowly, the anger, the exasperation, the sadness … all CodL's maladies began to seep away.

Poona knew it would take time, but it was a beginning.

It is a Genesis for CodL, she surmised.

One afternoon Princess Poona was surprised by a request from CodL.

"I do not wish to be called CodL anymore, Poona."

Poona considered this.

"It is not the name that defines the man, CodL. That said, I firmly believe you will never be the CodL as before."

"I believe that too," said CodL, "and because I am so sure of that, I wish to be called by another name. I never want to known as CodL again." Looking into Poona's eyes, he exclaimed, "CodL is dead, gone forever. He no longer exists, Poona."

Poona nodded, understanding, and thought for a moment.

"I can 'christen' you with another name, if that be your wish. But, remember CodL, as I explained, you must understand it is not the name that makes the Being."

"I understand," he said, affirmatively.

"Christen," he then questioned?

"Yes," answered Poona. "It is an ancient ceremonial term. One definition is to give a new identity, or as I would like to think in your case, a new name for a new man reflecting notable, and noble qualities. Among other achievements, I foresee you becoming a honorable and ethical man, CodL, and, yes, a new name for the new man is apropos."

A softer, but respectful name suits him, she thought.

"Aha! Inspiration once again reaches out to me," she said brightly. "I have a suggestion for you to reflect on. It is not entirely unlike the name you carry now, CodL, but worlds apart in meaning."

"A name which you must always honor and be worthy of."

"What is that name," asked CodL anxiously.

Poona softly smiled, and quietly spoke CodL's new name, and the meaning it represented.

CodL heard the new name. He heard it, and the more he thought of it, and repeated it out loud, the more he liked it … and it's meaning.

"What is your response," a glowing Poona asked?

"YES! YES," he replied assuringly! "It is symbolic of the man I am becoming." He withdrew for a moment, thinking.

"Let us assemble the crew as soon as possible. I want to make it official. I wish for those who choose to be in attendance to share in this new beginning, or Genesis, as you mentioned."

"I like that word, Genesis, too." He smiled happily.

"I have one further request, one more name change, Poona." He spoke it to her. Princess Poona responded with a glowing smile.

"Ginesthoi," she said.

"Ginesthoi," CodL remarked. "What does it mean?"

"It is yet another very ancient saying, CodL, basically meaning, Make it so!"

"I am finding this unbelievable, Poona. I am happy," CodL said.

"There are others CodL, who will undoubtedly find it unbelievable too. Along with your crew, these 'others' should be present ... as your guests."

"Who are you thinking of, Poona."

Poona replied with the names of five men.

"I feel it would be advisable to have them in attendance," she said. It would also be right to access the ceremony to the Peaceful Voyageur and the Black Widow, so those men aboard could be involved.

"Peaceful Voyageur," asked CodL, questioningly?

"Yes, CodL, the new name DrexL has christened the RogueRecon."

"Amazing!" This 'christening' thing is catching on, isn't it, Poona?"

"Yes, CodL, it seems so," replied Poona, inwardly chuckling.

CodL, considering the five names Poona had mentioned, closed his eyes, and nodding his head, said...

"Yes, I agree — Ginesthoi."

At this, Poona had to laugh out loud.

Later that evening, CodL sat in the Control Center reflecting on his state of mind, and watching the crew go about their duties, occasionally acknowledging them. It seemed they intentionally avoided coming to close to him, although he could certainly understand their apprehension.

Deciding to implement an act of kindness Poona had spoken of, he motioned to one of the crew. The man quickly, but nervously came and saluted.

"Yes, Commander CodL, my Emperor," he said.

CodL, recognizing a tinge of fear in the man's voice, felt sad for the first time.

"Second Starcraft Navigator, Lokk," he said, reading the officers name and rank badge.

"Yes, Commander," answered Lokk.

"To begin, Navigator Lokk, you may address me as Commander, and drop the 'my Emperor.' Is that clear?"

"Yes, Commander," Lokk said hesitantly.

"Wonderful, Navigator Lokk. Now, how goes the inspection of the Starlite Indicator Sensors, and Documentation Input Systems?"

Lokk was momentarily at a loss for words, but replied, "They are proceeding very well Commander. We are somewhat ahead of the designated schedule assigned to our department."

CodL smiled at Lokk.

"Well done, Navigator Lokk. I am pleased and I am putting you in charge of reporting all progress directly to me in a timely fashion. Thank you, and Lokk, thank your department for their efforts."

Lokk, feeling a little numb, and more than confused, nodded affirmatively and attempting a smile, saluted.

"That will be all, Lokk," CodL said softly.

"Yes Sir, Commander CodL."

Still smiling, Lokk saluted again. Turning, he walked away.

CodL, thought to himself...

That didn't feel to bad at all.

A hint of a smile formed on his face.

Chapter 75

I Christen Thee

Do Not Disappoint Yourself

The next day, vision and sound access to The Peaceful Voyageur, and the Black Widow was functioning, and all the men were gathered in the main assembly room of each vessel, waiting for, what they had been informed was an extraordinary announcement by CodL ... a christening!

Aboard the RogueEmpire Warrior I, Empress Poona, and CodL were situated on a small raised platform so all could witness this 'christening,' this 'transformation' being spoken of. An air of bewilderment permeated the surroundings.

Finally the moment arrived. All were gathered, and all were watching. CodL gave a long look at his men standing before him before lowering to his knees in front of Empress Poona. She, only concerned with CodL, payed no heed to those gathered and slowly and regally lowered the Scepter of the Moon and 7Stars to the head of the kneeling CodL.

The room became quiet in uncertainty and expectation.

She regally spoke ...

"In capacity as the Emerald Empress of the Moon and 7Stars, and by the vested sovereignty of the Goodness of All Things ...

for peace, and honor, and respect everywhere ...

for compassion to all Beings, and everything that is ...

I, Princess Poona, the Emerald Empress of the Moon and 7Stars christen thee ..."

"Code, Code, of honor."

"From this day forward, Code, compassion, honor, respect and goodness will encapsulate your ideals, guiding your actions to be worthy of your thoughts ... and your inspirations."

"Please rise now, Code and present yourself to all witnessing this affirmation, and this genesis."

Standing, Code presented himself to all present and to those watching.

Everyone stood in silence for a long moment stunned by this metamorphosis of CodL, and this transforming occasion.

Everyone had the same thought…

Could this actually be true? Has the menacing man who ruled over us these past years really changed? What will happen now?

Several anxious moments past. Empress Poona and Code stood, waiting, allowing for the momentous moment to sink in, and for the murmuring to cease.

Several Dark Capes, and others turned, exiting the large room.

"Apparently not to their liking," whispered Code.

"So be it," she replied. "It is their choice."

"I will not let those men, or any others who disapprove, sway me in how I now choose to conduct my life," Code stated with conviction.

Poona looked at Code, who, while continuing to stand assured, was appearing disappointed, and apprehensive to Poona's watchful eyes.

Leaning over she said discretely…

"Code, we knew that the possibility of an occurrence such as this was likely. However, look around, most have remained."

"Unfortunately, there are those aboard, and in the vast Heavens, who will continue to lead the lives they have become accustomed to. Some actually thrive on such a life. Hopefully, someday their thoughts, and principals will change. That will always be welcomed. But, Code, we cannot always expect to see a change in others because 'we' have resolved a change within ourselves.

That choice is theirs alone to make. Those souls that are lost need to seek the change, and need to listen to the message from within their own hearts. When the time comes, that message, that spark of the Source, that ability to change is in each being, Code."

Then it began.

FaLN was the first to step forward. He knelt down in honor.

"My Commander, it will be a privilege to serve with you in honor and for the Goodness of All Things. May your genesis be the catalyst for our genesis."

Raising his eyes to Princess Poona, he offered a thankful smile. Princess Poona noticing the recognition, and warm gesture, softly bowed her head in respect to FaLN.

Then TragL knelt, and one by one, and then in great numbers, they all knelt before Code.

Code stood tall before them, but, unlike before, he was now approachable. His eyes unashamedly glistened with tears.

Now he is truly a man of strength, and compassion and morality, thought Empress Poona, happily.

His convictions will be of Goodness.

She could see a resplendent energy radiating from him. Many men sensed this also, but were still wary, suspicious and confused by such a radical change.

How will this affect us?

Code, raising his arms to hush the crowd, spoke.

"For the first time I address you as, Code. Code of honor! Not a title, men, but a truth that I will earn by example as your Commander and also as an equal. You are all men of courage. I have witnessed your bravery and your loyalty under extreme duress. I speak not only of duress from battle, but immoral duress from me ... the man once named CodL."

"You, and innocent others endured CodL's madness for years. You all endured insult, humiliation, danger, and I, Code, am truly sorry for that.

Look at me, men. CodL is gone. CodL no longer exists! It may take time, but I will prove I am worthy of your trust. I, Code, choose to supplant anger, revenge, cruelty, and all that identifies with unfairness with ideals that nourish one's soul rightfully. I speak of honor, respect, integrity ... and compassion!"

"I ask for the chance to lead you."

"I realize many are thinking what will we do now that our 'old' way of life is ending. Where will we find the means to support ourselves and the facilities?

Well, that weighed upon my mind also, and I have given this a great deal of thought. I have an answer you hopefully will embrace. Listen, and think about this. It is literally right at our doorstep, situated right next to the RogueEmpireComplex."

"I speak of Trion."

There was a restlessness and shuffling of feet. Men were gesturing among themselves, and looking at Code in disbelief.

"Please hear me out," Code continued.

"I suggest a new beginning on Trion, a planet many are from and where many still have friends and family. Legal mining can be become a way for all of us to create legitimate lives."

"Good lives."

"On Trion, there are hardships that are deplorable, and yet the planet is rich in valuable ores. The people there desperately need help, and many are relatives. We can be that help. Instead of taking advantage of the situation — as we have in the past, we, together, can create a legitimate business, mining these minerals and making a profit doing it … benefitting ourselves, and our families."

"We can help provide for those unable to make it on their own. Think of GemCraft Corporation, and how they make money."

He could not help himself and ever so subtly, glanced over at LesterJonko who stood with arms crossed.

A few shouts of 'yes' from scattered areas arose.

Code looked out at the men, considering his words.

"It is also my wish that this fine vessel, our vessel, be renamed."

"Henceforth it is to be known as the 'Peaceful Warrior.' My goal is, that as 'we' change, we will create change! Let us begin with yet another renaming I have thought about, and that is the RogueEmpireComplex, orbiting Trion."

"The RogueEmpireComplex is no longer! From this moment on, men, we reside, and work on the complex we will call 'Genesis!'"

"It means 'Beginning,' men. A new beginning for us all!"

He beamed, again gesturing to all with upraised arms.

Waves of 'yes,' reverberated across the room, and many raised their arms to Code and his ideas. Some still stood bewildered and unsure.

"I don't want to overwhelm you, or myself, so the last thing I will bring up at this time is this — and it is important. I Code, propose, no, in this case I insist, that the creation of a council, elected by the crew, and for the crew, be established as soon as possible. This council will be responsible to, and for, all aboard the Genesis and anyone affiliated with our cause. If you have a complaint or suggestion — it will be heard!"

The men were beginning to listen carefully now.

"If you choose to follow another path, one that you feel suits you better at this time, you are free to do so as soon as we have returned to the Genesis."

"But, for those who are tired of the madness, the loneliness, the way of life we have lived for so long, I offer a chance to have a home, a wife, maybe children, a honorable way to make a living and help others at the same time."

"There may be many trials ahead in accomplishing this goal, men. It will undoubtably not be an easy task, but we can be the beginning … and we can make it work."

"Enough for now," Code said. "There are decisions we all need to make, and make them we will. Think it over carefully, men. We can do this.

As for me, I have made my decision, I will make this happen, and nothing will honor and please me more than having you join me."

Empress Poona, eyes glistening, looked at Code in respect.

"I had no idea, Code!"

"Nor I, Princess Poona, nor I!"

Code then stepped off the platform and into the midst of the men gathered.

He extended his hand to FaLN who immediately shared the grasp. TragL stepped forward, then DragO. A few were hesitant, but to a man they shared in the offering of congratulations to Code.

Later, as Code was walking back to Princess Poona, he saw them.

Off to the side stood Princess Poona and the 'five' others, LesterJonko, FinnJonko, DrexL, Salamar, and MorQ.

Princess Poona had arranged for their travel aboard a Starburst, and they had come aboard at Princess Poona's request shortly before a ceremony none of them could have anticipated only weeks before.

A ceremony they were wary of, even with Princess Poona's involvement.

Code walked up to them, emotional, but confident, somewhat unsure of the reception he was to encounter.

DrexL approached first, and looking Code in the eyes for a moment, spoke.

"Code, it pleases me greatly to wish you the Goodness you speak of."

He put forth his hand which Code grasped.

"In friendship," said Code, inquiringly.

"In friendship," answered, DrexL. "Honestly."

Smiling at DrexL, Code then turned, and approached MorQ.

MorQ was nervous, but he was not afraid ... just unsure of what to do or say.

It was Code who spoke first.

"MorQ, I ask for your forgiveness." He placed one hand on MorQ's shoulder while extending his other hand in hopeful forgiveness and friendship. MorQ could not help himself. His eyes brought forth tears as he took Code's hand.

A sight never before thought possible happened next.

They embraced in forgiveness.

Princess Poona was satisfied that this was indeed a Genesis — a new beginning. She reiterated to Lester and FinnJonko that ... "The past can not be altered, but the present moment could and would alter the future."

She closed her eyes in thankfulness and placed her hands, in her symbolic gesture over her heart.

LesterJonko gazed upon her, wondering about her gestures and about her.

Finn interrupted his father's thought.

"Father, now that your arc enemy apparently has become one of the good guys, maybe we can cut him some slack regarding the rewards offered to bring him in."

Raising his eyebrows a tad, LesterJonko looked at his son, answering ...

"We will have to make some very good decisions regarding just that, Finn, and soon. By the way, Finn, did you happen to catch the reference to the GemCraft Corporation that 'Code' mentioned earlier?"

Finn suppressed a smile.

"Do you actually think that was directed at you, father?"

LesterJonko looked at his son stoically, before smiling.

A soft voice then whispered into LesterJonko's ear ... "LesterJonko, it is so good to meet a man who has led such an exemplary life, that even words such as '*forgiveness*' are unnecessary!"

Glancing over his shoulder, he grinned at a smiling Princess Poona of the Moon and 7Stars who had quietly joined them.

"We should not forget to forgive, my friend."

"Believe me when I say to you that it is Code who will not forget his past, and will live with his deeds of infamy. Code will, however, go on, and eventually overcome those ghosts of yesterday as best he can. It is my belief he will be a leader of men and women who will forgive, and eventually trust in him."

"Well, this is indeed a moment I thought I would never experience," said LesterJonko, with eyes twinkling.

He looked at Princess Poona and FinnJonko.

"Who is to know, perhaps Code, myself and Finn here can do some good together from time to time, for the Goodness of the Universe."

"By the way, Princess Poona, regarding the Starburst we were brought here in ... I would really like to inquire about a few things I saw while on board — if you have the time!"

"We will see, LesterJonko. Perhaps we will discuss it at 'the Red Spot someday! May your days be filled with gratitude, enthusiasm and compassion."

Princess Poona, The Empress of The Moon and 7Stars, respectfully, and sincerely bowed to Lester and Finn in appreciation.

LesterJonko, grinning, nodded at his son, and they too went to offer their regards to Code ... Code of honor.

After all the handshakes, offerings, and promises of new beginnings, Code was once again at Princess Poona's side, looking a bit tired and overwhelmed.

"Princess Poona, practically everyone has expressed warmth and good wishes for me. I feel so ... well, proud, and somehow humble. I now understand pride is not necessarily a good attribute, Poona, but in this instance it is the closest word I can find to express my feelings."

Poona smiled warmly and put her hand on Code's broad shoulder.

"It is alright, Code, feel the warmth and the happiness around you. It has been a long, long time coming. Enjoy and relish this moment, and the promise of all the fulfilling moments to come that accompany compassion and kindness."

"Also, Code, remember when I mentioned you may even come to love a rock because everything is connected in life, even inanimate objects?"

Code thought for a moment.

"Yes, I do," he replied with a sheepish grin. "Why do you ask, Poona?"

Poona extended an open hand and upon her palm sat a little Geodie.

"This is for you Code. Do not ask me why, but I brought this along when I came for my visit with you."

"A rock! My very own rock," said Code, somewhat humorously, and looking at Poona curiously, waiting for an explanation.

"Actually, Code, it is a real little living Being called a Geodie. It just happens to look like a rock! It is your own pet to name as you please. It is quite calming, and needs very little nourishment — actually, only water," said Poona, smiling cheerfully.

Code gently took the little rock from the palm of Poona's hand.

"Is it a little boy or girl," asked Code.

Poona grinned, looking into Code's now amused eyes.

"Well, Code, from my understanding of Geodies, I do not believe they are either a boy or a girl."

Code's smile softened as he looked at Poona.

"Then, if you would not be offended, Poona, I will christen it, 'My Princess,' after you. I will comfort, and treasure it always. It will be my rock on which to lean during difficult times as it will always remind me of you. I thank you, Princess Poona, from the bottom of my heart."

"I am honored Code. 'My Princess' is a lovely name for a rock."

He smiled into Princess Poona's eyes.

"It is now time for me to walk into my present, and help create a future ... a good future, for all. I am certain many do not believe what has transpired, and the truth be known, Poona, I too would have deemed this an impossible feat. But, I will not disappoint you, I promise."

"Code ... do not disappoint yourself."

Chapter 76

XennaOne of the Voice of One

Hmmm, the Scent of Sandalus

HighPriestess XennaOne snuggled onto her large recliner situated on the balcony of the top floor of her comfortably appointed suite. She personally decorated the suite sensually … with warm colors, overstuffed comfortable furniture, art, books and sacred essential fragrances that continually wafted throughout the suite and balcony, carried softly by the ever present breezes in Spectrum.

Xenna enjoyed these scents.

Lavendrius, Sandalus, Eucalyphus, and Frankincense were her favorites. When inhaling these exotic diffused aromas Xenna found she was not only ushered to an exemplar state of channeling the healing powers of nature, but also experienced enhanced emotional, and mental well being. At present, she delighted in these very essences as the aromas floated out onto the balcony in a sensual smoky dance.

She had just finished a strenuous daily workout, a practice she had maintained ever since becoming the HighPriestess. She had indulged in a long, soaking bath before massaging wonderful essential oils onto her body.

Xenna felt glowingly refreshed.

Finding a relaxing position she felt a feeling of peace. Things were going well and later she was to have a rendezvous with her good friend, Poona. But now, she thought…

It is my time to think personal thoughts, here under the Heavens. Oh, it is always such a glorious array. I must never take this for granted.

Her thoughts wandered before focusing on the proceedings of a day filled with anticipation and expectation.

Hmmm, it was a rewarding, but arduous day. Lets see, I received permission and completed arrangements to transport Annuj's family from

312

Quin Lapesia to Oneness for the upcoming reunion with BucchaSim, Junnuj and TerraSim. My argument being that at the very least, the Council should approve to put these families together after the traumatic ordeal JunnaOne had suffered. The Council had agreed, and rightfully so!

Then I explained the extraordinary significance of the 'gathering' soon to take place in Oneness, including a brief synopsis of why the Council had not been informed earlier. That was touchy.

The turning point, Xenna remembered, while rolling onto her stomach, *was when I reiterated the importance of being extremely tactful to not disclose any knowledge concerning the upcoming 'gathering' as every indication reflects a monumental disclosure will occur that will have an imminent effect on all Amythesians! Yes, that little bit of intrigue definitely opened their eyes.*

I stated in my conclusion that, out of honor for King Luxxor, and Queen Liluuc of Neptuna, it would be the respectable thing, and the right thing to do. She smiled.

At that point, the Council halted the proceedings and called for a brief pause to converse amongst themselves. Returning, they acknowledged that given the extreme importance the 'gathering' promised, and out of respect for Neptuna, it was only right and proper that all the Council members be in attendance.

Oh my Goodness, she thought. *I had sat back in my chair in disbelief. Inside I was ecstatic and bubbling in joy. Nevertheless, I composed myself. I stood, and as the HighPriestess, I masterly complimented the Council on their sound decision.*

"Representing, and honoring the people of Amythesia, and especially Neptuna at this time is laudable. You are to be commended."

"I said and meant just that."

XennaOne rolled onto her back, a soft expression on her face. She became tranquil, quickly growing enchanted with the cloud patterns in the Heavens above her. Soft, billowy clouds, lazily floating by on their way to ...

Who knows where? Wherever the winds blow, she surmised. *I wonder if the clouds ever get tired of their continuous wanderings? So much to discover.*

"Hmmm," she murmured, "the scent of Sandalus ..."

Reaching over, she casually ran her slim fingers through water that gently and quietly gurgled out of a Trumpet's bronze spout water feature. It felt sensual, and it's warmth felt soothing compared to the coolness of the evening Amythesian wind. Slipping one foot onto the stone floor, she sensed it's coolness creep up into her soles ... *Ah, the stimulus feels so good. The antithesis of the cool breeze, and warm water,* she remembered, vaguely recalling memories from her distant childhood. Xenna continued gazing at the lazy clouds floating by, becoming transfixed on the vastness of the Heavens.

Oh Goodness, I feel so very alone, almost insignificant ... at least at this moment, she contemplated.

But I AM alone — I am truly alone, she realized.

"Perhaps a time will come when I encounter someone that I choose to share my time with," she whispered while reaching up to embrace the breeze.

"A companion, or, better yet, maybe a partner."

Sitting up, with elbows on her knees and her head in her hands, she tried to picture someone, anyone, here beside her tonight.

No one came to mind.

It must be someone I have yet to meet, she pondered. *But when do I have the time to actually meet anyone. I have important responsibilities to consider. My time is truly not my own.*

Xenna had purposefully not allowed for any possibility of a personal relationship prior to her induction as the HighPriestess of the Voice of One. From the beginning, she initiated a training and fitness regiment for herself, understanding the importance of remaining strong, mentally and physically, in order to stay strong emotionally. *The demands on the HighPriestess can be extreme, especially for one with a family, and, as laws exist a family is truly not a realistic option. I need only look to my sister, Junnuj.*

Xenna settled into the soft cushions once again, closing her eyes. She pictured JunnaOne's allowance into Dreamstate.

"So sad," she said softly. "So very sad.

You tried so hard, Junnuj. It was never your wish to give up so much ... everyone that truly mattered to you."

Well, my sister, I have begun to prepare the way so that the laws that led to this injustice will be rescinded and replaced. I give you my oath, and promise. Together, Junnuj, we will make this happen.

Suddenly the distinctive deep hollow ring from the wooden transpalmation chime hanging at the entrance of her royal suites three floors below brought her back to the present. It was a reminder that the time was approaching to meet her friend, Poona, at the Circulum, only a short distance away.

Her gaze became distant.

I will never forget my first encounter with Poona. It was far from ordinary, she reflected, rolling her ochre shaded eyes, and following yet another soft fluffy cloud drifting through the darkness above Amythesia.

She arose, hurried inside and selected a casual robe, tying it at the neck to wear over a traditional dark purple gown. She quickly completed the ensemble with warm mid calf boots.

Checking herself in the reflector, she affirmed...

"This will do just fine."

Chapter 77

Time For One More Essential Rendezvous

She softly uttered, 'Ginesthoi'

Princess Poona stood silently for a few moments gathering her thoughts.

This would be a wonderful time for 'SilentMind' right now, she mused. *But, the appointed time for my get together with XennaOne is quickly approaching.*

Another time, she vowed.

Poona, still standing alone, considered the time frame of up to two months for the 'Aloneness Vigil' the Initiates had agreed on.

Thank Goodness I still have ample time for one more essential, and paramount rendezvous before returning to Oneness. It was fortunate, a blessing and a gift of the One, that my encounter with Code took less time than anticipated. Except for Bocc momentarily being lost, which Pellona had straightened out, nobody needed assistance of any kind.

I need to contact Laurra again, soon, to see how she is progressing ... although, Poona thought, *I can tell she is ready — physically, emotionally, and mentally. The long journey for Laurra is almost over, and yet, only just beginning!*

Looking around the spacious room on the Peaceful Warrior, Princess Poona was happy and she was pleased. Before her were all the assembled men, former friend and foe ... all offering their wishes to Code. Granted, there were disbelievers, distrust, and many questions, but most were willing to allow for Code and his transformation to have its chance ... its opportunity.

Poona viewed the men, standing around in groups. She felt amazed at the inconceivable turn of events over these past several weeks and suddenly detected a slight sense of fatigue.

Well, she considered, *maybe it is a good time for a short SilentMind treatment after all. When I am on The Emerald Starburst I will have just enough time before seeing Xenna. It has been quite the journey, but what a glorious and promising result.*

Ambling away from the crowds, and into the shadows of the quiet places, Princess Poona leaned back against a cool wall for a moment, allowing for its coolness to massage her approaching fatigue. She whispered to unhearing ears.

"Until we meet again my new friends."

Then, creating the symbolic sign of the All, she softly uttered, "Ginesthoi — make it so, Mulon … destiny does not wait for long.

She dissolved silently, amidst a thousand Clinamen starlets … and alone.

Chapter 78

Listen, I Can Hear A Leaf Falling

The time of DOC is upon us

Princess Poona materialized just as the HighPriestess XennaOne reached the Circulum outside the Council Of the Voice Of One in Spectrum.

Their arrivals were welcomed by soft, clear, melodic chimes, and, as normal, the chimes were orchestrated by the gentle winds coming from the south.

It was evening in Spectrum.

All had long since gone home for the night, leaving a curious feeling of aloneness or abandonment permeating the setting. It was as if one had innocently wandered into an ancient, long lost and forgotten place of antiquity.

The evening was cool.

Poona was happy to see her friend. Smiling, she walked over to Xenna, and they warmly embraced.

"Oh, Poona, it is so good to see you, my friend."

"And you, Xenna," Poona said happily.

Taking each other's hand, they ambled over to a small wall supported by pillars. It sheltered and enclosed a private and comfortable seating area.

As they situated themselves so they could face each other they noticed the Heavens above. Distinct glows of varying colors from Crystola's galaxy flickered upon them like shifting shadows, lending to all a dreamlike quality.

Poona and Xenna both felt a sense of peace, thankful to be here with each other and knowing that a critical part of their mission had been successful.

"I am so happy you have time to share with me tonight," said Xenna.

"I must say you are looking well, Poona, although I can imagine it must have been quite an exhausting period of time for you aboard the RogueWarrior and having to deal with CodL. It is a blessing you have been

318

successful and all the significant Beings involved came around to seeing things in a peaceful way."

Poona nodded, agreeing with XennaOne.

"Under such pressure, I truly appreciate you took the time to keep me informed as often as you have. You have had much to deal with."

"My friend," Poona responded, "it is good to be back. The intensity and the task were indeed formidable, and unsure. I never knew how some would react. But, as to the danger, I honestly felt little risk for me during this time. Given there is always the possibility of the unexpected, those of Topaz have prepared well in arranging for my safety ... where ever I may be. And, my friend, I too, have substantial powers within to call upon. However, I must admit, it is as if a divine intervention prevented anything from getting out of hand."

"The Goodness of All Things?" spoke Xenna.

Poona smiled and blew a kiss to the colorful Heavens.

"Actually, Xenna, DrexL and LesterJonko, under the veneer of hardness they outwardly present, are good people. After listening to my proposal and intention, they agreed that the opportunity to reason with CodL first was worth the attempt. Also, somewhat to my surprise, CodL was in fact desperately needing and wanting help. After an initial show of belligerent authority, he willingly submitted himself to the healing I offered."

"As in many unfortunate cases, his duress came from decades of loneliness and abuse, beginning shortly after birthing. His pain and anger has been building ever since. It's not unusual. However, his intent to heal and make the transition to Goodness ... well, remarkable and perhaps divinely inspired would be appropriate descriptions."

"Perhaps one could say, miraculous," offered Xenna.

"Yes," Poona, softly said, "it was."

"You know, Xenna, I often am concerned that there are moments when I feel I am not being heard, or more importantly, not understood. There were occasions I felt that way with CodL. Sometimes I become apprehensive that perhaps an opportunity is slipping away, or that I am not considering all the possible paths to choose from. I remind myself that many of the disparaging situations I am involved with are monumental in scale and the lives of so many innocent Beings hang in the balance."

"I have truly come to believe that most Beings are grateful with just the possibility of 'hope' alone. Do I sound as if I am rambling?"

Xenna, contemplated for a moment.

"No, Poona, I don't. I feel your apprehension stems from feeling that perhaps you have not done your best. But I know you always do what you feel is just, and right, under any circumstances. You need never fear you have not responded with your very best for all involved, my good friend. The pressure you assumed for your role in the Heavens is immense, Poona."

"And yet," Xenna continued, "even burdened by these pressures, you continue to tirelessly provide a calm and a sanctuary for those distressed."

"You have answers for those with questions. Perhaps most importantly, you present yourself as one of compassion and certainty regarding your belief and faith in the Goodness Of All Things. It all comes down to Beings trusting you, Poona — and they do! They sense your integrity and your honesty."

Poona, leaned forward, resting her head in her hands.

"You know, Xenna, it is mesmerizing watching the colorful shadows flicker about your enchanting face."

"Yours is dancing in 'moonglow ochres,' responded, Xenna.

Poona lowered her head, a grin on her face.

"I have indeed dedicated my life to these very principles you speak of, Xenna. However, I do have misgivings regarding my methods at times." She sighed.

"I hope that the few times I need to disguise a truth it will not cloud Beings from their trust in me, and what my overall intentions are."

Leaning back into soft cushions, Poona reflected.

"Xenna, on the more personal side, I often wonder if I have the right to explore other feelings ... natural feelings that occasionally enter and linger. Feelings that, you know ... arouse my curiosity, my sensuality. I wonder. Do you ever wonder, or fantasize about any of these things?"

"Yes, Poona — often!"

Poona suddenly shivered, and pulled her wrap tighter around her shoulders, as the coolness of the evening quietly enveloped them. She glanced over at Xenna, who seemed to be shivering a little herself.

"Come, Xenna, we will share our wraps."

Moving over, Xenna snuggled close to Poona.

"It has become colder since you have been gone, Poona. The time of DOC is upon us."

"Ah, yes, DOC ... the Days of Cooling," Poona recalled.

"Yes, I do believe they have arrived."

"I have a question 'I' am curious about," Xenna said.

"Has there ever been a time when the Goodness Of All Things has not been there for you, or not answered your calling, Poona?"

Poona thought for a while, before answering.

"Actually, Xenna, I truly believe that the Goodness Of All Things always provides me with the capacity to formulate the answer I seek for a given situation. However, the answer, the faith to trust in this answer and make use of its message, all come from within me."

"It is our choice, Xenna. That is the gift!"

"Although I must admit that often I feel our decision has been imbued with, shall I say, Divine guidance."

"Well, for me, at times I do not always immediately comprehend what has been gifted to me, Poona ... so, I have determined that the answer is not always ours to necessarily understand, but ours to implement to the best of our powers, intellectually, spiritually and compassionately."

"In other words, Poona, as you just mentioned, to just trust."

"I agree. We must always remember that the Source, the Oneness we speak of, is also a part of everything that it created. It exists within each of us and in everything. And, it does not interfere or preordain. Events happen as they will ... or as we will."

"Yes, I believe that, Poona. The Oneness is compassionate. It would never purposefully allow pain, suffering, or injustice of any kind to come to anything created that carries the One's own spark of life and consciousness. All things that we consider evil, unfortunate, or questionable are either natural disasters, or brought about by those who have lost any connection to the Oneness."

Poona and Xenna became silent for a long time, sitting quietly, cuddled together ... considering, wondering, and watching the dancing light of the stars.

Finally, Poona rested her head on Xenna's shoulder.

"Xenna, have you ever wondered if we are actuality abiding by answers we 'feel' were gifted us from the Goodness Of All Things, or were the answers from our own feelings, our Ego? In other words how do we know the difference, because sometimes the Ego disguises its selfishness? Here is what I mean ... we have a conscience and we have free will, but we also have an Ego. Perhaps, the Goodness in each of us is speaking ... but are we sure? Are we prepared to differentiate between our Ego and a true message from the Goodness?"

"Exactly," exclaimed Xenna, "I believe that the individual Ego can be extremely selfish. If we think about it, distinguishing the honesty of our thoughts can be perceived by that fact alone. In my opinion, Goodness is not selfish."

"Also, Poona, a question can be raised, will the Goodness always impart the same answer to the same question, to you, as it does to me?"

Once again, Poona and Xenna sat quietly snuggled under the wrap in the warmth of each other's company for some time ... perhaps waiting for an answer from 'without' to answer them 'within.'

Slowly, they looked at each other and took a deep breath.

Exhaling, Xenna exclaimed, "Well, that was certainly exhilarating and thought provoking! But, you know Poona, one thing is for certain … when I am with you I never have to worry about the gray matter in my head becoming stagnant! My mind is exhausted!"

They both burst out laughing.

"Who knows, Xenna, some complexities are best left to faith and reason. We can only choose to believe in that which seems right and do what we can, as best as we can. For you and me, Goodness guides our thoughts, and actions."

"Yes, it does," Xenna said softly, "well stated, my friend."

Poona then asked, "Did all go well, in regards to my concerns here on Prismacia?"

"Well, most, if not all of your concerns can be put to rest, Poona."

Xenna then informed Poona that King Luxxor and Queen Liluuc, per her request, accepted the invitation for a special event requiring their presence.

"I told them that a part of the ceremony will recognize Neptuna, relating to its graciousness, its greatly appreciated dedication to all Amythesia, and also to Neptuna's future. The 'future' part certainly peaked their interest. They will also be bringing Tunnis, and Dolpho."

Poona nodded thankfully.

"I was also contacted by my sister, Junnuj, who is at SeaCliff with BucchaSim. She requested my help, or as she put it … she is using her pull — with me, to arrange for Annuj's family in Quin Lapesia to be sent to Oneness. Well, I arranged for that to be, with the High Council's approval, of course. Both families will meet with Annuj and they will share their 'first' reunion together. I, too, am truly looking forward to seeing all my family as well, Poona. After such a long separation, it is a good time to have all of us together."

"That will be a very joyful occasion for you all," Poona said, hugging Xenna tightly. "I know King Luxxor, and Queen Iiluuc, will be happy to see you too. I personally am ecstatic," beamed Poona.

"And," added Xenna, happily, "I am pleased to inform you that the High Council will be in attendance as well. I presented them with just enough details to stimulate their curiosity, and perhaps their sense of obligation."

"Xenna, you are a marvel," exclaimed Poona.

Then, Poona, suddenly said, "It would have been a lovely gesture to have invited Yogga! He could have met many more of the locals and explained about his practice. Maybe even give a demonstration, and talk."

Xenna, a smile crossing her face, replied cheerfully, "In fact we did think of that, Poona, and Solannuj actually sent Pellona up to his abode where she found a note attached to the entrance of the cave he inhabits."

"Yes, and ..." a curious Poona asked.

"And," Xenna answered, "the note informed us that should he not answer, not to be alarmed. He was simply in 'corpse' pose and may be for some time! Please do come back."

"Corpse pose," Poona said gleefully!

"Corpse pose," chuckled Xenna.

Imagining Yogga in a corpse pose, they broke into laughter until tears fell freely.

"You know the time is almost upon us, Xenna ... the one we have spoken of so often. That which has long been kept secret will soon be unveiled. The Initiates will all have returned from their Aloneness Vigil, and given your efforts, everyone needed, or who should be in attendance, will be there. The honor of your involvement is truly a blessing, my friend. All is in place."

Xenna nodded her understanding, and thanks.

"The ceremony will be small and intimate," Princess Poona added, "but the consequences will be immeasurable in their promise, and the benefit for Neptuna, Amythesia, and Prismacia is incalculable."

Xenna, softly said, "It is so quiet and peaceful here. The wind has stopped and there is hardly a sound."

Poona listened and whispered...

"Listen Xenna, I can hear a leaf falling."

"Yes," Xenna whispered back. "Yes you can."

Chapter 79

Poona And Xenna

Poona, what do you think of

Poona and Xenna snuggled for a long time, content in the warmth of each other's company, each in her own thoughts. Thoughts of hope, curiosities and dreams.

The night continued to become colder.

The Tallgrasses danced to and fro, keeping time with the unending echo of the chimes reverberating throughout the Circulum corridors.

It was mesmerizing, and it brought up questions … personal questions.

"Poona," Xenna quietly, but mischievously asked?

"Yes," Poona answered, curious about Xenna's impish voice.

"Poona, remember your curiosity about what a special relationship with another Being would be like for you? I mean do you ever have 'fantasies' regarding a special Being in your life, and just what that entails, or do you already have an interest? I must admit, there are times I want someone to share my life, my longings, and my Being with."

Poona sat, eyes distant, understanding.

Xenna continued.

"I understand, Poona, that given our positions and the responsibility therein, 'our time' is not really 'our time' for the most part. But, that said, a decent, well, no, let me rephrase that … a significant portion of my thoughts relate to the 'curiosity' I speak of and, quite frankly, would like to experience. Are you grasping what I mean," inquired Xenna, with eyes still twinkling mischievously.

Before answering, Poona, smiled, her own eyes gleaming too.

"Yes, I grasp the drift of your curiosities and dreams, Xenna, my good friend. Yours is a very good question and one I too admit to dwell on from time to time … and, yes, entertain fantasies of! You are correct, Xenna, our positions in life do have a direct effect on our wherewithal to follow through with thoughts and desires that are innocent, natural occurrences most Beings naturally aspire to.

Perhaps we need to put our heads together and consider how to expand our possibilities, and opportunities.

And, Xenna, as to all that a relationship entails, let us talk about just that!"

Chapter 80

The Gathering

It was time for truth to be known

They gathered at Oneness, by the oasis pool ... near the edge of the Carbonian Desert. Above them the Heavens were clear, and the desert's early night winds caressed cooling sands, buoying tiny desert dust balls, called Twinklings, upward, into their floating nomadic wanderings.

Another extraordinary evening approached. Stars, hidden and cloaked by the light now began to emerge into the advancing darkness. Enchantingly, distant and ancient beginnings of life once again unfolded before them ... their mysteries and as yet unknown origin lay somewhere beyond their gaze, impossible to comprehend. All gathered knew it was of the One.

Everything is of the One.

People were resting on rocks, reclining on the sands and some were standing. Many were enthralled by the silhouette of the slightly visible 'Pantheon,' grooming himself while sitting upon a large undulating dunne nearby.

To lessen the coolness that the evening promised, all had on their wraps for warmth. And, while a sense of calm and peace blanketed the small gathering, anticipation hung in the air. All were waiting in eagerness of just why Poona had requested their presence on this evening. The meaning behind the gathering drew near.

It was captivating.

Poona, intuitively felt the moment was at hand. Sitting next to Laurra and XennaOne, along with Junnuj and her extended family, she arose, squeezed Laurra's hand and made her way to the top of a small sand dunne.

Discarding her warming wrap and hood, she turned to face the people gathered, revealing for the first time, Princess Poona, the Emerald Empress of the Moon and 7Stars.

Poona had not hesitated in her choice. The ensemble she had chosen for this momentous and memorable evening was a pure white robe, and white gown. The gown was embellished with a dangling emerald waist sash adorned with gems, whose individual facets sparkled with each move she made. Soft, cooling winds gently blew about causing folds of her silk gown to sensually flutter, caressing her form. Her thick hair, free except for a small tiara inlaid with tiny gems of moonstones and emeralds, fell to beyond her bare shoulders.

She whispered.

"Oh One, white is for Truth, and tonight I will speak of truths. It is the time for disclosures pertaining to Prismacia to be brought to light ... and it is the time to present the Awaited One!"

Dazzled by Poona's appearance, a hush overcame the Beings gathered. Princess Poona's gown caught the last golden glow from the setting Mother Sunne Lavva, which had continued to send off warm shafts of light in its attempt to survive the dark, blanketing domain of night. And, as night follows day, cooler shades of blue from the night Heavens began to rapidly embrace the gathering where Princess Poona stood alone, upon a small black sand dunne.

Her eyes shone bright, and clear.

Lowering her head, Princess Poona raised her arms gently, and as she did, a radiance suddenly appeared. In the night sky of this black desert and before those gathered, 7 large Emerald Starbursts materialized, pulsating in white, magenta, and blue. Hovering in the distance were several small Emerald Starflakes, also softly glowing.

Everyone gasped in unrivaled astonishment.

The glow, now emanating from Princess Poona, standing in front of the hovering Starships, revealed a fantasy one could only imagine. The recurrence of tiny guardian 'Clinamen starlites' also appeared, dancing about Princess Poona. She had allowed them, not as a shield, but because the sparkle and mystical visual was always an important element involving wonder — and she wanted those gathered to understand they were a part of an unprecedented and extremely historic evening.

They did understand, and awaited, breathlessly.

Princess Poona, the as yet unknown Emerald Empress of the Moon and 7Stars, gazed across the sea of faces now tinged in a blue hue, graciously gifted by Mother MoonLunna.

She spoke...

"Please allow me to finally address you as the Being I truly am. I am Princess Poona the Emerald Empress of the Moon, and 7Stars."

Astounded, everyone was spellbound, and questioning within. Was this not Poona, the Caregiver from Emeralsia? It was obvious this was someone of unimaginable significance.

As they were to discover, this was only the beginning.

Both King Luxxor and Queen Liluuc were taken back in amazement, and bewilderment at this revelation.

Turning to Luxxor, Liluuc softly uttered...

"The Temple in Neptuna has the Sanctuary water feature we call the Fountain of Life, my Chosen One. It also indicates the Moon and 7Stars, and the prophecy!"

He took her hand in his and they began to slightly tremble in anticipation.

Chapter 81

Discretionary Dishonesty

Princess Poona Disclosures

Princess Poona, the Emerald Empress allowed a moment for her disclosure to settle, before stating...

"To many of you I am known as, Poona, which is my birthing name. What you have not been aware of is ... the StarCraft you see hovering about, the Beings within and myself, are from a galaxy known as Topaz. It is my home. It is an adjacent, and ancient galaxy, but in another dimension."

The hush continued from the assemblage. All listened intently to every word. It was totally quiet. Even the winds seemed to have stopped blowing.

"We, of Topaz, have been familiar with Prismacia for a long time. Prismacia has a function and a destiny previously unknown to you ... but one I will disclose this evening. You see, we are here to fulfill a 'Prophecy,' and protect what we deem is a 'Legacy for All.'

The time has come when much will be revealed. For the moment I will attempt to be clear, and keep it uncomplicated in explanation, emphasizing only, let us say — the highlights. More can be shared later."

"Let me begin with what I mean by protecting a 'Legacy for All,' and Prismacia's vital, but delicate involvement in this legacy.

The legacy, literally and simply, is the recorded history of events that has been discovered. It constitutes the entire known Universe that we, of Topaz, are aware of. Prismacia is one of three locations chosen where this knowledge is accumulated, maintained and protected by us, and it will continue to be a repository for ongoing history throughout time. *We of Topaz are among 'others' who guard this legacy, and given an unforeseen tragedy, which we constantly prepare for, we will continue to protect this legacy for the life of our lives, and all future lives."*

Princess Poona chose not to elaborate any further on the subject, especially the recent potential danger involving CodL which Topaz had prevented.

Why cause unneeded alarm to these Beings if not necessary. At the moment, they are of innocence. We of Topaz will continue to watch.

Quiet murmurs arose. She allowed a moment for them to cease.

"Prismacia, by reason of logic, was selected, as it consists of vast quantities of pristine crystal formations, which are transducers. A transducer creates conversion variations in it's physical make-up allowing for the storage of vast amounts of knowledge to be contained in a very small space. You can imagine the space needed for that of which I speak … that of all known time!"

"Here on Prismacia, we are all familiar with the crystal's ability of 'conduction,' or allowing messages to be sent by the mere placing on of hands. It is also widely known of a crystal's healing powers. These are relatively new developments — a few centuries.

But, the crystal's transducer capacity to store knowledge was discovered long, long ago. This innovation initiated a quest for planets consisting of immeasurable quantities of quality crystals, eventually leading to the discovery of your planet, Prismacia.

After a thorough exploration it was chosen, and its place in history … is now history."

Princess Poona bowed in respect to all those gathered.

"I will now speak of prophecy, destiny, and the withholding of truth. Yes, she emphasized, the withholding of truth!"

"We all understand, that often, things are not as they appear, but, is there ever a time to not be totally honest? An unusual question you may be thinking. 'I' would personally question that question. However, let me help clarify by presenting another question to you."

Could there be times when one is not truly honest … for a honorable purpose?"

Princess Poona gazed over the gathering, remaining quiet for a few seconds. Beings conversed between themselves…questioning, debating.

"One such scenario, my friends, which may allow for withholding the complete truth, would be to negate any distress people may incur should they come to know of an impending serious situation, out of their control, and which may or may not happen.

By shielding others from the truth, until all possible factors have been considered, and the issue hopefully eliminated, is it possible these actions could prevent undue concern, trepidation, and fear? All through discretionary dishonesty! And, would this be morally right, or wrong?"

"I ask you to trust me when I say that deep within my heart I believe it is never truly right to be dishonest! But, at times, is it possibly the compassionate, and thoughtful thing to do, given the circumstances?"

"One could argue, it is all in how you interpret the circumstances. Therein establishes — trust! We, of Topaz, have acted in as compassionate a manner as deemed prudent for the situation and time frame, believing your understanding and trust would rightfully surface later ... when all is revealed to you."

Lowering her head, Princess Poona created the symbolic sign of the One.

"You will now learn things about me, and others, that may surprise you, but hopefully not alarm, or offend you. At this time, I will speak of things that myself and others have kept secret from you, for what was determined the overall good of all ... the discretionary dishonesty I have been alluding to."

A slight murmur arose from the assemblage, spellbound before her.

"You have every right to understandably question, who are we to make these decisions ... especially in your absence, and without your knowledge and approval. As I mentioned before, unfortunately, time frames do not always allow for discussions and interpretations, especially when one must act not only prudently, but hastily. Time, and the events therein, wait for no one. It ultimately came down to who would and should be informed regarding what we knew to be the gift of a 'promise and prophecy' long awaited, and the time needed to bring that promise to fruition.

If we have offended anyone through 'discretionary dishonesty' by pursuing what we believed was the right approach for those of Amythesia, and Prismacia, and,

Neptuna ... then, speaking for all Topaz, we humbly and sincerely apologize."

Once again, bowing her head, Princess Poona gestured with arms uplifted to all before her, saying ...

"The worlds and Heavens belong to us all. It is for all of us to help mold a compassion, a compassion the Beings occupying these worlds and Heavens will respect, uphold, and truly believe in. And, if time and the situation allow, always giving consideration, and voice to the viewpoints, and suggestions of all these Beings, known and alien."

"I can assure you that among these various viewpoints, 'stardust', or ideas, will be found, that once nurtured, and refined, will contain even more promise for all Beings in all Heavens.

'We are the creators of today and seed the future of tomorrows, and indeed there will be a promising and bright future."

Chapter 82

The Explanation

She is known among you

Princess Poona placed her hands over her heart and softly declared …

"You are witnessing and hearing of extraordinary moments this evening, my friends. While all things are cherished by the Goodness of All Things, there are those Beings that have been chosen to be 'Watchers and Guardians' for the welfare of all as custodians of the knowledge of all time."

"Topaz is a guardian for the welfare of all Beings, and while it is a daunting task, it is one the Beings of my world have accepted unquestioningly. When I say, my world, allow me to clarify. As I have indicated, our Heaven's galaxy is known as Topaz. It is a far away place whose past is shrouded in antiquity. It is extrasolar and of another Dimension."

"I am here to assist in an ancient prophecy whose time is now and I an here to usher in the rising dawn of an extraordinary covenant. There are those among you who have faithfully and unwaveringly awaited this moment. We have attempted to fulfill this prophecy in as natural a way as possible under most unusual and trying circumstances. We of Topaz are known as truthful people, believing in the Goodness Of All Things. Thus, the way in which this exceptional situation needed to be accomplished presented us with choices and soul searching we are not accustomed to — nor ones we would normally condone."

"It began with the birthing of a girl child. It was determined by the High Priests and Elders that this child met the expectations of the ancient prophecy. The critical alignment of all the stars proclaimed so! Her birthing date, her Star sign

... *all were perfect and in accordance with the prophecy. In time, her demeanor and her innate comprehension of wisdom were found to be far beyond her young years."*

"Explaining the destiny that awaited on a far away planet in another Dimension, the High Priests and Elders gave her the choice of accepting to fulfill this prophecy — or to decline. You 'are' the long expected One, they told her, and at five years of age, she chose ... yes!"

"This led to much deliberation. In our opinion, being discreet was a needed ingredient in order to integrate this young Being into your society as naturally as possible. Given that this child was to remain here on Prismacia for most likely the rest of her physical life it was imperative she have the physical life patterns of one of Prismacia before disclosing her as the expected one from the stars."

"Involved were two contingencies. First, there was an extremely hazardous period of time, a growth period for this child from Topaz in which her growth cell patterns accelerated rapidly. This occurred as the result of the difference in rotations of Prismacia, around your Mother SunneLavva, and the number of rotations, we of Topaz are accustomed to, around our Sunne, the Star of Life."

"You see, we of Topaz physically age three years for every one year we are here on Prismacia. A precise number of years was needed for her to acclimate and become adapted to your cycle before she would age normally ... as you do."

"It was a situation she endured in order to become the correct age, with the corresponding level of mental and emotional maturity for a Being of a similar age on Prismacia. She needed to be carefully monitored, cared for and watched continually for years before the transition was complete ... and successful! It was a complex, painful, and potentially dangerous ordeal, which she underwent to fulfill this prophecy."

"Second of the relevant concerns was to introduce this individual as one of you. One who grew up experiencing and understanding life here. One who grasped and comprehended the total Being of an Amythesian — because they grew up as one.

To just arrive and present herself as the Awaited One

from the stars could allude to perhaps a separation, perhaps a superiority."

"Given the profound relevancy of that which you expected, can you understand, this was the only way she could fulfill the prophecy that was promised? She is now prepared to present and offer herself to you, as one of you. She is prepared to share gifts of Goodness and of counsel she deems wise and compassionate, if you will but accept her into your lives."

Both King Luxxor and Queen Liluuc had silently gasped at the mention of the individual being called her, and she ... and the Awaited One.

"Could it be," they whispered, "is Princess Poona speaking of the Silver Princess of the Moon and 7Stars ... Neptuna's long Awaited One?"

They held hands and waited.

Princess Poona paused, collecting her final thoughts and words. She ended with ...

"It is our fervent aspiration, that as you consider our thoughts and actions, you will understand that what I have brought forth, and revealed, were for the right reasons and with only honorable intentions. I will now address the prophecy which has been expected for so long. You see, this evening, is for the unveiling of one who was promised untold ages ago and has now arrived ... having chosen to accept this prophecy, this destiny — her destiny, and now yours."

Turning to face King Luxxor, and Queen Liluuc, the Emerald Princess Poona, bowed respectfully.

"King Luxxor, Queen Liluuc, as I stated, you and the Beings of Neptuna have patiently waited ages without number. We must remember ... all that comes to pass, occurs in it's time ... by the nature of things. We believe that time is now. I, Princess Poona, the Emerald Empress of the Moon and 7Stars, thank you, and sincerely hope I have explained our concerns and actions clearly and that there is some measure of understanding within your hearts."

Then, turning towards Laurra, Princess Poona gestured in her direction with open arms, and said ...

"It is now time to allow the One of Prophecy to offer herself to you ... the Silver Princess Laurra, of the Moon and 7Stars ... the Awaited One."

Chapter 83

Tears Of A Long, Long Journey

You are home Princess Laurra

The night had become cold, but no one noticed. All present understood the significance of this night. The truths and grandeur thus far expressed and the expectation of that yet to come had become intoxicating, almost unbelievable ... and yet, as Empress Poona indicated, it was coming to pass, at this moment, and before their very eyes.

Laurra, who had been sitting next to Tunnis arose slowly. Turning to Tunnis, she placed her hand upon his. Her eyes smiled warmly. Then she slowly ascended the dunne where Princess Poona waited.

A soft mummer circulated among the small crowd. Crying was heard.

Princess Poona, and Princess Laurra, embraced each other and faced the gathering. Bowing to Princess Laurra, Princess Poona, stepped aside, joining XennaOne and her mother, Solannuj, nearby.

Princess Laurra slowly gazed out at her fellow Initiates of Brightness, her friends, her acquaintances from along the way, those who had been invited to share in this evening ... and the King and Queen of Neptuna.

She waited for the right moment to speak, thinking ...

I choose to be one who is approachable to all. I will allow for the One to guide my thoughts, and the expression of gratitude I am feeling at this threshold in my life, this beginning for us all. It will be spontaneous and from my heart ... not my mind.

Laurra had chosen simplicity for her attire. She wore a light gray robe and gown, trimmed in silver, and falling to her ankles. Her feet were adorned with simple silver shaded sandals, and her long, wavy hair fell loosely, blowing gently in the breeze. Her eyes were clear and bright, the eyes of compassion and conviction. She did allow for two exceptions. In her hand she held a simple silver head band with 7 stars on the front. The

336

moon being represented behind the middle star. Each star held a tiny moonstone set in it's center.

She gently placed it on her head.

Secondly, she had applied the symbol of Topaz, the Moon and 7Stars, upon her cheek. As always, it was of rare Trolon.

Except for the night breezes it remained totally quiet. Everyone watched and waited.

Looking over to Princess Poona, Princess Laurra, eyes glistening with tears of a long, long journey, began ...

"Thank you, Poona, my sister. Many times it was your courage, your strength, your wisdom, your concern and your healing which made possible this memorable, altruistic moment we are all sharing tonight."

Then, looking back at all before her she stated ...

"Yes, Princess Poona is my sister. I am blessed."

With a soft smile on her face and in her eyes she turned to look in the direction of King Luxxor and Queen Liluuc.

She offered gently ...

"Look within! When we do, we will know the truth."

"It is a seemingly simple saying, but one that carries a virtuousness of worthiness. I have personally looked within for some time now seeking my own truth."

Pausing, and closing her eyes, Princess Laurra lifted her head to the Heavens, placed her hands in the symbolic gesture of the One and went within.

She allowed for her thoughts to form ... she spoke...

"I looked within when it was decreed, and I was told, that I was the Awaited One, the Silver Princess of the Moon and 7Stars."

"I looked within after the decree and thought of seeking my own destiny. A destiny of my choosing, my creation."

"I looked within as an Initiate of Brightness ... a blessing I am still humbled by."

"I looked within when illness seemed to be deciding my fate." "I thank you again, my sister for your caring and compassion."

"I looked within when visiting the extraordinary city of Neptuna and all its lovely and gentile Beings, and its incredible contribution of responsibility to all of Amythesia."

"I looked within and knew my truth! I am here to fulfill

what was never forgotten ... Neptuna's prophecy has finally come to be!"

A hush blanketed the already amazed and mystified group. Beings were understanding the phenomenal significance of what was being revealed and that they were a part of an extraordinary beginning ... part of an ancient, mysterious prophecy to finally occur.

As they stood watching and anticipating, a radiant glow slowly encompassed Princess Laurra. Ever so slightly, the Starbursts and Starflakes hovering above began to pulse in their communal colors of magenta, blue and white.

The impact caused murmurs and gasps of astonishment and delight.

Princess Laurra, yielding to the wonderment of the gathering, paused briefly.

"However," she continued,"to arrive at this moment is not the intention of my journey. The expectation in the greater promise of my journey yet to come is why I have chosen this path. My own truth, my friends, and what I offer to all, is the fulfillment of prophecy — and it begins in Neptuna."

Respectfully, Princess Laurra turned to King Luxxor, Queen Liluuc, Tunnis and Dolpho, all standing anxiously.

Her glow intensified.

"I look now to the Beings of Neptuna, whose ancestors were those of Netropia, and beyond. Their courage and achievements, both past and present, will be etched in the History of the Heavens ... the very history hidden and protected here on Prismacia."

With glistening eyes fixed on the King and Queen, she stated...

"You have waited for so long, never wavering in your faith that the truth and fulfillment of this Prophecy would someday occur. My King, my Queen, I stand before you, the embodiment of the prophecy you have valiantly and faithfully yearned for."

Once again, Laurra, the Silver Princess, paused, allowing for her thoughts, and emotions to coalesce collectively. She felt calm, assured and in her truth.

"King Luxxor, Queen Liluuc, will 'you' now look within, seeking not only your truths, but also that of what you understand to be the truths of all Beings of Neptuna. I humbly offer you my destiny and my all. I now present myself, my true Being to you. I am at long last here, my King, my Queen

— the Silver Princess of Prophecy promised so many, many eons ago."

The King and Queen were speechless, but ecstatic and happy beyond belief. As Princess Laura watched she recognized their answer in their smiles and tears. King Luxxor was literally bubbling with excitement and unashamed tears of joy were flowing down his cheeks. He could not take his eyes off of Laurra, the Silver Princess of Neptuna.

Standing nearby, Tunnis was silent. He could feel Dolpho's happy energy, as she hugged his arm in jubilation, but he was confused by the meaning and complexity of what this meant.

Will this affect a possible relationship between Laurra and me? Where will I fit in, or can I, now that this has all been disclosed? What can I do? Oh, this is truly a mixed blessing for me.

As if channeling Tunnis's thoughts and anguish at this turn of events, Princess Laurra, gracefully raised her arms, bringing a hush over the crowd.

The Silver Princess then stated with conviction...

"There is something I must make clear ... except for affairs where it is necessary that circumstances require I assume the formalities that my title, the Silver Princess of the Moon and 7Stars, represents, know that I will always be available to you all.

Also, it is my wish to be simply addressed as Princess Laurra.

And, for those of you who may be curious, I unequivocally believe and insist on the right to live a normal life in respect to a husband and a family ... should I so choose, or be blessed with either."

Tunnis felt the burden of hopelessness dissipate immediately and a wave of emotion flowed through him carrying joy and promise.

At least there hope, there is a possibility, he thought gleefully.

Embracing Dolpho excitedly, he ran to his father and mother leaving Dolpho speechless as to his actions.

Seven Starflakes moved directly above the Silver Princess Laurra, each glowing in the collective colors of Topaz creating a soft radiance on all standing before her. Everyone was now tightly gathered at the bottom of the small dunne as the Silver Princess Laurra slowly made her way down.

She sparkled!

A soft blue glow, emitting tiny sparkles of what could only be called Heavenly sprinkles, embraced her countenance. They floated and danced, interspersing with Carbonian dust Twinkles, showering all below in a playful display of pomp, pageantry, and joyfulness. Reaching the bottom of the dunne, Laurra and Poona stood before one another. With eyes of tears they embraced, both filled with thoughts of the goodness to come.

King Luxxor and Queen Liluuc approached in respect, in awe, and as her friends. Bowing his head, King Luxxor spoke.

"Princess Laurra, Queen Liluuc and I, Prince Tunnis and Princess Dolpho, and all the Beings of Neptuna are honored ... and so very happy! I know that we speak for all Neptunians as we willingly offer you our truths. It is you Princess Laurra! You are the embodied truth of the covenant and prophecy promised to our ancestors ... but it is we, who live now, that welcome you."

King Luxxor put his arms around his Chosen One, Tunnis and Dolpho.

"We gratefully offer to share this glorious, promised journey together. The journey you so longingly and lovingly spoke of. Since 'you' have so chosen, Princess Laurra, we give you our choice. You are home!"

Princess Laurra joyfully embraced them each affectionately.

She lingered ever so briefly with Prince Tunnis.

Queen Liluuc noticed — and smiled.

Chapter 84

For Your Communications Only

I will come again — I will it to be

The Emerald Empress of the Moon and 7Stars, looked on.

She reverted to the informal Princess Poona.

Her eyes glistened and twinkled from the kaleidoscope of light radiating from the Starbursts and Starflakes hovering above. She shook her head in wonder. Her hair swayed, leaving a small wisp lingering across her eye. She brushed it aside. Her thoughts lingered on this evening. Glancing around she spoke...

"I feel truly peaceful at this moment. It truly is an astonishing moment in time ... for Neptuna, for Amythesia, and perhaps unknown civilizations to come."

"Time will tell."

She moved towards the dunne.

Those Beings converging around Princess Laurra, now noticed a change taking place. Harmonious sounds emanated from the Topazian StarCraft above. They all turned towards the dunne where Empress Poona now stood.

Garnering everyone's attention, Empress Poona declared...

"The Emerald Starbursts are preparing for my departure, my friends. For me, it seems to have been but a fleeting moment ... but, it is now the time for me to say, our time will come again. The Moon and 7Stars of Topaz, my home, is waiting."

Then, returning to Princess Poona, she mingled, offering thoughts for each, including the High Council of the Voice of One who respectfully bowed at her presence and listened attentively.

She found the eyes of XennaOne, her friend, standing with her mother Solannuj. Bowing respectfully before them, she brought her hands together

341

in the symbolic gesture of the Goodness of All Things. Upon lifting her head, Princess Poona saw that XennaOne responded in kind. They both blew each other an 'until we meet again' farewell kiss. As she turned, she heard Solannuj whispering to herself...

"You would have loved to see this, Parley Luk."

Hmmm, Poona thought. *Interesting! I will remember the name Parley Luk!*

Princess Poona found the Initiates of Brightness and lovingly embracing each, offered a few thoughts to them. When she came to Annuj she whispered in her ear...

"If you choose to become AnnaOne of the Voice of One, you will become that of Legend, Annuj. It will be within your realm of influence to truly carry on the work of those preceding you.

Imagine the chance to continue initiating a consciousness of goodness and compassion permeating not only Amythesia, but the Heavens themselves. And Annuj, even if you choose otherwise, your life, and those of your influence, will always advocate for goodness, and compassion. It is a good choice either way ... and it is your choice, Annuj ... your life and your path to choose."

Patto was the last of the Initiates she approached. With somewhat sad eyes, Patto raised both hands in the symbolic gesture of Goodness. Poona, taken by the gesture, took his hands warmly.

"I do not know exactly how to address you," Patto said. I am sad and yet joyful, happy and yet unhappy.

"Oh Patto, just between you and me, Poona will do just fine, but there may be times when 'Princess, or Empress Poona' will be more appropriate."

"I totally understand, Poona. I am sure I will be able to distinguish the wheres or whens!"

Poona smiled warmly, squeezing his hands.

"You do have the crystal I gifted you," she teasingly questioned.

"Yes, Poona, I do," he replied, reaching into his bag and carefully bringing out a small, round, glowing, magenta/blue/white glowing crystal.

"It is an inter-tunessional communication crystal developed in Topaz. We call it the Intune," Poona said, with a grin.

"Just how does it work, Poona?"

"Oh, Patto, it is somewhat involved, but I believe they take a little of your galaxy's Heaven'sDust, and a little of our galaxy's Heaven'sDust, add a pinch of our dimension's energy make-up, and shake it all up!"

"Yes, right," Patto said, looking at Poona with a bemused expression.

They both began laughing.

"Actually, Patto, place the crystal in front of you, sit with the moon, or sunne behind the crystal, and gaze at the symbolic 7Stars that will appear within. Put both hands on the sides. The crystal will turn from white, to magenta, to blue. When it is blue you can remove your hands if you so choose. You can then speak to me, Patto, and, I to you. Here, let me show you."

Taking his hands in hers she placed them onto the side of the crystal.

Hmmm, his hands feel strong.

Hmmm, her hands feel soft and warm.

Slowly 7Stars appeared and the colors changed as she had said.

"You are right, Poona. It feels good ... pardon me, I mean it works!"

Poona lowered her eyes, pleased.

"However, Patto, it is for 'your communications only.' I will anticipate, and look forward to your messages."

"And I will eagerly await your responses," said Patto. "Although, I must say I miss you, and our star gazing, already, Poona."

His eyes began to mist, in both the joy and sadness he had mentioned.

Poona noticed immediately and her heart warmed from the genuine care she felt.

Embracing tenderly, Poona, with eyes twinkling mischievously, whispered,

"You won't miss me for to long, Patto. *I am a Princess, an Emerald Empress even, and I won't allow it.*"

She kissed him on the cheek and turned to depart.

Visioning

'I have seen wondrous things

throughout the vast, majestic Heavens...

from golden stars and myriads of moons

to twinkling stardust,

a full light year wide.

Glorious suns, planets of ice...

beauty and discovery without measure.

But, in all the moments I have been gifted

by the Oneness of All things

nothing has touched me more

than the Goodness of you.'

Princess Djuna

Princess of Topaz, artist, and poet, ancestress of Empress Poona
From an excerpt of The Topazian 'Book of Love'
Star I of the 7Stars
date origin unknown

Chapter 85

The Emerald Empress Of The Moon And 7 Stars Departs

I would not have the faintest clue

Princess Poona, taking Princess Laurra, King Luxxor, and his Chosen One, Liluuc by the arms, walked together to a nearby Starburst. She reached in, and uttering a few quiet and unknown words, brought out a glowing crystal, pulsating as a heart beats."

Why, it is shaped as a Starburst," exclaimed Liluuc.

Empress Poona gracefully presented it to King Luxxor, saying,

"This crystal starburst representing goodness and knowledge within, is for you King Luxxor and you Queen Liluuc — and for all the Beings of Neptuna, and Amythesia if so desired. You will discover it will explain many things. Answer many questions. I, the Emerald Empress of Topaz, thank you for your kindness and understanding. If ever need be, I can now conjure up the name of one King and Queen who I know to be compassionate, passionate and wise."

Slowly bowing, she promised, *"We will meet again. I will it to be."*

King Luxxor, still trembling and feeling a wave of tribute flow through him, lowered his head in thanks. Queen Liluuc took her Chosen One's arm and also lowered her head in respect to the Emerald Empress.

With a happy expression, Princess Poona turned to Princess Laurra.

"My sister, your new world awaits. As the Silver Princess Laurra, the Awaited One, you have chosen to create your true destiny and have offered your truths to those Neptuna. King Luxxor, and Queen Liluuc, representing all the Beings of Neptuna, have graciously, and lovingly accepted you as the Princess of Prophecy they have been waiting for."

Embracing and kissing tenderly, Poona said...

"Always remember, my sister, you and I are forever together in our hearts. We are as close as a thought."

"As close as a thought, yes," echoed Laurra.

Reaching into the hovering Starburst, Empress Poona then handed her sister a gift to be opened later.

"With forever love," she said softly, kissing Laurra once more.

She turned towards the awaiting craft.

Glancing back as she was about to enter the Starburst, Empress Poona remarked ...

"Actually, King Luxxor and Queen Liluuc, perhaps you will find delight in a visit to our Galaxy of Topaz. There is beauty unimaginable! Topaz, is of course in another Dimension, but our world is, shall I say, watery also ... and not entirely unlike Prismacia, especially Neptuna and the Sea of the Forgotten Place. As you will find, it is perhaps a slightly 'different' reality from yours, but nevertheless one I believe you will enjoy."

"Familiarity breeds friends," Empress Poona said appreciatively, *"and I am certain we of Topaz can arrange suitable transportation for you and yours."*

"Empress Poona, what do I do with this remarkable crystal?" asked King Luxxor earnestly.

Empress Poona, gesturing towards the glowing crystal he held in his hands, said...

"Somehow I feel the Fountain of Life, on an ancient wall in your Sanctuary, has a special place just for this, King Luxxor."

Luxxor looked down at the crystal, a broad grin emerged.

"The Beings of my world and realm await me. Ours has been, and continues to be, a journey ... as will be yours, my friends."

Empress Poona turned, and entering the Starburst, disappeared from their gazes. The Emerald Starburst changed to white, magenta, and then a blue glow.

Chapter 86

Farewell Pantheon

I have one last farewell

CrownStarBeing Mulon looked approvingly at Empress Poona, and asked,

"Engage dissolve" Empress Poona?

"No Mulon," she replied, "suspend dissolve ... for the moment. Let us leave slowly. A slow fade," she smiled. "I wish to say my goodbyes as long as possible."

"And, Mulon, I have one last farewell."

"Yes, my Empress?"

"Yes, and it is only a short distance away. Take me to Pantheon. He has settled just on the other side of the oasis."

Pantheon was lounging lazily on his back, as if star gazing. Purring softly, he caught the arrival of the Emerald Starburst, but barely budged. He just looked on curiously, continuing to purr.

Departing the Starburst, Poona slowly, but confidently made her way to Pantheon. It was never easy, walking in the sloping sand, but she was now quite experienced in the ways of sand things after her trek through the Carbonian Desert with the Initiates.

It is an adventure I will remember always, thought Poona.

Maneuvering up to Pantheon's head, she gently caressed his ink black fur and lovingly massaged his soft nose before giving it a gentle kiss. Pantheon, purring approvingly, rolled his mysterious, wise eyes in Poona's direction while rolling over to his stomach. Poona, looked into the dark, endlessly deep pupils of Pantheon's eyes and suddenly considered,

Oh my, not unlike the endless Heavens themselves. Hmmm, I must give that some thought.

"Well, my trusted and most unusual friend," Poona said, "I must leave for now. I will return though, so know that I fully expect to be in your

348

presence once again. I will lounge with you at the oasis and together we will trek into the desert to relive old times."

Pantheon looked thoughtfully at Poona.

I would like that, thought Pantheon.

"Perhaps even a jaunt into the mountains would be interesting?"

I would like that too.

"Maybe a party with the Initiates?"

That would be nice.

"What do you say? Are you up for it?"

Of course I am up for it, you are my friend, Poona.

Hmmm, just what are you thinking, my sweet Pantheon?

Pantheon blinked curiously, and his large tongue found the side of Poona's face. He licked her tenderly.

Perhaps a goodbye kiss, she wondered.

She sat with Pantheon for a short time, and then, kissing Pantheon on the nose once more, said...

"I must leave for now, but I will return, Pantheon. Take care. I love you."

Pantheon watched Poona return to the flying machine.

I will miss you, Poona ... my friend, I will miss you. Come back soon.

Poona was almost back to the Emerald Starburst when she stopped.

A thought seemed to be trying to materialize.

"What is it," she remarked?

"What is this feeling?"

She stood still for so long that Mulon came to check on her. It had become even colder. He brought a heavy robe.

Putting the warm robe around her shoulders, he asked, "Are you well, my Empress?"

She looked at Mulon. *"Yes, I am alright, Mulon."*

"A friend is sending me a message."

Poona turned to see Pantheon on a dunne some distance away.

"Pantheon is watching," she mummured.

"Is that what I am sensing...is Pantheon communicating with me?"

"Could Pantheon have telepathic abilities?"

She closed her eyes and concentrating deeply, replied...

Yes, until we meet again, and we will, my friend, Pantheon.

Yes, until we meet again, Ponna.

Poona, joyfully mystified, cast a last glance, turned and entered the Emerald Starburst.

CrownStarBeing, Mulon waited patiently for his Empress.

Entering, Empress Poona stood at the threshold, and took in a last look of Oneness, the Carbonian Desert, and the extraordinary display of Heavens above.

"It is now time, Mulon, our work is done ... for the moment."

"Topaz awaits."

"Although, Mulon, I will miss them all ..."

Tiny, moving Starlites began their continuing protective journey around Empress Poona's Emerald Starburst, accompanied by the remaining 6 Starbursts, plus myriads of accompanying Starflakes.

"Ginesthoi, Mulon!"

Slowly, they silently arose, until once uniting with the Heavens, they eventually appeared as one star — one very bright star!

And then...

Dissolve.

Note

Except for one poem, I would like to give thanks, and credit
to a friend for the poems he bequeathed to me
before his passing. May they be a part of his legacy.
They are poignant, touching, and relate to this story perfectly.
Thank you, my friend. You are missed.

As to the other poem, 'Visioning,'
I thank my lovely wife, for the inspiration.

Printed in the United States
By Bookmasters